Books by Jean Stone

A Vineyard Crossing

A Vineyard Morning

A Vineyard Summer

A Vineyard Christmas

Vineyard Magic

Four Steps to the Altar

Three Times a Charm

Twice Upon a Wedding

Once Upon a Bride

Beach Roses

Trust Fund Babies

Off Season

The Summer House

Tides of the Heart

Birthday Girls

Places by the Sea

Ivy Secrets

First Loves

Sins of Innocence

A
Vineyard
Crossing

JEAN STONE

KENSINGTON
PUBLISHING CORP.
www.kensingtonbooks.com

KENSINGTON BOOKS are published by

Kensington Publishing Corp.
119 West 40th Street
New York, NY 10018

ISBN-13: 978-1-4967-2886-9 (ebook)
ISBN-10: 1-4967-2886-6 (ebook)

ISBN-13: 978-1-4967-2885-2
ISBN-10: 1-4967-2885-8

First Kensington Trade Paperback Printing: August 2021

10 9 8 7 6 5 4 3 2 1

Printed in the United States of America

To my family and friends whose
Zooms, calls, texts—and shipments of cookies(!)—helped
get me through 2020 unscathed of heart and mind.
And most gratefully, in good health.

A
Vineyard
Crossing

Chapter 1

"I know you don't want me to go," her brother said as Annie pulled up to the curb in the departure queue at Logan Airport. "But thanks for staying out of it."

She touched his arm, wishing she could stop him, knowing she could not. "Have a good time," she replied with a forced smile.

He gave her a small wink, grabbed his suitcase and backpack, and got out of the Jeep. Then he disappeared into the terminal as her heart crumbled a little.

Kevin, of course, was right: she'd wanted to convince him to stay on Martha's Vineyard where he now belonged. But Taylor Winsted—the auburn-haired woman who had turned his head a year ago—now lived in Hawaii, having fled her unfortunate past. Annie never dreamed that he would join Taylor; she'd thought that the couple had uncoupled before the woman left. "She needs me," he'd said when he announced that she'd enlisted his help with renovations to her house on Maui. Annie had been stunned. She'd been happy when Taylor had packed her bags and gone. Relieved, in fact, as Annie had never quite warmed up to her.

That'll teach you, Murphy said from her place up in the

clouds. Murphy was Annie's old college pal who had died but remained with Annie in spirit. On occasion, she still offered sage advice. And mischievous quips.

Annie didn't respond, but fixed her eyes on the road.

The trip from Boston back to the ferry at Woods Hole took forever, every mile of highway thick with traffic, every vehicle intent on getting in her way. To top it off, it was August-hot. And humid.

Or maybe Annie was merely stressed about Kevin having left.

By the time she reached the boat, she was grateful it was loading. Once on board, she parked where she was directed, then climbed two flights of iron stairs to the upper passenger deck. Squeezing between a texting teen and a large, sun-hatted man, Annie stood at the railing, closed her eyes, and let the sun warm her face and soothe her soul. After all, she was going home. And Kevin would be back—he would, he would, he would. If she turned that into a mantra, maybe it would come true.

A few minutes later, the engines rumbled to life, and the *Island Home* pulled away from the pier, out to the harbor, into Vineyard Sound. As they glided past the emerald Elizabeth Islands, Annie's gaze drifted from the clear blue sky to the sparkling summer sea; the soft motion enveloped her, rocking away the heat and the onslaught of noise that had besieged her in the city. Since she'd moved to the Vineyard two years earlier, the sight of the Boston skyline alone gave her agita.

She could hardly wait to be back on the island where life was magical and beautiful and blanketed with peace, and where she could think straight again.

You can be such a drama queen, Murphy whispered.

Which, of course, made Annie laugh. Out loud. Then she glanced around, grateful that no one seemed to have witnessed her outburst. She mused at how, no matter how badly the city could assault her senses, she was never bothered by the cacophony of too many people or too much traffic on the island, not even during the upcoming jam-packed week of Illumination Night, the fireworks, and the grand finale of summer, the Ag Fair. She had, however, been annoyed that Kevin had chosen a "rental turnover" day—a Saturday, of all days—to take off.

Kevin. Him again.

Murphy made no further comment, though it was a good bet she would have told Annie to get over herself.

Then a small hand tugged Annie's wrist. She turned and looked down at the upturned face of a young girl. Judging by the empty space where her two front teeth belonged, she might have been six or seven.

"You going to visit someone?" the girl asked, her voice whistling the "s" in "someone."

"No," Annie replied. "I live on the Vineyard,"

"All the time?" Her freckled nose wrinkled.

"Yes." Annie didn't add, *Thank God*. "Today I brought my brother to the airport in Boston."

"Was he visiting?"

"No. He lives on the island, too. He's going to Hawaii now. To see a friend. A lady."

The child scowled. "His girlfriend?"

Annie laughed. "Good question."

"How long will he be gone?"

"A week or two." Or three or four, Annie supposed. Or more—he hadn't said. "Are you coming over to visit someone?"

"No. I live here, too. But Daddy says without tourists to support us, we'd have to move somewhere else. Like Cleveland. So I was hoping you were a tourist."

A man walked up behind the girl and put his hands on the crown of her head. He gave Annie a crooked smile that made him look like an apologetic emoji. "Sorry," he said. "My daughter is taking an unofficial passenger survey."

Annie smiled in return. "If this boat is any indication," she said to the child, "I think there will be plenty of tourists this week." As the man steered his daughter away, Annie noticed that a thirtyish woman—a petite brunette with a flawless bronze complexion—was standing at the bow of the boat, slightly turned, watching her.

"Excuse me," the woman asked as she stepped closer, "are you Annie Sutton?" She had captivating, cornflower blue eyes.

Though Annie had written several best-selling books, she wasn't yet accustomed to being recognized. Or approached. She folded her hands and knitted her fingers together. "I am. Do you read mysteries?"

The woman hesitated. "Um, no. Didn't you do an interview on *Best Destinations*? The TV show? You have a new inn, don't you?"

When the show's producer had contacted Annie for their segment on New England vacations, it had come as no surprise. Her editor, Trish, had arranged it as a chance to promote Annie's books. "I have an inn, yes. On Chappaquiddick."

The woman began to speak again, but paused, as if changing her mind. Then she glanced toward the opposite side of the deck and gave a slight wave of recognition. Annie followed her gaze, but did not see anyone return the greeting.

"Excuse me," the stranger said, her words rushed and befuddled as she slipped into the throng of tourists, dogs, and rolling suitcases, leaving a cloud of curiosity in her wake.

The line at the *On Time* was blessedly short; by late afternoon, few people were interested in venturing off the main island and over to Chappaquiddick—the eastern arm of Martha's Vineyard and technically part of Edgartown. Chappy had no restaurants—unless one counted Jerry's Place, the mini–mini store that featured freshly made to-go sandwiches and bakery items, salads and ice cream, and recently had added some local specialties. Nor was there much shopping—with notable exceptions such as Slip Away Farm for fresh-picked produce and bountiful flowers, and, again, Jerry's Place, with its stash of beach supplies, toiletries, and souvenirs. Though numerous houses and cottages were sprinkled around the island, most visitors who crossed were day-trippers: hikers, bikers, sunbathers.

With four cars ahead of her, Annie figured she'd only have to wait a few short minutes to board the tiny ferry that held three vehicles—two if one was a pickup.

Drumming her fingers on the dashboard of her Jeep—her favorite acquisition since she moved there two years ago—she tried to organize what was left of her day, a nearly impossible feat now that she ran The Vineyard Inn and all its lively components. Chances were, nothing significant had happened in the hours she'd been gone. She'd left Francine in charge, and Earl Lyons on call in case of emergency, though there hadn't been any during this inaugural season.

Some days, Annie couldn't believe how great things had been working out. Their three guest rooms had been booked all but five days, which only had happened because of a last-minute cancellation due to illness. September looked promising, too, with reservations already at seventy percent. More important, in addition to being low-maintenance, the amiable guests and the year-round tenants—who were ensconced in three additional rooms—were cheerful, engaging, and helpful whenever help was needed. In October, once the summer guests left, winter rental tenants would arrive to claim those rooms. Maybe then Annie could let out her breath. Except, of course, that her next book would be published around that time, so she'd no doubt have to leave the island for a publicity tour. She was waiting to learn the schedule; hopefully, it wouldn't be grueling.

Yes, she thought as the first three cars in line boarded the ferry and she inched the Jeep forward, life was hectic, but wonderful. She only wished that Kevin had waited to bolt for Hawaii until after Columbus Day. Or Christmas. Or never. Annie knew that she wanted to protect her over-forty, very grown-up, "kid" brother because he was the only family she had left. And because she'd only known him a couple of years after she'd connected with her birth mother.

As her thoughts began to slide toward a smidge of sadness again, she heard a sudden rap-rap-rap on the passenger door as it quickly jerked open.

"Hey, lady, how 'bout a lift?" It was Earl, the stocky, white-haired saint of all saints, who still enjoyed a good chuckle at seventy-five, and whose spunk, as he called it, still functioned well. A ninth- or tenth-generation islander, he looked out for his neighbors, the land, and the shoreline, and was often called the Mayor of Chappy. On any given summer day, it wasn't uncommon for Mayor Earl not to be driving his truck. Unless a situation made it necessary—a dentist appointment, an early morning run to Stop & Shop, a brother who needed a ride to the airport in Boston—few residents of Chappaquiddick brought a vehicle over to Edgartown when the calendar said it was not yet Labor Day: there were too many people, too much traffic, too few parking spaces in town.

"What are you doing here?" she asked with a grin. "Aren't you supposed to be on call for Francine?" Along with every-thing else, Earl was the Inn's "handyman extraordinaire," though Kevin did most of the bull work, thanks to Earl's ad-vancing years.

He seated himself and buckled up without waiting for an

invitation. Today he wore a pale blue T-shirt from Sharky's Cantina; he enjoyed advertising island establishments to summer people. Patting the pocket of his well-worn jeans, he said, "Never fear. Francine made sure I brought my trusty phone. She's on my case way more often than you are." He chuckled again. "And she's doing a fine job, Annie. We all should be proud of that girl."

"We are," she replied. Francine was their twenty-one-year-old go-getter who had become an island treasure. "So, did you come to Edgartown for business or pleasure?"

"None of the above." His spiky white eyebrows crinkled above his warm brown eyes. "My son required my services. You remember him? Kind of a tall guy. Edgartown cop. Handsome like his father but half-a-foot taller? Pearl-gray eyes like his mother?" Of course, Earl was talking about John, the guy Annie had met soon after she'd moved there and now was engaged to. The guy she would marry one of these days.

"Very funny. What kind of 'services' did he require? If I'm not getting too personal."

Earl shrugged. "Nothing life-threatening. I helped him move some furniture around."

Furniture? John had been living in his townhouse in the center of Edgartown for quite a while; a year ago, Lucy, his now fourteen-year-old daughter, had joined him when she'd decided she'd rather live there than off island with her mother and older sister. He might have rearranged furniture then, but now? Was he was making the place ready for when they got married and Annie moved in? Did he want to set the date now that the season was nearly over?

A wee speck of doubt poked her like a deer tick—undetected until it bit. She hadn't planned to marry again. Not for a third time. Now that she was a hairbreadth past fifty, she knew that marriage was more than champagne and cuddles, and that life was way more than romance. Which was why sometimes John Lyons fit the old cliché of being too be good to be true.

She looked back toward the water. The second ferry—two of them crisscrossed in summer—arrived from the other side of the channel; the captain was signaling the next vehicles to drive on. As Annie guided the Jeep over the sturdy planks, Earl waved at the captain and leaned out the open window. "I'm getting a free ride today. How 'bout that?"

Captain Fredericks (better known as Captain Fred) laughed and tore a coupon out of Annie's booklet. When he moved on to the next vehicle, Earl turned back to her and said he assumed that she'd delivered Kevin to Logan okay; he asked if he'd been happy to be going and if the traffic had been god-awful up there, too, and Annie knew it was too late to return to the topic of moving furniture at John's.

It was after four o'clock by the time Annie dropped Earl off at his truck on the Chappy side of the harbor, made her way to North Neck Road, and pulled into the clamshell driveway at The Vineyard Inn. She turned off the ignition, closed her eyes, and sat silently, glad to be home. Though Francine had the day-to-day responsibilities of running the Inn to allow Annie time to work on her next manuscript, Annie had to let her know that she was back. And she should text John to alert him, too.

But first, if only for a minute, she wanted to savor the light breeze that drifted in the window and listen to the gentle surf lapping the beach on the western rim of their property. *Their* property, hers and Kevin's, thanks to the gift from their mother. Earl would receive one-third of the Inn's annual profit and one-third of the net if they ever sold the place. God knew he'd put in enough time, sweat equity, and worry to deserve an equal share. And now, with their first full quarter about to end, Annie was certain that, after they set aside a chunk to keep them afloat through winter, there would be a generous profit to share.

It had been an interesting few months, with too much to do to grapple with issues that Annie would have spent too many hours grappling about, anyway. Most of the issues, like nuptial plans, could wait until the chaos slowed to a simmer.

The thought of John's kindness, his strength, his love for her, made Annie smile. So she reached for her phone and texted: **Home at last. Boston sucks. MV is paradise. Dinner?** She hoped he'd invite her to his place. She was too tired to cook, and besides, he was better at it. She could have a nice cool shower before she left, maybe a short nap. Then she could put on something prettier than the denim capris and T-shirt she'd tossed on early that morning because she and Kevin had needed to make the eight-fifteen boat.

And, she reasoned, as she got out of the Jeep and crossed the lawn toward the back of the Inn, if she went to John's, she could find out about moving the furniture. Maybe they could set a wedding date—perhaps around the holidays. By then she should be better prepared to be someone's wife. Again.

She wondered if Kevin would be there to give her away.

She was pissed; he knew it.

But his sister had no right to try and run his life—did she?

He sipped a Diet Coke and munched on little pretzels while he studied the screen on the seatback in front of him. The miniature outline of the plane looked to be over Chicago. Maui was a long way from there, but at least he wasn't hyperventilating the way he used to do when Meghan was buckled up in the seat next to him.

Meghan.

He closed his eyes and tried to think about the woman who was waiting for him in Maui instead of thinking about her.

Chapter 2

"You're back!" a familiar voice rang out.

Annie snapped out of her daydream and into her role as innkeeper.

Francine was on the patio, balanced on a lounge chair. Her ebony hair was pinned atop her head; her sleeveless denim minidress was protected by a canvas apron, which, though clean, was splashed with permanent badges of her delectable creations in the kitchen. A silver colander sat next to her—it was mounded with plump blueberries.

"Guilty." Annie spotted Bella, her little body huddled on her colorful play rug, her hands busily matching blocks of different shapes into corresponding holes that Earl had die-cut into the walls of a purple wooden castle that he'd somehow found time to build. When Bella saw Annie, she stood on wobbly, toddler legs, and cried, "Annie!" She held out her chubby arms, and Annie happily scooped up the two-year-old.

"Hello, sweet girl. Did you pick blueberries today?"

Bella nodded and nestled her soft cheek against Annie's neck. And Annie's heart glowed, if such a thing really were possible.

"Blueberry scones tomorrow morning," Francine said. "Our guests seem to like them."

"Yum," Annie said.

"Yummm," Bella echoed.

"So, you got Kevin there okay?"

"I did. He's well on his way to Hawaii by now." *Enough said*, Annie thought. There was no need to share her displeasure. "How were things here today?"

"Fine. The couple in room six checked out. It's cleaned and ready, but I'm still waiting for the woman who reserved it to show up. No rush, though. She'll be here for two weeks. She sent a cashier's check for the whole amount, so that's great." That had happened before; Earl said not everybody liked paying by credit card and having all their financial information floating around in outer space. "Tomorrow the birdwatching couple from Amherst will be leaving, but that room's reserved for Monday—two sisters from Indiana—so I have a day to get it ready. And the honeymooners will be here another week."

Francine had proven adept at shuffling and juggling and making sure that everyone was happy and settled and treated to special things like blueberry scones. There hadn't been a single glitch all season—at least, not since they'd finally received the go-ahead to open. Best of all, nearly every guest had rewarded the Inn with five stars online. The most positive reviews had come from newlyweds who praised the lovely, secluded suite with king bed, sumptuous Jacuzzi, and postcard view of the Edgartown lighthouse. Kevin had labeled it "the honeymoon suite" and suggested they promote the Inn as a venue for ceremonies and receptions. As intriguing as that sounded, they agreed to get through the first year before trying to tackle special events. Meanwhile, the year-round tenants added to the Inn's charm, and everyone "fit" into the tranquil enclave that Annie had hoped they'd create. Yes, she reminded herself, so far, everything was terrific.

"Jonas will be here for dinner," Francine continued. "You want to join us? He surfcasted this morning out at Wasque and landed a nice bass for the grill."

It pleased Annie to think that Taylor's son, the once shy young man, the burgeoning artist, was no longer shy and was, in fact, dating Francine. She was also happy that nearly two dozen of his paintings that they'd hung in the Inn had already sold; each time one was bought, Jonas replaced it with another, though that one was soon gone, too. Earl joked that they were going to need a revolving door for the canvasses. Jonas's work was good and, apparently, so was his fishing. Clearly, the Vineyard was a place of healing for him—as it was for so many wash-ashores, Annie and Francine included. If only Annie liked Jonas's mother half as much as she did him, life would be easier.

"Dinner sounds delicious, but I'm planning to see John. Thanks, anyway."

Then a woman rounded the Inn and stepped into the backyard. "Hello?" She was a petite brunette with flawless bronze skin and cornflower eyes—the woman from the boat.

Francine sprang up to greet her. "You must be Ms. Mullen?"

She nodded, then gave Annie a small wave. "Hello again."

"Hello," Annie said, trying to conceal her surprise. "You should have told me you were coming here. Welcome."

Ms. Mullen wore jeans and a light green T-shirt that looked new—it bore the logo of the Marine Biological Laboratory in Woods Hole. She offered a soft laugh. "I got distracted when I thought I saw someone I knew. But I was mistaken."

"Your first trip to the island?" Francine asked.

She nodded.

"Well, it's nice to meet you," Annie said. "And, again,

welcome to The Vineyard Inn. I'm Annie, but I guess you already know that. And this is Francine, our assistant manager. And our mascot, Bella." Bella diverted her big, dark eyes from the Inn's latest guest and burrowed them below Annie's collarbone. "She's shy until she knows you. Then she'll talk your ear off. In the meantime, Francine will get you settled. Do you have a car?"

"Yes. A rental. I couldn't get a reservation for mine on the boat."

"Right," Annie replied. "It's still August. And the island has a busy week ahead. But we'll tell you about that later."

Francine stepped forward. "First, let's get you checked in. I'll get your bags. Annie? Would you watch Bella for a few minutes?"

Annie nodded. "We'll go down to the cottage." She watched as Francine led the woman away. Annie hadn't asked what had brought her to Chappy for two weeks, though it was rather curious that she was alone. Most single women preferred to stay in Edgartown, Oak Bluffs, or Vineyard Haven where things like shopping and restaurants were within walking distance. But two weeks would leave plenty of time for chatter, especially over breakfast. Hoisting Bella higher on her hip, Annie whispered, "I'm going to take a nap. How about you?"

Then a text alert pinged.

"Ding-dong," Bella said, which Earl had taught her to do when anyone's text sounded.

Annie laughed and dug her phone out of her pocket. She smiled when she saw that the message was from John.

DINNER AT THE NEWES AT 6? I'M ON 8 TO 8 TONIGHT.

"Ugh," Annie said. So much for a nap. Or a bath. A quick shower would have to do. As she and Bella headed down the slope that led to the cottage where Annie lived and worked and loved her Vineyard life, she was reminded that being in a relationship with a cop meant having to be flexible. Especially in summer, when his shifts were long and he often was worn out. Then she wondered if, over dinner, he'd want to talk about their wedding plans. And if so, was she ready to make them?

"Abigail is coming back," John said. They were seated at a quiet table in Edgartown's renowned Colonial pub—established in 1742—a plate of bangers and mash in front of him; grilled tuna and island-grown veggies in front of Annie.

She flinched. She'd been toying with the sweet peas and mushroom slices, thinking about broaching the topic of the wedding, when he blindsided her. "What?" she managed to ask. Abigail was John's elder daughter, who recently had turned eighteen. After her parents' divorce several years ago, her mother had moved to Plymouth, which was nearly two hours from the Vineyard, counting the boat trip. Unlike Lucy, Abigail had preferred to stay there with John's ex, whose name was—what? Jane? Joan? Annie knew it began with another J—John once said their friends had called them "Johnny and J____" when they'd been a couple, which had made them sound like a seventies' singing duo. Sonny and Cher. Donnie and Marie. Peaches and Herb.

He swigged his root beer. "Jenn has decided to move in with her boyfriend."

Right, Annie thought. The ex-wife's name was Jenn. The singing duo would have been Johnny and Jennie. Yikes.

"Abigail said she *abhors* him," he went on. "She claims that though she also *loathes* being trapped on the island, the idea of living under the same roof with her mother's 'ridiculous boyfriend' is 'totally more *abysmal*.'" He pierced the bangers with his fork. "I can't believe that teenagers talk like that in Plymouth. Besides, when was she ever 'trapped' here?"

Annie tried to process what she'd heard. Would she now

be expected to be actively involved as a stepmother to both Lucy and Abigail? Would the four of them live under the same, two-bedroom roof? "I thought she was going to go to college." When Abigail had graduated from high school in June, John had gone to the ceremony with Lucy, Earl, and Claire—Earl's wife and Lucy and Abigail's grandmother. John hadn't said much about his elder daughter after that. Summers on the Vineyard were so hectic that the days and nights tended to eclipse everything else.

"She didn't get into BU."

Annie had a vague memory of already being told that. "What about Rhode Island? Wasn't that her backup?"

He shoved a forkful of potato into his mouth, shook his head, and waited half a minute. "Turns out, she never applied. She only wanted BU because that's where her boyfriend went. But he's long gone now. He was a year ahead of her so, no surprise, right after he got there, he hooked up with another girl. A *college* girl. End of high school romance."

"Oh, dear," Annie said, remembering how crushed she'd been when, at sixteen, she thought that her first boyfriend had found "someone else." He hadn't; they'd gotten back together, and a few years later they had married. But those days of feeling she'd been dumped had been shattering. "She must be upset."

"Yeah, upset enough to ask to come back here." As usual, it was difficult to tell what John was feeling. He kept his head bowed, his eyes set on his dinner.

"How does Lucy feel about it?"

"Let's say she wasn't pleased to see her grandfather and me haul the other twin bed from the basement. She ranted about having to share a room with her sister like when they were kids. Then she stormed off to Maggie's."

At least Lucy and Maggie were friends again; perhaps Maggie could serve as a buffer of sorts between the two sisters.

Then Annie realized she now had the answer as to why Earl had helped John move furniture. Good dad and granddad that Earl was, he'd left it up to John to break the news.

"We'll see how it goes tomorrow," John said. "She's coming over on the two thirty. And I don't want to talk about it anymore." He lifted his chin; Annie noticed that his eyes were clouded, not with tears but with a veil of distance. She'd seen that look before when he hadn't known what else to do, as if taking a step back from a problem was the only solution, a kind of self-protective detachment. "How's Kevin?" he asked, brightening. "I can't believe he took off to see Taylor."

The conversation about his daughters had ended. If Annie weren't so tired, she might have tried to resurrect it. Not that she could have helped. She'd only talked to Abigail a year ago over breakfast at Among the Flowers. Unlike Lucy, the older girl had been neither engaging nor engaged, perhaps because John had introduced Annie as an author, not as his "lady friend." And though he'd told Annie earlier that Abigail liked to read, as they chatted awkwardly over English muffins and beach plum jelly, the girl had been noticeably disinterested.

"My brother's gone, all right," Annie said now, forcing herself to follow John's lead, knowing they'd talk more about the daughter situation when he was ready, and, God knew, not one second before. Especially when a twelve-hour shift was ahead of him. "I can't control my brother's love life, if that's what he and Taylor have. He'd been despondent since his wife, Meghan, had that horrible construction accident, and I do think Taylor helped bring him out of that." Meghan had been seriously injured nearly four years ago. The last time Kevin saw her, she didn't know him; the doctors said there was little hope that her brain trauma would improve. About a year ago, Kevin had filed for divorce; Annie had vowed she wouldn't get involved in his relationship with Taylor unless he asked for help. Some days, like today, the challenge felt impossible.

Then another question struck her: The wedding! Would Abigail's presence delay the wedding plans? She put her hands on her lap and twisted her napkin.

"Taylor must be homesick," John continued, oblivious to Annie's agitation. "I wonder if she's trying to win him back."

She sighed and forced a smile. "I have no idea."

They finished their meals and shared a dish of ice cream. Then John had to leave for work, and Annie headed back to Chappy, the when, where, and how of their nuptials remaining unresolved.

Chapter 3

If blueberry scones could be dreamy, Francine's surely were.

"Deliciously sinful," the newly wedded, pink-cheeked, perky wife remarked the following morning.

"What she said," her husband, preppy and well postured, agreed as he reached for another.

The bird-watching couple—retired UMass professors; she, tall, lanky, and loquacious; he short, boxy, and ponderous—begged for the recipe.

Francine laughed and poured more coffee. "The key ingredient is a heap of locally grown Chappaquiddick wild blueberries. I'm afraid you won't find them in Western Mass."

Annie doubted that she'd ever tire of the intriguing mix of guests that the Inn attracted. No matter how different they were from one another, they bonded over muffins or scones, Francine's special egg-and-cheese casserole, or whatever she'd cooked up that drew them to breakfast table and caused them to linger. It had become one of Annie's favorite places and often her favorite time of day, listening to the stories of their lives—from the humblest to the most outrageous.

That morning, as most mornings, the year-round tenants had taken their morning meals to go because they had to get to work: a carpenter, a restaurant server/mariachi bandleader, and a young married couple who were elementary school teachers and who were helping get the school ready for September. Ms. Mullen—whose first name Annie had yet to ask—also had wanted Francine to wrap a scone for her; she'd said she wanted to get to Vineyard Haven and start doing research, something about sea turtles.

After the newlyweds and the birders dispersed for island adventures, Annie was clearing the table when it occurred to her she hadn't heard anything recently about turtles on Chappaquiddick, not the big ones, anyway. During the fishing derby in the fall there were occasional sightings; last winter there'd been an uptick of newborn gray seals, but not a noticeable increase in loggerheads or leatherbacks. Or maybe it hadn't made the news feeds or VineyardInsiders.com, the island's in-the-know online connection.

What Annie found more peculiar was that there were plenty of places where Ms. Mullen could have stayed that would be more conducive to doing research; if she worked for MBL, as her T-shirt suggested, surely they must have accommodations on the Vineyard for staff. However, like with Kevin and Taylor, Ms. Mullen's life was none of Annie's business.

Still, if something interesting was happening with turtles on Chappy, she'd like to know about it. Though her mysteries took place in a fictitious museum in downtown Boston, maybe a leatherback could make an unexpected visit. *The turtle did it*, she thought with a laugh.

Bringing the last load of dishes into the kitchen, Annie knew she had to put off the rest of her innkeeping chores, get back to her cottage, and get to work. She meandered toward the chef's room—the wonderful concept Francine had learned about in one of her university classes and had convinced Earl and Kevin to fit into their building plans. Because it was Sunday, Francine would be in there, checking the inventory for the coming week. In the few months since they had opened, their routines had grown nicely predictable.

Standing in the doorway of what looked like a giant walk-in closet, Annie surveyed the well-organized area: shelves on the right held tightly sealed ceramic crocks filled with flour and white sugar, brown sugar, granola, and grains—enough to assemble an assortment of baked goods for twelve people or twenty; on the left, rows of smaller glass canning jars stored spices and seasonings and what Francine called "add-ons"— baker's chocolate, pure maple syrup, an array of dried fruits and nuts. And more, so much more. Across the back wall, specialty bakeware and appliances were stationed atop deep marble counters that featured built-in electrical outlets so Francine—or whoever was prepping breakfast—could keep any mess or noise out of sight and earshot of their guests. With an oversized farm sink and a refrigerator/freezer, the chef's room had been a brilliant addition. The main kitchen had another farm sink, the baking ovens, and an eight-burner, cast-iron cooktop so guests would be treated every morning to inviting aromas wafting into the great room where the massive dining table stood in front of floor-to-ceiling windows.

The dream they had created was, in large part, why Annie still had trouble believing all the wonderful things that had happened in the past couple of years. With enough gratitude in her heart to rein in her worries about the future—if only for a moment—she stepped into the room and asked, "Can you use my help with anything?"

"All is blissfully under control," Francine replied as she closed a drawer and jotted something on her iPad. "Claire's still upstairs with Bella; they're having a tea party."

Earl's wife had signed up for what she called "Morning Bella Duty." Every morning at seven o'clock, either Earl or Kevin brought Claire to the Inn so she could take charge of

Bella while Francine tended to breakfast. Their small team had learned to make things work, or, if need be, improvise.

Annie suppressed a wince, aware that the balance would be radically tipped if Kevin didn't come back. But determined to stay positive, she pushed down her apprehension and said, "You've turned into a wonderful mom, Francine."

"Only because of all the help I've had. But thanks, Annie. I mean, who knew, huh?"

Annie snickered. "I, for one, am not the least bit surprised."

Francine lowered her dark, soulful eyes and gave Annie a cockeyed smile, as she did whenever she was embarrassed.

"Did you have a nice dinner last night?" Annie asked. "With Jonas and the bass?"

Tilting her head, Francine said, "Yes. And before you ask, I do like him. A lot."

"I figured that. He's a nice young man. He's been through a lot."

"I know."

"And so have you."

"Maybe that's why we like each other," she said, lowering her eyes again.

Annie nodded. "Whatever makes you happy, makes me happy." She gave Francine a hug. "Now, I'm off to my other job. I'll be in the cottage trying to channel Agatha Christie in case anyone needs me."

"Good luck with that."

Annie waved and turned toward the back door as Francine called out, "Oh! Before you leave, can you please check our calendar and messages? I was in a hurry this morning and forgot."

"Will do, boss," Annie replied, which was a joke because the team had collectively decided that at The Vineyard Inn, no one would be the boss. Instead, though they each had certain chores—Annie's were to socialize with the guests when she wasn't writing, to help out with the vacuuming, dusting, and reservations when needed, and take care of anything else that no one either wanted to do or did not have the time for—they all had a say in the overall operation. After all, they were more than a team; they were a family, most of them not bound by blood but love.

Retracing her steps through the great room, Annie circled toward the staircase in the commodious, two-story foyer. She stopped at the front desk—an antique that had belonged to Earl's grandfather and, like his ancestors, had been on Chappaquiddick as long as anyone remembered. It was crafted of vintage, gleaming walnut, with nooks, crannies, pigeon holes, and, most important, a center drawer that now concealed a laptop so the old-world charm wouldn't be blighted by a visual of technology. The laptop was essential; when anyone wanted to book a room online, they were automatically linked to the Inn's calendar where they could see up-to-the-minute room availabilities and instantly make reservations.

Kevin had researched the perfect software. He was much better at understanding it than Annie, and light-years ahead of Earl, who took pride in his Luddite leanings. Kevin did not, however, get involved with the actual schedule; he jokingly referred to administrative "stuff" as women's work. He also said he'd had enough of book work when he'd had his construction business.

It now appeared that a pair of four-night reservations had been added to September's calendar. Annie checked the grid; the month was nearly full.

Then she listened to voice mail: "You have three messages."

The first was a hang-up.

The second caller wondered if they were taking reservations for Christmas. "Not a chance," Annie whispered, but would return the call because hospitality wasn't always about making money. She would explain that islanders rented the summer rooms off season in winter. It was another vow the "family" had made in order to provide housing opportunities to Vineyarders as well as to summer visitors. Technically, Francine's room would be available once she went back to college after Labor Day, but they'd decided to leave it open in case someone showed up on their doorstep in dire straits. More than anyone, Francine understood that. Kevin, Earl, and Annie also had made sure that Francine knew The Vineyard Inn was her home. Hers and Bella's. For as long as they wanted. And that their room would never be up for grabs for the sake of added revenue.

"Yes, hello," the third caller, a man, said. "I need two rooms starting this Tuesday for ten days. I just found out I can't get a rental car until the following Saturday. I didn't realize I'd need to reserve one this late in the season." He had an authoritative, almost familiar voice. A nice voice. Still, Annie would need to find an equally nice way to say, "Sorry, we're booked."

But the caller kept talking so she kept listening.

"I'll need someone to pick up my assistant and me. I'm not sure how the taxi service works out there. I've been told if we can get to the Inn, we can easily get back and forth from Chappaquiddick into Edgartown until I can rent the car. My flight arrives on Tuesday morning around eleven thirty." He paused, then said, "It's a private jet out of Teterboro. Thanks. Oh, and this is Simon Anderson."

For a second, Annie froze. Simon Anderson? She waited to hear more, but the message had ended. She stood motionless, holding the handset. Could it possibly be *the* Simon Anderson, the internationally recognized and respected journalist from CBN? She considered his voice. Authoritative. Strong. Yes. It could be him. Years ago, she'd watched him every evening on a local Boston news channel, most memorably during his edge-of-your-seat, "shelter-in-place" coverage of the Boston marathon bombing and the subsequent hunt for the suspects, which he'd delivered with calming, steady composure. Back then, Annie had given up teaching and was working at home; thanks to writing mysteries, her mind tended to wander toward the perilous, so she'd been terrified. But she'd heeded Simon's advice on how to be vigilant without being afraid, despite that the city was locked down for days. It wasn't long after that was resolved when his voice—steady and resonating—and his face—chiseled, Viking-like jawline, penetrating, teal blue eyes—were catapulted to a larger stage, a highly rated cable network. From New York he then brought news of everything from political unrest and racial tensions to the pandemonium of the pandemic into far-reaching homes, his delivery as credible and reassuring as she'd witnessed in Boston.

She supposed she shouldn't be shocked if *that* Simon Anderson wanted to visit the Vineyard. Though any accent he might have had was erased long ago (no doubt thanks to an expert voice coach), she remembered hearing that he'd grown up in Beantown. Besides, the Vineyard was a well-known respite for all types of celebrities. No, his presence wouldn't startle anyone. But why—considering the number of more luxurious, better-established places from Edgartown to Aquinnah and every town in between—had Simon Anderson picked *them*?

Of course, his request wasn't possible. They were full until after Labor Day weekend. Someone as in-the-know as he was should have guessed that.

Standing in the foyer, staring at the phone, she contemplated her next step. Should she return his call and say, "Thanks for thinking of us. I've been an admirer since you started out. However . . ."?

Suddenly, Francine was at her side. "Why are you standing here like a statue? And why are your cheeks so pink?"

Annie managed a tight grin. "Simon Anderson called." She related the details.

And Francine joined her in staring at the phone.

Which was when Murphy whispered, *Batten down the hatches, my friend.* And she said nothing more.

"He's hugely awesome," Francine said after they'd stood there, staring, for more than a minute. "We have to figure out a way."

"We can't," Annie replied. "We're booked."

"Give him my room."

"No. It's your home. And Bella's."

"We can go to Earl and Claire's. Kevin's not there now, remember?"

Yes, Annie remembered. "But you only have one room. Simon needs two. We can't ask one of our guests to leave early."

"But I could call the sisters from Indiana and tell them we have a gas leak or something."

"Seriously?"

"Yeah, never mind. It would probably go viral."

God knew Annie had had enough of things going viral in the spring. "I'll call him and say 'I'm sorry, we don't have a vacancy, but please think of us when you plan your next visit.' End of story." She aimed a finger at the call-back button; Francine pushed it away.

"Stop," she said. "Let's think about this." She gnawed on

a fingernail. "Bella and I can go to Jonas's. You can go to Earl and Claire's. Simon's assistant—whatever that means—can have my room. And Simon could take your cottage."

"No! *Nobody* gets my cottage, Francine. No one. *Ever.*" The cottage was her home, her quiet escape. Her place to work. Her place to be alone with John without his daughter—or soon, his *daughters*—around. "Besides, both of us can't leave the Inn with no one to look after it. What if something happens during the night?"

Francine exhaled loudly. "Annie. It's Simon Anderson."

"No, Francine. Forget that he's a celebrity. Think of him as a kid who, if he grew up in Boston, should have known to plan his Vineyard vacation earlier."

"But he'd give us huge visibility. I bet we could get him to post stuff all over social. And our other guests will run home and tell their friends. We could become the overnight go-to place. Maybe even a household name!" Her cheeks were pink now, too.

Annie sighed. "None of which will help. The bottom line is we'll still only have three rooms to rent in season. Everything else is for islanders, remember?"

Francine started in on another fingernail. "But it might jump-start Kevin's idea for special events. Weddings and stuff. Can't we get him on the phone? And bring Earl over? I think we should decide together. We're a *team*, Annie. I don't think we should walk away from this . . . this marketing opportunity, for the sake of a little inconvenience on our part."

Sensing she'd regret it, Annie said, "It's too early to call Hawaii, but when Earl comes back from the dump, we'll call Kevin. He should have a say in this, too." *And maybe*, she thought, *it might help him know how much they needed him there.*

"You should call Simon back and say we're working on a few logistics for him."

"No," Annie said. "Not yet."

"But what if he calls somewhere else while he's waiting?"

"Then he does. And we'll be off the hook. He should be no more special to us than the sisters from Indiana."

Francine pouted. "But he'd be our first real live celebrity." She cleared her throat. "Not that you aren't famous, but . . ."

Annie laughed. "But I don't happen to be in his league. I do know, though, that he's a person. That's all. If it's meant to be, we'll figure it out."

Leaving Francine alone with her fantasies, Annie went outside to the patio, gazed across the harbor, and wondered if, as Murphy had warned, she should get busy battening the hatches.

Chapter 4

"It's easy," Kevin said over the speakerphone when Annie told him Simon needed two rooms. "Francine can move in with you, or with Claire and Earl. On second thought, she could bunk in with Jonas—you'd like that a whole lot better, wouldn't you, Francine?"

Francine blushed. Suggesting it to Annie was one thing, but admitting to the men that she and Jonas were in love—if that's what it was—must have been embarrassing. "I'll do whatever works for everyone."

"Good," Kevin said. "Then you all can put Bella's mattress back into the twin frame. It's a nice room. And it's big. Simon Anderson would be lucky to have it."

"But we don't know if sharing a room is an option for him," Annie said. "He specifically asked for two." She tried to keep from sounding argumentative. Or from letting Earl or Francine think that she was being cautious with Kevin. "On tenterhooks," her dad would have called it.

"Give Anderson the choice," Kevin said. "Let him decide."

"And if he says no?"

He laughed. "Then give him a tent and charge him half

price." He paused for the briefest second. "In any case, you have my permission to do whatever you think will work. Now if you'll excuse me, there's a surfboard with my name on it awaiting my attention. Aloha to all." With that, he disconnected.

Kevin had probably been joking about the tent and the surfboard. Earl had laughed; Annie had not. She knew if they were going offer space to a winner of multiple Emmy Awards, it was not a joking matter; it would behoove them to do it right. And though Annie very much wanted to make life easier by calling Simon and conveying her regrets, she also knew that the publicity could potentially do nice things for the Inn. And for Annie's book sales, which Trish would definitely tell her when she shared the news. Maybe a few strategically placed photos on social media would result in a preorder boost for her upcoming *Murder on Exhibit: A Museum Girls Mystery.*

"Never miss a chance to touch greatness," Trish had once told her. "Your readers will feel as if they've touched it, too." Annie thought that referring to Simon as having "greatness" was a stretch, but there was no disputing that he was good at what he did. Or that he had a huge audience.

Calling Kevin, however, had been a mistake: hearing his voice only underscored the fact that he really was detached from them, disinterested in their trivial problems. Perhaps she would have been, too, if she were in Hawaii with someone she cared about.

The only solution was for Annie to take charge. So she told Earl and Francine they would only need to reconfigure the twin bed for aesthetics, that if Francine really didn't mind going somewhere else, they could put Simon's assistant in her room. Then she added, "And Simon can have my cottage. It's the best solution."

Earl's eyebrows shot up. "You sure?"

"Not really. I'm concerned that none of us will be on the

grounds during the night, but if I can go to your place, I won't be far. And I'll post my cell number at the front desk."

Rubbing his chin, a habit that Earl often claimed helped him think, he said, "It's a good idea for you to go to my house. But how about if I drag a sleeping bag upstairs over the workshop and camp out here? It's only half-finished up there, but it would mean that one of us will be here twenty-four-seven."

"Are you sure?" Annie asked.

"No reason not to. My wife will be grateful to have a break from me. Besides, I expect that, like most women in America, she has a crush on Mr. Anderson. She'll want to know we've done everything possible to make him comfortable." He rolled his eyes a little, the way Lucy, his granddaughter, often did.

Annie laughed, her anguish over their conversation with Kevin starting to fade.

"He is kind of good looking," Francine chimed in. "For an old guy."

The "old guy" was perhaps Annie's age. Or close to it.

"Well, okay, then," Earl continued. "Why not let him use Kevin's pickup, too? Then our guest won't have to wait to rent something."

"Seriously?" Annie asked.

Earl shrugged. "Kevin left it up to us to figure it out. Besides, the truck sits in the driveway, taking up space. It's unlocked. The keys aren't in it, but I bet they're around here somewhere."

Leaving the keys in an ignition wasn't uncommon on the Vineyard, especially on Chappy. After all, if anyone dared to steal it, they'd first have to cross back to the main island via the *On Time*, then try and get it onto one of the big boats. Which meant they'd have to provide the vehicle number and an ID.

In short, stolen cars and trucks happened so infrequently that when they did, the thieves were typically caught long before they made it to the mainland.

However, Annie wasn't sure they'd find the keys, especially if Kevin had never gotten rid of the handgun that he'd kept locked in the glove box. She did not, however, mention that to Earl. Nor did she suggest they hunt for the keys. If she wanted to avoid making Kevin angry, giving Simon Anderson free rein with the vehicle wouldn't help. So she nixed the idea.

Earl said he'd come back later and help her move whatever she wanted to get out of the cottage to make the place guest-worthy for Tuesday.

Before thinking about the million things she'd need to pack and store, Annie called Simon. "We've been able to arrange accommodations for you," she said.

"Thank you," he replied in a voice that sounded sincere, which boded well with Annie, who'd half-assumed that he'd be cavalier, because he might have expected nothing less. She wondered if his visit might turn out okay after all.

A couple of hours later, Annie was nearly done layering her clothes into plastic tubs, leaving her closet empty for Simon's belongings. She had until Tuesday morning to finish looking through, storing, and/or securing whatever else she wouldn't want him to have access to, though she supposed he'd have more interesting things to do while he was there than prowl through her closets or the junk drawer in the kitchen. She decided to leave the abundant volumes of reading material in her bookcases; he might enjoy perusing them. Maybe he'd admire the small but weighty reproduction of a famous sculpture of Agatha Christie that Annie kept on the top shelf. Murphy had given it to her when she'd started writing her first mystery. "To help channel your muse," she'd said. Annie continued to consult it whenever she had writer's block.

She thought about the other items she should tuck away. The electronic files pertaining to her books and finances were on her computer; she'd take that with her. There also were scores of notebooks where she scribbled down ideas, but she doubted that he'd want to steal them. Still, she locked the notebooks and a few hard copies of personal files in her Louis Vuitton trunk that held treasured photos and memorabilia from her past. There was no need to let a journalist loose among the intimate details of her life—no matter how *hugely awesome* he might be.

Annie wished she could talk to John about whether she'd been too hasty in giving up her space. Her home. But Abigail must already have arrived and was hopefully enjoying catching up with John and Lucy. And though Lucy had invited Annie to join them (actually, she'd begged her), Annie had politely declined. As much as she wanted to meet Abigail again and try and figure out how they might be friends, she knew John well enough to know that he'd need time to convene, assess, and regroup. She also knew it was going to take a whole lot more than moving the girl's old bed up from the basement for harmony to emerge. Harmony between John and Abigail, and, as important, between Abigail and Lucy.

Murphy was the closest Annie had ever come to having a sister. But the key difference was that they'd chosen each other as best friends; they hadn't been tossed together thanks to the same parents and a helix of similar DNA. Instead, they'd met in the hallway of their dorm the day they both were moving in for their freshman year at Boston University. With a map of the floor plan stuck between her teeth, a giant cardboard box heaped high with pillows, clothes, and shoes,

Annie fast-walked around a corner toward room 507 and ran smack into a redheaded girl who'd also been fast-walking in the opposite direction, her arms overloaded, too.

They both fell on their butts, their worldly belongings shooting across the linoleum, transforming the hall into what looked like the sorting area in the back room of a thrift store.

The redheaded girl said, "Well. We have collided. Are you okay?"

"It was my fault," Annie replied. "I'm sorry. I'm okay. Are you?"

"Yup. But don't be sorry. I was going too fast, too. Let's forget about it and make a pact to be best friends. Unless you already have one?"

Annie laughed. "Hardly. I just got here."

"Okay, then. I'm Murphy."

"Annie."

"Good. Now let's clean up this crap and find something to do. Four years is a long time. If we're going to be best friends, we might as well find out where the fun is."

It had been that simple. They'd stayed best friends for more than thirty years; through the weddings of their youth and Annie's young husband's tragic death, through Murphy's giving birth to twins, and through Annie's unfortunate years with her second husband. They'd held each other's hands when their parents died. The only time Annie had gotten angry with Murphy was when she'd become sick and died, too.

"Some friend you turned out to be," Annie said now as she snapped the lid on the storage tub closed.

Oh, stop whining, Murphy retorted from above, with more insistence than her usual whisper.

"I can't help it," Annie sighed. "You'd be whining, too, if I was the one who was dead and you were left to figure out how to do stuff on your own." She'd said it half-jokingly, so she was more than surprised when Murphy replied, *No kidding. My life would have been a disaster without you.*

Though intellectually, Annie supposed she knew that Murphy's words always came from Annie's imagination (or did they?), she chose to believe that her stalwart best buddy was still with her, would be with her to the end. And who could argue with that when Annie was the only one who Murphy talked to? Smiling now, somehow comforted, somehow having gained the will and the strength to start layering the contents of her bureau into another tub, Annie kept enough things out to put into a suitcase to take to Earl and Claire's.

Then Earl's trademark three short knocks on the screen door interrupted.

"Hey," she said, peeking from the bedroom and quickly whisking away the remnants of her emotions.

He went into the cottage and took a seat at Annie's compact table. "Hey, yourself. You packed?"

"Pretty much. I locked my valuables—what there are of them—in the Louis Vuitton. You don't suppose he'll pick the lock, do you?" Donna, Annie's birth mother, had gifted the pricey antique trunk to Annie; it wasn't until Donna died that Annie found secrets hidden inside.

"I have the impression you're not excited about this."

"I'm fine. I think it will be okay. And, by the way, I tacked on a little extra revenue for the cottage, so maybe Kevin will be impressed." Tired of her chore, she dumped the contents of the bottom bureau drawer into the last tub and snapped the lid closed. Then she pushed it into the living room. "It's strange, though, isn't it? Things had been going so smoothly. And now look at us. Francine and Bella are going to move into Jonas's. I'm moving to your house. And you're going to camp out in a sleeping bag on a plywood floor."

He rubbed his chin, as he'd done earlier. "For starters, I don't think Francine has a real problem moving in with Jonas, do you?"

Annie couldn't argue with that.

"And a change of scenery might be good for you, too. Like maybe staying with Claire will not only give her a rest from me, but will give you one from this place." He chuckled. "And after nearly fifty years marriage, I'm not above admitting I'm happy to get away from my dear wife." Of course, he was devoted to Claire, and she to him, and everyone on the Vineyard knew it. "Still," he liked to say, "fifty years is fifty years." Point taken.

She plunked down on the chair across from him. "You want a cinnamon roll? A cookie or something?"

"Nope. Leave 'em in the freezer for our celebrity guest."

She uttered a small groan. "I hope we haven't been too hasty. I can't stop feeling that this is exactly what we agreed we never would do: chase the money. It's as if we're saying, 'Honestly, we're full, but if you need a room, no problem. We'll hang from the rafters because we want your cash.' Yuck. Sure, the Inn is a business, Earl, but we all agreed we wouldn't be greedy." She didn't mention that she'd also up-charged their standard rate to give Simon's assistant Francine and Bella's room.

"We did. But I've been thinking about this, too, and if I were a betting man, I'd say that having Simon Anderson at The Vineyard Inn will be so good for our image it outweighs the rest. Who knows? Maybe he'll want to get married here."

"He's not married?" Annie asked, then hated that she'd stooped to that kind of natter. "Never mind. The fact is, I don't want this to be a precedent. We only rent three rooms in summer because we didn't build the Inn to have it become a big money business but to help out with the island housing crisis, including mine. The money from summer rentals is supposed to help us get through the winter and so we can keep the rentals affordable for islanders."

He nodded six or seven times; they had discussed those goals and objectives over and over since he and Kevin had come up with the plan a year ago.

"But there's another upside you haven't mentioned, Annie. Simon will be here for, what, ten days? I don't think there's any question that during his visit he'll be pumping big bucks into the local restaurants and the shops."

"Are you implying they don't get enough in August?"

Earl stood up. "If I were you, I wouldn't ask any of them that. Now, if you're finished, let's get those buckets stored in the workshop, and I'll pick out a prime spot for my old sleeping bag."

After they'd finished moving Annie's things, Earl went home. Annie went back to the cottage and stretched out on her bed, trying not to think about the fact that, once again, someone other than her would be occupying it.

The next thing she knew, it was six o'clock.

She bounded out of bed as if she'd been caught dawdling by one of the nuns at the Catholic elementary school that her mom, Ellen Sutton, had made sure Annie attended.

"It's nineteen seventy-four, Bob," Annie had overheard her mom say to her dad. "This isn't the fifties. The world is scary now, and Annie will need a proper education or she'll turn into one of those hippie girls in a psychedelic miniskirt."

"She's only six," her dad had replied.

But her mom had stood her ground.

So Annie ran a comb through her hair now, brushed her teeth, and smoothed her jersey and her jeans as if Sister Catherine Aloysius was waiting in the living room to conduct the mandatory grooming inspection.

Moving into the kitchen, Annie poured a glass of wine and pondered where she would have gone to school if Donna MacNeish had raised her, if Donna hadn't given Annie up for adoption. As she retreated outside to the porch, Annie didn't think she was feeling sorry for herself; she was merely sad that she was going to have to leave her comfy nest, her writer's room, and the silence she cherished more than she felt she should admit.

There was, she knew, a fine line between wanting, needing to be alone, and wanting, needing to be with another, who in this case was John. And though she'd accepted that her living arrangements would change once she and John married, Annie had imagined that though she'd move into his place, she would return to her cottage every morning to fulfill her duties at the Inn and to write. It had made perfect sense in Annie's world of make-believe, which was a good place for her brain to be when she was writing fiction, but wasn't always in sync with real life.

For starters, her dream had not considered that John mostly worked at night so he often wouldn't be home when she was there . . . and it would never have predicted that both his daughters would be living there, too, which was going to add a potentially difficult dimension. Nor had her fictitious plan addressed who'd be on the property of the Inn throughout the nights, a factor that suddenly felt significant.

"Excuse me," a woman's voice called out.

Grateful for the intrusion, Annie turned and saw Ms. Mullen, their turtle-researching guest, heading toward the cottage.

Oh, good, Annie thought. Whenever her mood began to slither down a somber path, she always welcomed positive distraction.

Chapter 5

"Sorry to intrude, but may I ask a quick question?"

Annie set her glass on the wood decking and stood up. "How can I help?" She noticed that Ms. Mullen had changed into black linen pants and a white top and wore a soft aqua scarf around her neck. Rather than pretty, she looked almost exotic, as if she were from an island in the Caribbean or far west, in the Pacific.

"Is there a restaurant on Chappaquiddick that's open for dinner?"

"I'm sorry, but no. There's a catering company, but I think you have to order before noon. Other than that, you'll need to go into Edgartown. Or catch a fish. Or forage for wild blueberries." She hoped she sounded cheerful and not as dour as she was. "The truth is, though we're only a ninety-second ferry ride into Edgartown, Chappy's fairly remote. And we love it like that. Will you join me for a glass of wine?"

"How nice. Thank you, I will. Unless I'm disturbing you . . ."

Annie raised a hand. "No. Please. You have no idea how

badly I needed to be disturbed." She smiled and added, "I'll be right back."

Thankfully, she hadn't packed the wine, though she supposed she should. Simon Anderson certainly could afford his own libations.

Returning in a flash with an empty glass in one hand, a bottle in the other, Annie asked if Pinot Grigio was okay.

Ms. Mullen nodded and the two women sat on the Adirondack chairs that were positioned for perfect sunset watching.

Annie poured; they sat quietly for a moment, gazing across the harbor.

"What a wonderful view you have," the woman said.

"It's a gem, all right." Annie felt her body and her brain finally begin to relax. "We were lucky to find this property."

"You're facing west; the sunsets must be magnificent."

"And every one is different. Some are muted; some are blazing. Some are pink; some are orange. I never get tired of them."

"And the Inn is new, right?"

"We opened Memorial Day weekend. And we haven't had a single glitch . . . yet." She saw no need to add the reshuffling required to suit Simon Anderson. "But tell me about yourself," Annie continued. "Starting with your first name, if you'd like."

Her companion sipped her wine. "Mary Beth."

"I'll remember that," Annie replied. "A teacher at the school where I taught was named Mary Beth. She wanted us to call her Mitzy, though. She said Mary Beth sounded provincial."

"And was she? Provincial?"

"I have no idea. She had white hair. Her body was pleasantly rotund. She wore dark red lipstick and flowered dresses that fell below her knees. She also wore white stockings, well after they'd gone out of style. I think she was past retirement, so I suppose she could have been provincial. She was nice, though. She was soft-spoken and kind to her students. I used to hope she had a secret life. You know, schoolmarm by day, harlot by night."

Mary Beth laughed. "Well, you can forget about imagining those things of me. Believe me, I am neither."

Annie's cheeks grew warm. "Good grief, I didn't mean anything like that. I was only reminiscing . . . oh, never mind. My imagination sometimes forgets it should not be connected to my mouth." She took a long sip of the Pinot. "But seriously, tell me about yourself. You're researching the leatherbacks?"

Mary Beth, who was not Mitzy the schoolmarm, rubbed her thumb against the glass. Then she said, "I never realized they were in the waters here. I knew that they come out of the water on Florida beaches to lay their eggs in the sand; I guess I always thought they stayed down there. But they migrate here when the waters get too warm in the south."

"The water's getting warmer here."

"I know. Which is why there's a greater need now to keep track of the leatherbacks."

"So, you're a marine biologist?"

She hesitated again. "Not really. Not yet. I'd like to get a job at the biological lab. I hope my research will give me a foot in the door. I've always been fascinated by the big turtles. They're prehistoric, you know."

"I didn't know that, but it makes sense. They're huge. And it's amazing that they swim all the way up from the south." She wondered if John realized that. Lucy might, as she was so curious.

"They can weigh anywhere from half a ton to two tons,"

Mary Beth continued. "Imagine! A four-thousand-pound turtle. Swimming in Vineyard Sound!"

Their conversation drifted to climate change, and Annie
shared what little she knew about the impact it was having on
the island. Before long, one of the beautiful sunsets began to
tint the sky, and Annie said, "I have an idea. How about if we
venture over to Edgartown together and grab a bite to eat?
Some place casual like The Wharf?"

Mary Beth vacillated, then politely declined. She stood up
and said she'd bothered Annie too long as it was.

But Annie said she was hungry and she'd cleaned out her
refrigerator except for a few cinnamon buns that wouldn't
constitute a very nutritious meal. What she didn't say was that
she felt comfortable with her guest, and that that night Annie
needed a friend, or at least the makings of one. She didn't
think Murphy would mind.

Mary Beth finally agreed, and Annie went inside to grab
her purse and a sweater.

Sunday nights in August typically posed a challenge to get
seated for dinner. Like many islanders, Annie didn't eat out
often in summer, preferring to let festive vacationers enjoy the
lobster rolls and crocks of chowder. In addition, John's crazy
work schedule often made it impossible for them to dine together, let alone in a restaurant with a long line. That night, if
Annie had been Irish not Scottish, she would have thought
she'd been granted a dose of ancestral luck when, after less
than five minutes, the host led them through the lively bar
into the large dining room that also was crowded. To say that
The Wharf was hopping was an understatement.

Best of all, they were seated at a booth, not a table. Annie
thought booths were more comfortable for conversation;
Kevin would have joked it was a sign that his sister was getting old.

He'd been gone less than two days, but it felt like a million.

They scanned the wine list, then each ordered a glass. Annie already knew what she'd order for dinner: the Seafood Jambalaya was one of her favorites.

While Mary Beth looked at the menu, Annie glanced around the restaurant—sometimes it was fun to be immersed in the happy clatter of summer. All around, people were decked out in August finery: Lily Pulitzer pastel sundresses, Vineyard Vines classic striped polos, Black Dog T-shirts. Everyone seemed merry, except across the aisle, a few tables away, where a man and woman sat, engaged in what looked like somber dialogue. The man's back was to Annie; she might know the woman, but didn't know from where. Her hair was neatly cut and coiffed, and she wore oversized silver hoop earrings. But there was something about the couple . . . about the man. And then . . . oh, God. It was John. Annie squinted. She knew those wide shoulders. And the woman . . . yes. The woman was his wife. Ex-wife. Annie had only met her once, but she'd had the same visceral reaction then: a knot twisting in her stomach.

"How's the grilled salmon?" Mary Beth asked.

Beneath the table, Annie clenched her hands, her fingernails pushing into her palms. She pulled her eyes back to her companion. "Excuse me?"

"The grilled salmon. Do you recommend it?"

Annie wanted to leave. She wanted to run outside, around the corner to Dock Street, all the way to the Chappy Ferry. She wanted to jump on it and go home. Fight or flight.

Stop it, she ordered herself because Murphy hadn't. *You're not twelve.*

"Is there something I might like better?" Mary Beth asked.

Annie tried to hide her agitation. "The salmon's fine," she managed to say. Her gaze traveled back to John and Jenn's table. She did not want to stare, but couldn't help it. John hadn't mentioned that his ex would be coming with Abigail. Wasn't that something a fiancé should have told his bride-to-be?

From her vantage point, it was tough to see whether or not there were other place settings—perhaps Abigail was with them . . . and Lucy? That would be more understandable. But as Annie discreetly craned her neck, she couldn't see other glasses or plates. Which made it obvious that John and Jenn were alone. Just the two of them.

The waitress reappeared and set their wineglasses down. She asked what they wanted. Annie was barely aware that she'd uttered "Jambalaya"; she was too busy trying to rationalize the situation. Maybe John hadn't expected to see Jenn, either—she did, after all, have a new boyfriend and was supposedly moving in with him. Which meant that surely she'd be leaving on the late boat.

"Annie?" Mary Beth asked quietly. "Are you okay?"

Annie knew her reaction was ridiculous; she blamed it on the stress of too many changes in the past two days: Kevin, Simon Anderson, now this. But she was currently with Mary Beth, a guest whom Annie wanted to help feel comfortable.

"I'm fine," she responded with a genuine smile. "Sorry. I'm just a little tired." She raised her glass in a toast. "Welcome to the Vineyard," she said. "Where everything is magical and only good things ever happen."

They clinked the stemware, and Annie carried on what she hoped was a halfway intelligent conversation until their meals arrived. That's when, from the corner of her eye, she saw John and Jenn stand up. She refused to let her knotted stomach ruin what should be a good time.

Jenn passed the booth first. She was looking toward the bar, oblivious, not that she'd remember Annie from their one brief meeting.

Then John started to pass. Annie sat up straight, prepared to say "Hi, what brings you to these parts?" or something equally light. Breezy. Not accusatory. But John was following his ex-wife's gaze until, as if by instinct, his line of sight flipped to his left and landed squarely on Annie's. Their eyes met, then locked, for a flash of a second. Then, without so much as a nod, he turned his attention away from Annie and kept walking, following Jenn's wedge sandals through the restaurant and out the front door.

Later, she decided that part had been the worst.

Annie woke up at four o'clock Monday morning after what she figured had been three hours of sleep. She could have paced the floor of the cottage the way she'd paced the downtown Boston apartment the night her first husband, Brian, had been hit and killed by a drunk driver; when she hadn't known where to put herself, or how to stop her racing thoughts. Or quiet her trembling nerves. Back then, of course, she'd still been in her twenties. Innocent. Naïve. Absolutely heartbroken.

Now, for God's sake, she was an adult, a real adult, solidly middle-aged. She wondered if gut reactions were predestined, like the size of someone's feet or the color of their natural hair.

She could have sat outside and stared up at the night sky, which, in the darkness on Chappy, often presented a brilliant canopy of stars.

Pacing would accelerate her agitation; staring up at the sky might either soothe her or make her more wistful. Not wanting to tempt becoming wistful, Annie did the one thing she could count on to settle her anxiety: she opened her laptop and started to work. Writing would be far more productive than dwelling on John.

Three cups of tea and two thousand words later, when the

sky was no longer dark but morning-sunny, her email pinged. She glanced at the clock: it was seven thirty. The message was from her editor; the subject line read: UPDATE. Knowing that Trish liked to tackle correspondence before heading to her office in midtown Manhattan, Annie promptly opened it.

GOOD MORNING, ANNIE. PUB DATE FOR *MURDER ON EXHIBIT* IS OFFICIAL: SEPT. 21. ATTACHED IS YOUR TOUR SCHEDULE. WE CUT IT BACK TO SIX WEEKS, BUT WE STEPPED UP INTERVIEWS AND SIGNINGS. SO YOU'LL MAKE MORE APPEARANCES IN LESS TIME. ALSO, THE SOCIAL MEDIA DEPT. HAS ARRANGED FOR YOU TO CONTRIBUTE A NUMBER OF ONLINE ARTICLES AND BLOG POSTS, SO PLEASE GET STARTED WRITING THOSE. THE ATTACHED SPREADSHEET OUTLINES THE WORD COUNTS AND DEADLINES.

IF THIS IS OVERWHELMING, IT'S YOUR OWN FAULT. IF YOUR BOOKS WEREN'T SO POPULAR, YOU'D HAVE LESS TO DO!

PLEASE CONFIRM ASAP THAT THE DATES WORK FOR YOU. AND KEEP GOING ON THE NEXT MANUSCRIPT. THANKS. TRISH.

Annie quickly did the math; September twenty-first was about five weeks away. Inhaling a deep breath, she opened the schedule: Boston, New York, Chicago, L.A. Followed by St. Louis, Houston, Atlanta, Miami. Eight major cities, with festivals and book fairs in between in places like Charleston, Milwaukee, and Bradford, Pennsylvania. She'd need to step up her energy level about ten thousand times more than she felt in that moment. She'd need to find time to prepare for speeches and interviews, to write blog posts and articles. To work on her next manuscript. And breathe.

If there was a bright side to Trish's demands, it was that John's antics—or rather, his non-antics—of the previous night would have to officially take a back seat. Their relationship would be, or it would not; there was little Annie could do, other than not let it overtake her. She supposed that few relationships were as easy as the one she'd had with Brian. Then again, they'd been too young and in love to think bad things could happen. At least, not to them.

They hadn't considered there would be an impaired, seventeen-year-old boy behind a wheel. Annie had never seen his face or been told his name because he was a minor; she only knew he lost his license for a couple of years. Because the night had been dark and rainy, and Brian had been wearing dark clothes, it was implied that he'd contributed to his own death.

And Annie was left having no recourse, other than to grieve.

More than twenty-five years later, she still found it surprising that she'd made it through the weeks and months that followed. But she had. And after the big blip with her second husband, she'd learned to maintain her balance and take care of herself. And neither John nor Kevin nor Simon Anderson could take that away from her.

She lowered her head and counted to ten—she liked to think the exercise helped put her brain cells back into good order so she could deal with things one at a time.

When she reached ten, Annie knew that some pelting hot water might also help, so she decided to take a shower. After breakfast she'd look at the spreadsheet of the articles and blog posts she'd need to write and when they were due. And then she'd figure out where she could work. After all, she was not only losing her home to Simon for ten days—she was losing her writing space, too.

Chapter 6

After Annie showered, dressed, and felt sufficiently determined not to let the prickly parts of her past wreck her nearly perfect life, she went up to the Inn. She ate every bite of a delightful breakfast—Francine's sinfully indulgent French toast casserole with peaches and a maple cream sauce. The guests clearly enjoyed it, too. Mary Beth, however, had not joined them, nor had she asked Francine for something to go. Annie hoped she hadn't been put off by Annie's sudden distress at dinner. Then she remembered that not everyone liked to be sociable, especially first thing in the morning. Perhaps Mary Beth's reason for skipping the meal was as simple as that.

Annie helped clean up the kitchen, then quickly vacuumed and dusted the main floor. She retreated to her cottage, opened her computer and the spreadsheet, and counted her blessings that she had so much to do. However, she knew that trying to get it all done while staying at Claire's might be difficult: she could easily be tempted to linger too long over tea, talk about John, speculate about the future. Claire would indulge her, but Annie would accomplish zilch.

She could have sneaked into the wonderful little cottage next door where she'd lived the first year she'd moved to the island, and where she'd often hid from the construction noise when the Inn was being built. But the new property owners had torn down the old place; the demolition had distressed Annie, as if the sweet memories of her new beginning had been bulldozed, too.

So now, grateful to at least have one last day to be able to work in her own place, Annie got started. An hour later, with the sizable list of her online commitments already organized, she had a good idea: she called Lottie Nelson, the manager at the Chappaquiddick Community Center, where Annie also had escaped more than once for a change of scenery in order to write. Those times, however, had been off season when the center was quiet; Lottie might not be able to accommodate her now, but maybe she could offer a suggestion or two. If anyone on Chappy would know who might have an isolated spot where Annie could retreat with her laptop, it would be Lottie. Or Earl, of course, but Annie had bothered him enough.

"I'm desperate for a hideout for ten days," she said when Lottie answered the phone. "I have a book coming out next month, and I have to do a ton of things to promote it. The Inn will be hectic, so I need a quiet place to work in the afternoons."

"What kind of place?"

"An attic? A shed with Wi-Fi? I'm not fussy." She'd thought about the apartment over the garage at Taylor's house where Jonas had been living before Taylor departed. But with Francine and Bella staying with Jonas while Simon was at the Inn, Annie feared she'd be as distracted as she'd be at Claire's.

"You have to have Wi-Fi?"

"Preferably. Yes."

"Well, that ups the ante to nearly impossible."

"I know. But I'll need to do some research . . ."

"How soon?"

"Tomorrow."

Lottie laughed. "Well, that's doubtful, too, what with the fair and everything leading up to it. What about next week?"

"Too late."

"Too bad. You could always come here, but we're booked solid until after Labor Day."

"I figured as much. Well, thanks, Lottie. If you hear of anything, I'd appreciate it if you'd keep me in mind."

"No problem." Then Lottie hesitated. "Wait. What about the fire station?"

"The fire station?"

"There's a big room that they use for meetings, but those are mostly at night. There's a table and chairs. And a small kitchen with a microwave and fridge, so you could bring food or make tea or whatever. I know it's town property, but . . ."

"But if no one was told . . ."

"Well, then, no one would know."

It went without saying that "no one" referred to the politicos in Edgartown, because Chappy was governed by them.

"It will only be for ten days."

"I'll let you know. My husband's a volunteer fireman." The last sentence wasn't really news because, at one time or another, most Chappy year-rounders were.

"You're my savior, Lottie," Annie said.

"Let's hope it works. If not, I'll keep my radar on for something else."

They hung up and Annie vowed to get Lottie something special for her trouble. Maybe something handcrafted by Annie's dear friend Winnie Lathrop, an Aquinnah Wampanoag who lived up island—perhaps a piece of her pottery bowls or a pair of wampum earrings. Annie didn't think the gift would be considered graft . . . but on the outside chance that she could be wrong, she'd be sure not to mention it to law-and-order John.

Returning to the spreadsheet, she began to consider topics for the blog posts. Sometime after two o'clock there was a knock on the cottage screen door.

"Hey, Annie, are you in there?" It was Lucy, John's younger daughter, and she sounded in distress.

Annie closed her eyes, counted to five (Lucy wouldn't be patient enough to wait for her to reach ten), then said, "Come on in, honey. I'm in the writer's room."

"She's impossible. *Impossible*," Lucy said as she marched in.

As badly as Annie wanted to ask if Lucy was talking about Abigail or her mother, she suppressed it.

"I'm serious, Annie. I'm going to run away." She flopped down on the beanbag chair that Annie had tucked into the corner for when she wanted a timeout from the ergonomic office chair with lumbar support and headrest that she'd splurged on when she'd moved into the cottage. And for when Lucy visited.

"Where will you go?"

"I don't know." She coiled the end of her caramel-colored single plait that she'd recently started wearing draped over one shoulder. The small splash of freckles around her pixie-like nose was one of the few hints of childhood that, so far, she'd retained. "They'll find me if I'm on Chappy. Maybe I'll hitch a ride up island. Do you think Winnie can put me up in that big house of theirs?"

Annie smiled. "I slept on Winnie's floor one night with Bella, when Bella was a baby. But I'm not sure they have a spare room, what with Winnie's family—her 'clan,' as she affectionately calls them—growing every year. Do you want to tell me what happened?"

Lucy moaned. "It *really* sucks. *She* really sucks. Why can't I have a sister who doesn't suck?"

Wheeling away from the small desk and moving closer to the beanbag, Annie said, "Well, I never had a sister, so I can't help you there. Sorry."

"All she does is sit on the bed with her earbuds stuck in her ears, listening to music while she looks at stupid clothes on her computer. Like she needs a drop-dead wardrobe because she has somewhere special to go." She rolled her eyes. "She won't talk to me. And worse, she totally ignores Restless. *Restless!* Why would she ignore him? What'd he ever do to her?"

Restless was the adorable dog that John had adopted from the shelter. He had grown a lot over the summer; he was black and white and fluffy, and John was convinced he had a good deal of Bernese Mountain Dog in him. Most of all, Restless loved people, and people loved him back.

"I can't imagine he did anything. But I do know it must be hard for her right now. She cares a lot about you and your dad, but she made no secret about not wanting to live here. Things in Plymouth must have been really uncomfortable for her to have come back." Annie was rather proud of herself for sounding calm and understanding about the latest bit of turmoil that had arrived on yesterday's two thirty boat.

Lucy folded her arms and pouted. "Abigail, Abigail. Everything's always about her. She's always been spoiled because she can't find her own way out of a damn paper bag."

Annie laughed. "I don't think swearing will help resolve the situation. My dad used to say that, for better or worse, all things change with time. Until then, why not find something else to do? Did you bring Francine cookies today?"

Lucy nodded. "She asked for peanut butter this week."

As per their original agreement, Lucy provided the Inn with cookies on a regular basis; the Inn made them available to the guests, day or night. Her profits were going into her college fund—hopefully they wouldn't be diverted now to pay for her to run away from home.

"Did you make muffins?" Annie asked.

"No. Francine makes them better."

"What's the difference?"

She shrugged.

Annie stood up. "Okay, here's an idea. You have two weeks before school starts, right?"

"Yeah."

"Why not take advantage of it? I bet Francine won't mind if you help her with the baking. Maybe she can show you some things she's been learning at college."

Pursing her lips, Lucy seemed to ponder the suggestion. "I suppose."

"Don't suppose. Say yes. It will get you out of the house and away from the sister who right now really sucks."

She pursed some more. "I'm going to the fair with my friends on Friday."

"Good. Between now and then, maybe you can further cultivate your baking skills."

"But can I . . . can I stay here? Like here in the cottage with you until school starts?"

Annie sighed. "I would ask your father, Lucy, honestly I would. But I'm going to be staying at your grandparents'. We had an emergency situation and needed to make extra space for a guest, so I'm moving out of here for ten days."

Lucy stood up. She'd shot up over the summer and now was nearly eye to eye with Annie. "You mean there won't even be room for me at Gramma and Grandpa's? I figured if Winnie had no room, and if you didn't want me, then I could at least have gone there. With Kevin in *Hawaii*." She wrinkled her nose as she said "Hawaii" as if she didn't think that Kevin's trip had been a good idea, either.

Annie didn't want to mention Simon's name. Lucy was an avid viewer of the news but hadn't yet perfected the art of tempering her teenage exuberance with discretion. "I'm sorry, honey. Please understand, it's not that I don't want you here. I don't have a choice right now."

"Well," Lucy said, her voice cracking most likely from feelings that were poised to let loose, "that sucks, too." She then spun on her heels, left the cottage, and headed up the hill, hopefully to track down Francine.

The good part was that Lucy hadn't once mentioned her mother. So maybe Jenn had left last night after all.

Annie rubbed the back of her neck, hoping it would help her relax.

After resuming what she referred to as her "writing position" while at the keyboard—feet flat on the floor, backbone straight, two fingers on each hand arced in a highly unprofessional, yet effective-for-her, manner—Annie tried to come up with a few clever blog post ideas (she'd be happy if she only concocted one) that could somehow relate to *Murder on Exhibit*. But she was feeling glum, and her thoughts wouldn't gel. She wondered if other authors had trouble remembering the details of a manuscript they'd finished months ago when they were deeply embroiled in the next.

Several minutes later, she gave up, slipped into her flip-flops, and went outside for a walk. Instead of going toward the road, she turned and headed down to the beach, which she'd avoided most of the summer thanks to the tragedy it had wrought last spring. Like with other things, she needed to get over that.

The early afternoon was hot, the sun still filled with summer. She adjusted her sunglasses, tucked her hair behind her ears, and put her hands into the empty pockets of her sundress. She hadn't brought her phone; she hadn't locked the cottage door, so she didn't have her keys, either. Sometimes when she felt a need to focus, Annie paid little attention to minutia.

She tried to remember the types of questions that readers tended to ask at her previous appearances—maybe they would offer a few kernels that she could turn into guest blog posts.

"Do you write every day?" No, she decided. Too boring.

"Where do you get your ideas?" No. Too broad-reaching.

"Why do you write mysteries?" *Huh,* she thought. *That might be a good one.* Then she remembered it was one of the first questions Kevin had asked her. He later admitted he had been trying to decipher whether or not his newly found sister was a closet sociopath. Or worse. They'd laughed together over that because by then Annie knew he could be a comedian. He had, however, insisted he wasn't kidding until she threatened to stop feeding him, at which point he immediately confessed that yes, it had been a joke.

She slipped out of her flip-flops now and let the sand rise up between her toes, knowing it was not the right time to be thinking about her brother. She simply had too much to do.

Instead she watched the gentle waves lap the shore and the lovely, small *Pied Piper* as it entered the harbor, ferrying visitors to Edgartown from Falmouth on Cape Cod. The Inn had a coveted strip of beachfront that stretched over four hundred feet in each direction—Earl said they should tell their "fitness-fervent guests" that, from one end to the other, a mere three and a quarter round-trips equaled a mile. Annie hadn't checked his math, but assumed that he was right or, as he often boasted, he was "close enough."

Heading south, she began to pace the first four hundred feet, hoping the activity would recharge her brain. She wondered if she should open the blog with an amusing anecdote that her choice of writing murder mysteries had absolutely no connection to having taught third grade for over fifteen years. At her appearances, that tended to bring hearty laughs. She wasn't sure if it would have the same effect in print or if it would be creepy.

The truth was, Annie had no concrete idea why she'd landed firmly on mysteries. She supposed it was because, having been raised as an only child, she'd always loved to read. Agatha Christie—the woman whose 3-D head likeness graced Annie's bookshelf—had been a favorite. But so had Joan Collins and her steamy romances. And Maeve Binchy and her small-town, friends-and-family dramas. However, for the blog, she supposed she should stick to the Christie vein—she could include a photo of the sculpture and add a short comment about her best friend who'd wanted Annie to be inspired by it.

"Whenever I see you out walking alone," a voice interrupted her thoughts, "I'm not sure if you're getting fresh air or if you're working in your head."

Annie bit her lip. Then she turned and looked up at John, who was standing on the grassy dunes. "A little of each today," she said.

"Want some company?"

"Sure."

As he jumped down to the beach, Annie noticed he was wearing cargo shorts and a T-shirt, not exactly a detective sergeant's outfit.

"You're not on duty?"

He shook his head and caught up to her. "Not right now. I worked midnight to noon. I switched with Dan when Abigail texted to warn me that Jenn was with her. I didn't want to be in my house all night with . . . *her* . . . there."

"Oh." What else should Annie say? That seeing Jenn must have been a nice surprise?

Snarky, snarky, Murphy would have whispered though when John was around, she typically gave them privacy.

"I'm sorry about last night," John continued. "I didn't expect to run into you at The Wharf."

Annie nodded and resumed walking; he fell into step beside her.

"I didn't know what to say," he added. "I thought it would upset you. That I was there with . . . her."

"It did," she replied. "But only because I wasn't prepared. And because you didn't say hello. It felt as if you thought you'd been caught doing something you shouldn't have been doing."

"I know. That was pretty stupid."

She didn't feel a need to say she agreed.

"Jenn wanted to talk about Abigail. To tell me about some stuff she's been doing. Like smoking. Cigarettes, you know? Who the heck in their right mind starts smoking cigarettes these days?"

Annie nodded.

"You'd never know it, but she's a smart girl. Or at least she used to be."

Because Annie did not really know the girl, she didn't reply to that, either.

He stopped. He reached out and took her arm, so she stopped, too.

"I'm sorry, Annie. But everything happened so fast. I didn't know what to do. When Abigail said her mother was coming with her and would stay overnight, I only had time to call Dan." He huffed out a little air as if he'd run out of words. "I didn't see the message 'til I was on my way to get her. I was going to wait to tell you until after Jenn left. As soon as I got off duty today, I changed my clothes, rustled her into the truck, and dropped her off at the one fifteen. Then I drove here."

Annie pivoted in the sand until she faced him. She raised her hands, put them on his cheeks, and gave him a light kiss.

"I believe you. It's not as if you could have gotten away with me not knowing. Not on this island, anyway."

He smiled. "Man, that's the truth."

"Can we have dinner tonight?"

A thin veil of apology crept across his face. "Sorry. I'm back on four-to-midnight."

"I hate your job sometimes. Well, I hate the hours, anyway."

"Me, too. I'd come over after but I only slept a couple of hours before I went in last night and . . ."

"And you're exhausted. And you need to be home for your daughters."

"Just for now. Until I'm sure . . ."

She shushed him with another kiss. One way or another, they would find a way to work on their relationship. Or they would not. Perhaps the six weeks of separation that her book tour would impose might turn out to be a test. Because Annie knew her dad had been right that, for better or worse, all things really did change with time.

Chapter 7

By the time John left for Stop & Shop to buy food that Abigail had requested ("She's a vegan now and only eats plant stuff," he'd said), and then to go home and get ready to go back to work, Lottie called to say Annie could use the fire station's meeting room—as long as she didn't mention it to anyone. Lottie's husband, Joe, would be there that afternoon if Annie wanted to check it out.

Grabbing her laptop, phone, and purse from the cottage, Annie decided she might as well go and test the Wi-Fi connection. Being able to search for things—including proper spellings—had become an important time-saver as it meant she could write a draft that was close to a final version. With everything else she had to do, there would be little time to "lollygag." She loved that old-fashioned word; she'd often used it to round up her third-graders and get them indoors after recess because it made them laugh. Annie missed teaching sometimes, missed being a pseudo-parent for six or more hours a day. Pseudo, not like John, who was a real dad twenty-four seven. But Annie knew that he was trying. She also knew he would put forth his best effort to be a good husband, too. One day. Soon.

Before heading out, she dashed into the Inn to see when the sisters from Indiana would be arriving, and to ask if Francine needed help revamping her room for Simon's assistant.

Francine was upstairs, putting a downy white comforter on the twin bed Bella used in their special room. In order to make it toddler-safe, Earl and Kevin had moved the frame and headboard into the storage room and set the box spring and mattress on the floor. Francine had dressed it with bedding that was identical to what she had on her bed—and Bella loved it. But now, with the frame and headboard in place, and Bella's toys and dolls evacuated to the storage closet, it looked like a room for grown-ups.

Annie set down her things and helped make the bed. "Did you put the frame and headboard back together by yourself?"

Francine laughed. "Men are like cops. There's never one around when you really need one."

"I won't tell John you said that. But you could have called me."

"Don't worry, I haven't turned into a martyr. Lucy helped. We also made more muffins and put them in the freezer in case of emergency." Francine looked happy, almost radiant; Annie sensed that, these days, life was agreeing with her.

"Where's Lucy now?"

"She rode her bike to Earl and Claire's."

"Ah, yes," Annie replied. "Like many of us, she's in need of some major distraction."

"Loo–see," Bella mimicked from her seat on a tiny stool at her very own table (Earl's wood crafting again) that would soon go into the closet, too. She was drawing colorful lines and squiggles on pieces of cardboard that looked as if they'd come from cartons of supplies sent to the Inn. Clever and conscientious, Francine recycled the shipping material after Bella had repurposed it for artwork.

"Fow-ers," Bella said next and held out her masterpiece for Annie to admire.

"Very pretty!" Annie exclaimed. "They look like the flowers at Gramma Claire's."

Bella's large dark eyes—that mirrored Francine's—widened as she studied the picture. Then she started to draw something purple.

"I think Bella and I should go to Jonas's tonight," Francine said. "Now that the room's clean for Simon's assistant, I'd rather not mess it up again."

"Good thinking. I'll be here in case anyone needs anything. We could risk leaving the Inn alone for one night, but with the sisters arriving . . ."

"But," Francine interrupted, "the sisters have landed, and they might need help with who knows what. And Ms. Mullen's only been here a couple of days so . . ." Her words trailed off as she smoothed the comforter, plumped powder blue and lavender pillows, and then, lowering her voice, said, "Which reminds me, there's something odd about her."

"Mary Beth?" Annie said. "Her first name is Mary Beth."

"Yeah, well, she makes me nervous, so I don't care about being on a first-name basis. I really think that something strange is going on with her."

"What do you mean? She acts fine to me."

"When I was cleaning her room this morning, I came across a bunch of library books."

"So?"

"They were about turtles. The leatherbacks. The kind she said she's researching."

"People use library books for research. What's odd about that?"

Francine shook her head. "They were children's books."

Annie scowled. "What?"

"Children's books. Picture books, actually. If she's a scientist, why the heck does she want those? Doesn't she already know the stuff that's in them? And if she works at the marine lab, why isn't she staying at their housing? Don't they have housing here for researchers?"

Annie refrained from saying she'd wondered the same thing. "The truth is, she doesn't work there yet. She's hoping that her research will help her land a job."

"Really? Well, that raises the weird factor even higher. How is she going to get a job at a science-y place like that by reading kids' books?" Adjusting the pillows so the bed looked tended to by a professional decorator, she added, "Like I said, it's odd. Or maybe I'm taking it personally that she doesn't join us for breakfast."

Annie tried to recall if Mary Beth had said or done anything that could be construed as "odd." After all, the night before when they'd been at The Wharf, if either of them had acted strangely, it had been Annie. "I had dinner with her last night, and honestly, she was okay."

Francine shrugged. "Forget it. I'm overreacting, that's all."

But Annie pressed on. "Maybe she doesn't want a job at all. Maybe she's trying to write a children's book about turtles, too. Maybe she didn't want to tell us because, well, because she didn't want us to think she was going to impose on me for advice on how to get published. Not that I'd have a clue."

"Yeah. I suppose that's possible."

Francine then placed a bar of Annie's honey-and-sunflower soap in one of the large oyster shells that Annie had collected on South Beach, then cleaned and varnished and set on the vanity in each guest room bath. Though Francine didn't mention Ms. Mullen or the turtle books again, Annie couldn't shake the feeling that, with all the guests they had welcomed over the summer, it was the first time she'd heard Francine complain about anyone.

★ ★ ★

Lottie's husband, Joe, was a volunteer firefighter, a Chappy Ferry captain, and a guard at Wasque Point in summer. It was no surprise that, though Annie hadn't known his name, she recognized the barrel-chested, ruddy-cheeked, smiling man as one of the many unsung people who made Chappaquiddick run.

After Annie left Francine, she'd gone straight to the station to see if it would make a sufficient temporary office for her displacement from the Inn. Joe let her in the side door of the white-cedar-shingled station that featured three tall bays, and, as Earl had once told her, was a "giant hook-and-ladder step up" from the single-bay garage that had been upgraded some fifteen years earlier. Annie wasn't convinced his description made much sense as the equipment wouldn't have needed to be big (there were no high-rises on Chappy), but she understood the gist.

"Happy to accommodate you," Joe said once they were in a large room where a small truck and a rescue boat were anchored. "My wife's a big fan of your books."

That was news to Annie. It was also part of what she loved about the island—almost all of her readers who lived there allowed her to blend into the scrub oaks and be as anonymous as she wanted.

"Lottie says you need Wi-Fi. Not many people know it, but we get great reception here."

Annie decided to take his word for that. If she said she'd like to test it, he might be insulted.

He gestured for her to follow him past the vehicles to an open room.

Several folding chairs rimmed the space; an eight-foot table sat in the center; an easy chair was tucked in a corner. A small kitchen was on one side; restrooms were on the other.

"All the comforts of home," he said, "without kids, dogs, or chickens. Not that you ever have to worry about any of those." He chuckled the same way Earl often chuckled, as if it were a trademark of Chappy. "You think that brother of yours is ever coming back?"

His question startled her. "I certainly hope so."

"Now that your inn's done . . . and what with Taylor gone . . . there's been talk about trying to get Kevin to help out with the rescue team."

"Thanks, Joe. I'll mention it to him." *If I ever see him again*, she was tempted to add.

"'Course, you all have had a lot on your plate. Starting up the place and being full most of the summer. Lottie said she saw Earl the other day, and he's looking a mite haggard. The man loves to work, but, like the rest of us, I 'spect he's getting up there."

Annie was stunned. Was Earl "looking a mite haggard"? If so, why hadn't she noticed? Maybe they—she—had been expecting too much from a seventy-five-year-old man . . . who was about to sleep on a plywood floor for ten nights.

Clearing her throat, she said, "None of us is getting younger, for sure. I guess staying active keeps us going." She hoped she didn't sound annoyed. "Anyway, thanks for helping me out of a jam. I'll be back tomorrow afternoon."

"Ought to be a busy week for you. What with your special guest arriving."

Once again, Annie was amazed at how quickly news was broadcast around the island, no matter how hard one tried to keep a secret.

"Here's hoping Mr. Anderson's visit won't trigger any ambulance runs to your place," Joe added. "We've enjoyed the peace and quiet over there these past few months." He chuckled again and led her to the side door.

Annie laughed, but wished he hadn't said that. She wasn't ordinarily superstitious, but . . .

She decided not to think about it and followed Lottie's husband back outside.

It wasn't going to work. Annie sat in the Jeep that she'd parked on the clamshell driveway once she was back at the Inn. From there she could see two gray-haired ladies on the patio chatting with the young honeymooners, all of whom were drinking what looked like lemonade, all gazing toward the harbor and the sailboats and the lighthouse and its beacon that blinked red every sixty seconds. From where she sat, she could tell that the conversation was upbeat, the pleasant white noise of summer vacation.

But Annie wasn't on vacation; this was her life. And she knew that her plan to focus on her book promotions, at the exclusion of her other responsibilities, simply would not work. Not this week, anyway, which promised to be as busy as the week of the Fourth of July, with its pulse set to quicken the next day when Simon arrived. He and his assistant (whoever it was) would total seven guests, with the honeymoon couple, Mary Beth Mullen, and the Indiana sisters. Adding the four year-round tenants—two singles and one couple—the count increased to eleven people who'd be depending on Francine by day and Earl by night—both of whom, of course, must be worn out by now. Annie wished she'd paid closer attention to the state of their well-being. And as upset as she was about Kevin having taken off, she suddenly realized that she hadn't been carrying her share of the load, either; she'd selfishly expected that the place would run smoothly with her barely lifting a finger.

Shutting off the ignition, she faced the facts. The Inn was thriving, but she could not sit back while two people she loved were being run into the waterfront-property ground. Her writing life would never—could never—be more important than her island family.

So she got out of her Jeep, waved at the folks on the patio, and skipped into the back door of the Inn. Francine was in the kitchen, scooping batter that was bursting with cranberries into a loaf tin. Bella was in the corner, pretending to grill plastic burgers in her Fisher Price Food Truck, which Earl had bought, not built.

"Annie!" Bella squealed and threw open her arms.

Nothing is better than this, Annie thought and knew that Murphy—though her twin boys had often been lively and rambunctious—would have agreed. Swallowing the tickle that rose in her throat each time she thought of her old friend, she picked up Bella, gave her a quick hug, and turned to Francine. "Stop what you're doing," Annie said. "Right now."

Francine slipped her hand into a potholder mitt. "Yes, ma'am," she said with a salute. "Right after I stick this in the oven. I'm trying to get a jump on tomorrow. I'm betting we'll be busy, what with . . . you know."

"Yes," Annie said. "I know. I also know I told you to *stop*. Right. Now."

"Stop," Bella repeated. "Right. Now."

Francine frowned and brushed a runaway strand from her brow. "You look serious."

"I am," Annie said. "Get your things. You're going to Jonas's. You're not going to wait until tonight. You are officially on vacation for an entire day and a half. I don't want to see you until Wednesday for breakfast. As for tomorrow, it might not be brunch at the Harbor View, but I'll serve your cranberry bread, and I'll fix something else. Maybe something with eggs. Or yogurt and Cheerios. No matter what, I promise you, everyone will survive. I don't want to see you until Wednesday morning."

"But . . ."

Annie walked over and nudged her with her hip. "Out of my way, please. I have bread to bake."

"But we need more cookies . . ."

"I'll ask Lucy to come back and make them in the morning."

"But in the morning the rooms will need cleaning . . ."

"I know how to do that." Perhaps she'd give Lucy a quick training on how to run an inn beyond the kitchen. After all, maybe in years to come, Francine and Lucy would be the Inn's proprietors. She blinked, not knowing where that last idea had come from.

"But you have to pick up Simon . . ."

"I'll manage. And I'm giving Earl a day off, too."

Francine looked confused. "Why, Annie? Did we do something wrong?" Her big eyes glossed over.

With one arm holding Bella, Annie folded the other around Francine. "Oh, my God, no. You are amazing. But you deserve a break. Please let me do this."

Francine laughed, then stepped from Annie's grasp and untied the strings of her apron. "All right, you win." She set the apron on the counter, then held her arms out for Bella. "Come on, little one. We're being booted out."

But Annie held up one hand. "Not so fast. I said *you're* on vacation. That includes a break our little Miss. You are going to Jonas's, and I am going to babysit. End of discussion."

More tears welled up. "Seriously?"

"Seriously. But because I do believe this little lady has out-grown my bottom bureau drawer, you'll need to tell me where her travel bed is. Bella and I are going to have a sleep-over."

"Would you like that?" Francine asked, as she touched Bella's chin.

"Yes, please," Bella responded, as if she understood the word "sleepover." She was a happy little girl and, best of all, she clearly knew that she was safe with them.

* ★ ★

When the bread was out of the oven, cooled, wrapped, and ready for breakfast, Annie put Bella in the car seat she kept in her Jeep and drove to Earl and Claire's. He was outside, pulling weeds from the garden while Claire stood by, instructing.

With shoulders squared, chin elevated with what she hoped looked like authority, and Bella riding on her hip, Annie walked over and to Earl and announced, "I've decided that your services will be best utilized if you are not sleeping on the floor above the workshop."

He stopped weeding and stared at her. He did, indeed, look a mite haggard. "I disagree. Someone has to stay there."

"Which is what I intend to do. As long as you lend me a sleeping bag. Bella will sleep in the cottage with me tonight, but I was hoping you wouldn't mind if she stayed here for a few days? Maybe while Simon's at the Inn?" She knew it was a lot to ask—a few days with a two-year-old could test the most well-meaning people, let alone older ones who were accustomed to a more serene life. "I really want to give Francine a break. And you. I don't want you to show up at the Inn unless you're summoned."

Claire reached over and rubbed Bella's arm. "Oh, my, of course we'll take her. What I wouldn't give to have this precious one back in our house!"

Right, Annie thought. Earl and Claire were a different breed of older people. They were islanders who took care of their own and, often, everyone else's. "She no longer needs the crib," Annie said. "She'll be fine in the travel bed Francine brought from Minnesota. But tonight, she's all mine. We'll stay in the cottage and maybe make cookies."

"Cookies!" Bella said, and everyone laughed, and Annie knew that she'd done the right thing.

Perhaps the most important thing Annie had learned since moving to the island was that sometimes people simply had to step up for one another.

He was awakened by a sweet scent of wild orchids wafting through the window's louvered shutters. The last two days had been unimaginable, almost dreamlike. Maybe it was due to the rum punch, or maybe it was because of her—the woman who lay beside him now, her amazing auburn mane splayed across the now-wrinkled white bedsheets like incoming waves over the soft sands of low tide.

If Kevin told anyone, no one would believe that two days earlier marked the first time he'd slept with Taylor, the first time they'd had real, honest-to-God, passionate sex that had made him crazy with desire as that thicket of auburn heaven had swept every which way over every inch of him until the wee hours.

Until then, it had been nearly four years since Kevin had made love. In all that time, he never thought he'd want to again. And he had not. Until two nights ago. When the rum punch and the scent of those wild orchids and that hair*—the same hair she used to hide under knit, woolen hats—and those long legs and that lean-muscled, temptress body—that she used to conceal in jeans and quilted vests—had done all the work that he never dreamed he'd once again be capable of. Not until he'd left not only Boston, but the whole damn Northeast, including, God help him, Martha's Vineyard.*

And though he knew full well he was acting like a stupid, horny kid, he could not seem to stop himself.

So he rolled toward her again and dove, again, into her warm, welcoming space.

Chapter 8

Tuesday morning arrived, and with it came rain. Lots and lots of rain. Which meant that everyone was moving slowly and had stayed inside. Only Mary Beth had disappeared, having ventured into the torrents.

The others lingered at the table, happily picking at "one more" slice of cranberry bread and having "one more" cup of tea or coffee, all the while sharing stories of kayaking and restaurants and disagreeing with good humor over which shops up at the cliffs carried the most unique handcrafted treasures.

Annie was grateful that Earl had stopped by early and whisked Bella away, though the night before had been wonderful. Annie had made chicken and veggie meatballs with homemade marinara sauce that Bella had devoured; they'd baked chocolate chip cookies and shared a giant one while it was still warm from the oven. Then Annie read the story of the little mermaid, and Bella fell asleep in Annie's lap. It was perfect.

Things were not perfect now. She checked her watch—ten thirty, only one hour until Simon's plane landed. She willed herself not to wring her hands or drum her fingers on

the artisanal wood table. Finally, she interrupted one of the
Indiana sisters (Toni and Ginny Taft—Toni was a retired
flight attendant, and Ginny had been a schoolteacher—though
Annie had trouble remembering who was who). "I have a
small request," she said. "As everyone knows, this is the second biggest, if not the biggest week on the Vineyard. People
from all over the planet will be here. Well, not here at the
Inn, exactly, though we've been asked to squeeze in a couple
of extra guests. Francine is taking today off to gear up for the
rest of the week."

She smiled in an effort to reassure everyone that they'd still
be well looked after.

"So I need to ask our guests a favor," Annie continued.
"If you'd like your sheets changed today, would you mind
doing it yourself? And if you need clean towels, would you
please help yourself from the linen room upstairs? I hate to
impose, but after I clean up the kitchen, I have to make an
airport run . . ."

Her stomach tightened as she waited for someone to say
something. Anything.

Then the honeymoon bride stood up. "My husband
would be delighted to take part in domestic duties," she said
with a toothy grin.

Then he stood, too. "If my wife agrees to wash dishes, I'll
be honored to dry."

"And we'll put them away," one of the sisters said. "Tidy-
ing up is our pastime. Besides, there's nothing else to do
today. We hate going out in the rain."

Annie bit her lip to stop tears from rising. "Thank you . . ."

Then Greg Collins, a carpenter and one of the year-round
tenants, said, "I don't know what's left, but I'll help, too. Vacuuming is my specialty."

Then the other residents—Harlin Pierce, the waiter/mari-
achi bandleader, and Marty and Luke Amanti, the pair of

Edgartown Elementary School teachers—pitched in with offers to dust and mop, as if each was trying to outdo the other. And Annie could not help but laugh.

"Okay," she said, "Okay. Thank you all so much. I'll think of a way to make it up to all of you."

"No," the bride said, "this is our way of thanking you for having such a wonderful Inn. Jack and I already decided that we'll come back every year.

"We only got here yesterday, but already I don't want our visit to end," Toni or Ginny said. "We'll clear the table, Annie, so you can get to the airport. Come on, everyone, let's get started. This will be fun."

The next thing Annie knew, everyone—*everyone*—stood up and began to divvy up the chores. As badly as Annie would have liked to sit there and cry at the awesome group of veritable strangers, she knew she needed to get a move on. She suspected that Simon Anderson wasn't accustomed to waiting for much of anything, let alone an innkeeper in a Jeep on a rainy Vineyard day.

The small waiting area at the entrance for private plane passengers was crowded. Several people were grouped close to the door that led out to the tarmac; they held signs with bold, felt-marker names: Mr. Reynolds; The Franklins; Waterson Wedding Party. Annie wondered if she should have made one to let Simon know she would be his chauffeur.

The rain had let up a little, but the sky was still gray and moderately foggy, the air still damp and chilly. As tempted as she'd been to toss a yellow slicker on over her regular old jeans and sweatshirt, at the last minute she'd changed into a pale blue linen shirt and sweater, white jeans, and a Stutterheim Mosebacke navy raincoat that she'd bought for her upcoming book tour. She had no idea why she'd felt compelled to make a good first impression on the journalist, whose head was probably already larger than the plane that he was flying in on.

Airport personnel assured her that, yes, a private plane from Teterboro was due in at eleven twenty-eight, but they could not say if it was Simon's flight. Annie had no way of knowing if he owned the plane, had chartered it, or if it belonged to the TV station. The *network*, she corrected herself.

She glanced at her watch again: eleven twenty. She wondered if she should text John to let him know where she was and whom was she was picking up. Maybe Earl had told him. Or the island's mysterious, high-speed grapevine. Celebrities were no big deal on the Vineyard; if anything, the police stifled their groans when they learned that another high-profile tourist was en route. To them, it tended to mean one word: disruption. Having been born and raised there, John certainly had seen more than his share of famous people and was not about to become googly-eyed. She hoped the guests and tenants at the Inn would be respectful and give Simon space. Though Annie still had no idea why he was coming, or why he'd chosen the Inn, he—like all their guests—was entitled to privacy. For sure.

The trill of a small jet engine vibrated nearby; the necks of the bystanders crooked to see who would alight. After a few minutes, several young men and women strutted down the steps and onto the asphalt. The woman with the sign that read "Waterson Wedding Party" stepped forward. Perhaps she'd seen photos of her passengers beforehand.

The rest of the greeters, Annie included, moved aside to let the wedding party through the doorway.

"Welcome to Martha's Vineyard," their driver said.

"Which way to the bar?" one of the young men chortled and the others snickered as they crammed together, pack-like, and followed the driver through the terminal.

Annie quietly whined.

The next thing she knew, another plane had arrived, though through the din of the wedding party, she hadn't heard the engine. But when she looked up there was Simon Anderson, moving toward the entrance with a bit of a swagger, juggling a backpack and a duffel bag. The others in the waiting area moved apart again with nonplussed precision.

Annie stepped forward. "Hello. I'm Annie. From the Inn."

He was more handsome than he appeared on the small screen—if that were possible—with thick black hair that was faintly brushed with silver, teal blue eyes, and a smile that could light up a starless night on Chappaquiddick.

She wondered if he realized she had gulped.

His handshake was firm, confident, warm. He introduced her to Bill something-or-other as his able-bodied assistant, who also had a backpack and a duffel. Annie shook his hand, too, saying it was nice to meet them both. She was grateful she'd changed out of her island day-to-day wear.

As they made it outside toward the Jeep, the men walked with purpose and did not mention the soggy weather. Instead, Simon explained that they'd hitched the flight with a colleague who was en route to Boston—something about an in-depth story on the big casino that had made an historic comeback after having been shut down during the pandemic.

Annie told him they'd been fortunate to weather that storm fairly well on the island. For people who always stuck together, they'd quickly learned to socially distance.

Thankfully, she'd removed Bella's car seat, so there was enough room in the back for their gear.

Then the three of them got in, with Simon in the front. Much to Annie's embarrassment, they hadn't made it out of the parking lot before she said, "I watched you every night when you were in Boston. You were amazing in the aftermath of the Marathon bombing."

He didn't answer at first, but she noticed a thin smile cross his lips. Then he said, "Is this my cue to tell you that I've read your books?"

Annie steered the car down the airport access road toward Edgartown-West Tisbury Road. Her cheeks flushed, her stomach twitched.

Then Simon laughed. "In all honesty, I planned to, but I haven't had a chance. They take place in Boston, don't they?"

She nodded silently.

"Then I absolutely must. There's nothing like a good old hometown mystery."

With a mortified smile, she said, "I guess."

And *snap!*—Annie Sutton became a googly-eyed girl.

All the way back to Chappy, Annie tried to not talk incessantly, but whenever she was nervous she tended to "run off at the mouth," as her dad used to lovingly call it. Right then, it was hard not to. Once she'd learned that Simon had only been to the Vineyard once, years ago, she felt a need to point out the sights—*all* the sights: the transfer station, which most folks still called "the dump"; the library, that was so much more than books; Main Street in Edgartown, the picturesque eighteenth-century whaling village that had been captured in many photographs and on many artists' canvases. He asked a few questions about the town's history, though they seemed to be more out of courtesy than genuine interest. For Annie, the trip was mentally and physically exhausting.

She didn't relax until they boarded the *On Time* and the men were so enamored by the simplistic, harbor-worthy vessel that she finally took the time to shut up. And breathe. She wondered if Simon had that effect on all women or only on muddleheaded ones like her.

By the time they reached the Inn the sun was almost shining.

The honeymoon couple greeted them in the driveway and offered to take their bags. They were smiling and pleasant and extremely friendly: that's when Annie realized that, like Lottie's husband—and the others who'd stuck around the Inn that morning—odds were they'd heard that Simon Anderson was coming to Chappy. To the Inn.

The thought of which helped her right mind finally slip back into place.

Both men declined the offers to for help, saying thanks, but they could manage their gear.

"Bill, you'll be upstairs in the Inn," Annie said. "Simon, we're giving you the cottage, down toward the beach. I hope it works for you." She could have said it was the best they could do on such preposterously late notice and during the second-busiest week of the season. But she knew that an important part of being an innkeeper was to stay both friendly and positive, and if they received a poor TripAdvisor review, Kevin would be all over her case. That is, if he still cared.

"I'd like to see the Inn first," Simon said. "Get the lay of the land, you know?" Leaving his bags on the patio, he gestured for Annie and the others to go inside, and he followed.

For Simon, the highlight of the tour wasn't the media room, as Annie might have expected, but the reading room. "Very nice," he said, while his gaze skimmed the volumes that lined the shelves. "Eclectic." Apparently it didn't bother him that her tenants the elementary schoolteachers were sitting in the comfy chairs, pretending—*yes, pretending*, Annie thought, as she hadn't seen the pair in there before—to be reading. He said hello to them both; they twittered nervous replies.

For Bill, the best part seemed to be the great room with its wall of windows that, according to him, offered "a photographer's fantasyland." Indeed, as the sun struggled to burn through the leftover murky air, in the distance, the Edgartown lighthouse was bathed in a pale golden aura.

Simon suggested they get organized in their rooms; he told Bill he'd text him when he was ready to hunt for lunch.

He said good-bye to the honeymooners, who had tagged along for the tour; to Greg and Harlin, who were huddled in the media room playing some sort of game—also no doubt pretending because, again, Annie noted this was the first time she'd seen them in there—and to Toni and Ginny, who were still in the kitchen, scrubbing and disinfecting the stainless appliances and smiling the whole time. Annie wondered if Simon thought the ladies were members of the staff.

"Sorry about asking for a tour," Simon said to Annie as they went outside and he picked up his bags. "I've found that whenever I land somewhere new, it helps if I get the gawking out of the way. But I suppose you know what I mean."

Annie hardly considered that being recognized in bookstores or at the post office could be compared with what Simon had to deal with. Few best-selling authors would be picked out in a generic crowd—Stephen King, J. K. Rowling, Neil Gaiman, perhaps more. But Annie was fairly certain that countless more people turned on the news at night than picked up, or ever would pick up, one of Annie's mysteries and study her image on the back cover.

"This way to the cottage," she said with what she hoped was only the slightest hint of a smirk, then led the way down the sloping hill.

He used the word "quaint," when Annie opened the door. She'd been hoping for "homey" or "comfortable"; "quaint" reminded her of the peony wallpaper that had decorated her grandmother's dining room. He shoved his bags into the corner of the living room, plunking the duffel on the edge of her equally quaint braided rug. The one that her peony-wallpaper-loving grandmother had made.

Annie told him to help himself to anything he wanted in the kitchen; she then showed him the bedroom, the bathroom, and the writer's room.

"You live here?" Simon asked.

She laughed. "Don't worry. You'll have the place to yourself. We're a little tight this time of year, so we make do however we can."

"Please tell me you won't be sleeping on the beach. Remember the opening scene in *Jaws* that took place at night and that young couple . . ."

"Yes," Annie said she remembered. "Are you planning to make a film? Is that why you're here?" She hadn't intended to ask outright, but, well, there it was. There had to be a good reason that he'd left New York and come out to the island and brought an assistant who'd noted that the view was a "photographer's dream" and therefore might have cameras and equipment inside the duffels.

Simon smiled his several-million-dollar smile but didn't answer.

"I didn't tell our guests that you were coming," she added, returning the smile. "But it's a small island. Apparently, the word had spread before I'd hardly known. But though my audience is miniscule compared with yours, I understand your need for privacy. Most islanders do. Celebrities are everywhere here." She hoped she hadn't offended him, but she didn't want him to think that she engaged in gossip. "But please," she added, "let me know if any of them bother you."

"Don't worry. I can handle it. Besides, my reason for being here isn't terribly sensational. I'm laying the groundwork for a special report on how climate change is affecting our country's top vacation spots. I'd give you the details, but I wouldn't want one of my competitors to scoop me on it." He winked. She melted a little. Just a little.

Then, as she pulled her thoughts back to reality, Annie realized that the topic of climate change in top vacation spots didn't sound like one of Simon's cutting-edge, never-been-done documentaries; perhaps he had a shocking new angle to the story. *Of course there would be more to it,* she thought. No journalist won as many Emmys as he had by exposing too much about a project—to anyone—prior to the airdate. "We have a guest who's also interested in the influences of climate," Annie said. "She's actually doing a study of the leatherback turtles. Their patterns are changing due to warmer waters."

"Is it one of the ladies in your library?"

"No. You didn't see her." It occurred to Annie that, once again, Mary Beth had been absent. She hadn't seemed like a loner and yet . . .

"Perhaps you and I can have dinner one evening," Simon was saying. "I can tell you more about my concept and we can talk about how I might be able to tie-in a promotion for your Inn. It's the least I can do after kicking you out of your home."

Unsure if he were asking for a date, trying to drum up advertising sponsors, or simply tossing off a casual remark, Annie didn't know if she should tell him that she was going to be married soon. But that would be presumptuous, so she only said, "Perhaps we can." She smiled again and left him to settle in. Slipping off her rain jacket, she walked back to the Inn to tell everyone they were now free to get on with their day. After which there was one more thing she needed to do.

Chapter 9

Sitting in the reading room that Toni and Ginny had de-
serted, Annie penned an old-fashioned, ink-on-paper note
that she hoped sounded pleasant:

> Hi Mary Beth,
> If you haven't heard the news, I wanted to alert you that
> Simon Anderson of CBN fame is with us for the next ten
> days. He's in my cottage; his assistant, a fellow named Bill,
> is in Francine's room while she's elsewhere on Chappy. I'll
> be on the property 24/7, camping out upstairs in the out-
> building by the meadow. Don't hesitate to pop over if you
> need anything.
> Simon is here to work on a documentary about climate
> change. I told him you have a special interest in that in rela-
> tion to the leatherbacks, so if he asks you about it, you'll
> know why. Maybe he can help you get good exposure for
> your study and a job at the lab!

She signed it, tucked it in an envelope, then went upstairs
and slipped it under Mary Beth's door. Annie loved that the
Inn provided a chance to bring people together; maybe

Simon's extroverted personality would help bring Mary Beth out of her shell. Then she smiled at her choice of the word "shell" when thinking of Mary Beth, the turtle lady.

Her next task was to call Lottie at the community center and ask her to please extend her thanks to Joe, but that Annie had decided to decline his generous offer to work at the fire station. She said she had to stay at the Inn in case anyone needed her. After hanging up, she went to the workshop, where she parked her belongings and the sleeping bag she'd borrowed from Earl. Grabbing her laptop and her latest notebook, she retraced her steps, went into the kitchen, and taped a note saying she'd be in the reading room if anyone had questions. She put a copy of the note at the front desk. After all, Simon had said the room was "perfect," and he was right. The restful space filled with books would be an ideal place for Annie to write. Even about murder.

She wondered why she hadn't thought about it sooner.

Sitting at the square table, she turned on the brass lamp with the green glass shade—a replica of the hundreds of lamps positioned on the tables in Bates Hall at the Boston Public Library. Once having read that the green glass had been presumed to be "easier on the eyes," Annie had selected the lamp with its twin light bulbs for a different, more important reason: She remembered the weeks and months she'd spent reading and writing in that room as she'd studied the skills she'd later use—plot, character, conflict, and the rest.

She couldn't believe it had taken Simon's comment for her to see that she could gather inspiration in the reading room. Especially now that "the gawking" over him was out of the way, having left behind nothing but blessed silence. The way libraries once had been.

The first memory Annie had of the BPL as it was known, she must have been seven or eight. She'd gone downtown with her dad for some reason she did not remember.

"I know you love books," Bob Sutton had said, "and I know you love stories. So as a special treat I'm going to introduce you to a place that I expect, as you grow older, you'll return to often. And no matter where you live or where you go in life, it's a place you won't forget."

He took her to the library.

And she fell in love.

In addition to the endless shelves of volumes and the magnificence of Bates Hall, where countless hushed people were hunched over research volumes, scrawling line after line in spiral-bound notebooks, Annie remembered the dioramas—the intricate, three-dimensional miniature scenes that a woman named Louise Stimson had crafted out of cardboard, paper, and other materials. People, houses, workshops, streetlamps, carriages, and more were positioned in in tiny tableaux inspired by books: *Alice in Wonderland, The London of Charles Dickens, Printmakers at Work.* Scattered throughout the building, each diorama held a story; each was mesmerizing to her.

Her dad had been right; the library was a place Annie never forgot.

And now, by the light of her own green glass shaded lamp, she opened her laptop and got to work on the blog posts for Tricia. She began by writing about that first BPL visit.

She didn't know how long she'd been working—two hours? Three?—when she became aware of low voices and laughter drifting in from the great room. Checking her watch, she was startled to see that it was after six o'clock. Still, she kept at it, until she sensed that someone else had entered the room. Annie looked up and saw Mary Beth.

"Annie?" she asked. "Can we talk?"

"It's about Simon Anderson." Mary Beth sat across from her. The soft light from the lamp reflected worry in her eyes.

"What is it? Has something happened?"

"I read your note."

At first Annie thought she was referring to the notes she'd left in the kitchen and at the front desk that mentioned where she'd be. But that would hardly upset her. Then she remembered the one she'd slipped under the door of Mary Beth's room.

"The one about Simon?"

She looked away. "I don't want a TV reporter knowing what I'm doing."

Simon would be irked if he'd heard someone call him a "TV reporter." After all, his career had arguably grown into something much more than that.

"Oh, Mary Beth," Annie said, "I'm sorry. If I'd known your research was confidential, I wouldn't have said a word." There was no point in saying that Simon had hardly been interested in hearing about her work, that he'd been more intent on asking Annie out for dinner. Yes, she decided right then, he had, indeed, been trying to coax her to go on a date.

Mary Beth stood up. "It's no trouble. But I also wanted you to know I saw him in Edgartown this afternoon. At the library. It didn't look as if he was engrossed in reading up on climate change. Unless you wrote about it in one of your books."

A wave of apprehension rippled over Annie. "What?"

"At first I didn't realize it was him. I only was aware that someone was sitting in an overstuffed chair by the window, close to the bookshelves. But when I started to squeeze past him, the book jacket caught my eye: *Renaissance Heist*. Then I saw your name. It's as big as the title."

Annie had once been told that the more book sales an author had, the bigger his or her name would appear on the front cover. Trish denied it, saying that "Annie Sutton" fit nicely, which was why they'd bumped up the type size.

"Well," she said, "that's my latest. Not counting the one

coming out next month." What on earth had Simon been doing? He'd already admitted he hadn't read any of her books. Did he intend to try and impress her now? For God's sake, they'd just met; he barely knew her. She stifled a shiver.

Then she stood up, too. "Was he alone?"

"I think so. I didn't see anyone else near him. When I got back here and read your note, I thought it was a strange coincidence. But more important, I'd rather not be introduced to him. I'd be afraid he might want to learn more about what I'm doing. I'd hate to have the laboratory find out I'm such an amateur before I've applied for a job."

"No problem, Mary Beth. And again. I'm so sorry I mentioned it to him."

She averted her eyes back to the bookcase. "It's okay. You didn't know." Then she left as quickly as she'd appeared.

Annie sat back down at the table and stared at her laptop screen. All she could think about was Simon sitting in the library reading one of her books. Why? It almost felt like he was stalking her. She laughed. "Don't flatter yourself," she muttered. In person, he was definitely a year or two younger than she was; maybe he was John's age. But unlike John, Simon was far more worldly to want to be bothered with the likes of Annie Sutton. Still, there was something unsettling about him reading up one of her books in public. If he was so interested, why hadn't he asked her for one?

If only Murphy would add her two cents.

Mulling over the situation, Annie knew she had no control over Simon's behavior. But she could at least correct the faux pas she'd made about Mary Beth. So, after looking up his email address at CBN, Annie composed a note:

Hi Simon,
I wanted to let you know I was mistaken about one of our guests being interested in climate change. She'd

ONLY MENTIONED THE TOPIC IN PASSING, AND IT TURNS OUT IT'S NOT HER AREA OF EXPERTISE. SORRY FOR THE MIX-UP— SEE YOU AT BREAKFAST!

She re-read what she'd written and thought it would do the trick, so she clicked Send and turned back to the blog post she'd been writing before Mary Beth had interrupted.

Within seconds, however, Annie's email alert sounded: the message was from Simon, and it simply read:

THANKS FOR REACHING OUT. I'M PRESENTLY ON VACATION BUT WILL TRY TO CONNECT WITH YOU WHEN I RETURN.

Annie mumbled a little. Simon was on vacation. Right.

But as she returned to her writing, a spidery sensation skittered across her skin: Didn't most TV people say they were on assignment, not vacation? And wasn't he supposedly on the Vineyard to work?

Shaking her head, she knew she must stay as far away from him as possible. If there was something untoward about why he was there, Annie had no room in her life for it. She did, however, wish he wasn't staying in the cottage, where he would be living among everything that was part of her.

Then her thoughts drifted back to Mary Beth. Why had she been so concerned that Simon might upend her attempt to get a job? Did she really believe he'd bother to tell the whole world about her?

Mary Beth seemed like a bright woman, perhaps a little bashful but smart enough to be looking for a midlife career change. Annie could not fault her for that. After all, wasn't that what she, too, had done?

Then again, the woman hadn't shared what type of work she'd done before.

The more Annie thought about it, she was as baffled by

Mary Beth's behavior as she was by Simon's. But why on earth did she care about either of them?

Still . . . in spite of the hours she needed to work, Annie wanted to get to the bottom of the mysteries—if there were mysteries there at all.

Shutting down her computer, Annie left the reading room, took a shortcut past the media room, and emerged into the back hall where she went into the kitchen and ducked into the chef's room. She selected a bottle of wine, Chanel Bordeaux, which one of the guests had heralded as a new favorite from California. She took a corkscrew from a drawer while mulling her dilemma, when an unfamiliar voice called out:

"Got any more cookies?"

Annie looked up as Simon's assistant, Bill, stuck his head into the room.

"Sure," she replied. She moved to the counter, took two cookies from the canister, then slipped them into a waxed paper sandwich-sized envelope. "Did you work up an appetite this afternoon?"

"Yup. Pretty much." He took the cookies, said thanks, and started to head back to his room when Annie asked, "Were you able to accomplish any work today?"

He laughed. "If you call walking up and down Main Street, checking out the surf shop and a couple of bars work, then yup, I did some." He wasn't overly enthusiastic. Or maybe he was a little drunk. If either was the case, it was not surprising that Simon had requested separate rooms.

Annie laughed in return, hoping that a friendly manner would mask her intent to pry. "How about at the library? Did Simon get anywhere on his climate change research?"

His head bobbed back a little, as if he had no clue what she was talking about. Then he said, "Oh, yeah, sure. I guess. All I know is he points, I shoot."

So Simon's assistant was in fact a videographer. Which was about the only concrete thing so far that made any sense. "Sounds easy enough."

With a nonchalant shrug, he said, "It's only for the pitch. We'll be back with a crew if Simon gets approval." Then he held up the waxed paper envelope, said thanks again, and disappeared back into the great room. A moment later, she heard his footsteps ascend the stairs.

Pouring a glass of wine, Annie discerned that Bill had a name that was as nondescript as the man himself. He was average height, average looks, average everything; his hair was a dull shade of brown, same as his eyes. She supposed, however, she should have told him he'd spoil his appetite if he ate a cookie before dinner. It could have opened the door to casual camaraderie that she might be able to use later to gather information as to why Simon was really there. If she at least had that, maybe Annie could relax.

Then an afterthought jumped into her mind: the cookies. Because Mary Beth hadn't been at the breakfast table, she'd missed out on the packet of freshly made sugar cookies that Annie had wound up giving the guests as a thank-you in advance for helping pitch in with the pre-Simon housekeeping.

She inserted two cookies into another envelope and put away the wine. Then she made her way through the great room and climbed the stairs for the second time that day, though she rarely went up there. Annie knew that, celebrity or not, all of their guests deserved privacy. For some unknown reason, Mary Beth seemed like an exception.

Chapter 10

Someone was crying. Actually, it sounded more like a whimper.

Annie had reached Mary Beth's door and raised her hand to knock, but paused it in midair. She waited a moment, then knocked anyway.

The whimpering stopped.

Annie knocked again. "Mary Beth? It's Annie. I forgot to give you something."

There was no response for a few seconds, then Annie heard footsteps approach the door. The handle turned slowly; the door creaked open.

"I'm sorry," Mary Beth said, "I was napping." But her eyes told a different story: thin, jagged red lines laced the white areas around her pupils, and mascara was smudged on her lower lids.

"Are you all right?" Annie asked.

She nodded and started to close the door. Which was when Annie did what she'd read about thousands of times in books and seen in films and on quirky TV cop shows: she wedged her foot inside the door.

"Please," she said. "I brought cookies." She held up the

small bag. "I'm told they do wonders for curing sadness." She smiled with what she hoped looked like empathy.

Closing her eyes, Mary Beth said, "Okay. Come in. But you might regret it."

If Annie were anyone but Annie—like if she were someone with half a brain left in her head—she would have handed Mary Beth the cookies, bid her well, and left her the hell alone. Instead, Annie gently pushed open the door and stepped inside.

Mary Beth went to one of the small boudoir chairs by the window and sat down. Annie shut the door behind her and joined her guest by settling on the matching chair. She placed the cookies on the round tea table between them.

With her small chin tipped down toward the hardwood floor that still gleamed as it had gleamed when it was installed three months earlier, the young woman said, "This isn't how it was supposed to happen."

The declaration sounded portentous; it skated on the edge of mystery as Annie had imagined. Perhaps she hadn't been wrong.

Purposefully keeping her voice low, Annie asked, "This isn't how what was supposed to happen?"

"It's messed up. Don't you see? I'm worried about Simon Anderson. When I heard he was going to be here, I knew it could be a problem for me. So I figured I only needed to stay out of his way. But when I saw him reading your book . . . and I wondered if he was somehow connected to you . . . well, I don't know either one of you, you know?"

Yes, Annie thought, *she knew that*. She also knew that she did not know beans about Mary Beth or about what she was trying to tell her. But Annie said, "I know," in order to keep the conversation going.

"When I read your note I was terrified that he'd start asking me questions about stuff I don't know anything about. I

knew it wouldn't take long for someone like him to figure out
I was lying."

"Lying?" The question shot from Annie's mouth before
she had a chance to soften it.

Mary Beth nodded. Her voice fell to a whisper. "Once he
knows I'm lying, he'll start digging around. That's what re-
porters do, isn't it?"

Annie tried to choose her words more carefully. After all,
as Mary Beth had said, they did not know each other. She
suppressed a fleeting concern that the woman might need professional help, that she might be in danger either to herself or
others. Pressing her lips together, hoping to garner courage,
Annie asked, "If Simon starts, as you said, 'digging around,'
will he learn something so terrible?"

What do you have to hide? Murphy would have added if
she'd been in the vicinity.

"He'll find out who I really am," Mary Beth said.

Annie knew that as a writer she was naturally curious
about people, places, situations. Mostly people. How they
thought. Why they did the things they did. In short, what
made them tick. Because of that, Mary Beth's reply was one of
the last things anyone should tell a mystery author if they neither wanted nor expected the next question. "Who are you,
Mary Beth?"

"No one you know. No one you've met."

No, Annie thought. She would have remembered that exotic bronze skin and those cornflower eyes.

"Help me out, here, okay? You're not Mary Beth Mullen?
You're not here to study the leatherbacks to try and get a job
at the Marine Biological Lab?"

Mary Beth sniffled; she inhaled, then slowly exhaled. "I'm
someone who has a story. The kind of story Simon might
jump on. Especially since I'm from Boston like he is."

Annie stared at the cookies that sat innocently on the

table. She had a feeling she needed to brace herself for whatever was coming next. "Would you like to tell me about it?"

Mary Beth lifted her eyes; they were sad, sorrowful. The last time Annie had seen someone with that kind of look, it had been on Francine. And she'd been in big trouble.

"Can I trust you to keep it a secret?"

"Yes."

Sighing again, Mary Beth turned her gaze toward the striking island-crafted, felt-appliqued pillows scattered atop the bed. "My real name isn't Mary Beth Mullen." She paused again. Then she said, "My name is Meghan MacNeish. I am your brother, Kevin's, wife."

It took Annie a few moments to grasp the situation. Mary Beth was Meghan? Kevin's wife? But Meghan had traumatic brain injury from that horrible accident . . . the last time Kevin had seen her she hadn't known him . . . the doctors had little hope . . .

Annie drew in a long breath. "I don't understand."

"Of course you don't. Some days I don't, either. But it's true. Here I am. Almost totally recovered. And properly discharged from the rehab facility in Stockbridge where I spent the last few years. I still get headaches, but otherwise . . . like I said, here I am."

Annie tried to quickly sort through the information as if she were a professional and would not be personally affected by any ramifications. "Did you come to the Vineyard because you found out Kevin lives here?"

She nodded. "I wanted to surprise him. Mary Beth Mullen was one of my nurses; I used her name when I made my reservations, and I sent a cashier's check because the only credit card I have has my real name on it. I thought I had all my bases covered, until I saw you on the ferry, and I overheard you tell that little girl about your brother going to

Hawaii. To see a friend." She paused, lowering her eyes. "A lady."

"Ahh," Annie said. "Right." But how had Meghan known that Kevin was her brother? Annie had only known about him for a couple of years, and they hadn't exactly advertised it—well, not off the island, anyway.

"I made up the part about seeing someone I knew on the ferry, so I could get away from you. I was going to stay on the ferry and go back to Woods Hole. But then I decided it didn't matter," Mary—Meghan—continued. "I decided that even if he had another woman, he still had the right to know that I'm better. Which I wouldn't be if it hadn't been for the trust fund he set up for my care."

"He sold his business to do that." Annie hoped that hadn't sounded harsh.

"I know. Your mother told me. Your birth mother."

Of all that had transpired in the past few minutes—or, for that matter, in the past few days—Meghan's last comment shocked Annie the most.

"Donna?" Annie asked. "Donna MacNeish?"

"Yes."

Annie stood up. "I could use a glass of wine. Follow me, please. I need to hear details, and I need to hear them now."

They sat cross-legged on the floor of the chef's room. To avoid interruptions, Annie had closed the door. Then she'd uncorked the Chanel Bordeaux; they drank it out of pottery mugs from Morning Glory Farm because the good crystal was in the kitchen cabinets, and she didn't want to chance running into anyone out there in the open.

"Okay," she said. "Start with what I know. That the last time Kevin saw you, you didn't remember him."

"I'd been in a coma for something like two years. I didn't remember him because I didn't remember anything. Or anyone. Even after I was alert again, it was months before the wiring in my brain began to reconnect. About six months ago, I remembered everything. Well, almost everything. I don't remember actually falling off the scaffolding at the job site. Only that I'd been determined to go up on it because we had a deadline. Donna told me the rest."

Annie had been told that Meghan had loved working with Kevin in the commercial construction business. As the company had grown, Kevin wound up doing all the "office stuff," and Meghan became his foreman—foreperson—doing hands-on work. Then, one winter, with a forecast of bad weather and high winds, Kevin ordered his wife not to go up on the scaffolding at the site of a new mall. But they had a deadline, and Meghan was stubborn when it came to their customers' demands (Kevin's words). The next thing Kevin knew he was in the back of the ambulance with his wife, who was close to death.

"Tell me about Donna," Annie said. "How . . . when did you see her?"

"She came to see me every week. Except when she was in Switzerland having the treatment. And when she moved down here. I am so sorry she's gone, Annie. She was a very special lady. But I'm glad you finally got to know her. She once told me that having both her children in her life was the greatest gift she'd ever been given. That knowing you made her life complete."

Tears now welled in Annie's eyes, her hazel—not green—eyes that were replicas of Donna's. And of Kevin's, her half brother, whom she'd come to adore despite that he was now being a royal pain. She took another sip of wine and waited while its warmth traveled to her heart. "Thank you. What a lovely thing to tell me." She wiped her eyes and took another sip.

Then Meghan smiled. "You look like her, you know. More than Kevin does. But you both have Donna's eyes."

On occasion, when Annie was doing research, she'd come upon an anecdote or two about her subject that prompted her to get emotional. But they were always about other, unknown people. Not her. Not her family. Because she'd barely had one. She pulled herself together; she needed to hear more. "How did you find out Donna died?"

"Her doctor. She'd left word on the Vineyard that I was to be notified if—when—it happened. And that no one was to know about me. Not unless I said it was okay. It wasn't okay then; I wasn't ready."

Though Annie could not recall the doctor's name, she remembered how kind he'd been to them. And to Donna. "But . . ." she added, as hundreds of questions tumbled in her mind, "what about Kevin? He didn't know that Donna saw you all that time?"

Meghan shook her head. "Absolutely not. I made her promise not to tell him. I wanted to be fully recovered before I stepped back into his life. Donna told me how guilty he'd felt about the accident. It wasn't his fault; it was all mine. When I finally believed that I was going to get better, I wanted him to see me whole again, so we could cry and laugh together and hold each other and celebrate the miracle." She closed her eyes a moment, then opened them again, the traces of her earlier weeping now gone, replaced by a clear veneer that coated their lovely color. "I suppose not every miracle is meant to happen."

They talked for a long time. Annie learned that Donna had told her that Annie was a mystery writer; she'd told her about the Inn. She'd also phoned Meghan a few times from the island and updated her on the goings-on, including telling her to keep an eye out for the episode about the Inn on *Best*

Destinations. One of the last things she'd told Meghan was that Kevin missed her terribly.

Annie didn't know how to ask if Meghan knew that Kevin had divorced her. So she decided not to. There were some things that should remain between Meghan and him . . . if he ever came back. And if he did not . . . well, Annie supposed she could figure out what to do about it then.

After they'd consumed over half a bottle of the wine, Annie suggested that they comb through the refrigerator to see if they could find something for dinner; they settled on making omelets and toast and ate while sitting at the marble-topped kitchen island. It had grown late by then, the guests no doubt were in their rooms, so privacy was nearly guaranteed. So Annie felt free to ask yet another question for her, well, *sister-in-law.*

"How on earth did you come up with the story about studying leatherbacks?"

Meghan laughed. "When I was on the internet looking up the ferry schedule, I landed on information for Woods Hole. There was a picture of one of the giant turtles, his head sticking up out of the water in the Sound. Ahead of him, on the horizon, you could see the big, white ferry. The researchers had tagged the turtle and put a tiny camera on its back, so it looked like he was watching the boat. It was beautiful. And fascinating. So I Googled them too . . . do you know that the leatherbacks are the only turtles in the world that don't have a hard shell? Theirs is more rubbery—which is why they're called 'leatherbacks.'" She looked at Annie and smiled. "But I guess that's off-topic, right?"

"A little. But I love it. Writers are curious creatures."

"Okay, then. Do you know that leatherbacks only eat jelly fish?"

Annie laughed again and took another bite of her omelet to which she'd added cheese, a few slices of mushrooms, and several sprigs of herbs from the garden Francine had sowed. "Lucky them," she said with a small frown. "And now I completely understand why you didn't want Simon to start quizzing you. But from what little I've seen of him, I doubt he would. If he asks, though, why not simply say you're on vacation? And that you think the big turtles are interesting, but you're not studying them?"

Meghan paused then said, "Do you think that everyone who has something to hide shies away from journalists?"

"I expect so." Then something else occurred to her. "It was smart of you to pay for your reservation with a cashier's check."

She lowered her head. "I wasn't sure I'd get away with it, but Francine was really nice and said that the Inn was flexible. It was the only way I could think of to surprise Kevin. I didn't want to tell him over the phone."

"You are a clever girl."

"Not usually. For one thing, I didn't expect I'd actually have to tell anyone my name was Mary Beth. I guess I thought I'd just run into Kevin as soon as I arrived. Like he was in charge of taking luggage or something."

"Around here, we're all in charge of everything." It was easy to understand why Kevin loved her; Meghan was quick and bright and wonderful company. It would be nice to have her as a real sister-in-law, not one who was technically, legally, no longer part of the family.

"But speaking of my brother," Annie said quietly, once their meal was done and they lingered in the tall chairs, still sipping from their mugs. "Have you thought about what you want to do now? About him?" She knew she'd have many more questions, but she was getting tired. And so, she suspected, was Meghan . . . a name that suited her better than Mary Beth.

"No. And I don't want to know anything about his lady friend. Not now. Okay?"

Annie reached over and patted Meghan's hand. "Okay." With all her heart and mind, however, Annie wanted to call her brother. But she would not. Not yet. Not unless . . . well, not unless who knew what might happen. Instead, she would be patient. And let things happen as they would.

They finished the wine; it was after midnight when they said good night.

Chapter 11

She hadn't minded spending the night on the floor over the workshop. The sleeping bag held the scent of old campfires, which had been comforting, though Annie had never gone camping. John was probably the last one to use it when he and Kevin had gone up island overnight—ostensibly to fish—right before they'd opened the Inn. Before the season had begun and life shifted into high gear.

Pressing her face into the fabric, Annie inhaled the hint of John and felt a small purr of contentment. She wished she could glide back into sleep. But it was the third Wednesday in August, and Annie knew it would be beyond chaotic. Starting tonight, Illumination Night.

She didn't know what time it was; she'd forgotten the charger for her phone, not that it mattered, because the electrical work hadn't yet been completed upstairs. After crawling out of the bag, Annie went to the window. The meadow was resplendent with late summer blossoms of bridal white Queen Anne's Lace, delicate deep salmon Wood Lilies, and vibrant orange-and-yellow Butterfly Weed. She opened the window to the early sun and the fragrant air. She was looking forward to returning to making soap once the hubbub of the season had died down, and she could harvest the flowers and herbs that grew right on their land for her sumptuous collection. Maybe Meghan would enjoy soapmaking alongside her. If Kevin came back. And if Meghan stayed.

Then she thought about how, before Annie had moved to the Vineyard, she'd been totally alone without a real family. Since then, she'd gained her island family; more important, she'd gained her birth mother for a while, a brother forever (or so she hoped), and now, a sister-in-law for who knew how long. She wondered what John was going to think about this, once Meghan said it was okay to tell him.

John. John! In the craziness of the day before, Annie realized they hadn't so much as texted, let alone talked.

Flinging a sweatshirt on over her pajamas, she grabbed her purse that held her dead phone, then ran down the stairs and up to the Inn. But when she burst in the back door, she was struck by silence.

Then Annie remembered: Francine was at Jonas's. Was Annie supposed to make breakfast for everyone again that day? Wasn't Francine going to come back this morning? What time was it, anyway? She ran her hand through her hair and glanced up at the ship's clock in the kitchen.

"Good job," Annie, she said aloud. It wasn't yet six thirty; breakfast didn't start for two more hours. Still, it didn't leave much time to pull something, however basic, together.

That's when she heard a low rattling from the chef's room. Tiptoeing toward the door, she jumped back as Francine emerged, carrying a large oblong pan and heading toward the oven.

"Good morning," Francine said. "You're up early."

Annie rubbed her eyes and tried to will her heart to stop racing. "I couldn't remember if I was supposed to make breakfast or not. I slept so soundly that my brain's still fuzzy."

Francine glided the pan into the oven and set the timer for fifty minutes. "I don't suppose that could be connected to the empty wine bottle in the recycle bin?"

"Good grief," Annie said, "did we drink the whole thing last night?"

Francine laughed. "Don't include me in the 'we.' Was John here? Or did you spend the evening with dashing Simon Anderson?"

Then Annie remembered her phone. She dug it from her bag, found a charger in the electronics drawer, and quickly plugged it in. "No. I was not with a man. I was with . . . Mary Beth. Mary Beth Mullen. She's a little shy, but very interesting." *Well*, Annie thought, *that sounded lame.* So she quickly added, "As long as you're on breakfast duty, I'd better go get cleaned up for the day."

"Where? Is there water in the workshop?"

"There's an unfinished bathroom downstairs with a shower. It isn't pretty, but everything works."

Then her phone rallied back to life, pinging, pinging, pinging, like a xylophone let loose in a kindergarten class. She snatched it off the counter; the screen lit up. She had missed eleven texts. All of them from John. They'd started not long after midnight.

"Ugh," she said. Instead of reading them right then, she simply typed: ALL IS WELL. LOTS HAPPENED YESTERDAY. WILL CALL LATER THIS MORNING. She looked at Francine and gave her half a grin.

"Something is going on with you, Annie Sutton," Francine said. "I've known you long enough to be able to see through that silly smile. You're up to something, aren't you?"

"Not at all."

Francine rolled her eyes. "I don't believe you for a minute."

"Excellent. It's good to give the imagination a healthy

workout once in a while. Which is especially fun when there's no good reason." She left the phone to charge and skipped out of the room, back toward the meadow and the workshop, where she hoped that her brain would recharge as quickly as her phone.

Talk around the breakfast table centered on Illumination Night, which would take place that evening in Oak Bluffs, known to islanders simply as OB.

Ginny Taft, the Indiana retired schoolteacher, announced that she'd done her homework and now made it her mission to enlighten the others. "The first illumination celebration was to honor a visit from the governor in 1869. Imagine that! Over one hundred fifty years ago. The Camp Meeting Association was actually started in 1835 when Methodists came here and slept in tents before they built cottages and added pretty filigree that makes them look like gingerbread creations."

Toni nudged her sister. "Get back to the illumination thing."

"Oh, right," Ginny said. "Well, in 1869, in honor of the governor's visit, people decorated their gingerbread houses with colorful lanterns. Today, the festivities start at the Tabernacle, in the center of the campground, with a concert by the Vineyard Haven Band and a community sing, followed by lighting the ceremonial first lantern. Then all the houses follow suit and light their lanterns that are all different colors; it sounds delightful. Everyone must go. Toni and I brought Victorian hats for the occasion."

Toni smirked. She didn't seem as enthusiastic as her sister was.

"You're right on all counts," Annie chimed in. "It's wonderful to watch all the people strolling along in the glow. Something you might not have learned, Ginny, is that whenever someone sells their gingerbread cottage, they leave the lanterns for the next owners. It's helped keep the tradition alive."

"I'll bring my camera!" Meghan chimed in, and Annie smiled. She was glad that Meghan had joined them that morning, but wasn't surprised that neither Simon nor his assistant was there. Last night, when Annie had been crossing the lawn toward the workshop, she'd noticed that the lights were on inside her cottage; she'd heard low, male conversation. Perhaps Simon and Bill had worked late and now were sleeping in.

After clearing the table, she knew she'd better get in touch with John before he thought she'd run away with their celebrity guest, assuming that, yes, by then he surely would have heard Simon was there. She quickly cleaned the plates, loaded the dishwasher, turned it on, then took her phone outside.

Lucy answered, not John.

"Dad's asleep," she said. "He didn't get home until four this morning. He left me a note—he said there was a wedding reception that, in his words, 'got out of hand.' Anyway, he told me to answer his phone if I saw it was you."

"Well, then, hi to you. How are things going on over there?"

"You mean with my stupid sister?"

"Lucy . . ."

"I know, I know. I shouldn't call her stupid. Well, she did say I could go to Illumination Night with one of her old friends and her. Maggie's mother won't let her out after dark with me, no big shock, so at least I'll get to go. As long as Abigail doesn't lose me in the crowd. Which, of course, would be intentional."

Maggie was Lucy's best pal, though Maggie's mother— who had a dicey history with John that went back a few decades—wasn't keen on the friendship.

"Who's driving?"

"Jeez, you sound like Dad. Abigail's friend is picking us up."

"Well, don't worry. If your sister loses you, text me. I'll find you."

"You're going?"

"Yes. Some of our guests are, too. Do you want to come with me?"

"I'd rather do that, for sure. But Dad keeps saying he wants me to try to get along with what's-her-name."

"Abigail."

"Right."

Annie laughed. "It sounds as if you're not quite there yet. But keep at it. And maybe I'll run into you tonight."

They rung off before Annie thought to ask Lucy to please tell her father that she'd called. Then she went back into the kitchen and found Francine.

"Are you and Jonas going tonight?"

Francine shook her head. "Earl thinks Bella might have a cold, so I think I'll go spend time with her. Not that Claire doesn't have it under control but . . ."

"But she's yours." Annie smiled and waved, then circled into the great room. Just as she reached the staircase to go up to look for Meghan, Annie spotted her in the reading room, staring out the window.

"Hey," Annie said. "I was looking for you. If you're serious about going to Illumination Night, would you like company?"

Meghan's eyebrows went up; her eyes widened. "You want to go?"

"Of course," Annie replied, then whispered, "What kind of sister-in-law would I be if I didn't make sure you saw the sights?"

"Then it's a deal. What time does it start?"

"Lots of people go early and bring a picnic supper. I could wrangle up some food for us. There might be chicken in the freezer and . . ." Then Annie's phone rang. She almost didn't answer it, but it could be John. "Ah," she said, "excuse me a second." She pulled the phone from her pocket and quickly answered. But it wasn't John. It was Kevin. Calling from Hawaii.

"That was fast," Kevin said as soon as Annie said hello. "Were you expecting someone more important?"

A wave of warmth rushed into her cheeks. She stared at Meghan; her mind went blank. "What?" she asked.

"You answered really fast. I figured you thought it was someone important."

She winced. "Who could be more important than my brother?" She saw Meghan's face go slack.

"For starters, your fiancé."

"Well, I suppose that's true." She stood perfectly still, afraid if she moved something might break—like her promise to Meghan. She was glad Kevin hadn't called via FaceTime.

"Or the famous journalist. Who I expect is now an official guest at the Inn?"

She wanted to be out of Meghan's sight and sound. She wanted to wander into the reception area or the great room or, for that matter, Edgartown. She wanted to escape the despair on Meghan's face, her jaw now having gone from slack to tight as if she were in pain. Of course, she was in pain. Why wouldn't she be?

What had Kevin just asked her? Oh, right. Simon. "Yes. Mr. Anderson has arrived."

"How's it working out?"

"Okay. Fine." There was no point in saying that Simon was in her cottage, that he'd been seen at the library reading one of her books, or that his assistant was very different from

Simon. She would have shared all that if Kevin had been there, if they were sitting on her porch, him with a beer, her with a glass of wine. If he weren't detached by so many miles of land and sea, by a Band-Aid now taped over his heart.

Annie turned away but could not shake the feeling that those cornflower eyes were boring a huge hole into the back of her skull. "How are things going over there?" She said it as if Hawaii, not Nantucket, was the next island over. Or Cutty-hunk, if one went west instead of east. Or, she wondered, were the Elizabeth Islands closer to Chappy than Cuttyhunk? She shook her head, annoyed that her mind always felt compelled to get the facts straight.

"All's okay. It's beautiful. And you'll never believe it, but it looks just like its pictures. That was a joke." He paused, then added, "And you didn't ask, but Taylor's okay, too."

Without intending to, Annie turned around again; her eyes flicked to Meghan. "Oh," she said. "Well. Good." She knew she should say, "Tell her I said hello," but that wasn't possible, not right then.

She inhaled. Exhaled. "Is something on your mind or are you just checking in?" By then a light film of perspiration had formed on her brow.

"I can't call my sister when I'm six thousand miles away?"

"I think it's more like five. Five thousand miles. Six hours earlier." Details again. Facts.

"You win," he said. "Sorry I bothered you."

"No. No, Kevin, you're not bothering me. But right now things are crazy . . ." She would rather have told him that she was glad he'd called, that she missed him, that she loved him, that she was so sorry if she hadn't been as supportive as he'd wanted her to be. She'd rather tell him that the love of his life was standing in front of her, healthy and beautiful, waiting for him to come home. To her.

"I know you must be wicked busy. Which is why I called. Because, believe it or not, I feel guilty about having left."

She sucked in a quick breath. Did that mean he wanted to come back? "We all miss you," was all she could think to say. Then she added, "A lot."

"If you say so. But you sound weird."

Closing her eyes in order to avoid Meghan's, Annie said, "I'm weird? Well, thanks. I guess nothing's changed, then." She laughed. "Call anytime, brother. You should know that by now."

"Will do," he said. "In the meantime, I'll try to have a good time. Not that you mentioned that, either."

"Sure," she said. "Have a good one."

"Thanks," he replied flatly.

But she knew that he knew she hadn't meant it.

They hung up, and Annie flopped onto one of the tufted armchairs. "I blew my chance. I should have told him we needed him. And that he needed to come back. I should have made up a story . . ."

"Hush," Meghan said. "It wasn't the right time." Then she added, "Is he okay?"

Annie hesitated, then nodded. "He's okay."

She knew it wasn't fair.

Annie told Meghan she had to get some work done on the upcoming online promotions, but that she'd be back by six o'clock to pick her up. Then she put her laptop in the Jeep as if she'd been telling the truth. Instead, she parked in the lot at the *On Time*, crossed over as a walk-on, and stepped onto land again in Edgartown. Dodging tourists on the narrow sidewalk of North Water Street, she finally reached the Harbor View Hotel. Across the road, she sat down on an empty bench that looked out toward the lighthouse and Chappy. From there,

Annie could see the Inn as it ascended from the dunes, look-ing stately, majestic, welcoming. She sighed.

Her phone call with Kevin had been dreadful, as she'd been pretty much frozen from beginning to end. Not frozen like winters sometimes got during a nor'easter, but frozen stiff, like the bust of Agatha Christie in her living room unless Simon—or more likely, Bill—had ripped it off by then.

And though technically Annie hadn't been lying to Kevin, she felt as if she had. She was caught in the middle, in that thankless chasm between someone you cared about who'd taken you into their confidence, and someone on the other side who you cared about as well, and who needed to know the truth.

Annie had been in that position years earlier when she'd only been fifteen, and had seen her aunt kissing a man who wasn't Uncle Joe. They were on the "T" at rush hour; Annie was heading home from the dentist. And suddenly there was Aunt Sally, hanging onto a leather strap with one hand, her other arm wrapped around a man Annie didn't know, had never seen before. Their lips were pressed against each other's; their bodies were pressed, too.

"Aunt Sally?" Annie cried out before realizing it had been a stupid mistake to make her presence known, before she had the sense to slink off to another railcar. But Annie knew darn well it was Sally; she recognized the blonde-tinted hair, the ivory silk dress, the Etienne Aigner purse that draped from her shoulder on its long, narrow strap.

Sally had snapped her head toward Annie; the man did, too. With his open shirt, gold chain, and dark hair that hung over his collar, it definitely wasn't Uncle Joe.

At the next stop, Sally urged Annie to get off the train with her. They went to a Brigham's where Annie had vanilla ice cream with jimmies and Sally stirred an egg cream with a big straw.

"It was nothing," she said. "Just an old boyfriend from high school. We ran into each, and he kissed me. For old times' sake. Nothing more."

"Uh-huh," Annie replied, not sure why she was the one who was embarrassed.

"Please don't tell Uncle Joe. And, God knows, don't tell your mother. Okay?"

Annie nodded because she didn't know what else to do. But after that, she was uncomfortable being around Aunt Sally, and she hadn't been sad when Sally and Joe moved to Syracuse, and they only saw them on Thanksgiving and at the funerals when Annie's grandparents died. Then Annie never laid eyes on them again.

The hardest part had been keeping the secret. And having felt responsible for Sally severing the family ties.

The situation with Kevin felt much bigger, much more important.

She wondered if Donna found it tough to keep Meghan's secret. Or to keep Kevin's secret from Meghan after he'd filed for divorce.

A young couple strolled hand in hand up the narrow path from the lighthouse. They were smiling, happy, laughing as they moved through the sand that was edged on both sides by tangles of beach roses that were starting to fade with the season. She wondered if Kevin and Meghan had ever kept secrets from each other.

Then Annie remembered that right after she'd caught Aunt Sally kissing the stranger on the train, Annie told her dad.

They were outside on their usual post-dinner walk. Her dad put his hands in his pockets and walked quietly, the way he did when he was pondering. Then he said, "I'm sure that was upsetting to see, kiddo. But secrets are always better off when they're kept. Especially since, you never know, one day you might need to share one of your own. And you sure would want someone to keep it."

And though Meghan was hardly Aunt Sally, her dad's advice resonated now.

With a last glance at the young lovers, Annie stood up, walked back down to the Chappy Ferry, and went home.

Chapter 12

Ocean Park looked like a quilt whose squares had been stitched from hundreds of multicolored blankets that had motifs of people, dogs, and picnic baskets. Scampering along the seams, long-legged boys and long-haired girls maneuvered strings attached to kites of different sizes, shapes, and designs— all vibrant against the sunset sky. Meghan laughed when she noticed one shaped like a jellyfish. She asked Annie if she thought a leatherback might mistake it for dinner.

They feasted on cold chicken and salad, while sharing silly stories about their lives. Annie kept an eye out for Lucy and Abigail, but didn't see them. Their absence, however, gave her a chance to get to know Meghan better.

"May I ask something personal?" Annie asked as she poured cups of spring water for them. "Your beautiful face indicates a curious heritage. Would you care to share?"

Meghan smiled a radiant smile that accentuated the high cheekbones under her lustrous skin. "My mother was Egyptian, my father is Irish. Quite a combination, isn't it?"

"Wow. How did they meet?"

"Their families wound up being neighbors in Boston. My mother had emigrated with her parents from Cairo in the mid-seventies, not long before the famous bread riots when the government took food subsidies away from the poor. I remember my grandfather saying, 'They took the food from the people who needed it the most.' He was a carpenter; he worked on the last stage of the John Hancock Tower. They weren't poor, but many of their friends were."

"He was a carpenter. Do you think . . . ?"

"That my trade came from him? Absolutely. My mother recognized it early on. But neither she, nor my grandfather, lived long enough to see me get my degree in construction engineering."

"Your mother died when you were young."

"I was thirteen."

The somber moments that followed were then sparked by music from a guitar being strummed by an elderly man nearby.

Annie pulled her knees up and looped her arms around them. "How did you meet my brother?"

"That's easy. I needed a job. I answered an ad. I married the boss." Her laughter was relaxed and infectious.

"You're a lot younger than he is."

"Only four years. I turned thirty-nine in April."

"Oh, my gosh. You look much younger."

Meghan laughed. "Lack of stress. It's hard to be stressed when you're in a coma for a long time. Maybe it's the secret to stopping the aging process."

"But I doubt you'd recommend it."

"Not for a second."

"Okay," Annie said, "enough of my prying. The sun's almost down. Let's head up to the action."

They packed their picnic things, toted them back to the Jeep, then meandered past small children racing with pinwheels, smiling grandparents pushing strollers, and couples of all ages making their way toward the sounds of the Vineyard Haven Band. Over the festive clamoring, Annie raised her voice to explain that the Tabernacle was a nineteenth-century, wrought-iron structure and was listed in the National Register of Historic Places. She told Meghan that under its striking, octagonal cupola and dozens of clerestories, the open-air church boasted seating for up to four thousand. "Today it's used for high school graduations as well as concerts, church services, and all kinds of cultural events in the summer."

"You'd make a great tour guide," Meghan said, also increasing her voice several decibels.

"I'll keep that in mind if the book thing doesn't work out," Annie shouted back with a happy laugh.

Then the music shifted to lively antics of dual pianos, and the hundreds of people joined together, singing lively renditions of "Yankee Doodle Dandy" followed by "In the Good Old Summertime." Annie stepped back and listened, unable to stop smiling. This was the Vineyard at its best.

At eight thirty (or thereabouts), the Tabernacle fell into darkness; the crowd turned customarily silent; the ceremonial first lantern was lit. What followed were ethereal rainbows of light, one after another after another and another, encircling the grounds as each gingerbread house lit its lanterns—some paper, some fabric, some painted with flowers, some with clever, custom artwork. The effect was enchanting. Then Annie felt a tap on her shoulder.

"Would you ladies care to glow?" It was Simon Anderson, holding up two glowing, plastic necklaces.

"How nice," Annie said quickly as she took them from him and handed one to Meghan, who looked somewhat stricken. "Mary Beth, I don't think you've met Simon Anderson. Simon, this is my friend, Mary Beth, who's staying at the Inn, too."

Meghan fidgeted with the necklace, then slipped it on while muttering a small "Thank you."

"Here," Simon said to Annie, "allow me." He retrieved

the necklace, wrapped it around Annie's neck, then lifted her hair as he clasped it. He then rested his hands on her shoulders, leaned closer, and whispered in her ear. "The glow enhances your loveliness." Then he straightened up and said, "Enjoy the rest of the evening, ladies." He bowed slightly and walked away, vanishing into the crowd.

"What was *that* about?" Meghan asked once Annie had hustled her out of there and they headed back to Chappy.

"I have no idea."

Meghan sighed. "I guess the good news is that he was so busy hitting on you, he barely noticed me."

Following the line of vehicles that inched along as slowly as the great leathernecks as they trailed their way back into the ocean after laying their eggs on Florida beaches, Annie was reminded that no matter how congested the traffic became on the Beach Road or at other bottlenecks, like her, few people cared. At least, not with the kind of horn-blowing, road-raging antics often seen on the mainland. Summer traffic was part of the Vineyard experience, and though islanders occasionally grumbled about it, they rarely moved away.

If Annie was trying to focus on the traffic in order to distract her from the discomfort of Simon's attention, it wasn't working. "I'm sure he wouldn't have done that if John had been standing there."

"Will I get to meet your fiancé soon?"

"I wish. But it's August. He's always working. Or sleeping. Or, now, tending to his two daughters. I won't see much of him until after Labor Day."

"That stinks."

"Agreed."

They grew quiet for a moment, then Meghan said, "Annie? Do you think Kevin will come back?"

"I wish I knew. I really do."

"I don't know how long I should wait. Or if I should wait. Or if I should go and let him have his life. Donna gave me hope that he still loved me, but time changes things, doesn't it?"

"I suppose it can." To stop from telling Meghan that she'd often wanted to hold Kevin captive until she succeeded in planting some sense into his gray matter over his bizarre attraction to Taylor, Annie told her about Brian, about how his death had left her unhinged, how it was years before she'd been able to delete the last message he'd left when he'd said he had a secret to tell her. "I'd become obsessed with trying to find out what the 'secret' was. It felt like something I could hold on to. And it felt safer than to keep thinking he was . . . gone." She stopped speaking a moment, until she regained some equilibrium—speaking about Brian had a way of decentering her. "The truth is," she added, "I never thought I'd recover. At some point I went on with my life, but I it was a long time before I healed."

"Did you ever find out what he wanted to tell you?"

She shook her head. "No. At some point, I accepted that it didn't matter; he wasn't coming back." In the early weeks, months, after his death, she'd had to remind herself of that often.

"Are you trying to prepare me that Kevin might not come back . . . or that he might not come back to me? And that I might never know the whole story?"

"Oh, Meghan, no. All I know is that every time Kevin talks about you, he can barely get the words out. But change is part of life, and no matter what happens, we learn from it, and God knows we grow. But I don't mean to sound . . . pessimistic. Unlike with Brian and me, you still have a chance."

A wistful look crossed Meghan's face again. "Our marriage wasn't perfect, Annie. I'm not sure any marriages are.

But it was good. So I'll wait. If nothing else, I owe it to him to let him see that I'm okay. And because I've never been sure if I did the right thing by not letting him know I was recovering."

Annie nodded. "Where would the fun be if life was perfect?" She tried to be upbeat, for Meghan's sake. But all she could think of was Brian's beautiful face, and the four words he whispered to her each night before they fell asleep: "My Annie; my love."

If she'd been able to go back to her cottage that night, she might have opened the Louis Vuitton trunk and taken out the album that held the memories of Brian and her. She would have sat for hours, lightly touching the photos of him. She still did that sometimes. She knew she should stop once she married John because it would upset him and why would she want to do that? But she'd never forget how much Brian had loved her. That was how she'd finally found the courage to move on.

But of course, Annie couldn't go home that night, couldn't wallow in the past, because the cottage was now occupied by Simon Anderson, who might or might not think that Annie was fair game for his lair. If he had a lair. Which, if he did, would surely be sizable.

When they arrived back at the Inn, Annie said, "I'd love to suggest coffee or tea but I'm bushed. So I'll see you at breakfast?"

"Absolutely," Meghan said. "And I'm going to try not to be afraid of what's going to come next."

Zipped in the sleeping bag, not ready for sleep, Annie's thoughts drifted to Meghan—how much she had been through, how many years she had lost from her young life. Kevin once said that he'd wanted children . . . if they did reunite, was it too late for that?

From where she was lying, Annie could see stars outside the window; she hoped Donna was up there in the heavens.

It must have been difficult for Donna to have kept Meghan's secret, to not have told Kevin that his wife was healing. Maybe Donna's perpetual optimism that the couple would reunite had kept her going through her own illness, had kept her "staying positive," as had been her mantra. And maybe that optimism had contributed to Meghan's recovery, too.

Annie thought back to a rainy afternoon when she'd sat in the Black Dog with Donna, looking out at the big white ferry as it pulled from the pier, embarking on another crossing, another journey, another passage of time and people coming and going, weaving in and out of one another's lives. Between sips of hot tea and spoonfuls of steamy chowder, Donna had abruptly said, "I've had a bout with cancer." She admitted that her treatments had "not been pleasant."

"I wonder what other secrets our mother is hiding," Kevin had commented after Donna finally told him, too.

"Oh my wonderful brother," Annie said now into the night, "you are in for a giant surprise about that—if you ever unhinge yourself from Taylor and get your butt back here where you belong."

Entranced by the stars, Annie knew that as sad as she could get about the people she had lost, she liked to believe that those souls—including Donna—watched over her now. And that, yes, of course, Donna watched over Kevin, too.

Just then a silver comet streaked across the sky.

He could get used to eating fresh pineapple for breakfast. And mango. And papaya. Not the kind that had taken who knew how many days to be shipped to the mainland, then to the Vineyard, then onto the market shelves. Now that he'd tasted the real deal right from the source, he did not want to go back to the other junk.

"One day, you'll be happy again," his mother had said after

Meghan hadn't recognized him. "It will be different than before, but you will be happy. I promise."

His mother, however, hadn't known the whole story. That in addition to struggling with his own guilt, he'd also been struggling to forgive Meghan. He'd spared Donna the details, simply because he could not bear to tell her the rest. He had not wanted his mother to have to try and forgive Meghan, too.

Chapter 13

As with their vehicles, there were few reasons for anyone to lock the doors of their homes on Martha's Vineyard, even in the twenty-first century. Oh, sure, there was an occasional break-in that typically involved a rambunctious band of summer kids who were testing the limits. And sometimes off season, island kids would sneak into empty seasonal houses and have a party or two. But overall, the Vineyard remained safe from marauders, petty thieves, or worse.

Which was why, as dawn began to break, Annie's heart leaped into her throat when she was awakened by the sound of someone clomping up the stairs to her sleeping bag haven over the workshop. She clutched the bag up to her chin as if that might ward off the intruder by making her invisible.

She wondered if it was Simon, in search of payment for the glow necklace.

Holding her breath, she dared to open her eyes as the upstairs door opened.

Instead of Simon, she saw John. She smiled and rubbed her eyes.

"You awake?" he growled.

He *growled*? Was she dreaming? "I am now," she said.

He stomped across the room and stood over her, hovering, staring down. It didn't look as if he'd come to Chappy for romance—his eyes had narrowed, his jaw was rigid. "Where's your laptop?"

Her laptop? Had he barged into what was, for the time being, her room, because he wanted to Google something? Annie pulled herself halfway out of the bedding. "It's downstairs. Charging. There's no electricity up here yet."

He turned and thumped back down the stairs. She wasn't sure if he expected her to get out of bed and follow him.

She was, however, damned if she would. Not with the way he'd blasted in without an explanation. They hadn't talked since . . . when? Monday morning? Three days ago?

Unpacking herself from the bag, she decided she could think more clearly if she were sitting up. Or standing. She reached for her cardigan that was draped across a lone straight-back chair next to her quasi-bed. Pulling it over her cotton pajamas, she raked her hands through her hair in a halfhearted attempt to comb it, then stuck her feet into her Crocs with a single thought: What the heck was his problem?

Then he was back, laptop in hand. "Open it, please. Boot it up. To the internet."

At least he'd said "please." So Annie turned it on and waited for the screen to light. She plugged in her password, half-hoping that the fickle Chappy connection would not cooperate. However, that morning it decided to play nice, so she handed the computer back to the man who did not in any way appear to be the kind and loving person she'd agreed to marry.

She wondered if he'd gone bonkers like her brother had.

He futzed with the keyboard for several seconds then handed it back to her. "It's a Mac, not a PC. I have no idea how it works."

She wondered if that gave her an edge, though she had no idea why she'd need one.

"John," she sighed, "will you please tell me what's going on?"

"Oh, nothing much," he replied, arms crossed on his chest. At least he wasn't in uniform. At least he wasn't wearing his holster and his .38, or whatever caliber the Edgartown police used for guns. "Find VineyardInsiders."

VineyardInsiders was a private website for islanders, about islanders. It was a place of perpetual information that everyone who lived there should or might want to know. On occasion, it served as a kind of gossip column, publishing things that neither island newspaper regarded as newsworthy. Some anecdotes were funny; some were not.

Though Annie rarely looked at it, she had a sickening suspicion of what she would see.

She typed VineyardInsiders.com and awaited her fate.

The first (or more accurately, the latest) morsel in the newsfeed was about a pig that had been found wandering on the airport runway. "This is the kind of stuff that happened back in the fifties," an old-timer had commented and added a smiley face.

Annie scrolled to the next story: a photo of a silver pickup, complete with visible license plate; the author proclaimed that the driver had cut her off at the five corners, causing her to slam on her brakes and her shopping bag to propel to the floor, thus shattering nearly all two dozen eggs she'd bought at Ghost Island Farm. A thread of comments offered sympathies and agreed that the truck must belong to a tourist. One writer suggested that the woman "bring the pic to the police station and have them run a make on the vehicle," as if that wouldn't waste law enforcement's time.

And then there it was. A photo of Illumination Night.

With the shimmering rainbow of lanterns in the background. And Annie in the foreground. With Simon Anderson leaned in closely, whispering in her ear after he'd clasped the glow necklace at the nape of her neck. From the angle of the shot, it looked as if he'd been brushing his lips on her.

If, in Annie's previous life, she'd been a longshoreman or perhaps a lumberjack instead of a third grade teacher, she might have spewed a string of expletives that would have embarrassed the most heartless villain in her murder mysteries. In her mind, she hoped Murphy was spewing them for her.

"Did you read it?" John hissed. "Did you read the comments?"

She had not. She did not want to.

"Go to the one that says, 'Hey, Sgt. Lyons, see what your lady's been doing while you're on the night shift.' That's one of the good ones. Or, 'What's going on at The Vineyard Inn, John?' And be sure to read, 'A crack in the wedding bells?' Yeah. I really love that one."

Annie couldn't speak; she could hardly breathe. "No . . ." she moaned, "It isn't . . . it wasn't . . ."

"The worst part . . ." John stepped on her words, his tone methodical, as if he was working hard not to sound threatening, ". . . the worst part is that my daughter showed it to me." His voice cracked when he said, "daughter." "She greeted me with it when I got home from work."

His daughter? Of course Abigail would do something like that. It was no secret that she didn't like having to live on the Vineyard, that moving back had only been what she'd perceived as the lesser of two evils. For all Annie knew, Abigail had taken the picture to humiliate her father. Or her father's girlfriend. Or both of them. "No . . ." Annie insisted again, then said, "Abigail . . ."

John scowled. "Not Abigail. Lucy. Lucy is upset."

Annie was stunned. That the image conveyed a romantic

encounter was beyond a doubt. Of course Lucy would have been upset. But why hadn't she texted Annie and asked her about it first? Then Annie knew that as close as they'd become, Lucy would always put her father first. As Annie would have done.

"So what was he really doing?" John continued. "Other than sucking on your neck?" He'd unfolded his arms and hooked his thumbs into belt loops, a stance that Annie recognized as him trying to tamp down anger.

"John . . . please . . . it isn't like that . . ."

"Okay," he said. "Then let's look at it from my viewpoint. Step one: With all the places on the island, why did the illustrious Simon Anderson pick the Inn as the place to bed down?" Then his breaths became choppy and his words stuttered out. "Did he interview you for one of your books? Did he think it would be cool to do an exposé on a celebrity who actually lives on our supposedly cushy little island? Or . . . is he someone else from your . . . checkered past?"

He was clearly referring to an unfortunate incident that had happened in the spring, when an unwanted demon from Annie's past had showed up at her door. She wondered if John would always be jealous, and, if so, how she should handle it when he seemed convinced that he'd been betrayed. Should she get defensive? Should she cry? Trying to pull her thoughts together, she wanted to say she had no more clues about this photo than he did. Or that she'd only met Simon Anderson two days ago.

But as she started to speak, John huffed. "I'm going to go before you say something I don't want to hear." Then he bolted out the door and clomped back down the stairs, one clomp at a time.

Then Annie had another thought: While it was clear to her—and apparently to all of social media—that Simon's face looked snuggled on her neck, his assistant, Bill, was not in the picture. Nor had she seen him in the brief few seconds that the episode had lasted. Had he been lurking in the crowd with a telephoto lens, waiting for the chance to snap the photo? Had this been a setup? And if so, for God's sake, why?

Annie took a long, hot shower because she didn't know what else to do. But standing under the steamy water didn't stop the questions from swirling. She dried her hair and dressed in a pale green T-shirt and white capris, but didn't want to go anywhere. Though Francine would arrive soon to start breakfast, Annie did not want to see anyone, talk to anyone, be on stage. So she changed back into her pajamas, went back upstairs to the plywood floor, and crawled back into the sleeping bag, doubting that she'd fall sleep.

Staring at her laptop that rested on the chair where she'd draped her clothes from yesterday, she couldn't bring herself to look at VineyardInsiders again. Her only hope was that by eight or nine o'clock, other gossip would have flooded the site so the image of her in the supposed intimate moment would be emasculated by time. And hopefully lack of interest. But she knew enough to know that there would be comments followed by comments about the comments and so on and so on, bumping it back to the top. Annie had never been sure how the "thread" of online conversation technically worked; that was her publicist's job. She wondered if anyone could make it go away.

Could Lucy?

John's daughter had proved her expertise at dispensing with previous social media entanglements. But was she angry with Annie, too—so angry that she wouldn't try? Then again, maybe Annie should leave her alone and not put her in the position of having her emotions pulled between loyalty to her dad and friendship with Annie. Especially when Annie knew who would win.

Trying to ease the sensation that a fish bone was stuck in her gullet, she closed her eyes. But all she saw was a vision of John standing in her doorway, angry and accusing, not waiting for an explanation, as if it were too late for one.

It reminded her of her friend Lauren DelNardi, when they'd been in the fourth grade. The day before Valentine's Day, Annie's mother had made her stay home with a cold. Lauren had stopped by after school; Annie showed her the sugar cookies with dollops of strawberry jam—Annie's favorites—that her mother made for the class party the next day. But Lauren said that their teacher, Mrs. Landry, had announced that no one was to in bring cookies or cakes because everyone in school was getting fat. And there would be no valentine cards, either, because they were too old for that immature tradition.

When Annie arrived at school in the morning, Mrs. Landry greeted each student at the door and accepted sweet treats that mothers had made, and she displayed them on a long table that the kids had decorated with red heart-shaped doilies. Annie shook her head and murmured that she hadn't brought anything. Even worse, when she got to her desk, it was piled with valentines from the other kids.

Annie felt sick. "Did you lie to me?" she asked Lauren.

But Lauren giggled and said Annie should have known it was a joke—after all, Annie was the smartest one in the class, wasn't she? A boy who Annie liked overheard the conversation; he and Lauren exchanged smirks.

Back home, Annie and her mom and dad ate the valentine cookies every night for dessert until they were stale. Her mother threw the rest out.

And though Annie stopped being friends with Lauren, she was left feeling hollow and alone.

She felt that way now. The man who was going to be her husband—unless he'd changed his mind—had been more pissed over the gossip about him and the fact that his daughter had showed him, than he was interested in learning the truth. Or in trusting her. It was as if he, too, had betrayed her—not the way Lauren had, but it left Annie with the same kind of desolate feeling.

Then another question started to simmer: If John was this upset about a frivolous photo that had been neither her doing nor her fault, what would happen when she wrote more books and gained more visibility? How would he react about whatever inaccurate gossip might blossom from that?

She sat up as a lone question formed: Was this marriage meant to be? Would it prevent Annie from being her own person, having her own career, at the risk of John becoming jealous when it was unfounded? And why hadn't it occurred to her earlier that living on the Vineyard wouldn't protect her from that kind of nonsense?

She hung her head. She felt deflated and defeated, all because she'd wanted to have fun while getting to know Meghan better. She couldn't, of course, explain that to John because of her promise. Right then, however, she didn't think he'd listen, anyway.

Then Annie thought about Earl. He would no doubt be at the Inn early that morning. But Earl was patient; he was fair. He would want to know how the photo came to be. He would listen to Annie's side of the story and maybe later try to talk some sense into his son.

But right then Annie didn't feel like talking to him, either.

Claire would take John's side because, first and foremost, she was his mother. She might confront him in private, but she'd defend him in public, because that was what mothers did.

If Kevin were there, Annie could have talked to him, asked for his advice. But even if he came home tomorrow, he'd be too busy with his own predicament: Meghan.

Annie knew she had to think this through, talk this through, with someone. It was her mess and hers alone, no matter that she hadn't asked for it. As with what Lauren had done to her, whoever had snapped the photo and posted it likely had wanted to be vindictive toward Annie. Or maybe Simon. Or John. But the "why" was as elusive as the "who."

Murphy might have chimed in with a plausible guess, but she'd always been a late sleeper.

Annie knew that though this was a totally crazy week all over the island, there was only one person she could speak to. So she climbed out of the sleeping bag again, put her clothes back on, skimmed a brush through her hair, and headed down the stairs for the long drive up island to Winnie's.

Chapter 14

It was opening day of the annual Ag Fair, now in its 159th gathering, having been shuttered only once during World War II and again in the COVID-19 pandemic. The traffic on West Tisbury Road was bumper-to-bumper; many of the vehicles towed horse trailers or were small open trucks that were carrying pigs or alpacas. Annie supposed that the Ferris wheel, the Scrambler, and other amusement rides had already arrived along with a raft of food trucks, as had the crafts and produce displays, the 4-H exhibits, and much more.

The first year Annie had gone she'd had a booth in the hall where she'd offered her wonderful soaps that Winnie taught her to make. Since then, Annie loved participating in the fair and lots of festivals, but though she'd had high hopes, she hadn't been able to participate in any events since the Inn had opened; there had been little time to devote to her hobby. After the book tour she'd have to finish her manuscript-in-progress, but maybe there would be time to make enough soap for the Christmas Fair. It's not as if she might be busy doing other things, like making wedding plans.

As the vehicles inched toward State Road, Annie suddenly slammed on her brakes. *Winnie!* she thought. Winnie wouldn't

be up island—she'd be at the fair. She'd be showing and selling her lovely pottery that she made from the clay of the Gay
Head Cliffs and her special wampum jewelry that she buffed
and carved out of purple-and-white quahog shells that were
indigenous to the Vineyard. Though wampum was still found
exclusively on its shores, a few renegade pieces sometimes
washed in with the tide on Cape Cod or Rhode Island.

Luckily, the car behind Annie had been paying attention
and Annie's Jeep wasn't rear-ended.

When she finally reached State Road, she turned right toward the fairgrounds instead of left toward Aquinnah. Winnie
might be too busy to talk, but at least Annie would be assured
of a big hug, which she needed more than anything.

By the time she parked in the dirt-packed lot and walked
toward the Ag Hall, the fair was in full swing, the air was filled
with the sounds of music and people and life, mixed with the
country scents of farm animals that somehow pleasantly mingled with those of fried dough and clam fritters. All of which
served to remind Annie that no matter what, time would pass,
as would this latest crisis, and that being on the island remained far preferable to living in Boston.

Inside the cavernous building, a large crowd milled in uni-
son like the sheep outside that were patiently waiting to show
off their bounty in a shearing demonstration. Weaving around
the browsers and shoppers, waving at familiar faces, Annie
couldn't help but wonder how many of them had seen VineyardInsiders. Was there a chance they had but didn't care?

Dream on, she thought.

She passed a booth of gorgeous handwoven shawls, passed
the lavender lady who showed pouches and silk pillows filled
with her homegrown buds, and passed rows of artful cloth
handbags made by a young woman who did not look much
older than Lucy.

Then she spotted a girl with blond-highlighted hair

pinned on top of her head. She was standing in a booth across the aisle, thumbing through what Annie recognized as Sue Freshette's array of hand-painted long skirts and shawls— Annie knew Sue from artisan festival meetings. But Sue's work wasn't the only thing Annie recognized: though she hadn't seen the girl in over a year, she was sure that it was Abigail.

For a few seconds, it seemed that someone had hit the pause button in the Ag Hall, giving Annie the chance to study her not-yet-stepdaughter. She was a pretty girl, softer-looking than Lucy, perhaps because she was older. From this vantage point, she didn't resemble her sister, though maybe her grand-mother Claire. Mixed in with Jenn.

Annie wondered if she had the courage to approach her. Perhaps there, on neutral ground, she could come straight out and ask if Abigail had taken the photo, and if she had, what on earth had been her intention? Annie would do her best not to be menacing . . . to try and act as if she were interested for no special reason—no big deal. Maybe she could make a joke about it.

"Thanks for helping to boost my book sales!" she could say while flashing a big smile. "Some people might think I put you up to it!" Ha ha.

She could then suggest that they do lunch one of these days.

The muffled laughter that came from the high-pitched ceiling could only have been Murphy's.

Then Annie saw Abigail hold up a shawl that was woven with thin abstract ribbons in soft shades of green that made it look like beach grass. It was a lovely item; it appeared that Abigail made good choices in clothing if not always in actions. But as she reached to hand the shawl to the artist, Abigail's body shifted; if she raised her head, they would come eye to eye. Annie ducked behind a row of handbags as if she were a private detective who'd nearly been caught stalking her prey. Or more like a preschooler with her hand in that elusive cookie jar. And, Annie realized, about as mature. So she gingerly peered round the corner and saw that Abigail was examining a skirt that was painted in shades of gold like fields of hay waiting to be reaped in West Tisbury or Chilmark.

"May I help you?"

Annie jumped. She turned and looked—dumbfounded, she knew—at the young woman in the booth where Annie stood, the one who did not look much older than Lucy.

"Are you interested in a particular bag?"

Glancing around, Annie regained her bearings. *Right*, she thought. She was standing amid a sea of handbags.

"Yes," she said, grabbing the first one she spotted. It was made of linen-colored canvas and was adorned with a number of felt flip-flops, most of which had seashells and rhinestones glued onto them. Annie supposed that the third-grade girls she'd once taught would have loved it, especially with the glittery magenta words "Martha's Vineyard" that danced across the top and stood out like tourists up at the cliffs, binoculars and cameras dangling from iridescent cords around their necks. *Like glow necklaces*, she thought. She quickly plucked the bag from the peg. "This is lovely. How much?"

"Sixty-five."

Annie nodded as if she were considering it.

Then the girl said, "I know you, don't I? Aren't you Lucy Lyons's friend? Lucy and I are in the same grade. You came to school last year and talked to us about writing, didn't you?"

So, of course, Annie melted. "I did," she said, trying to keep her voice low. "It was a lot of fun."

The girl nodded. "Artists like us have to stick together, right?"

Annie wasn't sure what the girl meant, but in any event she fished into her purse and handed over her debit card.

But as the girl rang up the sale, Annie felt an eerie shadow brush past her, leaving a slight chill in its wake. She shivered; she glanced over to Sue Freshette's booth but did not see Abigail. If the shadow had been her, and if she'd seen Annie, she hadn't bothered to stop and say hello.

Annie walked away from the handbag booth, toting a paper bag that held her purchase.

"Annie!" Thank goodness, the voice that called her name was cheerful and familiar.

Whirling around, Annie stepped right into Winnie's hug. Oh. Yes. She had really, really needed that. By the time she pulled away, tears welled in her eyes.

Winnie frowned. "Let's go outside. Barbara's person-ing my booth, and I need fresh air." Barbara was Winnie's sister-in-law, part of the "tribe" who lived under Winnie's roof. She was also a nurse who worked at the hospital, but when it came to the fair, it was all hands on deck to manage Winnie's popular creations.

They went outside; Winnie led her to a quiet picnic table in the shade.

"So here we are at the fair. Again," Winnie said.

"How are you?" Annie asked. "It's hard to believe that summer's almost gone. How was yours?"

"Busy. The usual. Things going well at the Inn?"

"We've been booked almost every night. It's been great." She knew that sooner or later they'd dispense with small talk and get down to what mattered. The elephant in the room that loomed larger than the draught horses on display in the Ag Fair's back corral.

"Until now?" Winnie asked.

Annie's lower lip started to quiver. "I haven't seen you in weeks and you can still read my mind."

"I can also read the internet."

Of course Winnie knew. By now, everyone on the damn
Vineyard did. Closing her eyes, Annie dropped her head. "I
have no idea what happened. Simon Anderson is staying at the
Inn. I ran into him last night at the Tabernacle. He put a glow
necklace around my neck and wandered off into the swarm of
colored lights. And, suddenly, I'm a pariah. John is furious.
But he didn't give me a chance to explain. It was *nothing*.
Simon clasped the necklace, then he went his way, I went
mine. End of story."

"But someone snapped a picture."

"And posted it on that god-awful site."

"Was it a publicity stunt for him?"

"But why on earth with me?"

"You're not exactly a nobody, Annie."

Annie laughed. "Compared to him? Come on, Winnie.
Most readers who like my books might recognize my name.
Period."

"Has he had any bad press recently? Has his reputation
been tarnished? You're an attractive, successful woman, Annie.
It might help his career if people think he's connected to you."
Winnie spoke so fast she must have been thinking about this
before Annie had run into her.

"Seriously? Thanks for the compliment, but I'm sure Simon
Anderson can have his pick of ladies who are way more attractive and much more successful."

When Winnie smiled, her teeth showed bright white
against her copper skin. "Apparently your John does not agree."

Annie groaned. "*My John*, as you call him, is not being rational."

"In that case, forget about him. He'll come around. Right
now, it might be more important for you to talk to Simon.
See if he knows who's behind it. Let him know it's disrupted
your life. Maybe he does not understand what a tight-knit

place the island is. And that most of us don't care for the kind of gossip that hurts one of our own."

Staring off into the mass of fairgoers, Annie knew that, as much as she loved the womb of the Vineyard, sometimes it was easier to live in the city, where she could walk the streets, go shopping, or have fun, all while remaining anonymous. *Where I can get lost in the crowd*, she thought.

Then Winnie's sister-in-law appeared; she was holding one of Winnie's large, beautiful bowls and said a customer wanted to talk with her about it. So Annie's visit was cut short, but it was okay. She'd heard enough on the subject of Simon Anderson to help her carry on. So she thanked Winnie, got another hug, then headed toward the parking lot.

It wasn't until the light breeze caught the fringe of the shawl with the ribbon-like beach grass and lifted it into the sunlight that Annie noticed Abigail leaning against the Jeep, smoking a cigarette. By then Abigail was staring at her, so there was no chance for Annie to hide like a child. Again.

As Annie's thoughts quickly shuffled, rearranging themselves, it was Abigail who spoke first.

"He's going back to her, you know."

At first, Annie did not understand. Then she remembered an acting class she'd once taken that taught her how to get inside the head of a fictional character. "Learn to sense when another person wants to hurt you," the instructor had said. "You can see it in the eyes." Annie saw that look now in Abigail's glare.

"Nothing you will say or do is going to stop my dad from going back to my mom." She took a long drag, exhaled a slow stream of smoke, and ground the cigarette out in the dirt. Then she slid the shawl from her shoulders and sauntered away, twirling the billowing fabric in the air. And Annie was left standing, feeling as if she'd gazed into Medusa's eyes and had turned to stone, which no doubt was the effect that John's daughter had intended.

On the way back to Chappy, Annie tried to dismiss Abigail's ominous message—whether or not it was true. Her head already hurt from too much on her mind and from the bright sunshine that might be good news for the Ag Fair folks but often triggered a migraine for her. She tugged her visor down, adjusted her sunglasses, and concentrated on how to navigate the traffic without losing her mind.

Being on the cusp of a migraine, however, reminded Annie that Meghan still suffered from her injuries. If only there had been time to tell Winnie about her. Annie trusted Winnie implicitly; she would have liked to ask her for advice on what to do, or not do, about Kevin—like if she should go against Meghan's wishes and call him and tell him what was really going on.

Then again, this was about Kevin, and he was Annie's brother. Maybe she should try and figure it out herself. Later. After she'd rested.

But as hard as she tried, she could not shake Abigail's words. Nor could she shake Winnie's advice: ". . . talk to Simon. See if he knows who's behind it."

Simon, however, did not have a motive to be malicious to her. Unlike Abigail did.

She wished her thoughts didn't keep leaping back to Lucy's "impossible" sister—a clearly distressed girl who would know how to spray the word all over the island. Abigail hadn't succeeded in breaking up her mother's new relationship, so perhaps she'd decided to try and wreck her father's. But wouldn't she have cared that posting it online would humiliate him?

Deciding she could no longer stand her obsessive thoughts, when Annie reached Edgartown, instead of heading to the ferry, she drove into the center of the village and went to John's. It was almost noon: he might be awake, or he might not. There was a chance, however, that Abigail had made it home by now; Annie wanted—needed—to face her, hopefully in John's presence. No matter the cost.

Squeezing into the small driveway, she turned off the ignition and went up onto the porch.

Lucy opened the door. Restless, the dog, leaped and barked and wagged his tail, as he tried to push past Lucy and give Annie a proper welcome. At least someone was happy to see her.

"Hey," Lucy said. "Dad worked late. He's still asleep." She wasn't unfriendly, though her tone was guarded.

"That's okay. How about you? How're you doing?"

She rolled her eyes. "It's kind of weird around here, you know?" She did not invite Annie inside.

"We could use more cookies at the Inn. I tried to make some, but they weren't as good as yours." It wasn't true, as Annie had made her mother's recipe for the sugar cookies with the dollop of strawberry jam, which the guests had seemed to love. But Lucy did not need to know that.

"Yeah. Sorry. I haven't felt much like baking since what's-her-name got here."

"Did you go to Illumination Night?"

"For a while. Too many people, though." Her voice was quiet, as if she were depressed.

Annie looked around at the pretty flower boxes that Lucy had filled early in the summer but now looked dry, most of the blossoms "gone by" in the past few days. "Have you had lunch?"

Lucy shook her head.

"Want to do the Right Fork? My treat?"

"Can Restless come? Maybe he could go for a run in the field. I know a good spot that's out of the way of the planes."

"Sure. Let's do it." She decided not to ask if Abigail was home. Lucy's reluctance was more of a concern than having a showdown. Annie cared about the younger girl too much to risk losing her as well as her dad.

In less than a minute, Lucy was on the porch with a Frisbee in one hand and Restless's leash in the other, the metal hook safely attached to the dog's collar. The diner was only a couple of miles out of town; not in the direction of West Tisbury and the Ag Fair, so the traffic would be blissfully light.

Chapter 15

They carried their food to a picnic table on the fringe of the airfield. Restless either didn't notice or care that his leash was looped through the railing and he could not have chased a sea gull if one landed two feet away. He appeared content to watch the people and listen to the chatter and sniff the good scents in the air.

Lucy tucked into her blueberry pancakes; Annie had ordered a grilled steak salad but didn't have much of an appetite.

"I know you saw the post on VineyardInsiders," Annie finally said. "And I bet you read the comments."

Setting down her fork, Lucy looked out to the runway where a red biplane had landed and was taxiing toward the restaurant to let the passengers off and pick up more. It was a popular activity for summer people, a chance to witness the beauty of the island from the viewpoint of an osprey.

"My dad was really upset," Lucy said.

"I don't blame him. But it was nothing, Lucy. I went with one of our guests—who, by the way, is a woman. I had no idea Simon would be there, let alone that he would spring from out of nowhere and clip a glow necklace around my neck. Right after he did it he laughed, then took off. The whole thing was over in seconds. Unfortunately, someone took a picture that somehow wound up looking suggestive. Chances are, the same person who took it posted it. I can't imagine who would do that."

Lucy shrugged. "Me, either. It's pretty stupid. The only ones who'd be hurt by it would be you and my dad." She took another forkful of pancakes, chewed slowly, and swallowed. "And Simon Anderson's wife and kids."

Annie took a long drink of her iced tea, not because she was terribly thirsty, but because she needed to process what Lucy had said. "There," she said, "you see? He's married. So he has no inappropriate intentions toward me."

Lucy rolled her eyes. "I'm not sure that's how it always works, or if my dad would believe it, but it might help."

"I hope he knows me better than to think I'd get involved with a family man."

"Okay, so who took the pic and posted it?"

"I hoped you might have an idea."

"I have a weird feeling you're going to ask me if it was Abigail."

In spite of Lucy's protestations that her sister was "impossible" and that she made Lucy want to run away, Annie knew that the bond of being sisters might conflict with clear thinking. She knew she should tread lightly, as the old saying went. "I don't know Abigail well enough to assume she did it," Annie said. "In fact, I hardly know her at all. And she doesn't know me."

"She knows you're going to marry my dad. He told her when we were in Plymouth for her graduation."

"I didn't know that."

"I don't think he wanted to make a big deal out of it. Like he didn't want you to think he was asking for her permission."

Once again, Annie wondered if she really knew the man she had agreed to marry. And though it was true that people can't really know one another completely, it felt to her that as time passed she knew John Lyons less, not more. The good parts and the not-so-good. She wondered if he felt the same way about her now.

"What was Abigail's reaction? Was she upset?" As badly as she wanted to tell Lucy the news that her sister had imparted to Annie, she was determined to stay calm.

"I only heard his side of the conversation when he told her, 'cuz I was eavesdropping from the top of the stairs."

"Lucy . . ."

"Hey, no lectures, okay? I listened because it was about my dad. And you. I wanted to make sure my sister wouldn't stick her nose in it. But I don't think she took that picture."

"No?"

"Nope. As much as I'd love to be able to get her in trouble, I could see the Tabernacle in the background of the pic. She wasn't up there. We stayed down at Ocean Park; Abigail met up with a few more of her old friends from school and they hung out down there. Don't tell Dad, but they were drinking. I got bored and went up to the Tabernacle, but I didn't see you. It was late, though; the lanterns were still lit but the band was done playing. Maybe you were gone by then. I got a ride home with Helen Jackson. You know her? She works at the pharmacy and the hardware store. She's a friend of my grandmother's. Anyway, she said her arthritis was bothering her, so I helped her back to her car and hopped in."

Annie didn't pay rapt attention to the rest of Lucy's story. Instead she focused on the fact that Lucy didn't think Abigail had done it. And that Lucy had unknowingly given her sister an alibi, because the band had still been playing when Simon had pulled his stunt.

As for Abigail's declaration that John would be going back to his ex-wife, Annie would have that conversation with John, not Lucy. If he ever got over being angry.

"Lucy?" Annie asked. "I know it's a lot to ask, and I don't want you to feel pressured, but is there any way you can take down the post? Like you did those other ones?"

Lucy shook her head. "If there's a way, I don't know it. I only know how to delete something I posted myself."

The next logical step would be to ask Lucy if she'd sneak onto Abigail's computer and find out if she'd been the "author." Just in case.

But, as if Lucy had known what Annie was thinking, she added, "Even if we knew who posted it, I couldn't take it off their laptop unless I knew their password. And I don't know anyone else's password. Not my best friend, Maggie's. Or my sister's."

Annie got the message. She also got another message, as her text alert pinged. Thinking it might be John, either to apologize or to dump her, she glanced at her phone. The message was from her editor.

CALL WHEN YOU GET THIS. WE NEED TO TALK.

It was cryptic, but typical of Trish, who was usually in too much of a hurry to want to bother to type. Unless the sun was rising, she preferred one-on-one conversation.

Annie ignored the text and boxed up what remained of her salad.

When Lucy finished her meal they brought Restless to the far side of the field where he and Lucy played catch until one of them tired, though it was hard to tell which one. Lucy had grown up a great deal over the summer: her legs were longer, her figure curvier; her face no longer looked like a child's. Annie supposed those changes could be part of the girl's slumping mood, especially when combined with her sister's unwelcome presence.

When they got back to John's, Annie simply smiled and said, "Make some cookies for the Inn, okay? I miss seeing your face." Though Lucy already had been there earlier in the week, Annie sensed it was a good thing to say. Apparently it was, for when Lucy got out of the Jeep she smiled back and promised that she would.

Annie drove to the Chappy ferry where the line was August-long, so she decided to call Trish and get it over with.

"There you are!" her editor cried. "I'd begun to think you'd run off with Simon Anderson."

"Hardly. Simon is a married man. With children." Then Annie's brain cells aligned; she stared at the back of the SUV in front of her and wondered how Trish had learned about the incident when she lived and worked in Manhattan and Vine-yardInsiders was a private site. Islanders only, like a little kids' clubhouse.

"Trish?" Annie asked. "How did you find out?"

"Stop being coy, my dear. We've known each other far too long for that."

"I'm not being coy. Tell me what you know. And how."

"Seriously? You don't read the *Times* online?"

Annie laughed. "It's summer on Martha's Vineyard. I barely have time to check my email, let alone read the *MV Times*." Then it occurred to her that Trish had meant the *Times* as in *The New York Times*.

"You're on the front page of the Entertainment section," Trish replied, ignoring the bit about the Vineyard newspaper. The headline says it all: 'Simon Anderson Must Love a Mystery.' The subhead reads: 'Martha's Vineyard rendezvous with mystery author Annie Sutton.' Below that is a terrific picture of the two of you. It looks like you're in a nighttime embrace, surrounded by all kinds of glowing things."

The vehicles in front of Annie inched toward the dock; she was too shocked to start her car and move it forward. Behind her a horn blew, then two.

"Are you kidding?" she asked, finally turning on the ignition and inching ahead. "It isn't true!" A veil of moisture surfaced on her brow.

"Oh, hush, don't be foolish. Pictures don't lie. Besides, it's wonderful news. Nobody cares if it's true. The fact is, Simon's name is contagious. He's highly visible and so damn good-looking he makes hearts throb and juices flow. And now he's on fabulous Martha's Vineyard, clearly smitten with an equally fabulous women."

"He's a married man, Trish. And, believe me, I'm not that fabulous." She knew that in addition to being a topnotch editor, Trish had a great sense of building an author's image and audience. Which might translate into high numbers of book sales, but right then, it felt smothering. And personal. Too personal. Maybe she'd been wrong to think that city life was anonymous.

"The fact that he's 'married with children' only makes the story more titillating."

"For the last time, there *is* no story."

"Don't you understand, Annie? Women around the world are going to be jealous. If they're not already your readers they will be, because, my dear, you've been *noticed*. So, I repeat, this is wonderful news. And right in time for *Murder on Exhibit*. No matter what you think, it's a spectacular stunt. Our publicity department could not have done better."

A publicity stunt? That was what Winnie had suggested. But if it had been one for Simon . . . why with her? Annie thought about the picture on VineyardInsiders . . . obviously the one in the *Times* was the same. How did it make it to the Entertainment front page so fast? Sometimes she hated how information—especially the hostile kind—now spread faster than the speed of anything, and not just around the island. "I doubt that Simon is desperate for a ratings bump, Trish. Even if he is, he wouldn't get one from me."

"Never underestimate yourself," Trish reprimanded.

Then a cold, dull ache nagged at Annie's gut, as reality finally comprehended. She knew that all the talking in the world, all the speculating over whodunit and why, was not going to unravel the answer. She needed to get to the bottom of this, and she needed to do it alone. Because no one else had as much to lose.

As she watched the sunlight glimmer on the rippling water, Annie calmly said, "I'm sorry, Trish. I have to go. I'll call you later."

Quickly disconnecting, she stared out at the wharf and the water, at small groups of ice-cream-cone-licking children and adults who were not at the beach or the fair or in a sailboat circumnavigating the island. They were summer people, on vacation. Perhaps they thought, the way Annie once had, that one day, if they were lucky, they, too, could move to "fabulous" Martha's Vineyard and leave all their troubles behind.

Once back on Chappy, Annie didn't go home. Instead, she drove to the Indian Burial Ground, her favorite place to go for what she called "a good think." The first time she'd been there had been on Christmas Eve, not long after she'd moved to the Vineyard.

There was nothing fancy about the graveyard. It was a small plot of land atop a short hill that overlooked Cape Poge Bay. Not many summer people knew about it; hardly anyone ventured there, though sometimes they stumbled upon it when hiking the island. It was quiet and modest, with only sixteen gravestones indicating the graves of members of the long-ago Chappaquiddick Wampanoag Tribe; fewer than a dozen other markers were unreadable, though it was thought that they, too, were Wampanoags, and several unadorned fieldstones were thought to honor their earlier ancestors.

A narrow path separated a couple of dozen other stones

from the Wampanoags; they were from later years—several were Earl's ancestors, and, of course, John's. And Lucy and Abigail's. A few were unmarked; two only had initials—G. P. and D. B.—but Annie hadn't been able to see those in late December, as they'd been covered by a thick cloak of snow.

She'd gone to the burial ground that first time with Earl. Curiously, a path had been plowed, allowing them to trek to the Lyonses' stones. Earl had brought a miniature, potted fir that was decorated with a string of popcorn and small red birds fashioned out of birdseed and was topped with a star that was shaped out of suet; he set it on the ground in front of the memorials to his ancestors: Orrin, Patience, Silas, and others. Earl had removed his knit hat, knelt in the snow, and bowed his head.

It turned out that John had been there earlier that day and had plowed the path for Earl's visit. It was their family tradition. At the time, Annie hadn't yet met John, but she'd been touched by his caring and his respect for his father and for those who had come before them. Perhaps more than that, she'd been moved by the act that was between father and son, done in private in such a remote place, with no need to impress anyone.

As Annie stood in the burial ground now, she looked out at the vista of clear blue water that was not accented by a skin of wintery ice as it had been on that Christmas Eve, but by colorful, luminous kayaks. She thought about how she'd admired John before having met him, and how only a few weeks later, she'd fallen in love.

John Lyons was an amazing man. She didn't doubt that he cared for her. But they were not teenagers; they were not each other's first love. His ex-wife might have been his first, or maybe not. He might be planning to go back to her, or maybe not. No matter what the future might or might not hold, the road to commitment felt more treacherous now, paved as it was with past mistakes, lessons learned, and hesitations to take a chance again.

Or maybe it was just her.

Still, he should have listened to her explanation. It was the first time she'd been the subject of his anger, his jealousy, his doubt about her feelings for him. The timing might have driven his behavior; Abigail's return and trying to keep peace between his daughters must be stressful for him. Especially since he also needed to keep peace, day and night, throughout the crowded streets of the much-heralded town that had somehow gained a reputation for glamor, glitz, and, incorrectly, anything-goes.

In short, if Annie was going to be his wife, how much slack should she cut him? Was being a fiancé supposed to raise the level of the bar of tolerance? And if so, why hadn't he done that with her? Were his stressors so much worse than hers? They might be, she supposed, if one included a desire to move to Plymouth to reunite with his former wife.

Despite her questions, as she strolled through the graveyard, Annie felt the calming presence of the souls at rest. As she walked, her priorities came into focus. She knew it was time to gather the facts.

Fact one was that she could not pretend she hadn't been a teensy bit smitten by Simon, thanks to his attention—and perhaps his damn sexy charisma. But no one would know that, except Murphy, who probably was listening to her thoughts right then.

Fact two was that Simon was married. And had kids. Three of them. And though Trish had said it made the story more titillating, the comment had made Annie shudder.

But fact three might be the most important: Annie must figure out who had taken the picture, who had posted it on

VineyardInsiders, who had leaked it to the *Times*—as in *New York Times*, not the *MV* one. It had to be the same person. And though it would be convenient to believe that Abigail was behind it, Annie doubted that the eighteen-year-old had connections to national or international media, or a way to coerce the *Times* into including it on their site.

But Simon Anderson would know the right people.

Fact four was that Annie needed to find out if John really intended to go back to Jenn. Or if Abigail had been testing Annie.

Yes, Annie needed answers, starting with the photo. Her first stop would be Simon, as Winnie had suggested. Because, if Annie had the most to lose, did Simon have the most to win? Or at least did he think he might have?

Good question, Murphy suddenly whispered.

Leave it to Murphy to be hanging out in a graveyard. At least she hadn't commented on Annie's self-admission that she'd been a teensy bit smitten.

I would have been, too, Murphy added, most likely to prove to Annie that, indeed, she read her every thought.

"Ugh!" Annie cried. "What am I going to do, Murph?"

Talk to him, like Winnie said. And talk to those you trust. Winnie and I aren't the only ones who are on your side, you know.

Drawing in a long breath of Vineyard air, Annie really wanted to believe that.

Chapter 16

Annie made it to the Inn in record time. She knew she should find out if Francine needed her. But Francine surely had seen or heard the latest island gossip, and Annie didn't want to lose time—or her nerve—by commiserating with her. So she parked quickly, jumped out of the Jeep, and went directly to the cottage. She doubted that Simon could be far because it was only Thursday—he still didn't have a rental vehicle. Which also made her wonder who had given him a ride to Oak Bluffs the night before.

The screen door was closed, but the main door was open. Annie knocked on the doorframe. "Hello?" she called, trying to sound friendly. "Simon? It's Annie. Are you there?" She cupped her hand to the screen and peeked inside, but the bright sun behind her dimmed her view. Then she heard footsteps.

"Annie?" a voice asked.

It wasn't Simon. It was Bill. He was dressed in a wrinkled T-shirt and jeans that looked as if they'd been worn many times since they'd been washed. Compared to the care with which Simon dressed, Bill was definitely a production guy and not a news anchor.

"Is Simon here?"

He opened the screen door and stepped outside, but not before Annie caught a glimpse into her living room that surprisingly did not look trashed. Then she scolded herself for thinking it would be simply because Bill was there.

"Hey," he said, "that Illumination thing was pretty cool. When Simon first told me about it, I figured it would be hokey. You know, small-town stuff ramped up for the tourists."

Annie stiffened. "It's not hokey, Bill. It's an island tradition."

"Yeah, we figured that out. Like I said, it was pretty cool."

She forced a smile. "I'm glad you enjoyed it. But how'd you get there? You could have come with us." Sometimes being nice was challenging.

"We hitched a ride with some Chappy people—Lottie, I think her name was? Plus her husband and another woman. The ladies were decked out in red-white-and-blue like it was the Fourth of July." He scoffed, then scuffed his feet on Annie's pristine porch. So much for him being tidy. "We met them when they were crossing to Edgartown on that sad excuse of a ferry."

As badly as she wanted to suggest that he might want to be careful what he said about the people of Chappaquiddick or the beloved *On Time* in front of, well, in front of anyone, she decided not to waste her time or breath.

"So where's Simon? Sleeping off all the excitement?"

"Down at the beach. He took one of your porch chairs. I told him you wouldn't mind."

Of course she minded. Her Adirondack chairs belonged on her porch. Not on the beach where the paint could get scratched by the sand and scraped by broken pieces of shells.

Nonetheless, she smiled. "Okay, thanks. I'll go find him." She turned to leave.

"Annie?" Bill called. "You're not upset, are you? About the picture?"

She spun back around. "What do you know about it?" There was no point pretending she didn't know what "picture" he meant.

"Me? Not a thing. Scout's honor." He held up three fingers as if he were ready to recite the pledge to honor whatever. "All I know is everyone was talking about it at breakfast."

She cringed. "And what did Simon have to say to 'everyone'?"

"He wasn't there. He only had two boiled eggs for breakfast. He tries to do that every day. He says it keeps his mind sharp and his loins lean."

Annie wished he hadn't referred to Simon's loins as if she had—or wished she had—any kind of relationship with them. "Well, good for him. Did anyone at the breakfast table say if they knew or heard who'd taken the shot and posted it?"

Bill shook his head, but his mouth had twitched up into a slight smile that made her feel that he was mocking her. "Not that anyone admitted."

She was seething now.

"It could have been one of Simon's fans," the mocker continued. "They're everywhere. They suck up whatever gossip about him they can find. If you ask me, it's pretty lame, but it's part of the game. He knows that."

"It's hardly a 'game' if it involves innocent people." She wanted to add so much more. But she'd already said too much to someone who could diss the Inn with "one or none" TripAdvisor stars. Tossing him another fake smile, she started to leave again when he said:

"Wait."

She stopped but did not turn around.

"Maybe whoever did it was hoping to give a shout-out for the Vineyard Inn. Like maybe they thought they would help you. Free publicity, you know?"

Free, indeed. Except for the cost to Annie's relationship. And to Simon's family, not that she needed to care about them. Gritting her teeth, she replied, "I guess that's one way of looking at it." Then she flashed him the best innkeeper's hospitable wave she could muster and trotted toward the path that led down to the beach.

The Adirondack chair was burrowed in sand up to the pitch of its fifteen-degree-angled seat. Annie wondered if another inn would tack the cost of refurbishment onto a guest's bill.

"Simon," Annie said.

He looked up from the tablet he'd been reading and shielded his eyes against the sun. "Well, if it isn't my favorite mystery author."

Based on what he'd said when they'd first met—and until Meghan had seen him in the library—he hadn't read anything she'd ever written, nor was she one of his "favorite" authors.

"I'd offer you a seat, but as you can see, I only dragged one chair down here. Care for a spot on the sand?"

She could have told him they had plenty of real beach chairs available to guests up at the Inn. Instead, she ignored his remark and simply said, "What happened last night? And what did you have to do with it? Did you post it on the island website or get it to the *Times*—or both?"

He grinned. "It never ceases to amaze me how quickly word travels these days. You can have a good time one night and then—*boom!*—just like that, the whole world knows about it." He snapped his fingers when he said "boom."

"I'm serious, Simon. While my editor is delighted at the

publicity of the two of us supposedly being linked, it's causing a boatload of trouble in my personal life. And I can't believe it hasn't damaged yours."

"It's a well-known fact that John Wanamaker, who, in 1876, founded what became one of the world's largest retailers, once said, 'I know that fifty percent of my advertising dollars are wasted, but I don't know which fifty percent.' I remind my wife of that often."

Annie had no idea what any of that had to do with this. It was, however, becoming obvious that he was behind the photo. Though she still could not imagine why.

Simon turned off his device and donned sunglasses. "Neither you nor I have to 'advertise' in the old-fashioned way, but our ongoing visibility is as critical as if we needed to sell a line of fall women's wear. We are our own brands, Annie. You're the brand for your books; I'm the brand for my journalism. Like it or not, our brands need constant selling. In order to sell, we must advertise."

"You're a jerk," she wanted to say. Oh, how she wanted to. She tried to recall the young man she'd seen every night on the local Boston news, the rising star who once had presented himself as humble and truthful, not someone with an agenda. Perhaps he'd had one all along and had been good at pretending. "I let my books speak for my so-called 'brand,'" she said. "As for advertising, I leave that up to my publisher."

"Today's world is too competitive to leave your brand up to anyone but you. For example, don't you have another book coming out soon? You must know that this kind of PR, this widespread exposure, is going to help sales."

The sun was burning the back of her neck. The angrier she became, the worse it tingled. Without further invitation, she dropped onto the sand and draped the hem of her sundress discreetly between her knees. "We aren't in the same business,

Simon. Yes, our audience is important to each of us. But all I
try to do is give my readers a good story they can enjoy for a
few hours. I write one, sometimes two, books a year. I am not
on the evening news. Every night. Night after night."

He fell silent for a moment, as if letting her words sink in.
"You're originally from Boston," he said.

She hadn't expected that. And yet, she supposed she
shouldn't be surprised if he had Googled her in order to learn
all he could about her, brand-to-brand. Or maybe he'd just
read it on the book jacket in the library. She was beginning to
wonder if his ratings, indeed, had been falling, and if he were
frantically trying to invent a promotional pot wherever, whenever possible. Maybe she wasn't his first "hit."

"I am from Boston," she replied. "Born and raised there."

"As was I."

"I used to watch you on the local news. But I didn't know
you're a native."

"It took lots of coaching to get rid of 'chow-dah' and
'pahk the cah.'"

Annie would have smiled, but she was too intent on her
mission to let down her guard. Besides, if she did, Murphy
surely would give her a spirited tongue-lashing.

"I was brought up in the projects in Dorchester," he continued. "Columbia Point. Ever hear of it?"

She nodded, as if she cared. Though, from what she recalled, the disrepair and danger in that era would have made
for a frightening place to grow up.

"We got out before the end of revitalization. My dad was
dead by then—alcohol—and my mom, my two brothers, and
I went to live with her sister, my aunt Betty. We never figured out how it happened, but Aunt Betty married a guy who
was a big-shot city lawyer. They had no kids except us. And
everybody loved Uncle Harry. So while I spent a little more

than the first decade of my life in absolute squalor, in the second, I became a preppie. Rags to riches. Filth to frills. From Columbia Point to Columbia University School of Journalism. Worked my butt off because my mom needed to feel good about something in her life. And I've made it to pretty close to the top. Though I've had to slay a few dragons along the way."

She supposed she should comment that his mom must be proud of him, but Annie didn't feel like it. Besides, for all she knew, he'd made the whole thing up. "That's all very commendable, Simon. But I fail to see what it has to do with what happened last night. Or what *didn't* happen, as we both know it didn't."

After a pensive, perhaps intentionally well-timed, pause, he said, "Nothing. Never mind. It's crap, anyway." He lifted a can of seltzer that she hadn't noticed earlier. "Cheers to the old days. May they be forgotten. And to all our days. May they be forgiven."

"Is that an admission of guilt? Did you have Bill shoot the picture? And did you post it and send it to the *Times*?"

"Nope," he said. "I don't stoop that low. For starters, I never heard of that gossip thing you have here. And I have friends at the *Times*—all of whom texted this morning and wanted to know why I didn't give them the exclusive. I explained that it was bogus and asked them to track down where it came from; a few said they'd already tried and had gotten nowhere. But I had their word that the story or the photo won't be repeated, at least not there. Believe me, though I know my brand's important, I do have bigger fish to fry. No island reference intended."

Annie hated to admit it, but she thought he was telling the truth. She did, however, know how she might be able to confirm his denial.

★ ★ ★

On her way to the Inn to see Francine and try and correct the chatter that had infiltrated the breakfast table, Annie called the Chappy community center. She got voice mail.

She left a message: "Lottie? It's Annie Sutton. Could you please call me?" She left her number in case there wasn't a readout.

Then she texted John.

PLEASE CALL BEFORE YOU LEAVE FOR WORK.

She checked her phone and saw that in less than two hours he'd have to be on duty if he was on his normal four-to-midnight. Still plenty of time for him to comply. She slipped her phone into the pocket of her sundress and continued her trek up the hill.

Francine was on the floor in the great room, playing with Bella and half a dozen rag dolls that Annie suspected Claire had made. Bella was designating chores to each doll: the orange-haired one was to write a list for food shopping; the brunette was to pick blueberries for dinner; the blonde—whose yarn hair needed serious mending—was to mop the floor where a sippy cup had mysteriously spilled. Watching the little girl's imagination blossom grew more fun every week.

"Annie," Francine said, "I was thinking about you right this second." Her beautiful, dark eyes had lost some of their sparkle in the past couple of weeks; her once shining pixie-cut black hair had lost some of its vibrancy. Annie worried that a day and a half hadn't provided her a long enough break.

"How are you?" Annie asked.

"I have a little stomach ache. No big deal. Too much going on, I guess. But I'm the one who should be asking how you are."

Slumping onto one of the seaglass-colored wing chairs that

sat by the wall of windows that looked out to the harbor, Annie said, "I guess you're not the only one who's been thinking about me. Or rather, talking about me. Or so I've been told. What a nightmare." She scooped a few pieces of wampum from a small dish on the end table, closed her fingers around them, and tumbled them in her palm as if they were worry stones. Perhaps they were. "How upset are our guests?"

Francine picked up the doll that Bella had instructed to go shopping and smoothed its orange hair—Annie recognized the yarn as matching that in a sweater Claire had knit for Lucy last Christmas. "I wouldn't say they're upset. Curious, maybe. Mary Beth tried to set them straight, but I think they wanted to believe that you Simon are an . . . item."

It took Annie a second to remember that Mary Beth was, in fact, Meghan. Another one on her growing list of problems. "The picture made it into the *New York Times*. My editor says the timing is terrific, what with my next book about to come out." She toyed with the shells, grateful that Meghan had been standing beside her at the Tabernacle and, if questioned, could confirm the details of what happened. But if Annie used her as an eyewitness, she'd risk baring Meghan's secret if the police—namely John—interrogated her. And Annie would not do that. Ever.

"How are you?" Francine asked.

She blinked. "I thought I'd feel better if I got to the bottom of this. But so far I'm coming up blank. I've been told that Abigail didn't do it. Bill didn't do it. Simon didn't, either. It's tough enough to confront an enemy when you know who it is. But how can I defend myself when I don't know the culprit? Who hates me enough to want to ruin my life?"

"I can't imagine that anyone hates you," Francine said.

"One of John's old girlfriends?"

"From what Claire told me, after his divorce he was a hermit until he met you. He didn't have a single date. He was that upset—not about losing his wife, but about losing his family unit."

He'd used the same words when he'd explained his breakup to Annie, right after they'd started dating. She pushed away the thought that his "family unit" might be a strong enough incentive to shove him back to Jenn. She sighed. "Am I overreacting?"

"I have no idea. Maybe none of this was about you. Maybe it was about Simon. Like it could be someone who knows his wife, or knows he's married, and wanted to start trouble. You do know he's married, don't you?"

Annie planted her hands on either side of her head. "Oh, my God. Not you, too! Yes, I know he's married. And *no*, I have no interest in him. Nor would I if I weren't engaged to John—if, in fact, I still am. Simon Anderson is too slick for me." She was grateful she'd figured that out not long after they'd met.

"Look," Francine said quietly, "you might never know who did it. We both know the Vineyard is teeming with all kinds of people in summer. Maybe it was an arbitrary person with an iPhone who spotted you and thought it would be a hoot to post a photo on VineyardInsiders. Who knows how it got to the *Times* from there. There are plenty of people wandering around here who are connected with media from all over the world. Especially in August." Her words were wise, far wiser than her years. But as much as Annie appreciated them, she still felt a hole of uncertainty.

Dropping the wampum back into the dish, she stood up and stretched. "I'd much rather help with housekeeping duties than think about this another minute. What needs doing? Is anyone waiting for anything?"

"I think they've all gone out. I cleaned the rooms, which is pretty easy. Bill said he isn't fussy, so there was no need to do his. I gave Simon fresh towels yesterday, but he said the cottage was fine, and that he knows how to make his own bed. Who knows? Maybe he's a little miffed about the gossip, too. Maybe both he and his wife didn't appreciate it. Anyway, I haven't gone down there this morning. Maybe you want to try again to clear the air with him?"

"Thanks, but I already tried. He was pretty clear that he had nothing to do with it. I'll bring the towels, though. Save you a trip."

"While you're at it, are you going to ask him to leave?"

Annie touched her throat. "Why? Did someone suggest that?"

"Well," Francine began as she exchanged the orange-haired doll for the brunette that Bella handed her, "after Bill left the table, one of the Indiana sisters—Toni, I think—suggested that Simon should go elsewhere. She said, 'Whether or not this is true, why would anyone put such drivel online?' Did I tell you I found your books in their room?"

In spite of her all-consuming drama, Annie offered half a grin. "So the sisters are fans. How nice."

"They haven't asked for your autograph yet?"

"No. They're probably being respectful. Which doesn't mean they won't ask when they're checking out." She blew Bella a kiss. "Thanks for the talk, Francine. I'll bring towels to the cottage and see if Simon wants anything else. Other than to bake in the sun while wrecking the legs of my Adirondack chair."

"What?" Francine asked.

Annie waved it off. "Nothing. I'm being petty. Go back to Jonas's. I'll stay here and mind the palace. I've realized I like to work in the reading room."

"Jonas is painting out at Wasque today. He says those are the landscapes most people have bought. Maybe I'll bring a blanket, and Bella and I will go watch." Lately, whenever she mentioned Jonas, she smiled sweetly. "You'll be okay here?"

"Of course. Whoever is behind this might simply be vying for attention. I doubt if anyone is trying to blackmail me. Or kill me. So go. Enjoy. And please persuade Jonas to come to the fireworks tomorrow night. It's always a good time."

Francine smiled again, shyly that time, and lowered her head.

For the first time that day, Annie felt a little better—especially because the fact that she'd remembered about the fireworks must be a sign that at least a small part of her brain remained intact.

Chapter 17

Though she missed her writing space in the cottage, Annie did enjoy working in the reading room, where she was connected to the real world while immersed in her imaginary one. It was a nice combination, especially for putting together blog posts and "listicles"—a term she'd never heard of until recently; it meant that Annie had to come up with lists of items that in some way were tied to her novels and would be fun for her readers. Creating them entailed hunting for information on topics like:

—10 Museums with Unsolved Mysteries
—6 Must-See Museums in America
—12 Quirky Museums around the Globe

The research was easy and helped take her mind off everything else. Including the fact that by four o'clock, when John would be clocking in at the station, he still hadn't called. It was a silent, yet audible, message.

A few minutes later, Annie heard a light tap on the doorway. "Knock, knock?"

It was Meghan, alias Mary Beth. Or Mary Beth Mullen, alias Meghan MacNeish.

"Hey," Annie said. "Come on in."

"Sorry to interrupt."

"It's fine. I've been getting cross-eyed. Come in. Sit."

She came in. She sat. She looked woeful.

"What's up?" Annie asked.

"I looked for you this morning, but the Jeep wasn't here. I was wondering how you're doing since that absurd picture was posted."

"Ah, yes. That. I believe the term is I'm doing 'as well as can be expected.' In other words, I don't have a clue how I'm doing. John is angry. I'm angry that he's angry. I can't figure out who did it or why. So, yeah, I guess 'as well as can be expected' pretty much sums it up."

"Oh, Annie, I'm so sorry."

"Me, too. I heard you defended my honor during breakfast. Thanks for that."

"It's all so ridiculous."

"That it is." She shut down her laptop, closed the lid, and rested her arms on top. She leaned closer to Meghan. "But much in life is ridiculous, isn't it? Like how you happened to arrive here the very day that Kevin left."

Meghan studied her fingernails—clipped short, and nicely manicured with clear polish. "I haven't wanted to ask, but have you heard from him about the picture?"

"No." She did not want to tell her that she wouldn't be surprised if Kevin was not monitoring VineyardInsiders because he was otherwise occupied. "But I don't want to talk about it anymore. What I would love would be for you to come to the fireworks tomorrow night. They're really magnificent. They take place in Oak Bluffs, but I like to go to Fuller Street Beach in Edgartown. I went there last year with

Earl and Claire. It isn't as crowded, and the view is terrific. In fact, maybe I'll invite the honeymooners and the Indiana sisters, too. Not sure about Simon and Bill, though. Not after our last public outing." She'd added the last part in an attempt at a joke, hoping to elicit a laugh out of Meghan. It didn't work.

"That's the other reason I was looking for you," Meghan said. "Thanks for the invite, but I'll have to decline. I spent most of the day walking and thinking and thinking some more, and I've decided to leave the Vineyard. I'll check out in the morning."

It felt as if someone had sucked the air out of the room. Annie's whole body went limp. "No-o-o-o," she whimpered. "Please. Don't go, Meghan. You only just got here . . . I've only just met you . . ."

But Meghan shook her head. "I can't. That picture of you and Simon . . . I'm standing right there in the background. Thank God it was dark, and the lights pretty much blurred me, so I'm not recognizable. Which is good, because my bet is that if Kevin hasn't yet seen it, he will. But who knows what will happen next? Will somebody take another photo— that time with me in it, front and center? I can't risk it, Annie. If Kevin comes back it should be because he wants to. Not because he finds out I'm here. It wouldn't be fair. Not to him and not to that woman . . ."

Annie tried to listen patiently, to not interrupt. But the reference to Taylor made her stifle a grimace. "What really isn't fair is that he doesn't know."

Weaving her fingers together, Meghan said, "At some point, I'll get in touch with him—I agree, it's the right thing to do. But if I stay here he might find out by mistake. And I don't want to shock him. I've put him through too much as it is." She stood up, tears now coating her cornflower eyes. "I'm really sorry, Annie. You're so special, and I'm so glad Kevin has you. Under other circumstances, I think we'd be good friends."

"Not only friends, Meghan. Family. We are family, after all."

As Meghan pressed her lips together, a single tear trickled down her cheek.

Annie stood up and gave her a hug. "Think about it some more, okay? And let me know if there's any way on this planet I can get you to change your mind."

But Meghan slipped from her hug and from the room without responding.

Annie could not let Meghan leave, so she knew she had to act. It took all of five seconds to come up with what she hoped was the right strategy. But she couldn't execute it there.

Gathering her things, she left a note on the front desk saying she'd return in half an hour. Then she left the Inn and headed toward the meadow, where she quickly climbed the stairs to her temporary digs over the workshop and thanked God for the decent cell service up there. But before she could make the call, someone connected to her line.

"Annie?" an unfamiliar voice asked.

Instantly fearing it was a prank call—a woman calling to spout off about the picture of her with Simon, like maybe his wife who could have tracked Annie down, or one of Simon's enamored fans who thought she was entitled to have him for herself—Annie paused. And waited.

"Annie?" the voice repeated. "It's Lottie Nelson."

Annie sighed. "Oh. Lottie. Thanks for calling me back."

The woman paused, as if she'd heard the distress in Annie's voice. "Did you decide to use the space at the fire station after all?"

"No," she replied, shaking her head as if Lottie could see her. "I was wondering about something else. I didn't get to see you at Illumination Night."

"We were there. Along with Georgia, who I'm sure would have loved to see you."

The mention of Lottie's sister, a kind hospice nurse, an "angel of mercy," as she'd been called, triggered a tug of emotion. Annie cleared her throat. "I'm sorry I missed her. But I did hear that you picked up a couple of passengers at the ferry. A couple of guys who might have entertained you?"

Lottie laughed. "They sure did. Joe spotted them. Well, he spotted Simon. He watches him every night from eight to nine. Georgia was delighted when the men squeezed into the back seat. Simon sat next to her."

"That's nice," Annie said, as if she thought it was. Simon, on the other hand, would have been pleased to know that his brand had had a positive impact on Chappaquiddick, at least with Lottie's trio. "This is going to sound absurd, but do you remember if Simon's assistant had any camera gear with him?"

"You mean like a Nikon hanging around his neck and a tripod under his arm?"

"Something like that." She paced the plywood floor in the unfinished room, stopping at the window, where she looked out at the view that was so serene it seemed to ridicule her situation.

"Are you trying to figure out who took the picture that wound on the internet?"

A tiny thud thudded in Annie's stomach. God, she was getting sick of this. "I am."

"I bet John wasn't too pleased when he saw it."

"Never mind John. *I* wasn't too pleased." Her words snapped out. "Sorry, Lottie. I didn't mean to bark."

"No problem. I'm sure I'd feel the same way if somebody posted something like that about me. And Joe sure wouldn't be pleased."

"Right. But what about a camera? Did you notice one?"

Lottie sighed. "Sorry, but I didn't. I know that Bill—that's his name, right?—had a bottle of beer in one hand, but I don't think there was anything in the other. And no strap hanging around his neck."

"Oh." Though she was disappointed, Annie wasn't surprised. She turned from the window, walked to the chair by the sleeping bag, and sat. "And Simon?"

"He had a green map. You know, the kind with the illustrations of tourist attractions all over the island and how to get there? The ones you get free at the boat terminals and the airport and in lots of places?"

Yes, Annie knew the map. They kept a stack at the Inn's front desk in the reception area, and Francine put one in each guest room. "When you got to OB, did you drop Simon and Bill off or did you stay with them?"

"Oh, we wouldn't have stayed with them—that would have been pushy. Joe booted all of us out of the car at the foot of Circuit Avenue, then he went somewhere and parked. I told Simon to meet us at the carousel at ten if they needed a ride back to Chappy."

"Did they?"

"They did."

"But I take it you didn't see who took the picture?"

"Sorry, Annie. I wish I had."

"Me, too, Lottie. Me, too."

With all the things throughout her life that would go down in history as totally not worth repeating, Annie rarely felt sorry for herself. So she had no idea why, compared with the real struggles, losses, and challenges that she'd endured, something as relatively inconsequential as a stupid photo felt so monumental. Maybe because on the island she couldn't escape it; she felt marked as a topic of scorn.

Releasing a growl that was only as loud as Annie dared so no one except maybe Murphy would hear, she let her whole body shudder as if that could shake off any demons that came with needing to have a "brand." After all, Annie Sutton was not, did not want to be, a celebrity. She was just a writer who struggled with her work like many people struggled with theirs: good days, bad days, days of enthusiasm, days when she wondered why the heck anyone would care about what she did. Sometimes she still felt like a fake, that the notoriety she'd received in her genre was a fluke. She'd heard that other writers sometimes felt that way, too.

"Well," she said out loud once her shudder was done shuddering, "I do believe I'm feeling sorry for myself after all. I am such a brat." Why couldn't she be more like Meghan—stoic in spite of adversity? Understanding that the man she loved might no longer love her? After everything Meghan had triumphed over, it was both pathetic and embarrassing for Annie to think that she was the one with the corner on misery.

"My stupid brother," she muttered as she peeled her thoughts off herself because it felt safer to turn them back to him. "My foolish, stupid brother." She wondered what Kevin actually would do if he knew Meghan was well and was on Chappaquiddick, waiting for him to return. At least Annie had a plan. All she needed was the courage to pick up the phone.

He answered on the first ring. "If it isn't my celebrity sister," Kevin said with a playful cackle. "How does John feel now that you've dumped him for a journalist?"

So. He had seen the post.

Annie brushed off his glibness as an attempt to amuse her. At least he sounded goofy and cheerful. So he must not have spotted Meghan.

"Not funny," she said. "I can't figure out if I was set up or if someone was in the right place at the right time, so to speak, and thought it would be funny." Changing the subject was the best thing to do. She did not want to share John's caustic reaction—or suggest anything that might make Kevin look at the photo again, when further scrutiny might make him question if the blur in the background could possibly be his wife. His *former* wife, she corrected herself.

She tried to concentrate on her mission to communicate with her brother as if she weren't hiding the biggest imaginable secret from him. "How are things there?"

"Um . . . no different from when we talked yesterday."

"Sorry if I cut you off. I was with one of our guests when you called."

"Well, okay, as long as you're being nice now, I can tell you I'm making progress about Taylor's house. Excuse me, Jonas's house, seeing as how he's the one who legally owns it. I keep forgetting he inherited it from his father's family. Anyway, I'm at city hall right now, trying to nail down the protocol for scoring building permits."

So Kevin was dug in, which was not good news. She squeezed her eyes shut. "Is the place worth it?"

"It's run-down, for sure, but not so far gone that it can't be repaired. And forget about making it better to live in—if down the road they want to sell it, it needs to be in better shape. The location's good, and it could be worth a whole lot more than it would be now. Some carpentry here and there, maybe a new porch, a coat or two of fresh paint . . ."

Annie was trying hard to let him talk. But she only had so much patience, and she didn't want to waste what little she had listening to things related to Taylor. She opened her eyes. "Kevin," she interrupted, no longer able to hold back. "I really don't care. I need you to come home. Now."

The delay before his response could have been due to the miles and oceans and landmasses between them. Or it could have been because he wasn't accustomed to having Annie tell him what to do. He might have thought she'd already learned not to hassle him.

"Are you all right?" he asked.

At least he didn't act as if he thought she hated him. "I'm fine. Everyone's fine." She swallowed the words *Including Meghan*. Instead she said, "But there are things here that need your attention. It's too complicated to get into over the phone. Please trust me, I need you here."

He laughed.

Seriously? He laughed?

"You're kidding, right?" he asked. "I just got here."

"Technically, you've been there more than five days. Five of the busiest days at the busiest time of year." She prayed she could stick to her intention to be straightforward and firm, yet not hostile. Unless he provoked her. "I can't believe I agreed that you could go right now. It should have waited, Kevin. I'm sorry, but if we're going to be partners in the Inn going forward, I need to feel that we're on the same page and taking equal responsibility. Which I guess means you can't take off whenever you feel like it." Her voice had begun quivering, which she hoped he would think was because she was upset, not because she was riddled with anxiety for trying to trick him. "I didn't press you at first, because I didn't think you'd actually go. I thought you knew better." Her monologue tumbled out before she could reel it back in. She wished she could write a scene in one of her books so adeptly and as fast.

The lag time kicked in again. Then Kevin said, "Jesus, Annie. I knew you were pissed, but I thought you had everything under control. You always do, don't you?"

She really wished he wouldn't try to be rational. "That was before Francine and Bella relinquished their room for Simon Anderson's assistant, and before I turned over my place to Simon. I know I said I wouldn't do that, but there you have it. I felt backed into a corner. Your idea of a tent was asinine, though it might have been smarter as Mr. Anderson has already trashed one of my Adirondack chairs and God only knows what else. I'm sleeping on the plywood floor over the freaking workshop, where I don't have as much as a single electrical outlet to keep my phone charged." She had started to pace, her steps matching the escalation of her diction. She'd apparently forgotten her vow not to sound hostile.

"Are you more pissed about all that or about me being with Taylor? I know she's not your favorite person, Annie, but . . ."

"Stop!" she snarled. "This has nothing to do with her." For once, Annie didn't have a hard time lying. Meghan was at stake. And maybe Kevin's happiness. And the last thing she wanted was to hear him say anything related to his feelings for Taylor. "It's about your commitment here. To Earl and me. To our business. You knew before you left that I have a book tour coming up. Well, it turns out I'll be gone for six weeks. Francine will be back in Minnesota. So who's going to mind the store? We can't dump all this on Earl. I'm afraid we're already wearing him out. And probably Claire, too." When he didn't reply right away, she kept spitting words of bogus anger. "I'll say it again, Kevin: You need to come home *now*. You can go back later if that's what you want. When we don't have an Inn full of people. Let me know when someone can meet you at Logan."

With that, she abruptly ended the call, her scene spoken as she might have written it after all, if she'd ever created a character as heartbroken as Annie was about deceiving her brother, when all she'd been trying was to do the right thing.

Hopefully, when—if—he returned and saw Meghan, he'd forgive Annie for having stuck her nose into their business, where it clearly did not belong.

Depleted and depressed, all she could think of was that she wanted a drink.

Chapter 18

"It didn't occur to you that your brother would call me?" Earl stood at the top of the stairs over the workshop, his head cocked to one side, his stocky, solid frame silhouetted in the early morning light.

After her argument with Kevin, Annie hadn't gone in search of wine. Instead, she'd huddled inside the sleeping bag and stayed there, barely moving, through the night. John hadn't showed up unannounced. Or called. Or texted. At some point, either her mind had finally quieted or she'd given up trying to convince herself that it was okay that she'd called Kevin and misled him. She only wanted Meghan and him to be happy; not that Annie knew squat about mending relationships. Which was becoming clearer every day.

"Kevin thinks you're losing your mind," Earl added.

"Maybe I am," she muttered.

Earl guffawed as only Earl could do. Then he sauntered toward her, tugged his pant legs up at his knees and sat on the floor, which was a surprise, because he often said that one benefit of being over seventy was being entitled to sit on a chair. He wore a new T-shirt, that one turquoise and white, touting the MV Film Center. "You nervous about going on that book tour?" he asked.

"No. I've done them before."

"Not since we've had the Inn up and running."

While Annie's intention to put Kevin on a guilt trip had been without malice, she now wondered if she should, instead, have told him the truth. Or if she should at least tell Earl the truth, so he, too, didn't think she was losing what few marbles she had left. "We have a lot going on."

"We already knew that at some point you'd have to do your book stuff. When do you go?"

"Next month." Because she wouldn't be leaving until later in September, there was plenty of time to make arrangements at the Inn. But Annie didn't want to get specific. She already felt foolish enough for having bungled her mission to get her brother to come back.

"August will be over," Earl said.

"Francine will be gone."

"Did you expect Kevin should take her place and make breakfast for our guests? I ate his fried eggs once. 'Sunny-side up' was more like 'broken-side down.'"

One corner of Annie's mouth curved up. Earl knew how to humor her.

"Did you forget that Claire offered to babysit the Inn while you're away? And cook every morning?"

"Sorry. I guess I did." She was so tempted to tell him what was really going on. He might have a better idea about how to handle this. But Annie could imagine the forlorn look on Meghan's beautiful face if she learned Annie had broken her promise. Her trust. So Annie couldn't do it.

"Have you thought about not being so hard on Kevin?" Earl asked. "And let whatever he's got going with Taylor run its course?"

She smoothed the edges of the sleeping bag. Since Annie had moved to the island, Earl had been a wonderful friend. She hated that she was deceiving him, too; she hoped that once this was out in the open, everyone she loved would understand why she hadn't told them the truth about Meghan.

"For a summer that started out with so much uncertainty," she said quietly, "it's been amazing in so many ways." Cocooned in the zippered bed, she almost felt safe. "It's as if once we were under way, everything fell into place. But all of a sudden I'm sensing a shift: Kevin has abandoned us for God knows how long; I have to stop playing and get back to my other responsibilities; Francine will be off to finish her two-year college program. And John has both of his daughters now, and though they're teenagers, he's still responsible for them." She paused, needing, yet not wanting, to tell Earl how John's dismissive attitude was contributing to her unrest. "It's almost as if we've been like seasonal people—all summer, we've been surrounded by them, watching them have fun while loving life on the Vineyard. We've bought into the dream. But now our time is up, too, and we need to go back to reality. I guess I'm afraid of how that will turn out."

"Well . . ." Earl began, "'It ain't over 'til it's over,' said Yogi Berra—a smart and a decent catcher, despite that he played for the enemy. Anyway, we still have an Inn. We are a community; hell, we're a family. In other words, we figure things out. Together. I thought you knew that by now."

Annie sighed. Her eyes became teary; she could no longer hold back. "Even with all this ludicrous business with Simon? John won't give me a chance to explain."

Shaking his head, Earl said, "So you lashed out at Kevin because of John?" He scratched his chin. "Well, that would make more sense. John's my son, but he can be ornery. Takes after his mother—don't tell Claire I said that. Give him time to cool down, Annie. You know he's under a bucket load of stress this time of year; as much as he loves the gusto our tourists bring, he's counting the hours 'til August is over. It's the double-edged sword of living here." He rolled onto one side, pushed himself up, and brushed plywood particles from the backside of his jeans. "I expect you'll join us for the fireworks tonight? Fuller Street? Claire's making snacks."

"I was thinking about inviting our guests . . ."

"You know my motto: the more the merrier." He pondered a second, then added, "That's my motto, I think. Or maybe it was Shakespeare's. I don't think it was Yogi Berra's." He chuckled and turned and trundled back down the stairs.

Annie rubbed her eyes. She knew she had to get moving and go help Francine. She had to invite everyone to the fireworks and pretend she was in a glorious mood. It was, after all, time to start celebrating that, after this weekend, with the Vineyard summer "officially" finished, the Vineyard Inn would have closed the book on a highly successful first season. She knew she needed to focus on that. And not on Kevin or Meghan. Or John.

Everyone wanted to go, including Simon, who Annie could have done nicely without, but she figured there would be safety in numbers. She also felt fairly sure that no one in their group would dare reenact the incident of Illumination Night.

After breakfast was finished, the kitchen was cleaned up, and everyone went off in different directions, she got on the phone with Claire and coordinated what they'd make for what Claire decided should be not simply snacks but a "sunset supper": cold chicken and ham; lentils simmered in spices then tossed with sweet potato cubes, cilantro, and kale; red bliss potato salad; fresh green beans with red onion, feta cheese, and cherry tomatoes; roasted squash, zucchini, red pepper, and onions. And fresh rolls that Francine would make that afternoon and serve with sweet, creamy butter.

Next, Annie called Lucy and asked if she could come to the Inn and bake cookies—lots of cookies.

"And come with us tonight. Your grandparents will be there and Jonas and Francine and Bella. We'd love to have you." She quickly added, "And Abigail, too. If she wants." She stopped short of saying that of course John was also invited, and simply commented, "It's too bad your dad will be working."

"What kind of cookies? Chocolate chip? How about ginger? I saw a recipe for those online . . ."

"Either," Annie laughed. "Both if you want. Counting all of us, there should be around eighteen."

"Too bad Restless shouldn't come. Dogs are allowed on the beach after dark in the summer, but I think the fireworks might freak him out. Can I bring a substitute for him? Like a person?"

"Sure. If it's okay with your dad. And Maggie's mom."

"It's not Maggie. It's my friend Kyle. From school. He lives right in town."

Annie hesitated, glad that Lucy couldn't see her grin and be mortified. "Boyfriend?"

"Friend-friend. Maybe more. Not yet."

"Very nice."

"Yeah. What time should I tell him?"

"Seven-ish?"

"Great. And I'll come over in an hour or so to start baking. And Annie?"

Annie paused, bracing for the teenager's next words.

"I'm sorry my dad can be so lame."

So was Annie, but coming from his favorite daughter, who was also John's best cheerleader, it meant a lot. "He'll be fine, honey," she said. "This time of year must be wearing on him. But we'll have fun tonight. I'm glad you'll be with us." Somehow, that small bit of conversation calmed much of Annie's malaise. She hoped the feeling wasn't fleeting.

Aromas of warm ginger and chocolate wafted through the Inn. Annie had decided to make it a mental health day, which, for her, meant absolutely no work. No writing work, anyway. Bella left with Claire; Francine went off to see Jonas; and Lucy arrived—without Restless, as they'd be in the kitchen where dogs weren't allowed because, as Earl had explained, "They might muck up the works."

So Annie and Lucy were left to measure and mix together, to talk a little, laugh a little, and make sure that "the works" turned out successful. Lucy dubbed them "the dynamic cookie duo."

Annie loved being with her; she loved the girl's smarts, her energy, her flair for creativity. After more than an hour, with four sheets of oversized cookies ("Ginormous," Lucy called them) ready to go into the oven once the two sheets that were in there were done, Annie calculated that six dozen should be more than enough sweet things for their fireworks party.

Sitting on a high stool, watching Lucy survey the perfectly shaped creations through the glass oven door, Annie realized how comforting it felt to have someone else in the kitchen— which had no connection to any fond memories of baking with her mother. Ellen Sutton had always been nervous that Annie would make a mess, ruin the outcome of whatever recipe she attempted, and wind up crying, all of which would result in giving her mother a "sick stomach." As badly as Ellen had presumably wanted to be a mother, she'd rarely been able to relax. Except when they were on the Vineyard for summer vacations. Annie was grateful she at least had those memories.

Then the back door banged open, suspending her nostalgia, as Simon sprinted into the kitchen. His white polo shirt and crisp pleated shorts made him look more prepared for competitive tennis than for hanging out on casual Chappy.

"Where's Mary Beth?" he shouted as if there were a fire that only she could extinguish. He halted in front of the stove.

Mary Beth. Annie gulped. "I have no idea." What did Simon want with her?

"I passed her on North Neck when I was riding here on my bike," Lucy said. "She was walking, and she had a water bottle, so maybe she went hiking."

He frowned. "Damn. I heard that a leatherback was spotted off East Beach. They think it's tangled in fishing net—or plastic. I figured she'd want to know."

Right, Annie thought as her jaw tightened. "Thanks, Simon. We'll be sure to tell her if we see her."

"If I had a vehicle, I'd try to find her," he said. If he was hinting that he'd like a ride, Annie was not going to bite. The fewer times she was seen in his company, the happier she'd be.

"Sorry," she said, then gathered the mixing bowls and the measuring cups, brought them to the sink and, with her back to their guest, started to wash them.

"Do you have her cell number?"

Annie shook her head and said, "Sorry," again.

"Her room's next to Bill's, right?" Simon asked. "I'll leave a note on her door. She won't want to miss this."

Before Annie could stop him, Simon was in motion again, hurrying past her toward the great room and up the stairs.

Once he was out of sight, Lucy said, "He's kind of a weird dude, isn't he?"

Annie laughed, then the timer dinged, diverting her need to invent an answer.

Lucy pulled out the cookie sheets while Annie said, "As soon as we're done here, how about if we drive around Chappy?

I'd love to find Mary Beth before Simon does." It felt strange to call her Mary Beth again, but she congratulated herself for remembering to.

"Sorry, but I have to get home. Kyle's coming over; we're going to the beach before the fireworks."

A small tic of sorrow dinged in Annie's heart the way the timer had dinged on the oven. She knew it was a reminder that Lucy was, indeed, getting older and soon would be gone from John's nest . . . which might happen long before Annie had settled there. *If* she settled there.

"But you can take off," Lucy said. "I'll finish up here and pack the cookies. All you'll need to do is bring them tonight with the rest of the feast."

Annie thanked her, probably too profusely, then grabbed her purse and her phone and headed outside to the Jeep. She had no idea what direction Meghan had walked in, but she wanted to find her before Simon did. The man made Meghan nervous; being "outed" by a journalist—even if unintentionally—was not what Kevin's wife had had mind. Annie understood: her flailing relationship was proof of the damage that could cause.

He had no idea why Annie was so wigged out about a picture that Taylor said other women might be flattered to have. In fact, her exact words had been, "Simon Anderson isn't exactly chopped liver." Which was okay, until she'd added, "Then again, maybe your sister set the whole thing up and is embarrassed to admit it." Taylor was not always tolerant of others—she probably had the right, after the way folks had treated her—but he liked being with her. A lot. She was testament to that fact that Kevin MacNeish was alive, after all.

But it hurt to think that Annie might have lied to him.

He ordered a bottle of wine and tried not to dwell on Annie. He'd much rather think about how pretty Taylor looked that evening in one of the long, flowing skirts that she liked to wear now even when, unlike tonight, they had nowhere special to go. She also had a white orchid in her hair—the same one he'd picked earlier in the back-yard—and had rested it between her breasts while she'd been nap-ping. Naked. They'd made love again—the hundredth time in five days, or so it felt. Like him, she'd gone without someone to love far too long. But now the long drought was over for both of them. And life was pretty much perfect.

Was it wrong for him to be happy when his sister was miserable?

Chapter 19

Meghan was standing on the west side of Dike Bridge, the small footbridge that stretched across a channel that separated the lagoon from Poucha Pond. She lingered on the periphery, well behind a few dozen people.

Quickly parking the Jeep, Annie vaulted out and power-walked toward the gathering. "Mary Beth!" she called out.

Meghan turned. "Annie? You heard about the turtle?"

"I did," she replied as she caught up with her. "And Simon is looking for you."

Her face contorted. "He is?"

"He remembered about your interest in leatherbacks. If he had a rental car yet, he'd have gotten here first."

"And brought his cameraman."

"I guess."

Meghan glanced toward the bridge, then back to Annie, and braced herself as if preparing to flee. "Is he on his way?"

"I have no idea."

She looked back at the bridge. "The Trustees won't let us cross to the beach until they've cordoned off where she is. They said she's alive, but badly entangled. They want to free her without scaring her." The Trustees of the Reservations were part of the state organization that oversaw much of the protected land and all that entailed.

"You want to see her?"

She nodded. "Sure. They really are fascinating creatures."

"Agreed. And don't worry. I'll keep an eye out for our friends. If they show up with a camera, I'll make sure they aim elsewhere. Though I bet they already know that."

"And we can take off if we need to?"

"Of course."

Then one of the Trustees announced that it was okay to cross the bridge now. "Please stay outside the taped area," he added. "We still don't know how badly she's hurt or how long it will take to free her."

Annie and Meghan lagged behind the string of onlookers over Dike Bridge. As they crossed the portable walkway toward the beach, Annie frequently looked back, trying not to worry that Simon—crack journalist that he was—would figure out that Meghan was hiding her identity. And had a back-story that might be newsworthy.

As the boardwalk ended and they stepped onto the white sand, Annie knew that all this secrecy was exhausting. And unhealthy. She wondered if she should at least tell Meghan that she'd called Kevin and urged him to come home.

The turtle—"Let's call her Tillie," one of the thirty or so bystanders said—was entangled in what looked like plastic bubble wrap.

"She was spotted by the vigilant crew of a sailboat while she was thrashing in fairly deep water," the US Coast Guard representative said. "They called the Center for Coastal Studies in Provincetown and relayed the coordinates. The Center provides training in rescuing sea mammals to a team at the natural resources department of the Wampanoag tribe. They're out there in the rescue boat right now." He pointed to a small craft about twenty yards from shore. A woman and a man leaned over one edge close to the turtle; another man balanced the boat. The trio was working in precision, while the struggling mammal flipped and flopped in quick splashes.

"She's trying to free herself," the representative continued. "She doesn't understand that if she stayed still, she'd be free faster." His words were wistful as if he were worried. Then he turned back to the group. "The sailors who called in the alert gave her a wide berth and circled the area until the rescue team arrived. For any of you boaters, please note that this was perfect protocol. Sea turtles are common around here at this time of year, and we all need to watch out for them." He asked if there were questions, but the onlookers seemed immersed in the activity, waiting for Tillie to swim off and rejoin the others in her *bale*—a word Annie knew described a group of turtles, like a *murder* of crows or a *pod* of seals, both of which she'd seen on Chappaquiddick.

As the leatherback continued to thrash, Annie wondered if Meghan had felt trapped while she'd been recuperating: a prisoner in her surroundings, at the mercy of strangers, not always aware of her circumstance but knowing that her world had been turned upside down.

"Sea turtles have existed well over a hundred million years," Meghan whispered to Annie now. "Most don't make it to adulthood, but if they do, imagine the perils they've had to endure: weather events and climate changes; prey like killer whales and some sharks. They're the real survivors of life."

Annie wondered if that explained a large part of her interest in them. "You're a survivor, too," she said. Then, with their eyes fixed on the rescue, Annie touched Meghan's shoulder and said, "I called Kevin."

Meghan didn't move; she didn't even blink.

"I didn't tell him you're here," Annie continued. "But I asked him to come home."

Meghan folded her arms, her eyes still staring straight ahead. "What did he say?"

Annie had thought it would be easier to tell her while they watched the rescue crew murmur soothing tones as they struggled to hold onto their patient while they clipped sheets of plastic away as waves were dancing around them; that way, Annie could focus on what was going on in the water and not have to look Meghan in the eye. "He didn't say much. I told him he was shirking his responsibilities at the Inn, or words to that effect. I told him we needed him. Urgently. I guess he thought I was overreacting, because he called Earl and said I was losing my mind."

Meghan laughed. "I can picture him saying that."

Annie linked her arm through her sister-in-law's. "Won't you reconsider talking to him? Rather than taking a chance that he'll find out some other way? Just by virtue of you being here, your beautiful face could pop up on the internet. Simon is only one person—we have no way of knowing or control-ling what our other guests post—or where."

Before Meghan answered, a boisterous "Woo-hoo!" rose up from the rescuers; one of them brandished a length of gnarled plastic—proof of human negligence imposed upon the sea. "Go, baby!" he shouted toward the turtle, and the crowd applauded as Tillie splashed again, then dove below the surface and disappeared beneath a rolling wave.

Annie put her hand to her heart. "Wonderful," she said.

"Beautiful," Meghan added. Then she turned to Annie. "I appreciate your efforts, but I can't talk to Kevin. If he knows I'm well and that I'm here, he might not survive the flight. It's a long trip from there to here; trust me, he'd be a basket case."

One of the rescuers shouted to the Coast Guard that he'd seen the turtle resurface and head out to deeper water. He started his small craft engine and, with signals from the crew, he carefully steered away, southwest toward Aquinnah. The crowd applauded again, then slowly headed back toward the footbridge.

Meghan started to follow; Annie quickly caught up. "I'm sorry, Meghan. I only want both of you to be happy . . ."

But Meghan shielded her eyes from the sun and shook her head. "I know you do. But right now one of my headaches is coming on, so I need to get back to the Inn and rest." She traversed the boardwalk again, that time with her head bent, watching every step. "I know you want things to be different," she continued, "but not every story has a happy ending, Annie. Not everyone is like the turtle that got unstuck today and hopefully went back to her happy life. You might not know it, but Kevin is afraid of flying. In fact, he hyperventilates. Which made it hard for us to get work out of the Boston area. And now it tells me that he must really have wanted to see that woman to have screwed up his courage and flown all the way out there."

They traveled the short distance back to the Inn in silence.

John was on the patio, his sullen demeanor suggesting that a warm greeting wasn't going to be in store. Annie wondered if this day could get any more complex: the highs, the lows, the damn crosscurrents of it all. Meghan uttered a meek hello, made a limp excuse about going upstairs, and ducked inside. Annie wished that she, too, could claim a headache as a reason to avoid him.

"Hey," she said, offering a tight grin, an act of "bucking up," that she'd taught herself about a hundred years ago. "What brings you to Chappy?" It was an asinine question, seeing as how both his parents and his fiancé—her—lived and worked there.

At first, he did not reply.

Annie sat across from him on the rim of a stone planter that was packed with tall, orange day lilies that were bowing in the breeze. "What's up?" she asked.

He closed his pearl-gray eyes. "I need a break."

She didn't know if that meant he needed a break as in a vacation from the chaos of August and the pressures of his job, or from his daughters and their squabbling, or from . . . her. Her heart, however, expected the worst, as hearts often do.

"Care to elaborate?" Her pulse quickened.

Opening his eyes, he looked toward the harbor and the lighthouse and the August panorama of sailboats in the distance and kayaks being paddled close to shore.

"I never thought of myself as someone who crumbles easily," he said. "But now, I feel like I'm crumbling. I'm overloaded with too much responsibility, too many hassles. I'm trying to please too many people. And I'm not doing a good job at any of it."

"How can I help?"

He stood up, his height, his strength, his virility more visible than when he'd been sitting down, yet his body, his person looked sapped. Tapped out. Done.

"John . . ." Annie said as she stood up and took a step toward him.

He held up one palm, a barrier. "I need a break from us."

She supposed she should have seen it coming. The hours, the days, the nights that they'd been forced to be apart all summer; the addition of Abigail—and the sly insertion of the girl's disturbing statement to Annie—tossed into the lobster pot of their relationship; and Simon. Simon Anderson and that stupid picture.

But Annie had not seen it coming. Earl had told her that his son could be ornery. "Give him time to cool down," he'd said. It had been two and a half days since John had stomped up the stairs in the workshop and practically accused her of fooling around with Simon. If either of them should be angry, Annie thought it should be her.

But instead of being angry now, she felt a cold, gripping sensation enfold her chest, as if the air was being squeezed out of her lungs.

He ran his hand through the season's buzz-cut of his hair. "I can't do this right now. I can't do *us* right now. I'm sorry." He turned and walked from the patio, his footsteps crunching on the clamshell driveway. He was out of sight by then, most likely walking to the *On Time*, as Annie had not seen his truck.

She knew she could easily catch up with him. She could say that she'd give him all the space, all the time he needed. She could ask him not to leave her, not to be hasty. She could beg him to come back.

But as Annie stood, motionless, on the beautiful patio of the beautiful Inn that she and Kevin and Earl had fought hard to make happen, all Annie could think of was maybe John was right. Maybe they only worked as a couple when it was off season and fewer people were around and there were fewer distractions, fewer chances to screw up a loving relationship. Maybe they weren't made to be together for more than eight or nine months in a year.

She waited, hoping to hear a reassuring word or two from Murphy. But the only sounds were the soft cry of a gull, the distant hum of motorboats, and a haunting echo of Meghan's words: "Not every story has a happy ending."

Chapter 20

Whoever controlled the weather had painted a perfect Vineyard evening. As the group maneuvered along the winding path that was bordered by fragrant pink beach roses and tall grasses that swung ever so slightly as they brushed past, Annie was thankful that it was still summer and she had so many people and obligations. There still were a few weeks left of guests coming and going and needing attention; her book tour would follow. By the time she stopped being busy, busy, busy, maybe the fact that she'd come close to marrying John would be a distant memory.

At least she wouldn't have a chance to spend the next several weeks in isolation, curled up in a sleeping bag, feeling sorry for herself as she'd done the rest of that afternoon.

Pushing aside a lock of hair that grazed her cheek, Annie was determined to concentrate on the people around her and not on John. Or Kevin. Or Donna, Annie's birth mother, whom she missed more than she could have imagined. But she knew that dwelling on them would only make things harder. Besides, Annie was truly grateful for tonight's fireworks and this year's additions to their party: the tenants (except for Harlin, who had a gig in OB with his mariachi band), the guests (despite that she could have managed nicely without Simon's presence), Lucy's new friend, Kyle (who was shy but sweet), and, mostly, Meghan. Annie was both surprised and pleased that Meghan hadn't backed out of going to the celebration. Best of all, no one—not Earl, Claire, or Lucy—seemed to know about John's split from Annie.

She tottered behind her sister-in-law now; both were laden with food baskets and blankets. The tenants carried watermelons—their unexpected contribution. Simon had insisted on supplying the beverages, some with alcohol, some without. He hadn't said that he didn't imbibe, but whenever Annie had seen him during the week he was drinking plain seltzer. Perhaps his sins moved in other directions, like sparking gossip and then lying about it.

Earl spotted a perfect area that was large enough for the group without anyone being able, as he said, "to kick sand in somebody's face." Annie distributed blankets, then sat next to Meghan. Francine, Jonas, and Bella joined them, as did Earl and Claire, and then Lucy and Kyle. Annie wondered if they'd all crowded around her so Simon couldn't get too close. He and Bill had come over from Chappy with the sisters from Indiana, who for sure would return home with lavish tales for their friends and neighbors.

The group ate heartily and exchanged conversation from blanket to blanket. After dimple-cheeked, adorable Kyle had apparently consumed his fill that included two of Lucy's giant cookies, his shyness took a marvelous turn when he brought out a fiddle and revved up the party: Earl got up and did a surprisingly good imitation of an Irish jig with Claire; Jonas and Francine laughed and applauded, and then joined them. Everyone applauded, encouraging the young fiddler and the dancers.

"We'll keep you in mind for our next party!" Earl called out when he announced that he was "pooped" and plunked back down on the blanket. "Jonas, if your mother ever comes back, they'd make a great duo—Kyle on fiddle and her on cello. What d'ya' think?" It was a nonchalant reference to Taylor's early years in Boston, first at Berklee College, and then playing cello with the symphony.

Jonas laughed. "I'll be sure to tell her."

Annie glanced at Megan whose eyes were now fixed on the blanket.

Then Francine scooped up Bella and showed her how to dance. "We don't know if Taylor will ever come back," she said. "Unless it's with Kevin. Then we could have an outstanding party!"

The merriment continued, with everyone but Annie seemingly unaware that Meghan was sitting very still.

Annie leaned over to her and said, "Hey. How about a walk on the beach before the fireworks start?"

Claire had already packed up the leftovers, so Annie and Meghan bagged the trash, stored it in the back of the Jeep, then went down to the water. Once out of range of the others, Annie said, "I'm so sorry, Meghan. I wish you hadn't heard that."

Meghan shrugged. "Facts are facts, aren't they?" She put her hands in the pockets of her jeans, and kept her gaze fixed on the horizon as it tiptoed toward twilight. "I wonder what will happen if Kevin decides to appease you and comes back . . . with her. That would be a mess, wouldn't it?"

Annie did not know how to answer.

"It's funny, though," Meghan added, "It honestly never occurred to me that he'd be involved with someone else. But why wouldn't he? It's been years . . . and he is a loving, terrific man. Lots of women would want him." She pulled in a deep breath, then puffed her cheeks and slowly let it out. "I never thought I was a foolish woman, but I should have known better."

Wishing she could tell Meghan that she was wrong, that Kevin would absolutely dump Taylor and come back to her if he knew that she'd recovered, Annie could not promise that. She couldn't manage her own love life, never mind her brother's. So instead of giving false hope, she simply said, "You don't know what's going on with them. I'm not convinced that he does, either."

They walked on the beach until they reached a section that was posted as private property; they stood for a minute, looking up at the stars now sprinkled across a few small remnants of sunset.

"He loved me," Meghan said.

"I know," Annie whispered.

Then Meghan lowered her voice. "I have to go back to Boston. I have to start over without him."

Annie hadn't expected that. "But how can you? Where will you live? What will you do?"

"I'll be able to stay with my dad and stepmother until I find somewhere to live. Ogre that my stepmother is, I can't believe that she won't let me. And I'll get a job. I'm not sure what I'll do, but I'm itching to get involved in the working world again."

"And what about my brother?"

"All I know is I can't keep pretending. I'll need to use the trust until I'm on my feet again. I don't think Kevin will mind—after all, he never thought he'd see any of that money again."

Annie didn't want to get involved in their financial doings, either. So she reached for Meghan's hand and gently squeezed it. "How long will you stay?"

"My dad and his wife are in Kennebunk and won't be home 'til Sunday. And I don't have a key to their house." Which Annie supposed made sense, as they'd once thought that Meghan would never again be back in Boston, back in one piece.

"Okay, I'll stop badgering you. Let's change the subject. Tomorrow our honeymoon couple will be checking out. They want to be on the two thirty, but first, they have to return their rental car at the airport. I'll take them there, then to the boat. We'll need to leave the Inn by twelve thirty to allow for traffic. If you want to come with us, maybe you and I can do something fun after. Like go to the Ag Fair?"

"I can hitch a ride, right?" It was a voice Annie hadn't wanted to hear.

Against her better instincts, she turned around. Simon stood behind them, his grin as off-putting as his presence. She wondered how long he'd been listening.

"You turn up at the most inappropriate times, Mr. Anderson," she said, not trying to mask her irritation.

He sidled up next to her.

"Tomorrow is Saturday. I have to pick up my rental car, or did you forget? As long as you'll be going to the airport . . ."

So much for using someone else as her backup plan. "Yes, of course. You're welcome to come with us. Though it will be a tight fit, what with the luggage." She did her best not to grimace.

Then fireworks burst against the now-darkened sky, and Annie led the way back to the party, the once-pleasant evening now curdled, her mood once again spoiled.

The next morning, the breakfast table was full. Simon was there, too, perhaps having foregone his boiled eggs because he no longer was concerned about unwanted gawkers. The buzz was louder, more amiable than it had been before, thanks to the previous night's socializing. There was nothing like a little beer, wine, good food, and fireworks to put people in friendly spirits.

After homemade granola with deep purple elderberries and succulent peaches, cheesy chive-scrambled eggs, and warm oat nut toast drizzled with MV local honey had been polished off, Francine presented the honeymooners with a loaf of her seven-grain bread. Early on, she'd decided to start a tradition of giving bread to guests on their checkout day as a thank-you-for-staying-with-us gift. Tied with aqua raffia ribbon and a matching, bountiful bow, the gift not only looked lovely but also smelled scrumptious.

"Nice touch," the groom said. "Homey."

"Like the Inn," the bride added.

Then the couple went upstairs to pack, and the others dispersed to whatever activities they'd planned for their Saturday.

Annie cleared the table then began to scrape remnants from the dishes and into the compost bin. "There's been a change of plans for one of our guests," she told Francine. "Mary Beth will be leaving tomorrow."

"Oh, too bad. Did she finish her research?"

Annie hesitated before saying what would be on the shadowy side of a white lie. "I'm not sure. Apparently something's come up and she needs to get back to Boston." She was proud of herself that she hadn't said the thing that had come up was that Meghan had learned about Kevin's new life. Whatever it was.

Francine stopped loading the dishwasher and gazed out the window toward the harbor. "We have lots of names on the waiting list. I'm sure we can have the room rebooked by the time she leaves. Then we can reimburse her for the rest of her reservation. She paid in full up front, remember?"

But Annie shook her head. "Reimburse her. But let's not take another reservation, okay? I'm really tired. And you must be, too. Maybe I'll move into Mary Beth's room while Simon and his sidekick are still here."

"Or you could take the honeymoon suite. Our next couple won't be here until Thursday, the same day Simon leaves. Then you can go back to the cottage."

A flood of loss washed over Annie again. She would have hoped that by now she'd know how to handle her feelings when someone she'd grown to care about—in this case, Meghan, definitely not Simon—was slipping out of her life. It was bad enough to lose Meghan before Annie had really gotten to know her. But could Annie stay in the honeymoon suite? Without John? Right now, it would seem ironic. In a very dark, miserable way.

She scraped a cereal bowl that she'd already scraped. "Right now I need the rest more than we need the cash."

"Okay," Francine replied. "I get it. And yes, I'm tired, too."

Francine, of course, would be leaving soon. And Bella. The thought of more loneliness pressed a small bruise onto Annie's heart. "In a couple of weeks you'll be back in Minnesota. Back at your aunt's house. Back in school."

"Three weeks," Francine added, as she, too, grew pensive. "It's going to be hard to leave again."

"Because of Jonas?"

She nodded. "And the Inn. Bella will miss everyone, too. She's gotten spoiled this summer from the endless attention."

"It's been no more than she's deserved. Life is short, Francine. We need to love the people we love every minute."

"Like John?"

No, Annie thought. She was not going to go there. Not then. Not with Francine. "Actually, I was thinking about you and Bella. And how grateful I am that you came into my life. And I was thinking about Meghan. And how sad I am . . ." She stopped abruptly, hoping her small slip would pass by unnoticed.

"Who?" Francine asked because she was a smart girl and didn't miss much.

Without warning, tears spilled from Annie's eyes. Francine stopped fussing with the dishes, dried her hands, and took Annie by the arm. She led her into the tiny chef's room and closed the door after them.

"Annie? What's going on?"

Shaking her head, Annie said, "I can't."

"You can't what? You can't tell me something? Is it serious? Is someone sick? And who is Meghan?"

Annie could have made up another story—making up stories was her real job, wasn't it? But aside from the fact that she'd never been good at outright lying, Annie knew it would leave her feeling off-kilter. And ashamed. No, lying to Francine was not an option. Besides, Francine was a strong, capable young woman who knew how to overcome obstacles. And how to keep secrets. Despite their thirty-year age difference, Annie knew that Francine could help put the situation in perspective. And maybe help Annie weather her emotions.

Wiping her tears, she raised her head, set her gaze on the countertop, and said, "Meghan is Mary Beth Mullen. She isn't a scientist, and she doesn't work at MBL. I'm not sure if she even wants to. You were right when you questioned that. She thinks the leatherbacks are interesting, but don't most of us?" She realized she was stalling. "Her real name is Meghan Mac-Neish. She is Kevin's wife. Or at least she was until his divorce papers came through. But Meghan doesn't know about that. And I'm sure not going to be the one to tell her." Then her eyes met Francine's.

Francine was gaping at her. "*What?*"

Annie gave a short laugh. "Please don't make me repeat all that."

"But I thought . . ."

"I know. You thought Kevin's wife suffered a traumatic brain injury from a construction accident. She did. Years ago. She was in a coma a long time, followed by a bout with amnesia. The last time she saw Kevin she didn't know who he was. The doctors didn't expect that to change. It was painful for Kevin. And it took him a long time, but he finally was able to move on. That's when he came to the Vineyard. In the meantime, a kind of miracle happened; Meghan's brain function started to return. As you can see, today she's fine. She still gets headaches, but otherwise she does really well. And please don't make me repeat that, either."

Francine leaned against the cabinet where her griddles and skillets and bakeware were kept. Her large, dark eyes looked bigger and darker than usual. "This is amazing. But Kevin is . . ."

"In Hawaii," Annie said. "With Taylor. And he doesn't know about Meghan. She begged me not to tell him. She thinks that because of Taylor, it's not the right time for him to know. She says he's been through a lot, too, and that if he's happy, she doesn't want to upset that."

"But . . ."

"But nothing. End of story. I shouldn't have told you. Now it's your secret to keep, too. And that includes not telling Jonas. Okay?"

"I promise I won't breathe a word. But poor Mary Beth. Meghan. And poor Kevin! He'll be so upset when he finds out . . ."

"*If* he finds out. But it will have to come from Meghan, not us. Right?"

"Right. But, Annie, it's so sad. She must be so scared that Kevin will pick Taylor over her. Is that why she doesn't want him to know? Because she's afraid of how much it will hurt if he rejects her? Whether it's physical hurt or emotional hurt, hurting still hurts, doesn't it?"

Annie hadn't thought of it that way. But, of all people, Francine knew about hurt. Her early years had been loaded with it.

Chapter 21

Annie spent the rest of the morning performing as if she suffered with obsessive compulsive disorder, as her mother had once been diagnosed. She futzed (her dad used to call it) on the main floor of the Inn, straightening furniture that didn't need straightening, dusting windowsills that didn't need dusting, rearranging books in the reading room. She then moved to the front desk, where she aimlessly scanned the spreadsheets of the Inn's income and out-go; she reviewed the list of housekeeping supplies to determine what needed ordering; she counted their many stars on the online travel sites. The truth, however, was that she did not have OCD; she simply had no interest in working, no interest in doing anything except trying to invent a way to get Meghan to change her mind and stay. But everything Annie thought of was too close to meddling. As if she hadn't already done that.

By noon, she considered biting her fingernails the way Francine sometimes did. Which was when Earl showed up.

"You want to join us for dinner? Francine and Bella and Jonas are coming; Claire's going to repurpose leftovers from last night."

Annie suspected he'd at last learned about John's decision to "take a break." And maybe he felt sorry for her.

"Can I have a rain check?" she asked. "I'm taking the honeymooners to the airport to drop off their car, then down to the boat. From there Mary Beth and I are going to the fair." She prayed that Francine wouldn't slip and reveal Mary Beth's identity during dinner at Claire and Earl's, or that she'd mention that Kevin really, really needed to get home.

She looked back at the spreadsheet. "We've had a good season," she said.

Earl chuckled. "'To succeed in life, you need two things: ignorance and confidence.' My old friend Mark Twain said that."

"I'm not sure we had confidence, but we sure had ignorance," Annie said with a laugh. Earl was obviously attempting to lift her spirits—a sure sign he did, indeed, know about John.

"My wife thinks it might be time for us to start figuring out what we'll do if Kevin doesn't come home," he said.

So this was not about John, but Kevin. Annie didn't want to talk about either one of them.

"Maybe Jonas can pitch in?" she tossed out. "He was a big help in the spring, wasn't he?"

Earl fiddled with the brim of his cap from last year's fishing derby. He'd barely worn his Red Sox cap since Ortiz retired. "True. He was. But I wonder if the boy has other plans."

Annie scowled. "Such as?"

"Such as you'd better ask him. Or better yet, ask Francine."

The longer Annie lived, the more complicated life became. She turned off the computer, closed the lid, and returned it to its hiding place in the front desk. "Or I could ask you again. And maybe this time you'll give me an answer that will save me a whole bunch of time."

Earl chuckled. "I think we've been matchmaking without knowing it."

Cocking her head, she said, "They haven't exactly been hiding the fact that they're fond of each other."

"Fond of each other? Ha! You sound like a hovering mama."

"Do I?"

He rubbed his chin. "Well, I suppose you're entitled. I'm afraid, however, that this thing with them is beyond fondness. When she goes back to school, I think he wants to go with her."

Sometimes surprises were good. This one certainly was. But Annie was weary of trying to speculate about what was going on with the people she loved. Or wait until who-knew-when for clarification. So she excused herself and went into the kitchen to talk to Francine. But apparently the girl—correction, the young woman—had left for the day. Annie went back to the reading room and promised Earl she'd get to the bottom of things. It didn't matter if it would be inconvenient for Jonas to leave, too . . . Annie's heart swelled to think that he and Francine would be together. With Bella. A nice little family.

But before she could fully resuscitate a good mood, Simon ambled around the corner.

"Ready when you are!" he announced in his polished, news anchor voice. He was, of course, oblivious to the boulder that had just landed in Annie's stomach.

"Actually," she said as she flicked her gaze to Earl so quickly it surprised her, "I was about to ask Earl if he'd mind following our guests to the airport in his pickup. And bringing you to get your rental. I've been barraged by requests from my editor, so I have a ton of paperwork to do." *Please save me, Earl,* she thought.

Earl stepped up, not missing a beat. "Call me Earl Uber,"

he said. "Ever since I turned sixteen, I've chauffeured so many folks back and forth to the boat and the airport I ought to be on the payroll for the chamber of commerce." He grinned at Simon, his eyes steady on his, as if daring him to say, "No, thanks. I'll make other arrangements."

"Well, I'll be grateful," the celebrity guest replied. "It will be fun. When I was a kid, my dad delivered the *Globe* to the newsstands; my older brother and I sat in the bed of his pickup and heaved bundles onto the sidewalks. So our trip to the airport will bring back fond memories."

"Not to disappoint you, but you'll need to ride in the cab. We save the bed for the livestock." It was perfectly timed sarcasm, for which Annie wanted to hug him. Then Earl turned to her. "You want to let the honeymooners know that their Uber awaits, while I go clean my junk out of the back? We'll stash their suitcases there. Unless Simon prefers the hay." He chuckled again and meandered away without admitting that he did not own as much as a chicken, let alone livestock.

Then Simon said to Annie, "Too bad, though. I was hoping you and I would have a chance to talk."

"Sorry," Annie said, copying Earl's grin. "Duty calls." She swished from the room, then dashed up the stairs and ran into the honeymooners halfway up while they were heading down. She said good-bye and told them Earl was waiting for them outside. She took the rest of the stairs two at a time, feigning to clean their room, when instead she was hoping to avoid seeing Simon again.

Francine had brought Bella to Jonas's in time for a nap, so Annie arranged for Claire to babysit the Inn for a few hours, which would leave plenty of time for Annie and Meghan to spend the whole afternoon together at the fair. Over the past months, it was apparent that the Inn could run smoothly on its own for a short time, so she told Claire to leave by five o'clock if they weren't yet back.

Soon Annie and Meghan were strolling through sawdust, watching sheep shearing, horse draws, and pig races, and surveying the 4-H entries of roosters and chickens, rabbits, goats, and more. After a couple of hours, when they'd seen all the animals, they had veggie tempura on a stick from a food truck, sat at a picnic table and people-watched a while, and splurged on a big dose of ice cream. Meghan exclaimed that the fair was "wicked awesome," a testament to her Boston roots.

But Annie had saved the best for last: the Ag Hall. The building itself was a treasure—a century-old, post-and-beam barn that had been reconstructed on the new, more spacious fairgrounds nearly three decades earlier. They went into the barn to admire the abundant showcases of flowers and vegetables and the artful displays of watercolors, acrylics, and mixed media. Annie was determined to stay clear of the booth where she'd seen Abigail.

When they turned toward the pottery displays, Annie spotted Winnie ahead. "Follow me," she said. "There's someone I'd like you to meet."

Though she hadn't wanted to, Annie introduced her as Mary Beth.

They hit it off right away. As Annie watched Meghan examine Winnie's work while asking questions about the clay, the process, and the beautiful striations of the glazes, she wished that Winnie knew who Meghan really was. She'd be bound to agree that Meghan and Kevin were a good match.

Meghan selected a lovely bowl that highlighted the colors of the Gay Head Cliffs—red, orange, and gold.

"Not unlike the clay in the caves of your ancestors," Winnie said. "If I'm correct in thinking your heritage is Middle Eastern?"

Annie was again reminded of Winnie's far-reaching insight.

"I'm half Egyptian," Meghan said with a giggle. "I can't believe you guessed. People often ask if I'm Native American—like you."

Winnie scowled. "But your cheeks perfectly sculpted. They are like an Egyptian goddess, not like the fuller face of the Wampanoag."

Meghan grinned, perhaps embarrassed. So Annie said, "You never know whom you'll meet at the Ag Fair. Which is why anyone on the Vineyard in August must go at least once. I think it's a law."

"Speaking of the law . . ." Winnie said, "How's John?"

By then more people had converged around Winnie's wares, and Annie knew she couldn't say what she'd like to. So she merely raised her eyebrows, and Winnie nodded as if she understood. Then they hugged good-bye.

Once outside, Meghan stopped, seeming to revel in the clear, fresh air. "This has been so much fun, Annie, but you've worn me out. In my wildest dreams, I never thought I'd be here now. Sometimes it's still hard to believe that I've returned to the world."

"I can't imagine. But how you've managed to put it all behind you is remarkable."

With a small laugh, Meghan said, "It helps that I don't remember anything from breakfast the morning of my accident until more than two years later. I know that I'd made French toast; I wanted to celebrate that we were going to make the deadline for our project." She paused, as if searching for another splinter of her memory. "I also remember I'd decided to wait until after work that night to tell him I was pregnant."

The sights and sounds around them faded away. It was a moment before Annie could speak.

"Meghan . . ." she said, "I am so sorry . . ."

But Meghan shushed her. "Kevin wanted kids, but I'd kept stalling. I never wanted to be a mother. I loved our business; I kept pushing him to make it bigger. Anyway, I was almost three months along when I fell. I lost the baby." Surprisingly, tears didn't come to her eyes—over time, she must have shed them all. Annie knew from experience that that could happen. "Anyway," Meghan continued, "I never had the courage to ask the doctors if they told Kevin."

Annie had no words, not one. But she was reminded, once again, of how deeply secrets could not only scar but also change someone's life . . . forever. She wanted to ask if Donna had known, but perhaps it didn't matter now.

Waiving further conversation, they made their way to the car, with Annie holding back from crying for her brother, for the happiness he'd missed out on. She could do that later, when she was alone.

For now, the thought of painful secrets made her think of Brian again . . . and the cryptic message he'd left her the night that he'd been killed.

After the funeral, she'd asked his parents if they knew what he had meant. They said no. She asked his sister. She said no, too. Day after day, Annie asked anyone she could think of: his friends; the principal where Brian taught; the old man at the coffee shop where he stopped every morning. It had been less painful to focus on that than on the fact Brian was dead.

But no one claimed to know about a secret. Finally, Annie told a newspaper reporter who was writing an article after the accident; she'd hoped he'd mention it, and that someone, somewhere, might know what it was. But no one came forward. And Annie never got an answer.

Meghan's secret was far more earth shattering. And so much sadder. And unlike Annie, who'd yammered about Brian's secret to anyone who'd listen, or pretended to listen, Meghan hadn't told the one person who had a right to know.

As they walked, their gaits slowed, their legs weighed down by the past. Annie remembered how crushed she'd been when the *Globe* hadn't unearthed any clues. Maybe if the internet hadn't been in its infancy then . . . or if the reporter had done a better job . . .

As she recalled, he had been young, determined, and he'd been . . .

She stopped. Her whole body stiffened. And suddenly, two of Kevin's favorite words leaped into her mind: *Holy. Crap.*

No kidding, Murphy replied.

Despite that her adrenaline was pumping like a bilge pump on a lobster boat in a stormy sea, once they were in the Jeep and back on State Road, Annie tried to be kind to Meghan. "Are you okay?" she asked. "Do you want to tell me more about it?"

Meghan shook her head. "There's nothing more to tell. By the time my memory returned, so much time had passed it didn't seem as if any of it had been real."

"I am so sorry for . . . well, for everything." Annie's eyes bounced from Meghan back to the road, her thoughts unable to stop boomeranging from Brian to Meghan and back again.

"Thank you. That means a lot."

Pulling out onto Edgartown–West Tisbury Road, Annie stepped on the gas. "I'd like to stop at the library on our way back. But if you want to go straight to the Inn, I'll understand." Because it was Saturday, the library closed at five; it was nearly that now.

Meghan smiled and patted Annie's arm. "It's fine. And please, you don't need to treat me like a porcelain doll. I'm okay. Really I am. It was a long time ago."

"But you never got to talk to Kevin about it." She knew her brother would have made a great dad; she would not, however, say that, especially since Meghan had said she hadn't wanted kids. Annie didn't need to know more details about that; she firmly believed that everyone was entitled to do or think or be whatever worked for them.

"One of the reasons I came here was to tell him."

So, if Kevin returned, seeing Meghan would even be tougher on him than Annie could have predicted just a minute ago. "If it's any help," she said, desperate to change the subject, "the mere mention of secrets has led me to figure something out about Simon Anderson."

"Something good?"

"It depends. First, we have to get to the library before it closes." Now that some pieces had begun to gel, Annie needed answers. And she now knew where to start. With no cars ahead of her, Annie stepped on the gas. "I think I know who he is," she said.

"Simon? So do I. I remember when he was on the news in Boston. Especially when he covered the Marathon bombing."

But Annie was shaking her head. "Not then. Before. I think he was a newspaper reporter. I need to find out if I'm right. The library has access to the *Boston Globe* archives."

Unlike Meghan, Annie had never had amnesia. She had not forgotten anything about the night Brian was killed—or the aftermath. She remembered standing outside the hospital, nearly catatonic, the big red letters of the Emergency Room sign glaring at her, the double-wide, automatic doors opening and closing, opening and closing, each time an ambulance arrived and a stretcher was wheeled inside. She'd been awaiting word if Brian could be saved. She hadn't been able to stay in the waiting room because she couldn't breathe in there.

But now, despite that her stomach was twisting like beach grass in hurricane-force winds, Annie was elated. She supposed it was possible that Simon wasn't the reporter who'd interviewed her after the accident. She'd never seen the article; for all she knew it hadn't been published. She'd called him two or three times; each time he said he was sorry, but he had no leads. He said he'd let her know. But she never heard from him again.

Zooming past the airport and the transfer station and Barnes Road, she was grateful that a steady stream of traffic was heading west, toward the fair, not east toward Edgartown. She was barely aware of Meghan sitting beside her. All Annie knew for certain was that the reporter's name hadn't been Simon Anderson. It had been Andrew Simmons. She remembered the business card he'd given her. The one with his direct line at the *Globe*.

She supposed it could be a coincidence that the two names were so similar. Just as it could be a coincidence that he'd landed at the Inn more than two and a half decades later. But Annie didn't really believe in coincidences.

She wondered why Murphy wasn't chiming in. Then she wondered if her lead foot was freaking Meghan out. In the same instant that Annie thought she should slow down and chill, flashing blue lights appeared in her rearview mirror.

"Rats," she said.

Meghan looked behind them. "I wonder if you've been speeding," she said kindly.

"I was." The only benefit in having to pull to the side of the road was that her stomach settled a little, perhaps welcoming a reprieve from being on the fast track. Until she looked in the side mirror and saw the cop walking toward them. She recognized the stride, of course. How could she not?

"Annie?" John asked when he reached the window on the driver's side. "Jesus. Do you have any idea how fast you were going?"

She sighed. "Not really."

He hooked his thumbs into his belt. "Seventy-five."

She could have done nicely without knowing that.

Then he said, "License and registration, please."

If she'd gotten angry, that would only slow down her mission to get to the library before it closed. She reached for her purse, pulled out her credentials, and handed them to him. She bit down on her lip to stop from asking if he needed further proof of her identity.

"Sorry," he said. "Pete from the OB force called it in, so I have to write it up."

She shrugged. "Sure."

He leaned down and looked over at Meghan. "You two been at the fair?"

"It was wonderful," Meghan replied. "I bought a very nice piece of pottery from Annie's friend Winnie. But I have a terrible headache so Annie was in a hurry to get me back to the Inn."

The two of them chatted, their words floating back and forth across Annie, who remained perfectly still, staring at the pavement ahead. It was thoughtful of Meghan to lie.

"I'll only give you a warning," he said to Annie. "Okay?"

"Okay. Thanks." Thanks? Was she supposed to thank her fiancé for giving her a warning instead of a pricey ticket?

As he walked back to the cruiser to do whatever he needed to do (check her for priors? Search for outstanding warrants? Make sure her vehicle wasn't stolen?), she sat, numb now, only wanting him to hurry up and do what he needed thanks to Pete from OB. Or, more precisely, thanks to *her* for speeding. Yup. Her bad.

She sighed again.

Meghan reached across the console and touched Annie's hand. "This isn't easy for you."

Annie shook her head, grateful she had set a goal of getting to the library because it no doubt sidetracked her from totally breaking down.

In less than a minute John returned. He handed back her IDs and a slip of paper.

Then he squatted and looked over to Meghan. "I hope you feel better soon." He might have looked at Annie then, but she was busy shoving the paperwork into her purse and restarting the ignition. She gave him a dispassionate wave, and pulled away from the shoulder, back onto Edgartown-West Tisbury Road.

Chapter 22

There was a concert on the library lawn—Johnny Hoy and the Bluefish—a special Saturday night performance to honor library supporter and island icon Herb Foster for the publication of his latest book about the cross-culture of Yiddish and jive. It looked to be a lively gathering. But the library was closed.

So Annie slammed the gearshift into reverse, turned around, and headed toward the *On Time*.

She was angry. Angry at herself that the Simon Anderson/Andrew Simmons connection hadn't dawned on her earlier; angry that she'd been stopped for speeding, which had delayed her trip too long; angry that John had been the one to stop her, that he'd been so . . . professional, and that she'd responded as if she were a block of ice.

She was also angry that she wasn't able to focus on Meghan right then. All she said was, "Maybe some good will come of all this. Maybe closure is on the horizon for both of us."

When she reached Main Street, she slowed down: There was no point in causing more commotion.

"We might as well get back to Chappy," she said. "So you can . . . pack?"

Meghan smiled. "Only if I'm going to leave tomorrow."

Annie felt a spark of hope. "If?"

Pulling the bag that held Winnie's bowl closer to her chest, as if afraid it would fall and break, Meghan replied, "Let's just say I'm rethinking my impending departure. You might be able to find closure, but I won't have a chance unless I see Kevin."

Despite that there was little reason to think he'd be coming home soon, Annie decided it was important to have hope wherever—whenever—anyone could find it.

Navigating through the people-packed one-way streets of the historic village toward the dock, she spotted a parking space on Main Street and instantly claimed it.

"If you find a parking space in Edgartown in August, you have to grab it. Otherwise, you might never have good luck again."

"An old wives' tale?"

"Actually, I think it's one of Earl's. But as long as we're here, do you want to get a glass of wine or a bite to eat before we go back?"

"After our gourmet food at the fair, I'm not at all hungry. But I'll go if you promise to tell me what Simon maybe having had a job as a newspaper reporter has to do with you. It must be something serious for you to have dismissed John the way you did. And honestly, you were driving like the road was the Autobahn."

Annie ran her hands around the steering wheel, its circle perfectly harmless, unless one lost control of it and killed a twenty-nine-year-old on a dark street in Back Bay, Boston. "I think Simon was the *Globe* reporter who interviewed me after Brian was killed," she finally said. "And that his sudden appearance at the Inn is not a coincidence."

"If it's really him."

"I know. It's been years, and I was so rattled then I don't

really remember what he looked like, but in the beginning he seemed determined . . . and his name is too close to be a fluke . . ." Her words stumbled out. She blah-blahed the rest, including about how she'd enlisted the reporter to help her learn Brian's secret, but that he'd never responded. That he might have lost interest. Or moved on.

Then someone banged on the window. "Excuse me, lady."

Annie realized that the windows were still up, the engine was still running, the air conditioner still hummed. She put her window down.

A young woman in a taffeta pink sundress and carrying a matching pink clutch smiled and said, "Are you ever going to leave this spot? My husband is trying to find a place to park. We're supposed to be at a wedding at the Whaling Church . . ."

"Oh!" Annie said. "I am so sorry. Yes. We can leave right now."

"Can you wait until he comes around again? He's driving a silver Range Rover."

Summer people, Annie thought, *often didn't drive Jeeps.* "Of course," she said, then turned to Meghan. "While I wait for the Range Rover, how about if you pick up a couple of sandwiches for us? There's a takeout place down by the ferry in case we want something later. Once we get home I can rest and you can decide if you want to pack. We can meet on the patio after dark, eat sandwiches, and watch for fireflies."

"Sounds great." Meghan opened the door. "But I have to warn you, I really am getting a small headache. If I take a pill, I'll be knocked out for a while."

"I'll take my chances."

"Okay, we're on. But the treat is mine. Or actually, it's Kevin's, as I don't have a paltry red cent that I can honestly say is mine."

The sound of her brother's name threatened to sap Annie's

energy again. She couldn't let that happen; she had too much to figure out. "If you're not out of the shop by the time I have to cross, just hop on the ferry and sit on one of the benches. I'll wait for you on the Chappy side."

The grounds of the Inn were quiet: Saturday evenings were usually like that, with the guests meandering around town and the tenants often working their second or third summer jobs, trying to make enough money to eke it out over the winter. If they were lucky, they were done working and were enjoying some pre-sunset time out at South Beach, where by then the beach chairs of the summer folks had been folded up, loud music had abated, and children had stopped jumping in the waves.

After checking to be sure Claire had left, Annie walked along the still-vibrant meadow on her way to the workshop where, indeed, she would rest. And "chill," as Kevin might have called it. Whatever strength had propelled her across the Autobahn had nearly been sucked out of her when John had stopped her. At least it had been him and not an officer who didn't know her and was as weary of summer as she was.

Now, in her peripheral vision, she saw her cottage standing in silence, almost as if it were waiting. For something. For someone. For . . . her?

Maybe it was time. Maybe if Simon was alone . . . maybe he wouldn't be offended if she asked him outright if he was Andrew Simmons, and if so, whether or not he'd ever learned Brian's secret.

Or maybe this all was a dream from which she'd wake up any minute.

In the meantime, Annie stepped, one hesitant sandal at a time, toward breaking her unwritten rule about never disturbing a guest unless there was an emergency.

Maybe this was one. For her.

As she went up onto the porch, opened the screen door, and raised her hand to knock on the main one, another thought zoomed into her brain cells: Had Simon come to the Vineyard to finally tell her what he knew?

Before Annie totally unraveled, she knocked.

But Simon did not come to the door.

He did not say, "Hello?"

He did not ask, "Who is it?"

She waited a moment, then knocked again. Still, no response. So she did what she reasoned any man or woman who perceived they had been wronged might do: she turned the handle. The door opened.

She left her sandals on the porch—a signal that she was inside and had nothing to hide, that she was merely checking on something in her own home, or making sure her guest had enough towels in the bath and treats in the refrigerator. She could come up with a thousand excuses that would sound plausible. But the bottom line was, she was technically, and maybe—who knew—illegally trespassing.

The next thing Annie knew she was in the living room, her bare feet set firmly on her grandmother's braided rug. She moved into the bedroom, went straight to her nightstand, and retrieved a tiny key: other than her, only Kevin knew where to find it. Then she went to the Louis Vuitton where she might find the corroboration she needed.

She remembered the initial article in the *Globe*—the who, what, where, when, and how of the accident. She didn't recall if it had a reporter's byline; still, it was doubtful she had saved it because she'd wanted only happy mementos of Brian in her scrapbooks.

But maybe Donna had clipped it out and tucked it away as she'd done with so many other things.

It still amazed Annie that her birth mother had followed

Annie's life, had documented records and photos of her since she'd been born, a legacy of a mother's unconditional love that had never wavered, never died. When Annie first saw the trove of things concealed in the Vuitton, she unearthed the ones that she'd needed to know right then. But the Inn had been about to open, and there had been so much to do every hour, every day since then, she hadn't had time to finish exploring the contents of the trunk. Instead, Annie had kept everything intact, knowing the treasures would be there, waiting, if she ever felt sad. Or alone.

Right now, she'd be happy if she found anything written by Andrew Simmons, even the one with the who, what, where, etc. Maybe something between the lines would trigger a memory or two that could point Annie toward learning Brian's secret—the missing piece of her past.

Crouched on the floor, she spent the next couple of hours investigating every photo album, every scrapbook, every small cardboard box and 10" x 13" envelope that had been neatly clasped. Her jaw remained clenched, her pace was robotic; she did not allow tender emotions to surface; she could do that later. Off season, perhaps, when the luxury of time often permitted reflection.

But in spite of her diligence, Annie didn't find a shred of detail about the accident, just a lone copy of Brian's obituary that sent a lightning bolt straight from her head to her toes. Other than that, the only significant thing that happened was that both of her legs became cramped from crouching.

Closing the lid and locking it tightly, she wobbled to the nightstand to return the key to its place.

With a sigh of disappointment, she turned to leave the bedroom. Which was when she spotted Simon's messenger bag on the floor next to the bed. It looked like fine leather, soft and expensive. And old. A well-worn, well-used case.

Stepping closer, Annie wondered if it was a classic, the kind of item Donna would have loved to have had in her antiques shop. A small brass nameplate was fastened between two brass buckles; she bent to see if it might be the name of the designer—perhaps it was a Vuitton, like her trunk.

Instead of a name, she saw three initials.

AJS.

As in Andrew (whatever-his-middle-name-was) Simmons.

She stood for a moment, staring at what might be confirmation of who Simon Anderson really was. Or had been. But while her gaze drilled into the nameplate, she did not hear the front door to the cottage open, or footsteps crossing the braided rug and stepping onto the hardwood floor in the bedroom.

"Annie?" the voice asked. "Aren't you a little old to be snooping?"

Chapter 23

She might have reacted more casual, less contrite, if Simon wasn't downright red-faced angry.

"I'm sorry," Annie said, willing her voice not to tremble, though she knew it was on the verge. "I didn't mean to intrude. I needed to get something out of my trunk. You weren't here and the door was unlocked." Did that sound plausible? Acceptable? "I must have forgotten to ask you to please lock the door when you aren't here. Our crime rate is pretty low, but I wouldn't want to give everyone free rein to my personal belongings." She knew that her mouth was off and running, spewing out blah-blah-blah words again, something that often happened when she was embarrassed. Or nervous.

Why the heck was she nervous? This was her Inn. This was her cottage. There was no need to be nervous.

She was, however, standing with her back to the corner, with Simon blocking the doorway. Which made her feel like a trapped animal. A skunk. A raccoon. An opossum.

If he would say something—anything—maybe she'd relax.

"I wasn't looking through your things," she continued

rambling. "I was looking through mine. And I came across something interesting."

He responded with a steady glare from those teal blue eyes.

Then Annie had an unpleasant thought: Had Simon come to the island not to bring her information, but because he wanted to reveal her unhappy backstory to her fans? To boost his ratings with an exposé of a mystery writer's painful past? Annie's best friend might have whispered that she was *reaching*, if Murphy—the one voice she relied on more than anyone's— wasn't otherwise occupied doing God only knew what. *Come on!* Annie's thoughts muttered toward the ceiling. *Stop cavorting up there and pay attention to me!*

Then, at last finding her nerve, she returned Simon's glare and said, "I know who you are."

He shifted on one foot. His eyebrows scrunched. His mouth tightened, and he spoke through his teeth. "I'm the guy you watch every night on the news." As if it were a given that everyone in every household in America and beyond, would not miss the evening news with Simon Anderson.

She decided not to contradict him. "How did you find me on the Vineyard? And, for God's sake, why?"

His right eye developed a slight tic. "You're a popular woman. A best-selling author with a new business on Martha's Vineyard. What makes you think I wouldn't want to stay here when my work brought me to the island?"

"Bull," she said.

"No, it's not. I like to learn about people and places and connect them in ways that my viewers don't always get to know simply by watching the day-to-day news. Not to mention that I really am passionate about climate change. Some people call it having a global conscience."

It was hard to tell if he was schmoozing or preparing to do

battle. She decided to play his game and wait for him to say more.

But he didn't.

So Annie finally nodded, hoping that would help her manufacture another layer of courage as she asked, "You're Andrew Simmons, aren't you?"

He gestured toward the messenger bag. "That's an antique, you know. Belonged to my uncle Harry's father. He owned a manufacturing plant. Textiles."

Neither of them had moved, though Annie longed to, stuck as she was in the cat-and-mouse game.

"I'm surprised I didn't recognize you," she finally said. "From when you interviewed me. About when my husband was killed."

He bowed his head, then. Using his fingers he rubbed one eye, then the other, as if an eyelash or a grain of sand was scratching at them. But when he raised his head again, Annie realized why she hadn't recognized him: it hadn't been because she'd been so overwhelmed by grief that she hadn't paid close enough attention to the young reporter. It was because those striking teal blue eyes weren't teal blue at all. They were brown. Natural, ordinary brown. Now, he looked like an older version of Andrew Simmons. Andrew J. Simmons. Whatever the "J." stood for.

He held out his hand, displaying the tinted lenses. "This color makes me look better on camera. At least that's what the ratings' folks say." He bent his head again and popped the lenses back in.

It occurred to her that she should make a note to use the disguise in one of her plots. The change was so simple, yet quite effective.

"If you were one of my characters, I'd say that's a great way to travel incognito."

He looked back at her, his eyes teal again.

"You stopped taking my calls," she said. "And you never called back. Had you learned something you didn't think I should know? Something that might upset me more—as if that were remotely possible?" In her darkest hours, more than once she'd made herself ill rewinding the details of the accident, how the impact of the car must have felt, what might have happened to different parts of Brian's body—his arms, his legs, his handsome, still youthful face. While writing her books, she still had trouble including words like shattered, squashed, *spurting*. Remembering that now, Annie swallowed, unable to hold back tears.

He stiffened. "I was in grad school. I was an intern at the paper. When the summer was over, I left."

She looked back at the messenger bag. "Still, you could have called. I was desperate for answers . . . I was only in my twenties . . ."

"So was I, dammit!" His tone was sharp, his irritation flaring. "What did you expect? Did you think I was Sherlock Holmes? Or did you want me to make something up so you'd feel better?"

Annie shrank closer to the wall. Her throat started to close. "I only . . ."

"You 'only' what?" He was shouting now. "*What did you know?*"

"Stop!" she shouted back, her tears stinging, her voice cracking. "What are you talking about?"

His eyes narrowed into slits.

That's when she felt sure he was not there out of kindness. And that she had no other choice. She stood up straight. "Get out, Simon, or Andrew, or whoever you are. Get out of my house and off my property."

"I paid for this place."

"I don't give a damn. GET OUT. *Now!*"

Then another figure stepped into the room. Simon blocked

Annie's view; she only saw two arms: one was raised, its hand clenched in a fist; the other was holding up what looked like a gun.

"Do what the lady said." The voice was stern. And commanding. And it was Kevin's.

Dear God, Kevin was home.

Before she could speak, Simon spun around and grabbed Kevin's arm, the one holding the gun. They wrestled. They struggled.

"Stop!" Annie cried. "Please! Both of you!"

Then the gun went off. Of course it did. That's what guns did, didn't they?

Annie screamed. Her hands flew to her face. *Please, please, let it be Simon who's been shot.*

But the man who landed with a thump on the floor wasn't Simon. It was Kevin. And bright red blood was *spurting* from his chest.

"He attacked me," Simon said to John, who had come from out of nowhere, along with the EMTs who hustled around Kevin, phoning his vitals into the hospital, lifting him onto the gurney. He was unconscious. There was a makeshift pressure bandage on his wound; it was high up, closer to his shoulder than his heart. Annie had a vague memory that Simon had put it there. The same kind of vague memory that Simon had also called 911.

All she knew for sure was that there were too many people in her small bedroom. Too much commotion. And too much blood. Her brother's blood.

"He . . . came in . . . with . . . a gun. I . . . tried to grab it from . . . him . . ." Simon was stuttering.

It looked like John was taking notes. It was hard to keep everything straight from where Annie still stood, her back glued to the wall next to her bed, the messenger bag still at her feet. She had a quick flash of Brian in the road, how he must have been bleeding. She pushed it back, way back into the recesses where dark thoughts needed to burrow.

Then she had a vision of Joe Nelson in the fire station and how, after mentioning Simon's impending arrival, he'd said, "Here's hoping Mr. Anderson's visit won't trigger any ambulance runs to your place."

Annie wondered if she would go to hell for wishing that Simon, not Kevin, was the one strapped onto the gurney.

"Do you want to ride in the back of the ambulance with him?" It was John. Her John. The guy who once had been her friend, her lover, her fiancé. He was talking about Kevin, who was her brother, not Brian, who'd been her husband.

"Yes," she said.

But it was hard for Annie to move. Until John handed her the sandals she'd left outside by the front door.

"Thank you," she thought she might have added.

He put an arm around her, as if they were still a couple. Maybe he was only trying to steady her while she slipped into her sandals.

The next thing she was aware of was sitting in the back of the ambulance, holding Kevin's limp hand, wishing, praying that the driver would go faster.

But it was still August, a Saturday evening no less, so the streets must be clogged with traffic. The flashing lights, the siren, the blasting horn made little difference.

"Can't everyone get out of the damn way?" she cried to the EMT who sat opposite her, holding onto the tubing that snaked from an IV bag into Kevin's arm, his eyes fixed on a small monitor that was attached to white plastic circles pasted on Kevin's chest. An electrocardiogram, Annie supposed.

"We'll get there," the EMT responded. "Your brother's fairly stable, so that's good."

She searched his face to see if he was telling the truth, but

she could not be sure. Then she looked back at Kevin. His
face was peaceful, his hazel eyes that were exactly like hers,
exactly as their mother's, were closed. If Annie could only see
his eyes, she might be able to tell if he was in pain.

"Kevin, are you okay?" she whispered. "Don't be scared,
I'm right here."

His breathing was a little raspy. Was that indicative of
someone who was "fairly stable"? Annie had never done much
research about medical trauma—in her books the victims
were already dead. She supposed that was how she'd averted
the shattering and squashing and the rest.

"Don't be scared," she repeated. "Don't be scared."

Then she gasped. *Medical trauma.* The only one she knew
of who'd gone through such a thing was Meghan.

Meghan. Who was back at the Inn, packing or not packing to leave, not knowing that her husband had returned.

"I need a phone," Annie pleaded with the EMT. "Can I
use yours?"

"Sorry. It's not for public use. We'll be at the hospital
spoon enough." He was nice but not helpful. Meghan needed
to know what had happened. And she needed to hear it from
Annie, before someone else on the grounds of the Inn told her
first. If anyone other than them had been on the grounds.

Leaning toward the closed window that connected the
driver from the action in the back, Annie shouted, "Hello?
Hello, up there? Can you hear me?"

"He can't," the EMT said. "He has to focus on the road."

"But . . . can't you ping him or something? Please?" She
wanted to say that her brother's wife needed to be told what
had happened. But she was afraid if she said that much, everyone would find out the rest.

He shook his head. "Sorry," he repeated, then checked
the EKG again.

She didn't know where they were, how far from the hospital. She couldn't see out the back, as there were no windows. And though she squinted, she couldn't see through the small window to the front seat and all the way out the windshield. It didn't help that they were driving into the sunset.

So Annie bolted up, banging her head on the ceiling. Then she stooped and lunged toward the window, knocking on it with insistence. She'd moved so fast the EMT couldn't thwart her.

"Help!" she shouted through the glass. "I need a phone!" Her eyes were fixed on the back of the driver's head. Which made it all the more surprising when a man sitting on the passenger side suddenly turned and was eye to eye with her. It was John. Again.

Why the hell was John there? He was a cop, not an EMT.

He opened the window a couple of inches.

She shook off her surprise. "I need to make a call."

"You don't have your phone?"

That's when she realized she didn't even have her purse. What had she been thinking? Then she remembered she hadn't been able to think. "No," she replied.

"I can call someone for you. You want my dad?"

Dear God, no, Annie thought. She couldn't very well tell Earl that the woman he knew as Mary Beth was really Kevin's wife. Not now, anyway. Then she remembered that she'd told Francine. "Francine. I want Francine. Ask her to check on Mary Beth Mullen. Tell Francine what happened. And that I'll be at the hospital with my brother."

"Do you know her number?"

She did not. Damn cell phones, where links had erased the need to know details like that.

"You don't want me to call my dad?"

"Not yet, okay?" How could she say she didn't want Meghan to find out about Kevin from Earl. Francine knew the facts. Francine would know how to handle it. "I had plans with

Mary Beth tonight," she said. "I don't want a guest to think I've stood her up." It could have been the stupidest lie Annie had ever told. But it was all that came to mind. Meghan had to be told. Meghan had to know. If Kevin didn't make it . . .

Annie started to cry. She slinked back to her seat and took Kevin's hand in hers again. His palm was warm, callused from the manual labor that he worked at so hard. He looked a little tanned. Perhaps Hawaii had been good for him.

"Don't be scared," she said again. "I'm right here."

Her tears felt like the steady trickle of the water that passed from an upper shady spot at Mytoi Japanese Garden on Chappy, down to a lower pond. Slowly, methodically, never-ending.

She was grateful that the EMT didn't scold her for jumping up the way she had, for bothering the driver who was focused on the road.

John looked back through the window. "How about if I call my dad and ask for Francine's number? He'll have it, won't he?"

But Annie's brain had become fuzzy again, and she was having trouble trying to process if that would work. Then she remembered she could not control every outcome of every situation; that she could not always protect those she'd grown to love. John, however, had offered to help. If nothing else, she knew she could trust him. So Annie nodded, because it was easier than speaking again.

Then the ambulance made a sharp right turn. Annie grasped her seat; she knew it meant that they were now on County Road. And that it wouldn't be much longer before they reached MV Hospital. God knew she'd done this before.

If there was one thing Kevin hated it was a bumpy ride. This one was a beaut. Whoever was driving was going too fast and hitting every bump in the damn road. Not to mention that he kept seeing bursts of light. And something was squeezing his shoulder and he felt like he was being squished and he couldn't see anything.

It reminded him of the Fourth of July when he'd been five and he'd gone with his mother to the fireworks on the Esplanade on the Charles River where the Boston Pops was playing what he later learned was the 1812 Overture. He'd been scared then. He was too short to see over the heads of the people, so he couldn't tell what was going on. And people kept bumping into him, stepping on his feet, and the music kept booming, hurting his ears, but he didn't want to cry because he wasn't a baby.

Besides, his mother was having a good time. Taking his hand in hers, she said, "Kevin, are you okay? Don't be scared, I'm right here."

He heard those words again now, over and over, in what sounded a lot like his mother's voice. He felt her hand in his. And he wasn't scared anymore. Because she was there.

Chapter 24

"I need to take your statement." John had joined Annie in the waiting room, where she'd sat too many times over the past couple of years. This time was the most difficult. He was her brother, after all, her last remaining blood relative. Her true family.

She flinched. "Is that why you rode in the ambulance? Not to be here for me, but to do your duty?"

His gray eyes became quizzical, as if he did not understand. "No," he said. "I mean, I came for . . . both."

Annie nodded, wishing she could fully believe him. She looked around at the smattering of people in the room. "Where's Simon?"

"At the station. Linc took him in for questioning." "Linc" was John's friend Detective Lincoln Butterfield.

She nodded again. Now that her tears had stopped, she wished she could feel something other than . . . numb. "Go ahead. Ask what you need to. Get it over with so I can go back to praying for my brother."

He angled his body so he was facing her, his muscular frame bulkier in his uniform with the walkie-talkie on his shoulder, his belt, his badge, his gun, and, she speculated, a bulletproof vest under his short-sleeved shirt. She remembered him once saying that he always, always wore one when he was on duty. *He must be hot in that*, she thought, then realized it was no longer her place to worry about his comfort, not while he was "taking a break." From her.

She tried not to take it personally that he'd left one seat between them. Or that the distance felt as wide as the gap from the Vineyard to Hawaii, where she'd have to call at some point. To tell Taylor.

Pulling a pad and pen from his pocket, John drilled his eyes onto the paper, not on her, as he began.

"Why was Simon Anderson in your cottage?"

Well, that was a loaded question. Especially since chances were, he would have preferred to ask, "Why was Simon Anderson in your *bedroom*?" Did he expect her to say, "Since you ditched me, I've been sleeping with him"?

"He was renting it from us. All our other rooms were occupied." As soon as the words sprung from her mouth, Annie wondered if that was against the law, if the zoning board permit only allowed the rooms inside the Inn itself to be rented. If she'd thought of that earlier, she could have stopped Simon from coming, and what happened tonight would not have happened.

Her hands felt clammy, as if she'd been digging for quahogs with Lucy. *Lucy!* She suddenly remembered. Lucy was going to be upset. More than once, she'd said Kevin was the *absolute best*. Annie stared at the floor.

"Okay," John continued, "then why, if Simon was a guest at the Inn, were you in the cottage with him?"

At least he hadn't mentioned a permit for rentals. It wasn't like him to forget those kinds of details. Maybe he was anxious being next to her. Or maybe he planned to ask her that later. Like when they weren't sitting in the hospital waiting room.

Still, he had asked a perfectly understandable question.
Annie supposed if she could think straight, she might be able
to come up with an answer that might help her evade the
truth. But she could not.

So, moving her gaze from the floor up to her lap, she said,
"I needed to get something of mine. Simon wasn't there. I
went in anyway. Then he surprised me."

"You went into a guest's room when the guest wasn't
there? And you weren't there to do . . . housekeeping? Or
due to an emergency?"

"That's correct. If you want to get technical, I had no
right to be there. Except that it's my home."

In her peripheral vision, she saw him set his pen down,
then turn to her. "That doesn't sound like you, Annie. Invad-
ing someone's space."

"It isn't his space. It's mine." She hoped he didn't state the
obvious that Simon had paid for privacy. She bit her lip so she
wouldn't cry again.

"But . . ." John started to say, then went back to his pen
and pad. "Did you find what you were looking for?"

That time, she was able to swallow. "Yes. In a way, I did."

"In a way? What's that supposed to mean?"

She folded her hands and looked down at her fingers. She
did not have an engagement ring; they'd foregone that tradition, having chosen to save the expense for quality, handmade
wedding bands that they hadn't yet ordered. She blinked, then
looked back at John.

"What?"

"I asked what you meant when you said you found what
you'd been looking for 'in a way.'"

She went back to studying the floor. "I thought he was familiar. You know how it happens when you see someone in
person that you think you've met before but you can't quite
place them?" There went her mouth again, running, running,

spouting words before she'd thought them through—because, if she waited until she did, she'd only get confused. "In the mid-nineties, Simon Anderson was a reporter for the *Globe*. He interviewed me about Brian's accident. Simon was in grad school and was working there as a summer intern. That's why he looked familiar to me. Anyway, it brought up painful memories; I went into the trunk in my bedroom to see if I'd saved any clippings so I could read them again." In spite of being in a mental fog, she decided not to tell John about Simon having changed his name. She knew she wasn't done investigating whatever it was about him that she couldn't quite put her finger on. Yet. And she didn't want John butting in.

She closed her eyes. "Are you almost finished? I really want to sit here and be quiet until someone can tell me something about Kevin."

He raised his hand as if he wanted to reach out for her arm, her face, her hair. But he hesitated before making physical contact.

"One more thing for now," he said. "Do you have any idea why Kevin showed up at the cottage with that damn gun?"

She shook her head. "Not unless he heard Simon shouting at me. I had startled Simon; he thought I was going through his things instead of mine. So he yelled. Maybe Kevin heard him and thought someone was trying to hurt me." Yes, she thought, that actually made sense. She hadn't been able to rationalize that until then.

"I didn't know he was back," John added.

"Me, either."

"He still keeps that damn gun locked up in his truck?"

She shrugged. "I guess."

"And his truck was on the property the whole time he was gone?"

Annie sighed. She was weary. Exhausted. She wanted to

use the ladies room and submerge her face in a sink filled with cool water. "I guess. Please. Are we done now?"

He started to say something else when a pair of sneakered feet raced into the entrance and sped over to them.

"Annie!" Lucy cried. "Is it true? Has Kevin been shot?"

Behind her, Earl and Claire hoofed into the waiting room.

John put away his pad and pen and stood up to greet his family.

"Francine will be here shortly." Earl was the first to speak to Annie after John told them what had happened and that Kevin was "fairly stable," using that ambiguous term again. "She'll be here after she's given Mary Beth your message."

Annie stood up. "Will you all please excuse me a minute? I need to use the restroom."

Claire offered to go with her, but Annie said no thanks, that she really needed a few minutes alone. She hoped she hadn't hurt Claire's feelings.

Annie headed toward the restrooms, but halfway there, she veered off into the massive foyer at the hospital's main entrance. It was, as always, a quiet place, soothing and restful. No one was there; she sat out of sight, on the opposite side of the sleek grand piano, in a spot where she could look out the vast windows and down the hill into Vineyard Haven Harbor. Much larger than both Edgartown and Oak Bluffs harbors, Vineyard Haven was the year-round port for the comings and goings of residents, in- and off-season visitors, and trucks, lots of trucks, that carried food and drink and medical supplies and building needs and furniture and packages and mail—and everything required to sustain a vibrant, healthy community.

She watched the *Island Home*, her cabin lights aglow as she started her slow crawl out of the harbor, blasting her antique whistle. Annie checked her watch, it was the nine thirty boat, the last one out that night. The boats—"the lifeline of the is-land," as they were called—were as much a part of daily living as high winds in winter and traffic in summer. She wondered which one Kevin had arrived on and why he hadn't phoned to say he was coming home.

The weight of the past week pressed down on her. Kevin leaving. John breaking up with her. The secrets: Simon's. Meghan's. Even Brian's. Especially Brian's. The unfinished business about Simon—and Annie's persistent need to know why he was there. Most mystery writers, like cops, investiga-tors, and district attorneys, often sensed instinctively when there was "more to the story." And there was more to Simon's story. She would have bet on it.

An ache gnawed in her stomach. Or maybe it had been there all along, since the gun went off, since she saw Kevin's blood ooze over her bedroom floor. As she watched the big boat set off on its latest crossing—every trip, every journey a new story—Annie knew she needed to tell Meghan's story to the others: John, Earl, Claire. And Lucy. Because Kevin was the one who mattered now. And if he was going to get better, Annie knew he'd need everyone to rally around him, talk to him, show him that they loved him. And as important as Annie knew she was to him, Meghan no doubt would be the real catalyst to help him to get well.

Unless he was so shocked by her presence that it made him worse.

You can't control everything, Murphy whispered, then added, *Or anything, really.*

"I know," Annie said quietly. "If I could, you'd be right beside me now."

Then pretend I am. You can do it. You pretend all the time, re-member?

Annie felt her mouth curve just a little, into a half-smile.

"Thank you, my forever friend." Then she rose from the soft cushioned chair and made her way back to the waiting room, finally knowing what she had to do next.

John had left the hospital to return to the station. Annie's first thought was regret that he wouldn't be there to hear the truth about Meghan. Her second thought was that she wouldn't relish having to repeat it to him, to watch his eyes narrow as she told him while he silently questioned why she hadn't shared it sooner. Like as soon as she'd found out.

She hoped that he would not take notes.

Claire and Earl and Lucy listened dutifully to Annie's introduction, when she said she had news that was going to come as a shock, but that it was good news. She guided them to a cozy corner of the waiting room; she asked them to please sit, then take a deep breath and slowly let it out. The ladies complied; Earl did not.

"Get on with it, lassie," he said. "I'm not getting any younger."

So Annie said, "I think you all know the story about Kevin's wife?"

The small group exchanged quick glances with each another.

"She was killed, right?" Lucy asked.

"No," Claire chimed in. "She had some sort of accident at work. Construction, wasn't it?"

Annie nodded. "Scaffolding collapsed underneath her, and she fell several stories. She was diagnosed with traumatic brain injury; she was in a coma a long time. A couple of years."

"And when she came out of it, she didn't know who Kevin was," Earl added, scratching at his chin.

Nodding, Annie said, "After the accident, he was devastated. He found a really good rehab place for her in Western

Mass.; he sold his business and put the money into a trust fund for her care."

"Yup," Earl said, "he told me."

"I didn't know that part . . ." Claire said.

Annie smiled. "It was difficult for him. He loved her very much. But several months later, when she still didn't know him, the doctors advised him that his visits agitated her. They also said that chances were, her condition was permanent. So Kevin stopped going. I can't imagine how tough that was for him. A long time after that, he knew he needed to get a new life."

"Is that why he came here?" Lucy asked.

"Yes. Well, it was a while before he was able to pull up stakes and leave Boston. But all that time in between, unbeknownst to him, Donna had been going to see Meghan. She became her support system."

"Donna, as in your mother?" Earl asked.

Annie nodded.

"Cool," Lucy said.

"I liked that woman from the day I met her," Claire said.

"It must have been difficult for her, though, because Meghan made Donna promise not to tell Kevin; she said no one could predict what her chances were going forward, and she didn't want him to get his hopes up. She also said that if she ever got to see him again, she wanted to be whole—as whole as she could be. She didn't want him sitting by her bed, waiting for the minutes to slowly tick by until she was able to walk again and be healthy again. She said she'd rather have him find someone else who would make him happy than to think she was causing him more misery." Annie did not mention that Meghan had been pregnant. As far as Annie was concerned, that would remain between Meghan and Kevin, where it belonged.

Silence filled their little corner of the waiting room. Silence, framed by anticipation.

Annie looked away from the little group. She hoped what she'd say next would be all right, and that Meghan would know she'd done it out of love. Clearing her throat, Annie set her jaw and turned back to them.

"Meghan has recovered," she said. "Both her body and her mind."

"Oh, my God!" Lucy shouted. "And now Kevin's with . . ."

Earl put a finger to his lips and said, "Lucy, darling. Shush."

She shushed.

"There's more," Annie went on. She closed her eyes, breathed, then opened them again. "Meghan is here on the Vineyard," she said. "In fact, she's staying at the Inn under the name Mary Beth Mullen." The silence that followed only lasted a few heartbeats.

"The turtle lady?" Lucy was the first to speak.

"The one and only."

"With the beautiful eyes," Earl said.

"Oh, my," Claire said, as she raised a hand and grasped the silver chain around her neck, the one Earl had given her when she'd been recuperating from a stroke.

Earl shuffled his feet, no doubt needing to pace. "Well, isn't this somethin'."

"Isn't it, though?" Annie said.

"And Kevin has no idea?" Claire asked.

Annie shook her head. "No. It's how she wanted it. The only trouble is, she found out he's in Hawaii with Taylor. She doesn't want to intrude on his life, so she's going to leave for her father's place in Boston."

"She's not gone yet?" Earl asked.

"No. Maybe tomorrow."

Lucy jumped up. "She can't leave! Not now!"

A wave of sorrow washed over Annie. "It's not up to us, Lucy. Especially now, with so much . . . uncertainty." In spite of her will to remain stoic, small tears began to form.

Claire got up, went to Annie, and hugged her. "Oh, dear. You've had so much to deal with lately."

Which told Annie that Claire and Earl—and maybe Lucy, too—knew about John's decision to take a break from her.

"Kevin is all that matters now," Annie replied.

Then the big glass doors into the Emergency Room squished open, and Annie, Claire, Earl, and Lucy all turned at once, as Francine walked in with Meghan.

Chapter 25

"I told them," Annie said.

Meghan looked at her a moment, then lowered her eyes. "Thank you."

Annie chewed on her lower lip, fresh tears forming.

Then Earl went to Meghan and gave her a hug. "Welcome to the family," he said, and the ladies started to cry.

Claire hoisted herself from the chair and swatted him with the thin scarf she was wearing. "Stop that, you old coot. You've got us all blubbering when we need to be thinking about our poor Kevin. And how long it will be before we find out anything." Then she smiled at Meghan. "It is, however, nice to meet you, dear. We've heard so much about you."

Which gave Annie a brilliant idea. "Meghan, come with me."

Without hesitation, Meghan followed Annie to the registration desk.

"Hi, Cynthia," Annie said. She'd recognized the woman at the computer not only from previous trips to the ER but also from the warming shelters at Vineyard churches where they both volunteered in the winter. "You know that Kevin MacNeish is my brother?"

Cynthia nodded and looked sympathetic. "They just brought him in . . ."

"I know. I was with him in the ambulance. We're really anxious to learn what's going on . . ." Then she turned to Meghan. "This is Meghan. Kevin's wife. Do you think that the doctors—or someone—can talk to her? So far, all we know is that they're 'doing tests.'"

Cynthia's eyes widened and her eyebrows shot up. Annie wondered if she was a friend of Taylor's, not that it mattered, as Taylor now lived on another island in a distant ocean. Sooner or later, everyone at least in the 02539 zip code would know that Kevin's wife had returned from practically being dead; announcing it now wouldn't make a difference. It might, however, help them learn more about his condition. And faster.

Cynthia restored her professional posture. "Well, hello. I didn't know Kevin was married."

"Twelve years next month," Meghan replied with a smile.

Annie hadn't known they'd been together that long, but she supposed the count included the last four.

Meghan handed over her driver's license, which looked brand new. Her old one must have expired while she was in rehab. "It doesn't say I'm married, but you can at least see my last name. And the address was our home in Boston before . . . before Kevin moved down here."

Wishing she could have applauded Meghan's determined spirit, Annie interrupted. "So she's entitled to talk to a doctor, isn't she? And maybe to see Kevin?"

"I have to check," Cynthia said. "But I'll do my best. It's nice to meet you, Meghan. We've all grown fond of your husband."

The comment surprised Annie, until she remembered that Kevin had woven his way seamlessly into Vineyard life. Of course, people had "grown fond" of him; he was a great guy. *Is* a great guy, she corrected herself.

Cynthia finished something she'd been doing on the computer, then stood up, left the registration area, and disappeared through a door marked PERSONNEL ONLY.

"Come on," Annie said. "Let's sit."

But Meghan did not move. "Thanks, Annie. For forcing me to go public."

"I did it for both of you. And for the rest of us, too. We all love him, Meghan."

Then it was Meghan's turn to cry. So Annie led her back to the corner in the waiting area and they sat across from Francine and Lucy, Earl and Claire. Together, they all waited. Hopefully, not for long.

In less than five minutes, a man in a white lab coat with a stethoscope dangling around his neck pushed through the "personnel only" doors. He was followed by a young man with a clipboard. And Cynthia, who directed them to the group.

"Mrs. MacNeish?" the doctor asked.

Meghan stood up; the others did, too.

He introduced himself, then quickly continued. "The bullet has fractured your husband's clavicle. No organs seem to have been damaged. But he needs surgery." He spoke rapidly, as if the procedure was urgent. "The bullet didn't exit, so we need to try and get it out of there pronto. We also have to remove a number of bone fragments before we'll know the full extent of his prognosis, such as if there's been any impairment to the neurovascular bundle or the subclavian artery. I'm sure you could tell he lost a lot of blood."

They stood, silent. Annie would have bet that none of them—including her—had a clue as to what either the neurovascular bundle or subclavian artery were, but she didn't think it was the right time to ask for details.

"Any questions?" he asked Meghan.

Annie wanted to ask for his name again, as he'd spoken so fast she had missed it. He did not look familiar.

Meghan shook her head. She was clearly overwhelmed.

"How long will surgery take?" Annie asked.

"Hard to know. Maybe several hours."

The onlookers hung on his every word.

"Is he going to be okay?" Lucy asked, her voice small and scared.

The doctor turned to her. "We're going to do our very best. I'm sorry I can't be more specific. Not until after the surgery."

Then the young man with the doctor thrust his clipboard at Meghan. "We need you to sign this as his next of kin. It's consent for the operation."

Meghan took his pen and the clipboard. She hesitated, and then asked, "Have you performed this type of operation before?"

The doctor smiled. "We don't have many gunshot wounds on Martha's Vineyard. A hunting accident now and then, but that's about it. Working on an island, though, we're trained to be versatile. And without the surgery, your husband's chances are, at best, poor. We don't recommend airlifting him to Boston. It would be too risky to lose the time."

With a slow nod, Meghan raised the pen and sighed the form. "I'll wait here," she said. "I don't care how long it takes."

Perhaps, Annie thought, *with all Meghan had been through, she was better equipped than the rest of them to navigate the hospital environment.*

Then Annie realized something else: Meghan had signed the consent form as Kevin's wife when, technically, they were divorced. She wondered what legal liability Meghan might incur, and if the fact that she hadn't known would make a damn bit of difference.

★ ★ ★

Annie convinced Earl to take Claire and Lucy home. She promised to let them know as soon as Kevin was out of surgery. Lucy announced that she'd sleep at her grandparents, if they'd have her, which, of course, they would. So the trio set off. Like Annie and Meghan, they must have been afraid for Kevin, and now they also knew the truth about his wife. It was a lot, Earl said, to reckon with; Annie expected they would talk nonstop on the way back to Chappy.

Francine did not go with them. "How about if I run over to the food truck at ArtCliff and pick up a couple of sandwiches? It could be a long night."

By then, Meghan had retreated to a seat that gave her a clear view of the door from which the doctor had emerged.

Annie hesitated, then remembered that her dinner—the sandwich from the shop by the Chappy Ferry—was still in her purse, along with her phone, back at the cottage. A tremor shivered through her when she thought of Kevin's blood puddled on the floor. "I have no purse," she said. "No money."

"I'm buying," Francine said. "And come out to my car for a second, okay? I have something to show you."

Annie told Meghan she'd be right back, and then followed Francine out the big glass doors. When they were outside under the portico, Francine suddenly stopped.

"I have nothing to show you," she said.

Not in the mood for guessing games, Annie asked, "So, what's up? And who's staying with Bella?"

"Jonas is on babysitting duties."

Annie couldn't help but smile.

With a carefree shrug, Francine said, "We all pitch in in an emergency, right?"

"Right," Annie replied.

Then Francine's dark eyes darted around, scanning the

cars, shifting to the harbor, then moving back to the hospital where she stared at a pillar of the portico, looking anywhere but at Annie. It was obvious that she was holding something back.

"I have to tell you something," she finally said. "And I didn't want Meghan to hear me."

Then, a bolt of lightning—or a message from Murphy— struck from high up in the starlit sky, leaving Annie with an ominous feeling that this was important. Her belly churned and nausea loomed as she waited for Francine to speak.

"Taylor came back with Kevin."

Murphy must have stepped in and stopped Annie from screaming. She muttered a word she did not even use in her mysteries, no matter how gritty they became.

"I was at Jonas's when she came in," Francine went on. "The first thing I thought about was Meghan. I didn't say anything, though. I promised you I wouldn't. Taylor said she was exhausted and was going to bed. Which was also strange because that's where Jonas and I have been sleeping. Anyway . . ." she seemed to lose her train of thought for a moment, "she went to bed. Jonas and I went outside, while I tried to decide what to do about where I should stay. I was going to call Earl and ask if Bella and I could bunk in there until Simon and his sidekick are gone and we can have our room back. That was when you called and told me about Kevin."

"Did you tell Taylor that Kevin had been shot?" Annie's question sounded harsher than she'd intended. After all, Francine was an innocent party.

She hung her head. "No. I didn't tell Jonas, either. I was going to ask him to come to the Inn with me and hang out there so someone would be on the premises. Then I realized if he found out about Kevin, he might insist on telling his

238   Jean Stone

mother. So I decided not to tell him. Because I didn't think you'd want Taylor to show up at the hospital and come face-to-face with Meghan."

"So Jonas doesn't know, either."

"No." She raised those big eyes again. They were troubled, sad. "I told him that Earl and Claire had cancelled our dinner plans, so I might as well go back to the Inn until you got back." She bit a fingernail. "I can't believe I lied to him. And I told him to stay at the house with his mother. And to please keep Bella there because I'd already put her to bed." She fidgeted with her small earrings, a gift from Jonas for, as she'd told Annie, no special reason. "Oh, Annie, I hope Kevin's going to be all right. And I hope I did the right thing."

Annie reached out and hugged her. "You absolutely did. You are positively the best. I love you."

"And I love you. Every one of you. And I don't want anyone to be hurt."

"It'll be fine. But I expect that after Taylor wakes up, it won't be long before she knows. Which gives me between now and then to figure something out."

Annie let Francine go, watching as she walked to her car to go get the sandwiches, grateful, so very grateful, that she was in her life. Then, before going back into the hospital, Annie leaned against one of the portico's tall white pillars and looked up at the sky. "We need a lot of help down here," she said. "In case any of you are listening. Murphy? Donna? Mom? Dad?" She paused then whispered, "Brian?"

Conversation between Annie and Meghan was minimal while they sat, nearly holding their breaths, waiting for the message that Kevin was out of surgery. That it had gone well. That he was doing great.

"I'm sorry," Meghan said at one point.

"Sorry for what? This isn't your fault."

"I didn't hear the gun go off. My headache pill knocked me out. I was asleep. I never heard the shot."

"It doesn't matter. Simon called 911 right away; there's nothing you could have done."

"But Kevin wouldn't have come back if you hadn't called him because of me . . ."

"Stop. Don't blame yourself, okay? You have enough to worry about right now." It was easy for Annie to say.

Later, Annie coaxed her into splitting one of the sandwiches Francine had bought, though they each only had a bite or two. The rest of the time Annie sipped water and flicked her gaze from the "personnel only" door back down to the floor. She couldn't shed the shame that this was her fault. And hers alone. True, she didn't know that Simon would be a jerk or that Kevin would blast into the scene with his stupid gun. Hell, she didn't even know he was on the East Coast. But if she hadn't gone into the cottage in the first place . . .

The guilt, the remorse would not abate.

Not long after midnight, the outside doors whooshed open again; Annie barely noticed. It was, after all, still August, so they'd whooshed often that night.

Then Annie heard Meghan say, "Hello."

"Any word?"

It was John.

"Not yet," Meghan said.

Annie raised her eyes; John stood in front of her. He set down a suitcase and a large canvas bag.

"Francine updated me about Kevin being in surgery. I figured you'd want to be here all night, so I asked her to pull some stuff together. She put it on the last ferry; Captain Fred dropped it off at the station for me." He turned to Meghan. "This suitcase is yours, right, Meghan? That's your name, right?"

"Yes," she said weakly. "To both questions."

"Nice to meet you. My dad explained your situation. I think I can speak for my whole family when I say I'm really glad that you're here."

She smiled tentatively.

"Francine said the suitcase was in your room, that it looked packed, and that it saved her from having to go through your things to pick out . . . whatever."

Annie did not want to consider that Meghan's suitcase had, in fact, already been packed. That she had planned to leave in the morning. For real.

"Annie, the canvas one's for you."

Off duty, out of his uniform, dressed in ordinary shorts and a T-shirt, he didn't look as menacing. He looked like John again, *her* John, though he no longer was. "Thank you," she said.

Now that he'd delivered the goods, he seemed unsure what to do or say. He folded his hands in front of him and asked, "Do you mind if I sit down?"

"No," Annie said. "Do you need to interrogate both of us?"

He sat next to Annie, on the far side of Meghan. As earlier, he kept an empty seat between them. "I'm here as . . . I'm here to give you some support, Annie. I care about Kevin, too, you know."

She nodded. "I know." She rested her hands on her knees and took a long breath.

"Annie . . ." he began.

But she shook her head. "Please don't, John. I'm trying to hold myself together. I can't do a long discussion." She fully expected that he'd get up then, say good night, and leave. Instead he reached across the empty chair and took her hand in his. As tired as she was—and as dazed as she'd thought she was—she was unprepared for more tears to splash out of her eyes.

John moved to the chair next to hers, put an arm around her, and pulled her toward him. Her head tipped down and rested on his shoulder.

"It's my fault," she whispered. "If I hadn't been . . ."

He shushed her, then kissed the top of her head. "Kevin shouldn't have had the gun. Simon shouldn't have wrestled him for it. And, yeah, you shouldn't have been in there. But it was an accident, Annie. Open-and-shut."

She wanted to say, "Tell my heart that."

"I asked Simon not to leave the island until we've spoken to Kevin."

If you're able *to speak to Kevin,* Annie thought, but did not say.

Then a man in blue scrubs came through the "personnel only" door. The surgeon. Annie and Meghan simultaneously leaped to their feet.

"Doctor?" she asked, aware that John was right behind her, perhaps ready to catch her if she . . . fainted?

"He's out of surgery," the doctor said. "It was trickier than we'd hoped, but so far so good. We'll going to keep him under sedation for at least twenty-four hours, maybe longer. We removed the bullet without much of a problem, but there were a number of bone fragments—one of them had nicked the subclavian, which is where all the blood came from. We were able to fix it, but we need to keep him immobile for a while to be sure."

Annie and Meghan remained quiet, as if they didn't realize that the doctor had finished speaking.

"Thanks, Mike," John said. "I'm glad you were on duty."

The doctor reached around Annie and shook John's hand. "I'm happy it went well. We never know with these kinds of injuries."

Annie moved away from John then and wrapped her arms around Meghan. Stalwart, strong Meghan, who started to cry.

"It's okay," Annie said. "He'll be okay."

"He'll be in ICU," the doctor—Mike—continued. "Whenever we decide to wake him up, we'll let you know ahead of time, so you can be here if you want."

"I'm not going anywhere," Meghan said.

"Then I won't, either," Annie added.

"He's in recovery now; you won't be able to see him until the morning . . ."

Then John interrupted. "Mike, is there somewhere near ICU where the ladies can stay tonight?"

"Man, it's August. We're okay right now, but I'm not sure we have enough beds for whatever else might happen the rest of the weekend."

"What about the extra portable beds you brought in during the pandemic? Are they still in storage?"

"Not my department, but probably."

John smiled. "I'll check it out. I'm sure the ladies won't mind sleeping in a closet if they have to."

Chapter 26

While John was pulling whatever strings he had to pull, Annie texted Francine and Lucy about the surgery results and asked them to let Claire and Earl know. Then, because John was Annie's hero, he once again saved the day with beds and linens and a supply closet that he set up as if it were a bedroom. He even procured a vase of fragrant pink roses that he'd coerced out of one of the nurses. According to John, they'd come from the nurse's back yard, but she was happy to donate them to Annie and Meghan. He was Annie's hero, indeed. But though Jane Austen might have been proud, Annie found the idea a little worrisome, not knowing what it meant, if anything, about their future.

Before one o'clock in the morning, she and Meghan were nestled in the closet, each in a twin bed that was remarkably comfortable. They set the roses on a wire rack that held boxes of latex gloves and surgical masks and agreed that they added a nice touch. Yes, Annie mulled, John had done a good deed.

So had Francine; she'd put a change of clothes and a few toiletries in Annie's canvas bag and had thought to include Annie's laptop and charger. The girl knew well what would be most important if Annie was sequestered for a day or two.

After saying good night to Meghan, Annie closed her eyes and willed sleep to come. It did not. Instead, her mind started spinning again, that time with thoughts of Simon. She wondered if he was sleeping in the cottage. If she were him, she'd be holed up in the other twin bed in Bill's room. Or somewhere remote up in Aquinnah.

Then she remembered the explosion: the sound—as if the world had blown up. The gunshot: the reverberation—as if an earthquake had shaken the cottage. And Kevin's blood: the stain—the floor of her beautiful bedroom now marred forever by this awful night. She sucked in her cheeks, clenched them between her teeth, and tried not to cry out.

"Annie?" Meghan whispered into the darkness. "Are you asleep?"

"Are you kidding? I can't stop thinking." She didn't want to tell her that she couldn't erase the images from her mind. Or how she had become paralyzed with fear as Kevin had lay . . . bleeding.

"Do you think he'll be okay?"

"I do. Your husband is a strong, healthy guy." She knew she shouldn't have referred to Kevin as Meghan's husband, not in light of the divorce. Which Annie wondered if she should warn her about now. It was one more thing to worry about. One more slice of torment.

"Thank you for everything you've done, Annie. Thank you for being so nice to me."

"How could I not? I liked you before I knew who you were. I did think it was a little strange that you were reading children's books about turtles, though."

Meghan let out a short, little laugh. "I'm not very good at trying to be someone I'm not."

"Neither am I." Annie's knew that her years with her second husband had proved that.

In the darkness of the supply closet, they fell silent as the scents of cardboard boxes mingled with the roses in the air.

Then Meghan said, "Annie? What will he think when he sees me?"

Annie had no answer. So she was honest. "I've been wondering the same thing. Have you thought about how you want to do this? Or what you should say first?"

"No. But I guess I should."

"It's going to be a shock for him when he sees you."

"And that I know who he is. And that I'm okay."

Annie prayed that the confusion wouldn't be too much for him.

"I think I'll try and sleep now," Meghan said. "I don't want to be exhausted in the morning. And at least I know he's peaceful now."

There was no need to mention they did not know that for sure. *Tomorrow*, Annie thought, *could not come soon enough*.

She awoke at dawn, not to sunlight, as there were no windows in the supply closet, but to the sounds of a hospital beginning a new day: footsteps pattering in quick precision, muffled wheels of carts, the low chatter of take-charge voices. Annie found it comforting, a gentle cloak of life resuming. She wondered if Kevin had slept uneventfully through the night. The fact that they hadn't been alerted otherwise must mean that, so far, he was stable.

She closed her eyes again as questions began to nag her. Why had she been so hell-bent on trying to figure out what Simon Anderson was doing there? What had she been trying to prove? That her amateur investigative skills could unearth a sinister motive? And, most important, would she ever learn to stop treating real life as if it were fiction, as if she could create a plot with twists and turns that felt like the real stuff, resulting in an ending that she wanted?

While a mystery might offer readers a pleasant escape, being able to write one didn't mean Annie could control what was really going on. And if she hadn't been so damned inquisitive, this "accident," as John called it, simply would not have happened. Not to mention that all she'd learned was at some time between working at the *Globe* and moving into broadcasting, Andrew Simmons changed his name and the color of his eyes. Big whoop. Who cared? The information hadn't been worth the outcome.

Maybe there had been nothing sinister involved, and he'd only changed his name because he thought Simon Anderson suited him better, sounded more successful. Still, if Annie hadn't been so edgy, so ashamed that she'd been caught, she could have asked him. Plain and simple.

Weighted by guilt, worried for her brother, she would have let out a loud sob if she hadn't known it would awaken Meghan, who, hopefully, had slept peacefully.

Slowly opening her eyes, Annie turned toward the other makeshift accommodation. It was too dark to see if Meghan was awake; if she, too, had been ruminating on what-ifs and if-onlys.

Then a burst of fluorescence lit up the space.

"I know no one is in here because that would be against hospital protocol," a woman declared. "But it's five thirty, and as the nurse supervisor, I must check to be sure everything is in proper order." She closed the door, and Annie heard the pattering of footsteps fade.

"Oh my God," she said. "Meghan. You're awake now, right?"

But Meghan didn't answer.

Fumbling for her phone, Annie quickly lit the icon of the

flashlight. "Meghan?" She beamed it to the other bed, which had been neatly stripped. And Meghan's suitcase was gone.

Annie tried her best to smooth her hair. Then she pulled the linens off the bed, grabbed the vase of roses and her canvas bag, and made a quick escape. On her way past the nurses' station, she left the roses on the counter. With a hurried thank-you wave to the nurse supervisor, she headed for the ladies room. Her next stop would be ICU; she prayed that Meghan had wound up camping out in the waiting room.

Meghan wasn't in the ICU waiting area. Annie turned in the opposite direction, walking past the elevators and the stairwell. Then she saw her curled up on a love seat in the waiting room across from maternity; someone—a caring nurse, perhaps—had covered her with a thin hospital blanket. A heavy ache pressed down Annie's heart.

Meghan did, however, look as if she were asleep. Or perhaps in a stupor of emotion and exhaustion.

Annie quietly sat in a chair next to the love seat. No one else was there; with only three ICU beds in the hospital, she guessed it was a well-monitored place year-round, controlled by a bustling medical staff whose presence blended with the beeping of technology and the random sounds of machines that were keeping patients, keeping Kevin, alive. And might have kept Meghan awake if she'd been in the waiting room over there.

"Annie?" Meghan's voice was small, timid.

Quickly moving to where Meghan could see her, Annie stooped and touched her shoulder. "I'm here. I wasn't surprised that you snuck out of the closet."

Meghan gave her a half smile. "I wanted to be close to him. I went into the ICU waiting room first, but it was noisy. And this was roomier. They let me stay."

"How is he?"

"I saw him. He's hooked up to monitors and IV bags, but he's asleep. He has a breathing tube. Which is hooked up to a ventilator. But he looks comfortable enough." She sat up; she twisted her hands together. "His hair has gotten gray."

"That must be my fault," Annie said with a smile. "The stress of his having a big sister." She straightened the edge of Meghan's blanket. "Do you think they'll let me see him?"

"Sure. Go ask. Lorna is the head nurse on duty. Only one of us can go in at a time, and you can only stay a few minutes. And you're not supposed to touch him. To help prevent infection."

Annie stood up. "I don't know what time the cafeteria opens, but it's on the first floor . . ."

"Thanks, but the staff is wonderful—the nurses tried to wait on me all night. I had tea, but I haven't been hungry."

"You snuck up here early, then."

"As soon as I figured you were asleep." She smiled again, an inconsequential gesture but one that helped ease the heaviness that Annie felt.

Still, as she went to the ICU nurses' station and waited to be noticed, Annie wasn't sure that she deserved to see her brother. But when Lorna saw her, she led her to the doorway of his room, repeated the directives Meghan had already shared, then squeezed Annie's hand and left her alone.

It was peaceful in the room; the lighting was dimmer than it would be if he were in crisis. In spite of the breathing tube, he slept, his respiration steady. Thank God, or whoever was in charge.

Annie pulled a chair next to the bed and sat. And, for the first time since she'd received confirmation in the Anglican Church of Greater Boston, Annie prayed—really prayed, not merely the "Please, God, get him through this and I'll do anything you ask of me." Instead, she simply asked for help. For a swift and permanent recovery for Kevin. And that she'd be forgiven.

After a few minutes, she was aware of a figure standing in the doorway. Lorna stood there, silent.

Annie got the message. She stood up and went into the hallway. "Thank you," she said.

Lorna nodded. "The doctor will be here soon. I'm sure it's encouraging that your brother had a good night."

Annie thanked her again, then headed back to the waiting area and Meghan. But just before she reached the stairwell, the heavy door opened, and an imposing figure tramped out, heading toward ICU. The mane of auburn hair that bounced with each determined step belonged to Taylor. And she was on a rampage.

Chapter 27

"No one told me!" she growled. Thankfully, Taylor knew to keep her voice down in the hospital, especially in the ICU. An EMT, after all, would be well aware of protocol. "No one! I had to pull it out of my son, who apparently is more important in Kevin's life than I am!"

"Taylor," Annie said, grateful she was headed toward the nurses' station and not the waiting room where Meghan was. "Please. Let's go somewhere quiet."

"I want to see him. I'm entitled to see him."

"No," Annie said, her voice as low as possible, "actually, you aren't." She scanned the area. "Let's go out to the garden." Without waiting for consent, or for an argument, Annie took Taylor by the elbow and swiftly steered her through the ICU unit, hugging the wall of windows to obscure the view inside the rooms, parading the irate woman down the hall and out the door to the rooftop garden.

They were greeted by the early morning sun, melon-colored in the dawn of day. Annie led her to a seating area, careful to take a single chair rather than a long bench made for more than one. She didn't want to be that close to Taylor. She motioned her to sit on the other side, a small table between them. Then she noticed that, like Kevin, Taylor sported a golden tan; Annie didn't want to think about them together on a blanket on a tropical beach.

Taylor sputtered, then sat down. She crossed her legs, her long, pink-and-white-and-orange-striped gauze skirt draping in loose folds. Her wardrobe was noticeably different from the jeans and flannel shirts that Annie was accustomed to seeing her in on Chappy. Her whole appearance was softer, more feminine, as if Hawaii had transformed her.

"I had to pay extra for Fred to bring me across," she said. "The first run's not 'til six forty-five."

"I know," Annie said. She'd lived on Chappaquiddick long enough to know the *On Time* schedule better than the one for the big boats.

Staring out at the water, Taylor asked, "Why didn't anybody tell me? Jesus. I'm a freaking EMT. Maybe I could have gotten to him sooner . . ."

"Taylor, please. It all happened so fast. Simon took control and . . ."

"Who?"

"One of our guests. Simon Anderson."

"The TV guy?"

"Yes."

"The same guy who shot him?"

Annie knew she had to fill her in on a few details before Taylor heard a version of the story that might have become altered from a lengthy chain of telling. She started by explaining that Simon had been staying in the cottage, and that Annie had gone inside to try and find an envelope of research that she needed for her book. It was, of course, a lie, but Annie had no intention of telling her the whole truth. She went on to say Simon was shocked when he came in unexpectedly and saw her in the bedroom after she'd been prowling through her trunk. She said he shouted at her, and Kevin must have heard him. That part was true, including that Kevin must have raced up to his truck and grabbed his gun before he'd run back to the cottage. She told her about the scuffle, and how Simon had been the one who'd called 911.

The abridged account was conceivable.

Taylor was mute. In the time Annie had known her, she'd never seen the woman so quiet for so long.

"I'm sorry you didn't find out right away," Annie said. "It had nothing to do with you—I didn't know you were here. And as I said, everything happened fast."

Taylor toyed with one of the folds of her skirt. It looked as if she was trying to pleat them according to the pastel stripes.

"I heard that John arrested that guy. Simon."

Annie shook her head. "No. He questioned him. He also questioned me. Our stories were the same. John's going to wait until Kevin wakes up, of course, because he wants to question him, too. But as of now, it's being called an accident."

Flipping her mane back from one shoulder, Taylor snorted. "I've heard more believable tales that turned out to be lies."

Aside from providing good health care, one of the nicest parts about the hospital was that it sat up on a hill that overlooked both Vineyard Haven Harbor and Lagoon Pond. Annie looked past Taylor to the harbor now, where one of the big boats was visible behind a Black Dog tall ship—the vintage schooner *Alabama*. The vessels rested on still water—seeing the peaceful image calmed her.

"Taylor," she said, "nothing ominous happened. Three of us were there. So far, two of us have explained the details the same way. As, without a doubt, will Kevin. Please, don't try to stir up trouble where there isn't any."

Taylor stopped pleating the stripes and stood. "I want to see him."

Annie jumped up. "No. You can't."

"Of course I can," the woman grunted. "For one thing, I'm an EMT. I can get access if I want. For another thing . . . I feel partly responsible. Kevin didn't want to come back; I talked him into it."

Of all the things Taylor could have said, Annie hadn't expected that. "Okay," she said. "Then please hear me out."

Taylor paused.

"The reason no one told you last night is because we were trying to protect you."

"From what? A little blood and chaos? As if I haven't been around that most of my life?"

Annie sighed. "No, Taylor. We were trying to protect you from finding out that Meghan is here. Meghan. Kevin's wife."

The tanned complexion paled. "But . . ." She didn't seem able to continue.

"It's a long story," Annie continued. "And it's taken a long time. But she's healthy now and doing well."

Taylor shook her head. "So Kevin has played me for a fool."

Annie leaned forward. "Kevin? No! He didn't know. The last time he saw her she didn't recognize him."

"And suddenly she's better?" She flipped her mane again, her attitude returning. "Well, then. It's a bloody miracle."

She hurried away as Annie called after her. "Taylor. Stop. Please don't make a fool of yourself. Now isn't the time."

But she stalked off, a woman scorned.

Annie stayed on the rooftop garden, trying to regain her mental balance, if she had any left at all.

Not your circus . . . Murphy whispered, letting Annie know this was neither her show nor her responsibility. It was nice to know her old friend was back to hovering.

Tipping her head up to the heavens, Annie wanted,

needed, conversation. And no one was around to see her talking to the air.

"But we're talking about innocent people, Murphy. Meghan was doing what she thought was best. She didn't know until recently that she really was going to be okay. And she felt guilty about losing the baby. And Kevin . . . well, Kevin's been trying his damnedest to make a new life. God knows that what he's been through before today has been tragic, too. The bottom line is, Taylor's never been my best friend, but she's an innocent party, too, caught in the middle of something no one was aware of. So this is no circus, Murph. It's just life, I guess, and people—none of whom set out to hurt anyone, or to be hurt."

Um . . . I already know those things. I see everything from here. And I think it's time to let love happen—or not happen—as it will. Then Murphy's words trailed off, drifting up to the orange sunrise sky. Though Annie didn't feel much better about the situation, she at least felt as if she were no longer on her own in this . . . whatever "this" turned out to be.

She took her time going back into the hospital. When she stepped into the corridor of the ICU, she fully expected to see Taylor in Kevin's room. And that Meghan would be standing in the doorway, watching.

Moving stealthily, Annie went to the glass wall of the room. Kevin was lying in the bed, his face turned in her direction. His eyes were closed. And he was alone.

"He looks peaceful, doesn't he?"

Annie jumped. She pivoted on one foot and saw Meghan approaching.

"Sorry," Meghan said. "I didn't mean to startle you."

Shaking it off, Annie replied, "I'm just . . . it's just . . ." She knew she had to tell her that Taylor had been there, that she'd had come back with Kevin.

Meghan reached Annie and stood next to her, her eyes

fixed on the figure in the bed behind the glass. "I know Taylor's back," she said. "I know she was here."

Annie's throat started to flutter; it felt as if she'd swallowed a tiny bird. She feared if she spoke, her words would come out in small chirps. "I'm so sorry, Meghan," she managed to say. "I had no idea that she'd come back with him."

Unlike tall, lofty Taylor, Meghan was petite; Annie hoped that the contrast between what looked like strength versus fragility was deceiving.

"I told her," Annie said. "I told her you're here."

Again, Meghan nodded. "I know. She told me. She saw me in the waiting area. She introduced herself."

The bird inside Annie threatened to take flight. "How did she know who you were?"

Meghan shrugged. "Kevin's the only one in the ICU. She saw me. She must have figured it out. Maybe he'd told her what I look like—my eyes, my skin color, who knows?" She turned from the glass and put her hand on Annie's arm. "It's okay, Annie. I'm okay. What will be, will be, right?"

Part of Annie wondered if Meghan had been talking to Murphy, too. She looked back at her brother, thinking how upset he'd be if he knew he was causing so much anguish to the people he cared about. "Can I interest you in coffee? Somewhere outside the hospital? I think it's safe to safe to assume that Kevin isn't going anywhere."

"Maybe." She pressed a palm against the glass. "But let's wait until the doctor comes, okay?"

"Absolutely."

They went back to the waiting room and sat, passing the time with minimal conversation. It was mid-morning before Doctor Mike arrived.

"He's doing okay," he told them. "I'm still concerned about the possibility of bone fragments, so let's see how today goes before we wake him up." It looked as if he was smiling behind his mask. "Patience isn't always easy, but sometimes it's the best medicine."

Annie figured that Meghan already knew that.

After seeing the doctor, a nurse let them shower and clean up in the staff locker room. Then they left their belongings at the nurses' station along with their phone numbers in case anything happened to Kevin while they were gone.

Because Annie had arrived in the ambulance and Francine had driven Meghan, they went outside and hopped the bus to Vineyard Haven. They got off at the Steamship pier and walked up Main Street to Waterside Market, where they shared a breakfast egg wrap of cheese, spinach, tomato, and avocado. It was as energizing as it was colorful.

After a second cup of coffee, Annie said, "The library is right up the street. It's the only one on the island that's open Sundays. Maybe I can do some of the research I wanted to do yesterday."

"About Simon?"

"Yes. I'd love to find anything he wrote about Brian's accident. I was in such a fog for so long I could have missed something important. Some clue as to why Simon's here."

"You don't think it's a coincidence, do you? Even though it's been more than twenty years?"

"I don't. It's too strange, and he's acted oddly since I picked him up last week. Besides, I need to do something constructive right now. Instead of worrying about my brother." She paused. "Would you like to come with me?"

Meghan placed her napkin on her plate. "Thanks, but I'd feel better if I were in the ICU, trying to be patient. I know he'll still be sleeping, but . . ."

"There's no need to explain. I'll join you in a while. Do you know how to get back from here?"

"I think so. I saw a bookstore on Main Street the other

day. I'll pick up something to read, then make my way back to the ferry where I can catch the bus back to the hospital—can't I?"

Annie nodded. "It's bus thirteen," she said, not sure how she knew that since she'd only traveled by bus a few times since she'd lived there. "Just tell the driver you're going to the hospital."

They stood and hugged, then cleared their plates. Once outside again, Meghan walked down the hill and Annie went up, hoping that her mission wouldn't be in vain.

The library was quiet, which wasn't surprising. It wasn't only the final day of the Ag Fair, it was also a great-weather beach day. Lots of seasonal people would be heading home thanks to the unofficial end of summer. And islanders would start to regroup again.

Annie went past the desk and the shelves of fiction toward the tables with the computers that provided digital access. Though she supposed she didn't need total privacy, it was more relaxing to be alone. She signed on, went straight to the *Boston Globe* website, then to the newspaper's archives. Taking a deep breath, she clicked the cursor on the Search bar and typed the name Andrew Simmons.

One–two–three. She waited, wondering if a question would show at the top: *Did you mean Simon Anderson?*

Finally a page loaded. She scanned it quickly. A number of entries for Simmons were obviously wrong: an Andrew Simmons had graduated from CalTech the previous year; another was an insurance agent who had to be at least seventy; another boasted a link to an indie rock band's Facebook page.

The name was too common, her search too broad. She went back to the top of the screen and added "Boston" after his name.

Several Simmonses came up; the first was Andrew. It was an obituary, dated Oct. 13, 1984:

*Andrew J. Simmons, 42, of the Columbia Point section of
Boston, died in his sleep, Thurs., Oct. 11. He leaves a
wife, Margaret (McKenna), and three sons, David,
Andrew, and Christopher. No calling hours; burial is
private. Doherty-Jones Funeral Home is in charge.*

It had to be Simon's father, who Simon said died of alco-
holism. Annie wondered what the man would have thought
about his namesake's success.

Next on the list was a plea from Boston Latin School,
Class of 1990 Reunion Committee, that was searching for
missing classmates, including one Andrew Simmons. Annie
did the math in her head and decided that would make him
around fifty now. Which meant it could very well be Simon.

She did another quick search for Simon's Wiki page: *born
April 3, 1972, Boston, Massachusetts.* Close enough, she thought.

She went back to the previous page and continued the
search, but nothing was relevant. Until she reached another
obituary: *Christopher Simmons.*

Simon's younger brother?

She clicked on the link. The article was brief; it was dated
Sept. 14, 2018.

*Christopher M. Simmons, 40, of Dorchester, died Friday
from an accident sustained in his home. He leaves a brother,
David Simmons, of Brookline, and a nephew. Services are
private.*

Short, but not terribly sweet, Annie thought. Sad. An accident "in his home" could mean many things: a fall down the
stairs, an electrical shock, or, she imagined, one of about a
million things. There was no mention of Christopher's parents
or of Andrew/ Simon. No mention of Simon's three daugh-

ters. It was as if he had vanished once he'd taken to the air-waves. Once he'd changed his name.

"Cheers to the old days," Simon had told Annie. "May they be forgotten."

The remaining links on the page did not include Andrew, either. And there was no reference to any articles he'd written for the *Globe*. Perhaps he hadn't been granted a byline. Or . . . he'd never worked there. Which, of course, was impossible, because he'd given Annie his business card.

It was as baffling as it was exasperating.

However, Annie now knew she needed to confront Simon again and get him to confess to the real reason he was there . . . and if it was, in any way, related to why he had divested himself of all things "Andrew Simmons." Including his brothers and his nephew.

And while none of it might be connected to why he'd cut off communicating with her about Brian's accident, she was now haunted by the question Simon had asked her back in the cottage: *What do you know?* It had now become more important to Annie to learn what it was that she *didn't* know.

But as she logged off the computer, Annie wondered if Meghan had been right, that the whole thing was a coincidence. Maybe Simon didn't even remember the scared young widow he had interviewed. He'd had a new name for many years now, and a whole new life. In a bigger city. On a much bigger stage. With his grad school days long gone and probably forgotten.

Then she remembered his toast when she'd approached him on the beach: "Cheers to the old days. May they be forgotten. And to all our days. May they be forgiven."

Whatever that meant.

Chapter 28

Annie walked the two miles from the library back to the hospital, wanting the exercise, wanting to think. Somewhere between the five corners and the drawbridge, she knew she needed to refocus on the present, on Kevin, and on Meghan. The old days were done. And, as Simon had further noted, "It's crap, anyway."

When she arrived in the ICU, Meghan was sitting in the same chair in the waiting room where she'd spent the night. Next to her was Earl. He was holding her hand.

Annie smiled. Earl was such a kind, caring man. He would have made a perfect father-in-law.

She sat down on the other side of Meghan. "No news?"

Meghan shook her head. "Earl's been telling me how hard Kevin worked on the Inn, especially on the actual hands-on building. That's what he always loved to do. When our business got so big that he had to stay in the office, he hated every minute of it. He was happier when he was hammering."

"Yes, Kevin's a hammering fiend," Annie said. "And I've had enough headaches to prove it."

Meghan laughed a sweet, gentle laugh. A laugh so much nicer than Taylor's.

"I brought Kevin some clothes," Earl said. "Not that I think the kimono isn't attractive on him."

"It's called a johnny, Earl," Meghan said. Her disposition seemed lighter, which was likely due in no small part to Earl's company.

"Speaking of johnny . . ." the jokester said, "here he is now."

Annie didn't catch his meaning until a voice from the doorway said, "Hey, Dad."

She counted to three before turning her head.

"Annie," John said, then looked over at Meghan and nodded. "How's he doing?"

"The same," Meghan said. "So that's good."

"Great." He looked back at Annie. "Can you give me a minute?"

She closed her eyes for a second, then stood up. "The garden okay?" Not waiting for a reply, she said, "Excuse us." She left the waiting room, knowing John would follow but not wanting to think about why he wanted to talk. Maybe he was there merely in a professional capacity.

It was hotter on the rooftop than it had been earlier; the sun had inched across the sky, its rays now flared up from the cement walkway. "How many eggs did you fry out there?" her dad used to ask whenever she came inside after playing hopscotch in the driveway on a steamy summer afternoon. She wondered how many dad-isms he'd said over the years; she wished she remembered all of them. Especially now, when she'd rather be thinking about that than the impending conversation.

"How 'bout here?" John said. "No sense walking all the way to Aquinnah."

She stopped at a bench; she realized then that they'd already passed a few. He must have thought she was losing her mind, as Kevin had told Earl.

He sat down next to her. "Man," he said, "this has been one lousy way to end a summer."

"I had a lot to do with it. For starters, I practically browbeat Kevin into coming back."

"Does he know about Meghan?"

"No. She didn't want me to tell him. So I told him he was shirking his responsibilities at the Inn. Which probably made things worse. He must have been exhausted from rushing to get a flight, then coming all this way. I never knew he was afraid of flying." She lowered her head, stared at the concrete squares that were laid out in a great grid for hopscotch. If she wanted to play, she'd only have to number the squares and not draw all the lines. She wondered how many eggs she could fry on it. She sighed. "God knows how long he went without sleep—which must be why he grabbed his gun when he heard us arguing."

"Annie," John said. Then he paused.

Ordinarily, his pause might have been disturbing, might have stirred up her insides. But her senses were still dulled from the night and the day to evoke any more emotion.

"I'm sorry for everything that's happened," John said. "Most of all, I'm sorry for being a jerk."

She supposed he was referring to their relationship. "We all need a break sometimes, John. Even me."

It was so hot the gulls weren't bothering to squawk; the drawbridge seemed too lazy to rise up; there was no breeze to filter the buzz from jet skis on the Tisbury side of Lagoon Pond. It was as if everything and everyone was either cooling in the water or at home in front of a fan.

"Is it too late to say I made a mistake? That I overreacted because of Abigail, who's known how to push every one of my buttons since the day she was born? Or because I'm jealous about a guy I've seen on TV for years but have never met?

Or because last night I realized how much you've been going through, and how I've been so stuck in my own crap that I haven't been very nice to you—of all people?"

She didn't know how to answer. It might be the perfect time to tell him about Abigail's assertion that he was going back to Jenn, and to ask if it were true. Or she could turn toward him, lean into him, kiss him, and say that everything would be fine. But her numbness felt as if the weight of a thousand concrete squares like those in the garden were parked solidly upon her chest. And she felt nothing else.

"John," she said. "I appreciate what you said. Honestly, I do. But right now . . ." From out of nowhere, or from out of everywhere, tears came again. She wrapped her arms around her waist and hugged herself.

He kept the distance of about two feet between them. But he reached over and brushed back her hair. "I was afraid you decided you don't want to marry me," he said. "We hardly see each other anymore. And when I said I needed to take a break, I didn't mean for you to think I don't want to marry you. Or that I don't . . . love you."

Choosing her words carefully, then wondering why she needed to do that, Annie said, "I can't talk about this right now. Can you understand that? I can't think about anything except Kevin. Okay?" She looked out at the harbor, wishing one of the big boats was coming or going so she'd have something to focus on other than her feelings, or rather, her lack of them right then.

John stood up. He stuffed his hands in the pockets of his uniform. Which was when Annie realized he was, in fact, in uniform, and he'd be on his way to work soon. Four to midnight. Or later if summer got out of hand.

"I keep thinking about him, too, you know."

No, Annie thought. She hadn't known.

"I guess I've said what I needed to say," he added. "I'll check in later. To see how he's doing. Unless you don't want me to."

It was an odd thing for him to say. Or maybe it wasn't. "I'll be here," she said.

Then he left.

And she stared down at the cement squares again.

The rest of the afternoon was a blur of people and nurses and hushed conversations in the ICU waiting room. Lucy came with Claire. Francine came without Jonas, which was understandable. By then, most people must have heard the truth about the Inn's enigmatic guest Meghan, aka Mary Beth Mullen, aka Kevin's wife. Jonas must be torn between his friendship with Kevin and loyalty to his mother. Annie hoped it hadn't caused a rift between Francine and him.

Winnie, blessed Winnie, came, too. She suggested that Annie and Meghan get out of the hospital and go for a drive with her before sunset; Meghan politely declined, but Annie agreed. Life, after all, always felt safe when she was with Winnie.

They went to West Chop, not far from the hospital, yet removed from the whispers of people and the hums of machines and the faint scent of disinfectant.

Standing at the tip of the chop, where the west side of the Vineyard sloped south toward Aquinnah, they watched the sun deliver its end-of-day spectacle. Annie gazed at the green mounds of the Elizabeth Islands and told Winnie about John's visit and his apology and her reaction, or rather, her non-reaction. She could have predicted her friend's reply.

"Give it time," her friend said. "Making important decisions when life is in turmoil often yields regrets."

The only breeze of the day flittered past them then. Or maybe it was Murphy, underscoring Winnie's wisdom.

In addition to advice, Winnie also had brought wine. Annie allowed herself a small glass; she sipped it slowly, savoring the taste and the way it helped melt her anxiety. She then told Winnie what she'd found out about Simon, though, in truth, it hardly mattered now. At some point that day, her interest in the mystery had slipped away. At least for the moment.

Winnie listened. She was good at that.

After an hour, Annie felt better.

But when she arrived back at the hospital, said good-bye to Winnie, and returned to the second floor, Annie's mood shifted again. Meghan was alone in the waiting room, her head down, the calves of her legs swinging back and forth.

"Meghan?" Annie asked. "What's wrong?" Her palms began to perspire.

Meghan lifted her beautiful face, her cheekbones chiseled like an ancient goddess's, though her eyes had faded in the twilight that now seeped into the room.

"The doctor wants to wait until tomorrow morning to wake him up."

Annie asked as she took the chair next to her, "I suppose the longer he sleeps the better he'll heal . . . ?" Had Doctor Mike explained it that way? Or had Annie made it up? She decided it wasn't important; what counted was that Kevin hadn't needed another surgery. So far.

Meghan shrugged. "Supposedly, he's stable, and his vital signs are strong. The doctor isn't expecting any problems, but he did say when it comes to the body—especially with trauma—they can never be a hundred percent sure. But I know that from experience."

Annie put her arm around her. "The doctors here know what they're doing, too. Kevin will be fine. I believe that." Right then, she actually did. "Why don't we go back to the Inn and get a good night's sleep? We can come back early. Did he say what time they'll wake him up?"

"Seven o'clock."

As Taylor had pointed out, the first trip off Chappy wasn't until six forty-five. In spite of that early hour, chances were they wouldn't make it to the hospital and upstairs by seven.

She thought about texting John to ask if he could pull a few strings. But Winnie's words echoed: "Give it time." So Annie called Earl instead.

"Be at the dock at six," he said. "I guarantee someone will be there to bring you across. It might be me in a kayak, but I'll get you there."

What with Winnie and now Earl, they might get through this after all.

But when they got back to the Inn, Annie's optimism faded when she saw the light burning in her cottage. For some reason, she'd really hoped that, though John had told Simon to stay on the island, he had found other accommodations.

Deciding that in order to keep a modicum of well-being, right then Annie also needed to give the situation with Simon some time. So she summoned all her courage, looked away from her cottage, got out of the Jeep, and followed Meghan through the back door of the Inn where she intended to put together a quick and healthy meal. She did not expect to see a large shopping bag on the kitchen counter.

There's more in the refrigerator, an accompanying note read. It was signed Claire and Lucy, with several X's and O's under their names. The bag was stuffed with freshly baked brownies, a batch of peanut butter cookies, a loaf of home-baked sourdough bread (which must have been Francine's doing), a box of oyster crackers, and a bottle of Chardonnay. A quick peek in the refrigerator revealed barbecued chicken breasts and thick slices of ham; pasta salad, broccoli, cole slaw, and potatoes au gratin; and a large container of creamy clam chowder.

"Enough to feed all our guests and residents for a week,"

Meghan said with a small laugh. It felt like days since Annie had heard her laugh.

"The intention is more than enough to lift my spirits," Annie said.

"Mine, too. I might have a slice of bread and a small piece of chicken . . ."

Annie retrieved clean plates from the dishwasher just as Francine scooted in from the great room.

"How is he?" she asked.

"The same," Meghan said.

"Stable," Annie added. "But they won't wake him up until tomorrow morning."

"So will you sleep over the workshop again tonight?"

"I suppose so." She took utensils from a drawer and set them next to the plates.

"Don't forget that the honeymoon suite's available. It might be good to pamper yourself a little. Get you prepared for the future, you know?"

How had it happened that Francine had missed the grapevine about John needing a break? Or perhaps she had but was being optimistic. Annie sighed. Then she realized that, yes, she could do with some pampering . . . a nice, warm Jacuzzi, a giant, comfortable bed . . .

"Okay," she said before she started to dwell on John. "I'll take it. Shall I change the sheets?"

Francine smiled. "Everything's ready for you. All you need are your jammies and whatever you'll want for the morning."

Annie could have kissed her. So she did, right on her forehead. "I have those, thanks to the bag you brought to the hospital for me. But I'd like to get clothes for tomorrow. Maybe I'll run down to the workshop now; we'll be leaving for the hospital early in the morning. Meghan, help yourself. And if you don't mind, I'll have what you're having. Maybe with a little pasta salad on the side. And a cookie. Francine? Can you stay? Will you join us for food and wine?"

"Absolutely."

And Annie was reminded that no matter what was going on, life was best when love was shared.

With an unexpected surge of happiness, she rushed from the Inn and headed toward the workshop. On her way, she glanced over at the cottage where the light still glowed; it would be a decent human gesture if she updated Simon on Kevin's condition. After all, chances were the guy was still upset from having shot someone. They could talk about Andrew Simmons tomorrow. Or the day after that. Or never, if he didn't want to.

Her resolve now in place, she stepped onto the porch. The main door was open, but thanks to the light of the lamps, Annie had a clear view through the screen: Simon was on his hands and knees in the bedroom, scrubbing Kevin's blood up off the floor.

Chapter 29

Annie's first instinct was to run. Far from the cottage, from Chappy, from Martha's Vineyard. But she couldn't very well run with her feet glued to the ground.

She must have cried out. Or gasped. Or shrieked. Whatever the sound she'd made, it alerted Simon. Before she knew it, he was at the screen door, looking at her. Shamefaced. Sheepish.

"How is he?" he asked.

Her heart was beating faster than it should. She took a breath before she spoke. "He came through surgery okay. But they're not going to wake him up until tomorrow morning." She was amazed that she sounded so coherent.

He closed his eyes. "I am so sorry, Annie. I thought he was going to shoot me."

The feeling began to come back into her feet, her legs, the rest of her. "I know, Simon. I know."

He opened the screen door; she backed up a step but stopped before nearly falling off the porch.

"He's going to be okay, isn't he?"

"He'll only need another surgery if more bone fragments break loose." Her words were medical, scientific, logical. They did not reveal that, basically, she was still scared to death for her brother.

Simon stepped outside onto the porch. "You want to come in? Have a glass of wine or something?"

She shook her head more insistently than necessary. She gestured back to the Inn. "I'm having dinner with Francine and one of our guests."

"It's clean," he suddenly said. "The floor."

Annie's toes and fingers wriggled as if she were trying to stave off a seizure. "We would have called a cleaning service . . ."

"Bill did it. By the time I got back from the police station, he'd . . ." His gaze drifted toward the meadow, toward the Inn, toward the ground. ". . . he'd taken care of . . . it." Simon was visibly struggling for words; Annie wondered if his toes and fingers were wriggling, too.

"I saw you on the floor . . . I thought you were scrubbing . . ." They were tough words. For a tough situation.

"I was touching it up. To be sure . . . well, you know."

She knew, so she nodded. "I need to go now."

"I'd like to talk with you, Annie. I need to clear a few things up." He couldn't seem to look at her; perhaps he was vying for time, attempting to summon his own form of courage. "Maybe tomorrow evening?"

"Here?" she asked.

"How about somewhere neutral? Like a restaurant in town?"

Of course, a restaurant was out of the question. Annie didn't need for John to see her out with Simon. Or for anyone to see her with him. Especially if "anyone" had a camera with a flash and a zoom lens. Though Annie had no idea where, if anywhere, her relationship with John was or wasn't going now, she didn't want to intentionally derail it.

"It's probably not a great idea to be seen in public together."

He nodded. "Right. Here, then?"

"Let's meet on the beach. Around six o'clock?"

"Six is good."

"As long as Kevin is awake and he's okay."

"Fair enough."

She started off toward the workshop.

"Annie?" Simon said.

She stopped. She turned around.

"Thanks for not calling me Andrew."

Under other circumstances, his admission might have been confounding. But basically he'd validated Annie's discovery, and she couldn't resist giving him a tiny smile. Then she gestured thumbs-up and continued on her mission to get clothes, and he perhaps went back to "touching up" the floor.

The Jacuzzi was incredible. After a glass of wine, a little dinner, and a lot of girl talk, Francine shooed Annie and Meghan upstairs to their rooms so she could tidy the kitchen. It was only ten o'clock, but morning would come soon enough—*early* morning, in order to catch the "custom-scheduled" ferry, as Earl called it when he'd phoned to say it was arranged.

However, with the night ahead of her, Annie wasn't yet ready to try and sleep. Instead, she luxuriated in the churning water that slowly massaged her aching muscles. She added a few dashes of lavender oil that Winnie once told her was the best antidote to a difficult day.

Closing her eyes, allowing the bubbling jets and the scent to soothe her, Annie thought about how much she'd missed not having been able to gather herbs and wildflowers that summer; not having been able to craft her soaps: beach roses and cream, buttercup balm, fox grape and sunflower oil, and more. Her favorites were violets and honey, and her newest creation, snowdrops, both of which were unique discoveries that she'd blended with a good dose of imagination. She missed wrapping each bar in the collection in pastel netting, tying it with coordinating ribbon, and adding a label that read, *Soaps by Sutton*. Each time a customer purchased one (more often they bought three or four), Annie felt as proud as if she'd sold one of her books. The most important aspect of her life now was to do things that brought joy to others, whether through calming, sudsy scents or giving her readers permission to curl up with what she hoped they'd feel was an engaging mystery.

Until she'd moved to the island, though, she had no idea that real, not made-up, mysteries would permeate her days.

When Kevin had learned that his big sister was an author, he wondered if writing could be genetic, and if so, he thought he should try his hand at it because he said that sitting around all day, making stuff up, must be a lot easier than building buildings.

It hadn't been long, however, before he decided not to try writing a book after all. He said he had enough trouble putting together an intelligent email.

As time went on, he'd finally shared the details about Meghan, about how "ripped up" he'd been about the accident, and about his guilt.

"The weather had been lousy all month, and we'd lost a lot of time," he'd explained. "That day, the forecast was for more snow; I asked her to stay home." But he said that, in addition to being great builder, she had a "fierce head" for the bottom line; she was determined to finish before Christmas in order to meet the deadline and ensure final payment by the end of the year. "She also heard that the client was planning another mall on the South Shore," he'd continued. "She wanted us to get the job. So even though I begged her not to, even though I told her the last thing we needed was another job that size, she wouldn't listen. That's why she was on that damn scaffolding when the wind kicked up and the whole damn thing collapsed. I never should have allowed her to be up there."

He'd also said it had taken him a while to believe the doctor's prediction that she wouldn't recover.

He'd never mentioned whether or not he'd learned she'd been pregnant. Or if his guilt had turned to anger because she'd taken such a risk. Perhaps the doctors hadn't told him about the baby. Maybe Donna had told them not to.

The irony, however, was that now the situation had been reversed: Meghan was the one waiting for Kevin to recover.

A gruesome twist of fate. A dreadful coincidence.

As Annie smoothed the lavender water over her arms and legs, the word *coincidence* lingered a breath too long, swinging her thoughts back to Simon. She now was fairly certain it had not been a coincidence that Simon had come to the Vineyard, to the Inn. The only piece still missing was why.

Tomorrow evening would be interesting. Perhaps he only wanted to apologize for dissing her years before, for upsetting the young widow more than she already was. As if there could have been any chance of that.

Suddenly, the comforting bath lost its dreamy allure; the water had gone cold.

She turned off the jets, opened the drain, and got out of the tub, knowing that if Kevin woke up in the morning without complications, she would be happy beyond measure. And that any mea culpa Simon might later impart would almost not matter; it would not be able to rattle her joy.

But if anything bad happened to Kevin . . .

She grabbed the thick terry towel and held it to her face, trying to snuff out any tears before they dared to start. Then she slipped into her nightgown and went straight to bed.

That night she dreamed she heard Donna calling out to her.

★ ★ ★

Sunrise in the third week of August came early to Chappaquiddick: it officially occurred at the same time Annie's Jeep rolled onto the *On Time*. She'd packed a Thermos of coffee, two slices of Lucy's fresh sourdough bread, and a small container of strawberry jam made from this summer's crop. It wouldn't be much of a breakfast—not compared with the ones Francine was growing famous for—but Annie figured that she and Meghan at least would have coffee to help them stay alert.

Meghan looked pretty in a pale aqua linen sundress and white, skinny-strap sandals. When Annie complimented her, she said the outfit belonged to Francine, who'd let her borrow it so she'd look extra special for her husband. Annie nodded and agreed that Francine was thoughtful.

It was the last bit of conversation they had for a while; there would be plenty of time for talking later.

The channel in the harbor was choppier than usual, which Annie supposed might be due to the early hour. As she recalled, Captain Fred had a wife and a grown daughter; she made a mental note to drop off a few of her soaps and perhaps her latest book at Fred's house. Though Annie was certain Earl had given him a decent tip, it never hurt to do something personal.

She knew her mind had drifted from the purpose of their mission because it was less scary than thinking about where they were going and what was going—or not going—to happen. Whatever was playing out in Meghan's mind she was keeping to herself as she sat, her head turned toward the window, either transfixed by the sunrise or frozen with fear, as Annie was—not only from the odds of what might happen when Kevin awoke, but also about how he'd react when he saw his wife. *Ex-wife*, Annie corrected herself.

The more she hashed through innumerable possibilities on

their short journey across the water, by the time they landed in Edgartown, she was tempted to ask Captain Fred if he would ferry them back.

But they kept going, because Annie once heard that sometimes the best way to face anything is simply to plow through it. She'd forgotten if she'd heard it from her dad, Murphy, Earl, or Winnie—the attentive sages in her life.

It was quiet in the hospital when, mere minutes later, they walked silently into the entrance. They moved past the receptionist's desk where no one was on duty yet, then past the grand piano and down the hallway that was lined with museum-quality art pieces: island paintings of quiet rowboats and up-island landscapes of stone walls and sheep. Across from the paintings were poster-sized, iconic photographs of celebrities, including one of Barack and Michelle Obama that had been taken when they might have been in their thirties, long before they could have guessed the responsibilities that lay ahead for them. *Even then*, Annie thought now, *they'd looked like leaders.*

As for Annie and Meghan, Annie was just grateful that they were still upright and moving forward. Until they got into the elevator. That's when Annie's legs grew weak and Meghan started to cry.

"What if . . ." she began to say.

"Shsssh," Annie whispered as if someone were listening. "Let's only think positive thoughts, okay?"

She nodded meekly. But as they stepped out onto the second floor where the ICU was, Annie noticed that Meghan's eyes were clouded.

Of course they are, Murphy reassured her.

Now that she knew Murphy was there, Annie was able to get her bearings, square her shoulders, and advance directly to the nurses' station.

"We're here," she told Lorna, who was on duty again.

"The doctor isn't in yet," Lorna said. "Would you like to sit in the waiting room? I'd offer you coffee but it looks like you've come prepared." She nodded toward the Thermos.

"Yes. Thanks. We'll be in the waiting room." Then Annie's nerves began to quibble again. She took Meghan by the elbow and escorted her to the small room next to the stairs as if Meghan didn't already know where they were to wait, as if she hadn't spent far too many hours there already.

Twelve minutes later—Annie knew that because she'd kept checking her watch—Doctor Mike appeared. Three others in lab coats were with him. Annie realized that they, too, were early. Maybe they wanted to get this over with as badly as Annie and Meghan did.

Doctor Mike explained that they needed a few minutes to remove the breathing tube and "other things" that would "no longer be necessary." He said one of the nurses would be back to get them once Kevin was awake.

"He's been out of surgery less than thirty-six hours, and he's been sleeping the whole time. He won't be completely cognitive right away," he added. "So bear with him, okay?" He smiled and set off for Kevin's room, the other lab coats trailing behind him.

Annie was tempted to sneak furtively to the end of the line, to stay out of sight but listen. But even if she could manage to remain undetected, she knew it wouldn't be wise. If Kevin cried out in pain, or worse, if something went wrong and chaos erupted, resulting in the doctor having to fire off orders and the nurses to scurry around, she knew her heart would explode into thousands of pieces, scattering its shards all over the polished floor.

So Annie sat next to Meghan and both of them remained perfectly still. And waited.

★　★　★

They looked like a miniature gang of voyeurs, clustered around Kevin's bed: the doctor, his three lab-coated ducklings, two nurses, Annie, Meghan.

Kevin's eyes had opened several times, but he'd looked directly at Doctor Mike, who gently said, "Kevin? Time to wake up now." Then Kevin closed his eyes again. Mike repeated the exercise over and over; each time Kevin's eyes opened, they stayed that way a half a second longer; he made soft, guttural sounds, like the kind a dog made when he was dreaming. Still, it seemed hopeful.

Minutes elapsed; Annie felt as if she'd been standing in motionless limbo for hours. She didn't know how much longer she could pretend that her brother's occasional blinking and mutterings were "good signs," though the doctor kept insisting that they were.

Meghan stood beside her as stalwart as Annie, though no doubt she was as unsteady. While they'd been in the waiting room, she'd confided to Annie that she didn't remember much about waking up from her coma except that, in a random instant, for no reason she'd either known or later learned, she'd sat up, looked around, and cried out, "Hello? Does anyone have any ice cream?" She said her voice had been raspy, and she'd had a sore throat. Otherwise, she was fine. A nurse flew into her room and gasped, "Meghan?" Then the nurse laughed, raced out into the hall, and cried, "She's awake! Meghan's awake!"

According to her memory, it had been that simple. It had not been like this.

Suddenly, however, Kevin's eyes opened without prompting. He stared at the doctor. His gaze then traveled to the other lab coats, to the nurses, to Annie, and, finally, to Meghan.

His brow furrowed.

His face contorted.

He cowered.

An emergency alert screeched from one of the machines still tethered to him: a red light started flashing incessantly like an angry lighthouse beacon. And Kevin let out the howl of a freshly wounded animal.

He used to tell people he'd hired her because he thought it was so cool that Meghan's grandfather had worked on the John Hancock Tower. The real reason was because from the moment she'd walked into his office for an interview, Kevin was in love. Sure, he'd had his share (maybe more) of girls, but nothing, no one, had come close to causing that rush of heat that went from his eyes straight to his heart.

Sure, she'd been young and drop-dead gorgeous, but it was those eyes—those hypnotic blue eyes—that drilled into him like a jack-hammer and left him unable to move.

He'd been stuck to his chair the whole time he'd interviewed her, the whole time she'd answered his questions, not that he remembered what she'd said.

Until now, he never thought he'd see her again. Unless they both were no longer breathing. He'd hoped that one day they'd meet up in heaven, and he could ask her why she'd done what she had done.

Was that why she was here?

Was he already dead?

Chapter 30

One of the nurses rushed Annie and Meghan from the room, saying over and over that Kevin was fine, that what happened was nothing to be afraid of.

Reassurances aside, Annie knew that the sound Kevin had let loose with would be forever rooted in her mind.

"Perhaps come back later?" the nurse suggested. "Give him a few hours to adjust to his surroundings. He wasn't aware that he was shot, was he?"

Annie shook her head. "It happened so fast. I think he was unconscious before he landed on the floor."

The nurse smiled. "I know his reaction was startling, but . . ."

"No," Meghan said, "it wasn't a surprise. He didn't expect to see me. He probably thought he was hallucinating . . ."

The nurse looked bewildered. Annie said, "It's a long story. We'll come back later."

By then Meghan had opened the door and was trouncing down the steps, her footsteps echoing in the stairwell.

"He's awake," Annie announced as soon as Earl opened the back door of his house. "He's okay." She'd wanted to tell him in person rather than with a phone call.

Earl began to speak but clearly got choked up, his words stuck in the muck of his emotions. "Claire! Lucy!" he called out.

The ladies came running, and Annie repeated what she'd told Earl. Claire covered her face with her hands—she was either crying or thanking God. Lucy said, "Way cool. Does my dad know?"

"I'll text him now," Annie said, embarrassed that she hadn't thought to let John know first, saying she'd been sidetracked by Meghan, who'd developed "a nor'easter of a headache," as she'd called it. When they'd arrived back at the Inn and Annie had pulled into the driveway, Meghan had said, "I don't know what I expected. Of course he was upset when he saw me. I was only thinking of myself; I should have had you break the news to him first. Stupid me." She'd climbed out of the Jeep and gone inside to rest.

Annie's next thought had been to get over to Earl's.

John hadn't crossed her mind.

She pulled out her phone now; if she texted and didn't call, he'd see her message when he woke up and wouldn't know he hadn't been her first choice.

Texting, however, would be a cop-out.

No pun intended, Murphy could have said, but perhaps she'd decided this was not a good time to joke.

Claire wanted Annie to come in "for coffee and a decent breakfast," but she declined.

"I'll go tell John in person," she said. "I came to Chappy first so Meghan could go to bed. She's been through so much in these past few days alone."

"As have you," Earl added.

Annie waved, got back into the Jeep, and headed to the *On Time* for the third trip that day, despite that it wasn't yet nine o'clock.

Her good intentions, however, were thwarted when she reached John's house in Edgartown and Abigail answered the door. She was dressed in a striking white, gauzy jumpsuit that was splattered with multi-shades of summer yellows.

"Dad's sleeping," she said and began to shut the door.

"Wait," Annie said firmly. If there had ever been a right time to be the grown-up in the room—or rather, on the porch—it was now. "I need to see him about something important. I think he'd want me to go upstairs and wake him." Kevin was who mattered then, and John deserved to know.

Abigail might have rolled her eyes—it was hard to tell with her Cleopatra-like makeup—but she stepped aside. "Whatever."

"I like your outfit," Annie said as she pressed past her and headed to the staircase. "The colors are stunning."

"I made it. I did the tie-dye, too." If she was surprised by Annie's calm demeanor, she didn't let on.

Three steps up, Restless bounded down the entire flight to greet her properly. Annie gave him a quick pet, knowing that he hadn't seen much of her lately. With the dog now on her heels, she made it to the top landing, where she ran into John.

"Kevin's awake," she said.

"He's okay?"

Because she hesitated, she sensed that John would know she was going to say something that was not totally true, but would be as close as she could come, what with Restless entwining himself around her feet and Abigail staring up from the living room. "He needs time to acclimate to everything that's happened, but the doctor said that physically, everything looks good."

John reached down and petted the dog, which Annie recognized as a way to redirect his feelings. The Lyons men had trouble expressing theirs. "That's good. Kevin's a good man. And," he added, as he stood again, emotions now in check, "Mike Hoffman's a good surgeon." He looked into her eyes. "You want to come upstairs and tell me more?"

She was about to say yes, because she wanted to tell him what had really happened, how Kevin had screamed when he'd seen Meghan; she wanted to tell him about Simon scrubbing the floor and that she was now certain he'd been the one who'd interviewed her for the *Globe*. Mostly, Annie wanted to find out if her love for John was back, intact, if her withdrawal had been merely a knee-jerk reaction because he had hurt her, despite that he'd since said he was sorry. She wanted to ask about his ex. But as badly as Annie wanted to talk—really talk—to John, right then her text alert went off.

The readout said: **MVHOSPITAL.**

MIKE HOFFMAN HERE. KEVIN IS CALM NOW. HE ASKED TO SEE YOU. ALONE. ASAP.

Annie's flip-flops slap-slapped on the hospital floor as she hurried toward the staircase. She didn't want to bother waiting for the elevator—climbing would keep her in motion, pushing forward as quickly as she could, getting closer to seeing her brother, to actually talking with him.

"Kevin," she said once the nurse had cleared her to go into his room. "God." She put her fist to her mouth and bit down, trying to deflect her tears.

Then he opened his eyes, looked at her, and said, "Hey."

She decided not to give a "seagull's crap"—as Earl like to say—about crying, so she removed her fist and released the dam.

"Jesus," he said weakly, but still smiling. "I'm the one who should be crying. I got shot. Not you." Then he frowned. "You didn't get shot, too, did you?"

She smiled. "No, I did not get shot." She dragged a chair to his bedside, sat down and took his hand, the one that no longer had tubing attached to it. "Are you in pain?"

"Not if I don't move. I think I'm pretty well drugged."

"Good." Wiping her tears, she took a long breath.

"Now," he said. "Will you please tell me what happened? Did I shoot myself with my own gun?"

"You don't remember?"

"Kind of, but it's spotty. I was in your cottage . . ."

"And Simon Anderson was there."

"Right! He was shouting at you! I ran to get my gun so I could scare him off."

"You scared him, all right. He thought you were going to shoot him."

"Me? Shoot anyone?" He laughed, then coughed.

She waited until he was calm again. "Simon tried to push you to the floor. You guys struggled. The gun went off."

"Sounds like a movie."

"Not one based on any of my books. It was too much of a cliché."

Kevin coughed twice. "Boys with toys, huh?"

"Will you please get rid of that ridiculous gun now?"

"You bet. I meant to before . . ."

"But you forgot."

"We got busy!"

She sighed. "We sure did."

He closed his eyes again. Then he tightened his grip on her hand. "Annie? I need to ask you something."

By the knots that sprouted inside her stomach, she was pretty sure she knew what he was going to say. "Anything," she said.

"When I . . . when I woke up . . ." He paused.

She wasn't sure how she could make this easier for him. She wasn't sure that even would be possible. "When you woke up, what?"

He opened his eyes slowly and turned his head to the doorway. "Right over there. I thought I saw Meghan. So these drugs are wicked powerful, right?"

She could have laughed and said something benign like,

"No kidding." Then she could have told him to get some sleep, that she'd come back later if he wanted. But he was her brother and she loved him immensely and she couldn't do that to him. Or to Meghan, who also must be feeling pretty crummy.

"Kevin," she started slowly. She lifted his hand to her lips and kissed it. "There's something you need to know." She didn't give him a chance to respond. "You weren't hallucinating. Meghan was here. She's out of rehab. She wanted to surprise you."

His eyelids drooped. He stayed quiet for what seemed like the longest time. Then he said, "You're making this up, right? Like, you're really here in the room with me now, but you're making up stories, aren't you? Is it some kind of psych evaluation the doctor asked you to do?"

She sighed. "No, Kevin. I'm not making this up. It's not one of my stories."

He scrutinized her face, then zeroed in on her eyes.

"She's doing well." Annie kept going, praying her strength—or her guts—wouldn't fail her. "It took a long time . . . well, you know how long it's been."

"Four years this Christmas," he replied, his voice having dropped and become quieter. Much quieter.

"Right. Well, she's here. And she wants to see you. When you're ready."

That's when Kevin cried.

Annie scooted as close to the bed as she could get. "Are those tears of joy? She's come back to you, Kevin. She's doing well. There's so much to tell you . . . I've gotten to know her a little—we hit it off right away. She registered at the Inn under a fake name, and then she told me the truth, which is why I called and pretended I was angry, and I begged you to come home and . . . Oh, never mind, there'll be time for all that. You're happy, aren't you?" She was blah-blah-blahing again, but she couldn't help it.

He rolled his head from one side to the other. He groaned.

Annie let go of his hand and stood up. "Are you in pain? Should I call for the nurse?"

"No," he squeaked out. "It's Taylor."

Oh, Annie thought. *Her.* She sat back down, took his hand again. "I'm sure she'll understand, Kevin. You and Meghan were together a long time."

His tears leaked freely now. "It isn't that." He groaned again. "It's because . . . Taylor and I got married."

Blindsided was a good word. A most appropriate word. For starters, Annie never dreamed Kevin would marry Taylor. Not to mention that he'd only been in Hawaii a week, so how could it have happened so fast?

After a couple of minutes of protracted silence, Kevin spoke again. He told Annie there was no waiting period to get married there. She listened as he asked her what he should do, for which she could not reply because she had no idea. And because she'd been blindsided.

That's when he said that his marriage to Meghan had fallen apart long before the accident. She was ambitious; she worked hard. She liked money, but more than that, she craved success. "Every year, her goal grew higher and higher. She wanted to buy more property, build more buildings, feel like she could own the world. Sometimes it made me a nervous wreck. I even got afraid to fly; I knew that every time we went somewhere it was to bid on a big project I didn't really want. All I wanted was to do good work for nice people and have a little family. Including kids."

Annie tried to coax him into thinking he should rest, that they could talk about this later. But he just shook his head, as if now that he'd started, there was no way that he could stop.

"She was pregnant when she fell. The baby died." He let out a somber rush of air. "She was on the pill, so I don't know how she got pregnant in the first place. I don't think she fell on purpose, though. I don't think she would have tried to have a miscarriage." He fell silent a minute, then added, "I didn't even know she was pregnant until after the accident. Until Meghan was in a coma, and the doctor told me he was sorry. But I never told anyone. Not even Mom."

All Annie wanted then was to crawl into the bed in the next room, pull the sheet over her head, and make this go away. Like with other things, it wasn't her place to tell him that Donna had known about the baby, that Meghan had told her. Maybe he'd learn all that some other day. Maybe not.

"I know you've never liked Taylor much," he continued, "but she helped me come to terms with all of it. She showed me that maybe my marriage to Meghan hadn't worked because our values and our needs weren't the same. Neither one of us was wrong; we were just too different."

And then his pain broke through—*no surprise*, Annie thought. She called for the nurse and asked if his meds could be increased, and the nurse said he was due for the next dose. So at least that was one miracle.

It wasn't long before he drifted back to sleep, thank God, and Annie got out of there fast. As soon as she reached the hospital lot, she called Francine.

"I need to talk to Taylor," Annie said, "but I don't have her number. Do you? Or does Jonas, if you're with him?"

"Sorry, I don't, and I'm not with Jonas. But I know where she is. Jonas brought her to the boat. She's on the three forty-five out of OB. How's Kevin?"

"He's okay. We talked. Where's Taylor going?"

"Back to Hawaii. She got a flight for tonight. Do you want me to call Jonas?"

Annie didn't know if Francine knew about the Hawaiian nuptials, but she didn't want to put what might be a wedge into anyone's relationship. So she said, "Never mind. But can you hold down the fort a little while longer?" It was already three fifteen. If Annie hurried, she could make it to Oak Bluffs before the three forty-five left port.

Annie jumped into the Jeep and peeled out of the hospital parking lot. Anywhere near the OB pier in August that close to boat time meant the traffic would be backed up and parking would be deplorable. Not to mention it was the Monday after the last big week of summer. Tourists would be leaving, having figured if they waited until the weekend was over the mass exodus would have lessened. Seasonal folks who had closed up their houses would be heading home, too. And everyone would be mingling with the day-trippers on bicycles who'd be grasping the green island maps they'd picked up at the terminal. But Annie knew she had to try. Because it absolutely, positively, was the right thing to do.

When she reached the area, it was every bit as jammed as she had feared. So she did what she never thought she would: she double-parked, got out, and locked the doors. If she blocked traffic, she didn't care; if she was ticketed and fined an exorbitant amount, she didn't care about that, either.

Tuning out everything and everyone around her, Annie zigged and zagged through the people and the vehicles while she mad-dashed up the sidewalk and down onto the pier where the line of walk-on passengers was backed up what looked like the length of a football field to the street. They stood four abreast, not counting their suitcases, bikes, and dogs, with no room to spare between the barrier on one side and the water on the other.

"Sorry!" she shouted repeatedly while weaving in and out. "Coming through! Emergency!" Most people accommodated her by stepping aside; she didn't notice, or care, if anyone was upset—she was too preoccupied scanning the crowd for the telltale auburn mane.

And then she caught a glimpse of it far ahead: the hair was thick and long and shining in the sun, the color of deep ginger, careening back and forth as Taylor moved up the gangway. Which meant she had already handed off her ticket to the Steamship ticket-taker in the fluorescent yellow vest.

Cupping her hands to her mouth, Annie shouted, "Taylor! Stop!" The sea of people parted then; she raced ahead, saying "Thank you" in all directions until she reached the ticket-taker who stopped her from going farther. By then, Taylor was only a foot or so from stepping into the boat.

"Taylor!" she railed in one last effort.

But Taylor must not have heard, as the auburn mane vanished inside the doorway.

Annie stopped. If there had been a wall nearby, she would have slumped against it. The line moved politely around her and the passengers held out their tickets. And all Annie did was start to cry.

The man in the fluorescent yellow vest scanned another barcode. Then Annie heard him say, "You looking for Taylor Winsted?"

Lifting her head, she said, "Never mind. She just boarded." Too distraught to explain why she'd caused such a scene, Annie turned and started to trundle back up the pier.

"Wait," the ticket-taker called after her. "I'll get her."

Annie stopped. She quickly moved back to where he was busy on his walkie-talkie. She heard him say Taylor's name, then add, "Yeah. The redhead."

Less than thirty seconds later, Taylor was walking down the gangway. She stopped at the check-in spot. She looked summery and fashionable in a pastel, citrusy Hawaiian way. But her face was twisted in apprehension.

"Annie? What happened?"

"Kevin told me you got married."

"He's awake?"

"He is. He'll be okay. Please don't leave. Please stay until this can be sorted out."

For a moment, Annie actually believed that Taylor would do as she had asked.

But the woman turned her gaze out to the water and said, "No. Kevin has been good to me. He helped me break away from this place and have a life again. I love being in Hawaii, with or without him. But getting married so fast was my idea, not his. He was lonely and vulnerable. I knew that long before I knew that she was here."

The "she," of course, was Meghan. Annie couldn't blame Taylor for not wanting to say the name.

Then Taylor shook her head. "Tell him not to worry; I'll have it annulled as soon as I get back. Kevin belongs here. But I don't. Not anymore. I like being five thousand miles away from my old self." With that, she turned and walked back to board the three forty-five.

Five thousand miles, Annie thought. She had to give Taylor credit for getting the details right.

Watching her walk back up the ramp, Annie wondered if she'd ever given the woman a fair chance. She'd first seen her as a harsh, rough-and-tumble, disgruntled loner; as time had passed, Annie came to understand that, like so many people, Annie included, Taylor had been beaten down in many ways—some were her own doing, others were not. And Kevin, Annie's sweet brother, had showed Taylor that life could be good again. He was so special, that brother of hers.

Annie stood, still watching, as the auburn mane dipped into the doorway of the boat; then the last car was loaded, the ferry whistle blew, and just like that, Taylor was gone.

Chapter 31

Annie was so tired she barely made it back to Chappy. She found Francine on the phone at the front desk, telling yet another caller that she was sorry, but the Inn was booked. She waited until Francine hung up before issuing the idea she'd come up with on her trip back to Chappy.

"Call Jonas. Tell him to get his butt to Boston and bring his mother back. I'd drive up there myself, but right now, I couldn't handle the traffic." She tossed Francine a smile, then went upstairs to the honeymoon suite and stretched out on the king bed. She closed her eyes and tried to settle her mind. She thought only of Kevin, that he was alive, that he would make it. And when Taylor returned and Meghan found out they were married, that she no longer was . . . Oh, Annie was tired of trying to figure out what would or should happen next.

The next thing she knew, the sun was lower in the sky. She checked her phone: six o'clock.

She sighed, and rested her head back on the pillow. Then she sat up with a start. "Simon!"

Bounding off the bed, she ran into the bathroom, quickly

brushed her hair and teeth, and tried to smooth the wrinkles from her crop pants and her top, not that it mattered. Still, she applied a coat of lipstick to help prevent her from looking as exhausted as she felt.

She made it down to the beach in record time.

Simon was waiting, standing by the shoreline, gazing toward the lighthouse.

Kicking off her flip-flops, she slipped her hands into her pockets and walked down to the water. She stood next to him. "I never get tired of this view."

He nodded. "What's it like in winter, though?"

"Different. But still as captivating. Maybe more, because it's unpredictable. The water, the light, the wind—they can be different every day."

He nodded again. "How's your brother? Francine told me he woke up."

"He did. And he's doing better." Despite their challenging moments, Simon seemed nice enough, whatever that meant. Evidently, however, he was one of those people who held their troubles deep.

"I didn't come to the Vineyard to do a special report on how climate change is affecting top vacation spots," he said.

Annie drew in a long breath. "I guessed that by now."

He flinched, but did not look at her. Instead he watched a sailboat glide out of the harbor. "Do you suppose they're headed home because the season's over?"

"Yes."

"I live in Manhattan now," he said.

She didn't say she knew that thanks to Wikipedia. "I guess you have to. For your job."

"My wife's a New Yorker. My kids are, too. They tease me because I'm still a Sox fan."

Annie smiled. "I suppose there are more of those around

these parts than in Manhattan." As badly as she wanted to ask him to get on with whatever he wanted to say, she was at least grateful that he hadn't brought a blanket and a bottle of wine.

"My brother killed your husband," he said suddenly.

She paused for a second, maybe more. Then her head slowly swiveled toward him. An ice-cold chill slid from her temples down the length of her body. Annie stood, now frozen in the sand, unable to feel the granules sifting between her toes. "What?" she finally asked.

"My brother Christopher was seventeen. He was drunk. He hit your husband, Brian."

Annie's lips began to quiver. She wrapped her arms around her waist, then dropped onto the beach, keeping her gaze steady on the view, as if its presence would ground her and stop her from fainting. Or screaming. Or from clawing at her chest where her heart now felt as if it had been ripped out.

Simon sat next to her. He pulled his knees up and rested his hands on them. "It's haunted me for years, not that you need to hear that."

"I . . ." Annie began, but had no idea what to say next. So she fell silent. In fact, they fell silent together.

After a few minutes, Simon went on. "It's true it was dark, and that Brian had on dark clothes. It's true that Christopher was a minor. I think you knew those things. It's also true that I went to grad school in New York, but that I was home in Boston and interning at the *Globe* when it happened. I told you that my uncle Harry was a big-shot attorney. He called in every marker and pulled every string he had so nothing leaked out that could link the accident to my family."

Annie let out all the air inside her lungs. Her quivering had stopped; her chest pain had eased. Perhaps it was because of how Simon was speaking: gently, with what sounded like genuine sorrow. "No one would tell me his name," she said.

He nodded. "I know. My uncle said it was the law, but I

wasn't sure about that. He was pretty corrupt. That always bothered me."

"But you were working at the *Globe*? When you interviewed me?"

"I was. I begged the city editor to let me talk to you—of course, he didn't know the connection. What I really wanted was to tell you what had happened. But when I met you that first time, and I saw how broken you were, I told myself I couldn't betray my brother. The truth was, I didn't have the guts." He turned to her but didn't touch her, for which she was glad. "I am so sorry, Annie."

She stared down at her feet. "It was an accident." Like Kevin being shot. Though the outcome that had been far worse.

"It was an accident, yes. But still . . ." His words trailed off.

"Is that why you changed your name?"

"Yes. After Columbia, I was offered the job in Boston. I didn't want to go back; by then I hated my whole family. But I needed a job, and it was a good place to start my broadcasting career. I told people who knew me that I had to change my name because there was another Andrew Simmons in the broadcasters' union. It was a crock, but as far as I know, no one ever figured it out. Or they couldn't imagine that I'd lie about something as stupid as that. But I was ashamed of my brother. I was ashamed of my uncle. And my other brother, my mother, my aunt. And of me. Christopher might have been behind the wheel, but all of them—all of *us*—covered it up." He reached down and scooped a handful of sand. "The contact lenses changed my appearance; I did that intentionally. They have nothing to do with me looking better on camera. I only knew I couldn't take a chance that anything would get in the way of me rising to the top. I felt like the higher up I went, the farther away from them I'd be. And it worked. My brother David never forgave me for that. God knows he couldn't out me to the media, because he knew I could ruin them all."

Which explained why Simon's name—or Andrew's—hadn't been included in Christopher's obituary. "And you never forgave him?" Annie asked.

"I never forgave any of us."

The feeling slowly came back to her body. "After all this time, why did you track me down now?"

"Christopher was a good kid. But he was an alcoholic, like our dad. Or maybe he became one out of guilt over your husband. When Chris died a few years ago, I realized what a selfish bastard I'd been to you. I am so sorry, Annie. About everything. I looked back on Brian's obit; I saw that your maiden name was Sutton. So I Googled Annie Sutton. Once I saw that you're an author, you were easy to find. It took a while for me to convince myself I needed to do this—apparently, not having guts is one of my many flaws—but here I am." Then he smiled a reluctant smile. "I wasn't being truthful when I said I hadn't read your books. I've read them all—the latest one at the library the day I got here. Sad to say, but I wanted to find out if you made any kind of reference to my brother."

"I write fiction."

"Writers write what they know, don't they?"

Using her toes, she carved little trenches in the sand. "Did you come here looking for forgiveness?" She wasn't sure why he would, since his brother, not him, had killed Brian. Then she had a sudden, alarm-bell kind of thought, the kind she might have given one of her characters if this were a novel and not real life woven with human complexities. Before he could answer she asked, "Simon?" She kept her voice calm and considered; she didn't want to offend him, but she wanted, needed, to know the truth. "Were you in the car? When Brian was killed?"

He looked back at the harbor and the lighthouse. "I was."

"Oh, God," Annie wailed. She started rocking back and forth. "And you let your brother drive drunk?"

He lowered his eyes, his chin, his head. "I'd been drinking, too. After that night, I never touched alcohol again."

She didn't respond; she wept, as the truth slowly started to sink in.

He waited until she'd quieted. "I called nine-one-one that night. The same way I did with Kevin." Then he added, "I don't think Brian felt any pain, Annie. I really don't."

She shook her head; she didn't want to hear this. She'd been told that the driver was alone, that a passerby had called the police. She'd been lied to, lied to, lied to. Thanks to Simon's pompous uncle. And to everyone who had covered it up. Including the man sitting next to her now.

"He told me something," Simon continued. His words grew more sullen, his voice cracking. "Before Brian closed his eyes, before he passed away, he asked me to tell you something. He said it was a secret."

Annie yelped. It was not the howl of a wounded animal that had erupted from Kevin had, but rather a yelp of loss that had festered all these years. The *secret*. Simon knew the secret that she'd never learned.

Shifting on the sand, Simon pulled his knees closer to his chest. "Your husband said, 'Tell Annie I got into grad school at USC. Tell her we're moving to Southern California.'"

Annie spent the rest of the evening burrowed beneath the comforter on the king-size bed in the honeymoon suite, her thoughts bobbing like buoys in the harbor during a storm. At least she'd had the strength to call Earl and ask him to visit Kevin, to say she was tied up at the Inn, but she'd be back at the hospital in the morning. She wanted to tell Meghan that Taylor was gone, but Annie didn't have the strength to help her untangle anything. She wouldn't even be able to help her brother, if he'd asked.

She didn't recall what else Simon told her. Her mind kept

sprinting from wondering if he'd only said what he'd said because he'd been trying to ease his guilt, make amends, or if he
genuinely felt that she'd want to know.

Southern California had been Brian's dream—an ideal
reason to get away from his family, the expectations of his
parents, the never-ending control levied on him by his
know-it-all sister. He wanted to earn a postgrad degree in
school administration that would put him on the path to becoming an elementary school principal. "The principal is your
pal," she remembered from a spelling lesson when she'd been
young. She'd shared that with Brian when he'd shared his
dream. They'd laughed as young lovers laugh, as if everything
was bright and happy and going to go their way.

Southern California was about two thousand, six hundred
miles away by air, nearly three thousand by car. It had been
Brian's dream to go; it became Annie's dream, too. She knew
she could teach anywhere: she wanted that, she wanted children, and mostly, she wanted Brian.

It had been a long, long time ago. And now, it was an odd
coincidence—perhaps those really did happen sometimes?—
that Brian had wanted to flee from his roots, yet Simon was
the one who'd wound up doing that.

When her tears finally abated, Annie closed her eyes. The
next thing she knew it was dark outside and someone was
edging under the comforter, someone who carried an aroma
of salty sea air mingled with a touch of furry dog.

"John?" she asked.

Then a rough little tongue tickled her face. Restless. Surely,
the sweetest dog ever.

Annie laughed. "What are you doing here? How did you
find me?" She cuddled Restless, rubbing his fluffy ears and his
belly.

"I figured you might want to throw me out, but you'd
never say no to the mutt."

She reached across the wide bed and said, "I would never throw either of you out."

John climbed under the covers and moved close to her. "I love you," he said. "And I think I love Bill, too."

There was only one "Bill" in Annie's world then. "Simon's friend?"

"Yeah. I ran into him downstairs. He told me where to find you. My dad called and said you asked him to go to the hospital. Lucy insisted on going, too; my bet is they'll stay there all night. Anyway, he said you needed some time alone."

"I'm not alone now."

"I noticed. You have a dog on your chest."

"And you're here, too. I'm glad." She shifted Restless to the end of the bed and rested her head on John's shoulder. Then she told him about her conversation with Simon. When she finished, she simply said, "So that's why he's been here."

He stroked her hair and kissed her neck. "Are you okay?"

"I am," she said and realized that she meant it. "But I'm ready for summer to be over. For life to begin again."

"It will. Soon."

She couldn't yet tell him the details about Kevin, Meghan, Taylor. Not until . . . well, not until she had her own priorities in line. "But the end of the season also means Francine will be going back to Minnesota. Then I have the book tour. Six weeks. From the third week of September straight through October."

"Maybe you'd like company?"

She raised up on one elbow. "You want to come on the book tour?"

"I've racked up a ton of vacation time. I can take at least a couple of weeks off. Where are you going?"

"Chicago, L.A., Bradford, Pennsylvania . . ."

"Count me in. I've always hankered a trip to Bradford. Where the hell is it?"

She laughed. "I'm not sure. But I think it's cold there. And I know I'll be awfully busy."

"All night?"

"No."

"Then let's consider it a pre-honeymoon. Which goes nicely with where we are right now—in the honeymoon suite."

She touched his face, his stubbly beard that she loved so much when it grazed across her cheek. "What about Lucy and Abigail?"

"Don't worry, they won't be joining us."

She laughed. She also loved how he could make her laugh at the strangest times.

"Lucy can go to my mom and dad's, though she'll tell me she's old enough to stay by herself."

"Alone? But won't Abigail be there?"

John emitted a little snort; he rolled onto his side and propped himself up on one elbow. "My older daughter will be busy commuting to the Cape. I told her she either had to go to college or get a job."

Annie blinked. "What?"

"She picked college. Cape Cod Community for now, because it's too late to get into RISDI."

Annie knew that RISDI was the abbreviation for Rhode Island School of Design.

"She'll get some core classes out of the way," John continued, "while she gets her application in. She says she really wants to learn art and fashion design. When my dad hears that, he'll probably say she must get his fashion sense from him."

Annie laughed. "Wow. This is a surprise."

"No kidding. I'm not sure her mother's happy about it, but who cares what she thinks. Abigail seems happier than she was a week ago."

A week ago? Had his daughter only been back a week? *Oh*, Annie thought, *what a week it had been.*

"Maybe if she's happier she and Lucy will get along better. And maybe you'll wind up having a better relationship with Abigail."

"Who knows? Part of our deal was I'll pay for college and get her a car to keep over on the Cape as long as she quits smoking. She agreed. So let's see what happens. I do know I feel better."

This was hardly the time to tell him about his daughter's announcement that her dad was going to be reunited with her mom. Maybe it would be best for Annie to leave that alone. Forever.

Then John grew more serious. "I do love you, Annie. And I want to be with you. Starting now. I'm off tonight; I'm going to stay here with you. In the morning we'll go see Kevin together. Sound good?"

"Sounds great," she replied as she nestled against him. "And you may join me on my tour if you carry my books."

He laughed a hearty laugh. "Seriously? I thought you were a celebrity. Doesn't your publisher pay someone to do that?"

She thought about Simon. "From time to time, even celebrities have to deal with reality. It's part of . . ." She almost told him it was part of the job, but decided it was way more than that. "It's part of life," she said. "So we never forget where we came from and who we really are." Then she thought of Kevin again, and Meghan, and Taylor, until John kissed her again.

"And you're sure you're okay about everything Simon told you?" he asked.

"I am," she said. "I really am. I have all I want right here."

It wasn't long before they fell asleep, with Restless cuddled between them.

Chapter 32

Annie slept through the night and woke up to the motion of the dog wriggling and the scent of bacon sizzling. She quickly checked her phone: no one had called, no one had texted. Kevin must have had a good night. The crisis might really be over.

After kissing John awake, she told him she wanted to get to the hospital. She tossed on her robe, ran downstairs, and brought Restless out the front door; when he was finished she picked him up and went back inside. And saw Meghan sitting at the bottom of the stairs. Her suitcase was by her side.

"What's this?" Annie asked. She knew she needed to warn her about the Taylor situation. But how much should she tell her? She ran a hand through her bed-head hair and remembered Francine's words: "Whether it's physical hurt or emotional hurt, hurting still hurts, doesn't it?"

If right that second Kevin had been there and asked Annie what he should do, she might advise him to let Meghan go back to Boston and Taylor back to Hawaii and let everything sit for a while. And wait for the best solution to evolve.

She knew, however, that was the kind of ending that looked good only on paper.

"I'm leaving," Meghan said. "I went back to see Kevin last night. He told me we're divorced. He told me he married Taylor. So I have no business being here."

"Meghan . . ." Annie sat next to her on the staircase, not knowing what to say or how to feel. Restless wiggled in her arms; she scratched his ear to quiet him.

"He said you knew. I figured you were protecting me, so thanks for that."

"I didn't know he'd married her. Not until late yesterday . . ."

"But you knew about the divorce."

"I wasn't positive it was final."

She stood up. "Oh, it is. The good news is that I get to keep the trust fund. All of it. So maybe I'll start my own business with it. Whenever I figure out what that business will be. I only know it won't be turtles. As interesting as they are, I only made that up so no one would wonder why I came to the Vineyard by myself."

Annie readjusted Restless on her lap. "I'm so sorry . . ."

"Me, too. But he's right. We're far too different for either one of us to be completely happy. We always were. I'd stopped taking the pill—I'd hoped a baby might help fix our marriage, but I don't expect that really ever works, or at least, usually not well. Anyway, I was sorry that it died. Sadder than I would have expected." She picked up her suitcase. "I told him I signed the consent form for his surgery as his wife. He said if anybody barked about it, he'd take care of it. Kevin's a good caretaker, you know." She offered a little smile. There had been good parts of their lives together, that was clear. "Francine agreed to follow me to drop off the rental car, then she'll take me to the boat."

Annie stood up and hugged Meghan, the dog taking turns to lick both their faces, and Annie taking a moment to look one last time into those lovely cornflower blue eyes. She did not suppose their paths would cross again. With a teary sigh, she hugged Meghan again, then said told her that she and Francine needed to get a move on, if they wanted to make the eight fifteen.

After showering, dressing, and acknowledging a tiny hole that saying good-bye to Meghan had left in her heart, Annie tried to concentrate on Taylor—her new sister-in-law. If offering a "decent human gesture" to be kind to Simon had been important, perhaps Annie should also extend an olive branch to Taylor. If Kevin and Taylor loved each other and planned on staying married, Annie would work hard not to ruin that for them.

She told John that she'd meet him downstairs. Then she headed toward the kitchen to grab coffee to-go.

The table already was set, but, with Francine having taken Meghan to the boat, who was in charge of breakfast? It was ridiculous that Annie had been so distracted she hadn't checked to be sure the basics of the Inn were being covered. But as she moved from the great room into the kitchen, she heard voices coming from the chef's room—the sisters from Indiana. Ginny was providing instructions; Tina was piling muffins into a basket.

"I know how to serve people," Tina barked at her sister. "I was a waitress, you know."

"Just because you waited tables at our church tent at the State Fair doesn't mean you qualify to call yourself a waitress. For one thing, it was forty years ago."

Toni set down the basket. "Forty years? That long?"

"Closer to fifty," Ginny said.

Annie smiled. She expected that, now and again, the sisters squabbled. "Hello, ladies. I see you're helping out this morning?"

The women turned to her, both looking a little nervous, as if they'd been caught with their hands in the muffin tin.

"Actually, Francine already put eggs and bacon in the chafing dishes, and your nice young man, Jonas, was supposed to help serve," Ginny said. "So you could say right now, we're helping out him. Bella had a fussy night. She rode with Francine and Jonas to Boston. We have no idea why they went, but when they got back, Bella woke up and wouldn't go back to sleep. She kept saying, 'Bella go for ride!' That little one is so adorable. Anyway, he's driving her around the island hoping she'll fall asleep again."

Annie wasn't sure what part was more "adorable": Bella, or the way that Ginny told the story.

"Well, I'm sorry, but I won't be joining you, either," she told the sisters. "I only came in for coffee, but now I think I'll bring those delicious-looking muffins to the hospital. I have a feeling my brother will be having visitors. You probably know there's plenty of homemade bread for toast if anyone wants it, and cookies in the freezer if they want something sweet. Okay?" She didn't know why she was confirming with the Inn guests that taking the muffins would be okay, but Annie supposed she'd been raised to be polite, and some parts of the past simply had stuck.

"But is there any dog food?" John came into the kitchen, Restless in his arms. "Like bacon and eggs? He really loves those."

The sisters from Indiana ooh'ed and ahh'ed over Restless (and John) and fixed a bowl for the dog while Annie bagged the muffins and poured a Thermos of coffee. Which was when Bill walked in.

"Morning," he said brightly and looked squarely at Annie. "I hope it's a happy one for you?" He was dressed in khaki shorts and a golf shirt; his hair was neatly in place, and he was clean-shaven. It seemed that, like Taylor, he'd undergone a transformation.

Annie took a step back, her defenses apparently still on alert. "So far," she said.

Bill gave her a wary smile. "If you have a minute, could we go outside on the patio? I'd like to discuss a couple of things."

She looked at John, then back to Bill. She avoided glancing at the sisters, whose eyes were glued to her. "Okay." She moved outside to the patio, grateful that John was behind her. And Restless, too, of course.

"I took the photo," Bill announced after they regrouped. "At Illumination Night."

Annie's flicked her gaze to John then back to Bill. "Why?"

"Look," he said, "Simon and I talked last night. I know he finally told you the truth about the accident. He didn't tell you the truth about me, though. I'm not his loyal assistant. We've been friends since grad school. He called me the night your husband was killed. I know the guilt he's carried all these years. So does his wife. When he told us he'd found out where you were, he asked me to come with him for backup. Moral support. Whatever you want to call it. It was my idea to come incognito as his major domo. Anyway, once we got here, I could tell by the way he was acting stupid-nasty that he was getting cold feet. Stupid-nasty isn't who Simon is."

By then, Annie's mouth was dry. She was glad to feel John's hand resting on the small of her back.

"I called his wife—her name's Tracy, by the way. We decided I should do something drastic to make him face the music. Or at least to make him have to face you. I told her I'd be on the lookout; then I saw my chance at Illumination Night. I'm really sorry for the nightmare it caused."

"The people you hitched a ride with said you didn't have a fancy camera," Annie said, as if that mattered now.

Bill laughed. "I'm not a cameraman. I'm in advertising.

One of those guys who still wears suits and works on Madison Avenue. I had my iPhone, though. Those little buggers take great shots."

So that was why the two men hadn't been laden with camera gear that night.

"How'd you know," John interrupted, "about Vine-yardInsiders?"

"The day we got here, Simon went to the library; I visited a few pubs, pretending to be fascinated by the island. It's amazing what you can learn when you belly up to a bar, order a beer, and be friendly."

"And you put it in the *Times*?" Annie asked.

"Not me. That was Tracy's doing. She figured if Simon had more exposure it would make him nervous and shock him into telling you what he'd come to tell you before you— or the tabloids—started prying into his past, digging around for any kind of other 'indiscretions.' She wanted me to apologize to you, though. And to say she'd always known that if she'd been in your shoes, she would have wanted to know what really happened back then."

"For which you may thank her for me." She closed her eyes. "I think my editor would like to thank her, too."

Then Jonas came around the corner with Bella, and John asked if he'd mind taking care of Restless, too, so they could get to the hospital.

Jonas said he'd be happy to. He really was a nice young man, as Ginny had said. And Annie had a feeling that Francine would agree he was a keeper.

After thanking Bill again, Annie left the Inn in Jonas's capable hands. Then she and John got into his truck and buckled up, and Annie was catapulted back to the present, back to reality, back to Kevin, who was the one who mattered now.

On the way, she explained the latest Kevin-Meghan-Taylor development; John sat very still as he took in every word.

★   ★   ★

Kevin had been moved out of ICU and into a regular room, which was good, because he was allowed more than a single visitor for more than a few minutes. When Annie and John arrived, those visitors included Earl, Claire, Lucy, and Francine, who didn't mention that she'd taken Meghan to the boat. Taylor was there, too, sitting close to Kevin's bed. His eyes kept drifting over to her, his mouth set in a soft smile. He looked happy, which counted for . . . everything. And though there might have been too many people in the room, it made for a nice family portrait of sorts.

Even more surprising was that Simon was there. He'd brought a bucket of flowers that he'd picked in the meadow. Annie smiled at him and nodded.

"I have muffins for everyone," she said, setting them on a table. "Enjoy."

"Not for me," Francine said, patting her small belly. "I'm on a diet."

Earl laughed. "You're the last person who needs to be on one of those."

"Oh, hush," Claire said. "Leave the girl alone. She wants to eat healthy now."

Annie frowned, then looked back at Francine. "You're such a great cook. You already eat healthy, don't you?"

Francine shrugged. "I want to do better now. Because I'm eating for two."

It was another of those old clichés that Annie loved. And this time, it was the best of all.

Exclamations filled the room, followed by joy, tears, and a smattering of applause. Claire started chattering about knitting baby things; Lucy offered to babysit; Earl said he hoped it was a boy because, no offense, but it was beginning to feel like there were an awful lot of females on Chappaquiddick.

"Hello?" Kevin interrupted. "May the patient say a word?" Everyone shut up.

He reached over and took Taylor's hand. She hesitated at first; she wasn't one for displays of affection. Perhaps she simply wasn't accustomed to someone loving her that much. "My wife and I . . ." he began, but then he got choked up because he was an old softie just like Earl. "My wife and I are going to be grandparents," Kevin said. "There'll be a brand-new baby in our family." Then he cried because he couldn't help himself. Earl said it must be because of all those narcotics Doctor Mike was giving him.

Everyone laughed, and everything was good.

Then Francine said, "Stop all this nonsense! Before the baby comes, I'm going back to school. Jonas is coming with me. My aunt and uncle insisted that he'll stay with them, too. Jonas will paint and look after Bella; I think I can finish classes before the baby's born in the spring. Then we'll be back. This is our home."

Annie had a hard time holding back her happiness. She looked at Kevin and wondered if he'd told Taylor about the baby Meghan lost, but Annie supposed she needed to stay out of that, too.

"I have one question," Earl said. "Kevin, if you and Taylor are going to be grandparents, how're you going to do that from Hawaii? All this internet stuff is fine, but a baby needs his family."

Kevin looked back at Taylor, who shook her head a little, as if she were resigned. "Every time I try to leave this island, something drags me back," she said. "I'm afraid it's karma; maybe it's time I stopped trying to fight it."

"We can spend time in Hawaii in winters," Kevin said. "Now that I'm no longer afraid to fly." As usual, he was trying to make someone he cared about happy. It wasn't a bad trait to have.

"But you can't go until after the holidays," Claire said. "We need family here for the holidays."

Sometimes Annie wondered if anyone actually remembered who were the blood relatives and who were not, though by now she knew none of that mattered.

She looked at Simon—a newcomer to the group, but she had a feeling he might be back, too. Maybe he'd bring his family; she thought that would be nice. Then Annie glanced back to Francine, who was beaming, and wanted to tell her to hold on tightly to the happiness that she felt now, to savor every second of her time with Jonas and their bewitching young love.

Then Earl signaled Annie to join him in the hall.

"I told him Meghan left," he said. "Francine called me from the boat after she dropped her off. She also told me about Kevin and Taylor being married." He lowered his head and let out a low whistle. "I did not see that one coming. Anyway, Meghan told Francine it was for the best. Who are we to say otherwise, right?"

Annie agreed. The sad part was, it was clear that everyone liked Meghan. Of course, they did not know the whole story—and they'd never hear it from Annie.

"Sometimes things happen for a reason," Annie said. "Even if it's years before we understand what the reason was." Her dad had said that the night Brian had been killed. She thought of her dad now: he would have loved Kevin; he would have loved John. He would have thought Taylor was curious, but he'd never judged anyone, the way he hadn't judged Aunt Sally. "If you'll excuse me, Earl, I think I want to go up to the garden for a few minutes alone, okay?"

Because he was Earl, he simply nodded and didn't ask questions.

★   ★   ★

It was called the Healing Rooftop Garden. And though Annie had no physical pain, she realized she'd kept her emotional hurt buried inside for too long. Now that it had been lifted, she was able to see that the trauma from Brian's accident had stopped her from doing so many things, mostly from trusting that life could be, would be, good again.

She sat on a bench and gazed past the pots of beach grass, out to the harbor. The *Island Home* was making its way back to Woods Hole, crossing Vineyard Sound to that other world, "the mainland," some islanders called it, "America," others said.

Letting her thoughts drift back to Brian, she wondered how things would have been different if he hadn't died, if they'd moved to California, if he had become a principal. She imagined they would have had a family, children of their own to share their love. She would have kept teaching third-graders, because she'd loved that, too. But Brian was gone before any of that had happened.

As the air stirred, softening the heat of the August sun, Annie supposed that maybe sometimes things really did happen for a reason— even if we could never be sure what that reason had been. All she knew was that she now had wonderful people and wonderful things all around her. Regardless of what Simon's brother had taken away, she would have missed out on more than she could have imagined.

Getting to know Donna.

Meeting Kevin.

If Annie had gone to California with Brian, she would not have been able to be with Murphy at the end of her life.

She would have missed out on knowing Winnie, which Murphy must have arranged so Annie could have a living, breathing version of her to lean on.

Nor would Annie have had Earl, Claire, Francine, and

precious Bella. Or Jonas, and the new life that he and Francine were expecting.

And Meghan. Annie would never have known her, nor would she have met Simon. But with them had come unforeseen challenges that ultimately helped shape Annie's vow to embrace Kevin and Taylor's marriage. Challenges, after all, would always be part of living.

If things had turned out differently, Annie would not have had the chance to love John. She would not have met Lucy. Or Abigail, who would always be in John's world. Annie would try hard not to judge her.

But perhaps as significant as the new people and all the love now in her life, was that if Annie had gone to California with Brian, she might never have written a book. She would not have moved to Martha's Vineyard, this magical island that had taken hold of her heart. And there be no Vineyard Inn.

It was because of both the good and the bad that Annie had finally found harmony—that she'd learned the real meaning of gratitude, and the importance of having hope for whatever would come next.

Surprisingly, Murphy did not toss down her opinion from high in the crystal blue summer sky. But then Annie felt her old friend's hand rest gently upon her shoulder, and together they sat in silence, looking out to the sea.

Don't miss Jean Stone's next Vineyard novel . . .

A VINEYARD WEDDING

After months of procrastination and doubt, Annie Sutton has finally set the date to marry John Lyons—Christmas Eve on Martha's Vineyard. But though it's already the end of November, Annie knows a lot can happen between now and then, especially on the island where life, like fishing nets, often gets tangled. This time it will be worse. Because a much-loved member of her island family suddenly goes missing, sending shockwaves from Chappaquiddick to the Gay Head Cliffs.

Love and betrayal, vengeance and trust, among family, among friends. A VINEYARD WEDDING tackles the challenges of how to navigate it all. How to know when it's safe to be happy. And when to walk away . . .

To be published by Kensington Publishing Corp. in Summer 2022

Connect with Us

Visit us online at
KensingtonBooks.com
to read more from your favorite authors, see books
by series, view reading group guides, and more.

Tell us what you think!

To share your thoughts, submit a review,
or sign up for our eNewsletters, please visit:
KensingtonBooks.com/TellUs.